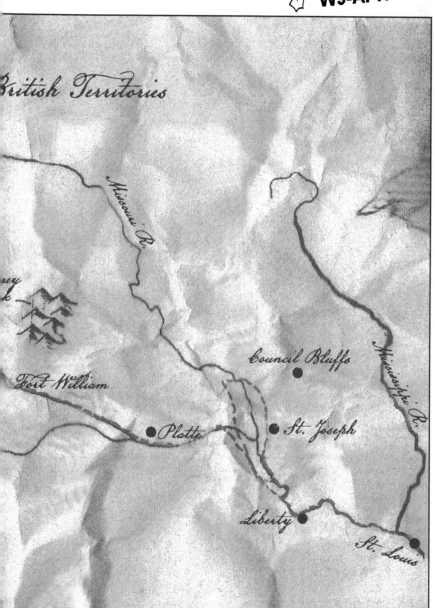

"Catherine Brakefield has carefully woven several genres of fiction into a singular, well-crafted, narrative...Rachael is strong, independent, and committed to her beliefs, she is also a product of her times and susceptible to the pressures of the day (such as an arranged marriage). While reminiscent of other works (Shakespeare's 'The Taming of the Shrew' comes to mind), Brakefield's work is never derivative and [is] well-paced."

— CHRISTOPHER BLUE, technical preservation specialist,
Western Historic Trails Center

"Historically accurate and exciting, *Wilted Dandelions* is a great story of missionaries going west to minister to the Indians. Catherine Brakefield creates a tension filled tale about the Oregon Trail that is fraught with danger and a marriage that is in name only."

— MARCIA (MITCHELL) LEE, author of *Surviving the Prodigal Years*

Columbia

Whitman
Mission

Spalding
Mission

Umatilla
Mission

Hell's Canyon

Snake R.

Rendezvous

Ft. Hall

South
Pass

Wilted Dandelions

CATHERINE ULRICH BRAKEFIELD

CROSSRIVER
BREWSTER, KANSAS USA

This book is dedicated to those early missionaries who sacrificed wealth, comfort, and life for the gospel of Jesus Christ. To my modern-day readers and missionaries, may God grant America another Awakening that will set ablaze His Holy Word.

"Go ye therefore, and teach all nations, baptizing them in the name of the Father, and of the Son, and of the Holy Ghost: Teaching them to observe all things whatsoever I have commanded you; and, lo, I am with you always, even unto the end of the world. Amen." (Matt. 28:19-20)

acknowledgments

"Ⓕor whatever things were written before were written for our learning, that we through the patience and comfort of the Scriptures might have hope." — *Romans 15:4 (NKJV)*

For a struggling, hurting world, no one but our loving Savior, *Jesus Christ*, will do. To Him belong the glory, honor, and inspiration of *Wilted Dandelions*.

If not for the insight of my publisher, *Tamara Clymer*, *Wilted Dandelions* might have laid within the dark crevices of my drawer gathering dust for another year.

Editor, *Debra Butterfield*, thank you for your dogmatic endeavor to wrestle out the best my writing could be. Not being content until it sparkled with its own vitality.

Thank you my *CrossRiver author family* for your encouragement, and most of all, your expertise, and blessed friendship.

Special thanks goes to *Christopher Blue*, Museum Technician of The Western Historical Trails Center, and to author, minister and speaker, *Marcia Lee*, for taking time out of their busy schedules to endorse *Wilted Dandelions*.

"A friend loves at all times . . ." Prov 17:17 (NKJV)

Laura Brestovansky, you believed I could rise from stomping the sidewalks as a news reporter to becoming an author. *Matthew Seymour*, your knowledge and expertise led me to the next step in getting *Wilted Dandelions* published. Thank you ACFW and HACWN for your writing conferences and adrenalin-pumping enthusiasm, especially when *Wilted Dandelions* won second place in the 2010 HACWN Writing Contest.

"...come, take up the cross, and follow Me." (Mark 10:21 NKJV)

These were the words my husband and I thought of as we traveled the dedicated footsteps of our American evangelists. The love and encouragement found in the Scriptures encouraged our former evangelists, and I pray will give my readers hope during these trying times.

My utmost respect and appreciation goes to the people I met traveling the *Wilted Dandelion* route. Thank you for your stories, experiences, and friendship.

"Blessed is the nation whose God is the LORD, *The people He has chosen as His own inheritance." (Ps. 33:12 NKJV)*

Most importantly, I want to thank my husband, **Edward Brakefield**, for his continued support and willingness to travel out west with me, just like Rachael and Jonathan. Well almost. We traveled in a comfortable car, stopped at plush motels, and panicked when we lost our cell phone power going through the Rockies.

To my daughter, **Kimberly Warstler**, thank you for your marvelous input and recommendations. Many thanks go to my son, **Derek**, his wife, **Alta**, and my son-in-law, **Brett Warstler**, for their encouragement. To my three grandchildren, **Zander, Logan**, and **Annabelle**, I pray and bequeath that this book will enlighten you on a part of history not often read about, nor often spoken about, and which your generation knows nothing about.

Lastly, thank you, my loyal readers, may *Wilted Dandelions* inspire you to endure through life's trials, and grant hope to your future. Never stop being the missionary that our Savior, Jesus Christ, has called us to be. God Bless!

Buffalo, New York
April 1837

"*S*pinster Rachael picks weeds, hoping someone will pick her.*" Rachael Rothburn glanced over her shoulder and into Bobby McGuire's gleaming eyes. His infatuation for her bordered obsession. Bobby elbowed his buddies and whispered.

She hurried onto the wooded footpath that edged the dirt road, then ducked behind a budding lilac bush and waited.

Bobby, Davy, and quiet Ralph walked past her poking each other and laughing. Like a reverberating sonnet, Bobby's words bespoke what her friends and family whispered behind her back. *Spinster Rachael hoped someone would pick her...*

With the prattling tongues of every matchmaker from Buffalo to New York gossiping over her unwedded state, Father wanted to hire an escort for her. If he learned of Bobby and his bullies hounding her heels, Father would put his threat into action.

She didn't want an escort or a husband. She wanted to become a missionary and bring the salvation message to the Indians west of the Rocky Mountains.

Walking down the hill through the mist, she spotted some flowers. Like misplaced stars, over twenty dandelions shimmered in the green grass, bravely cheering the dismal overcast day. "Lord, let me be like those little dandelions. Grant that my remaining years will be my finest years and that the trials of life will not conquer my joy for the Lord."

The dandelions stood in two inches of rainwater and the only way to reach them was across a fallen tree trunk. She set down her basket, gathered up her skirts and petticoats, and started across the makeshift bridge.

Whispered shushes and the scampering sounds of three pairs of boots running down the hill met her ears.

Rachael ignored them, bent over, and plucked the largest flower. She wove the dandelion onto her hatband and placed the hat on her head.

"Here, Spinster Rachael, here's one for your bonnet." Bobby's fingers closed around a whittled-down branch, and wedged at the fork was a wilted dandelion. He stretched out his arm and chuckled with glee as he jabbed her full bodice with his crude stick. Bobby's hard working mother would be mortified at his actions. "I can just imagine what it would be to feel them."

Rachael's temper ignited like gunpowder, and she thrust the stick away. "The rod and reproof give wisdom: but a child left to himself bringeth his mother to shame."

"Child?" Davy snickered. "Child? I don't think we should tell Mommy what Bobby's doing. Do you, Ralph?"

Bobby's face went crimson, his lips twisted into a snarl as the red freckles peppering his nose grew more predominant in the hazy light. "I'll show you."

"Look at this basketful of goodies, Ralph." Davy opened the lid, elbowing Ralph. "That drumstick looks good."

"Leave that alone," she demanded, but Davy bit into the chicken anyway. She gritted her teeth, and the soft flesh of her fingers felt the rough edges of the branch as she wrestled against Bobby's continued jabs.

Davy held up a large glass jar. "Tea. Yuck."

"Don't you know that's what old maids drink?" Bobby kept his eyes fastened on Rachael's bodice.

Davy stuck the half-eaten drumstick in his mouth, then kicked her wicker basket into the water.

"You ruffians." Her anger spilled out like the contents of her basket had in the murky rainwater. "I wish I was a man. I'd show you a thing or two."

"What's going on here?" A tall, well-built gentleman stepped from the footpath that led to the road. In one fluid motion he grabbed at

Bobby's stick, but missed. Bobby jumped back and forth, lithely dodging the man as if in a boxing match, and then threw the stick at him. "I claim first rights." Laughing, Bobby and his cronies ran up the hill with the stranger running after them.

Reaching the hill, the stranger watched the boys run toward the road, then he stopped and turned back toward Rachael.

No, don't come back. "I must resemble an oversized pelican perched on this tree trunk," Rachael muttered and straightened her bonnet. Oh — here he comes.

With her first step, the heel of her boot caught on a branch. Bending over to free herself, the hem of her petticoats wedged in beneath the toe of her shoe. She began to lose her balance and fanned her arms backward looking for something to grab onto.

"Hang on, I'm coming," the stranger hollered.

"I… am…" The rainwater slapped her face like a misplaced wave off the Atlantic. She gasped… the warmth of the stranger's arms encircled her waist, locking her into his tenacious grip and sweeping her up in his powerful grasp.

"Are you all right?"

She tilted her head back and looked at him through the drenched brim of her bonnet. A strong jaw, a rugged cleft chin, and the brightest blue eyes she had ever seen smiled into hers. "Yes," her voice but a whisper. Her heart skipped a beat when his eyes swept her face a second time. *Who is he?*

He carried her to a budding cherry tree and set her down beneath the spreading branches.

Rachael's wet bodice felt like a frozen dishrag next to her skin. She shivered. At least only the front of her was wet. She removed her bonnet and wiped a ringlet of curls from her eyes, then peered at him though wet eyelashes. "I… lost my balance."

He pulled a clean handkerchief from his pocket and leaned toward her. She tried to back away only the tree was in her way. "I'll get your handkerchief dirty."

He hesitated, and with gentle strokes wiped away the mud from her cheeks. "I almost made it to you in time," he said, his voice low and soothing.

Rachael bit her bottom lip. "You were only an inch —"

"Short." The stranger's lips parted to display even white teeth, his grin widening, he handed her his handkerchief. His fitted, black cutaway and white shirt displayed the fashionable white cuff a half inch beneath his sleeve, and bespoke of his gentry, his impeccable dialect, and his upper social status.

Rachel guffawed. "You act like it's a part of your morning routine, rescuing distraught women wallowing face down in yesterday's storm water."

"Actually, you are my first damsel in distress this month."

He made light of rescuing her. But for her, it would be a moment she would never forget. The man of her dreams now had a face. All that was missing was his prancing white horse and shining armor.

The sounds of carriages and horses from the road leading to Cheektowaga and the revival brought her back to reality with a sodden dress chilling her skin. What self-respecting knight would give a sloppy wet spinster a second look? She stuttered a half-hearted explanation, attempting to divert the stranger's eyes from her soiled brocade. "I… I mean, I am on my way to the revival."

"Indeed? Most everyone on the road this morning is, too."

"Only I became distracted by the dandelions." Rachael reached for her bonnet and placed the hat on her lap. Did Bobby McGuire's words hold some truth? Did she hope the right someone would pluck her? She shook her head. Nonsense. "Perky little things, aren't they?"

"They give a touch of brightness to your bonnet on this overcast day."

Laughter bubbled from a place deep within her as she placed the bonnet back on her head. "I spotted one immersed in rain water and decided it needed to be woven with my other flowers."

"And how do you determine which flower deserves that honorable recognition, to ride on such a beautiful head?"

Rachael felt the warmth of a blush creep into her cheeks. Her tall stature and well endowed figure always attracted the wrong response from the opposite sex. Usually the opposite sex's roving eyes stopped two inches below her neck. "I picked the dandelions that stood in defiance to last night's storm without wilting beneath the adversity."

He chuckled deep down in his throat. "As you did with those ruffians. The only thing I can fault you for is wishing you were a man. God knew what he was doing creating you a woman. You are the first brave gentlewoman I have ever met."

He reached for her arm to help her up. Her heart pounded wildly at his touch. She wasn't used to such kindness coming from a man of his social status.

His eyes were so blue… as blue as the Atlantic Ocean… as blue as the Niagara River after the morning fog burned off. "I… I need to retrieve my basket."

He kept her hand in his, stilling the trembling of hers with his touch. "I cannot allow you to leave until you answer me honestly." His voice had a melody all its own.

She shook her head attempting to clear it.

"No?" he asked.

"I mean, no… I mean… Sir, what is your question?"

"What is your name?"

"Rachael Rothburn," she said, her throat dry as a hot summer day in July. She didn't know how she managed to say her name at all. No matter how tightly she fastened her undergarments, her stays never flattened her bosom enough. Yet this man scarcely gave her figure a second glance. As if he saw beyond her outward appearance to the woman within.

Wading into the water, he scooped up her dinner and her mother's china, carefully placing them in her basket. "Miss Rothburn, my carriage awaits your bidding." He bowed, carrying her basket on one arm, as he placed her arm safely within the crook of his elbow with the other.

As they walked to the carriage, her only awareness was of him. His horses' neighs broke the spell. Startled, she looked up into his gleaming ebony carriage. Within its shadowed interior sat a lady adorned in a light blue dress with matching hat carefully poised to one side of her golden curls. The lady turned.

Rachael blinked. Isabella DeSimone. The belle of New York was sitting in his carriage. Standing alongside Isabella, who resembled their dainty, high-stepping and sleek-lined hackney ponies, Rachael felt like one of her father's oversized draft mares.

Isabella's gaze swept Rachael's soiled appearance. "You don't need to say a word, Jonathan," she said with a disdainful lift of her arched brow. "Rachael, I see you're up to your usual antics of collecting weeds."

"You have had such mishaps before?" Jonathan asked.

"Really, Jonathan, sometimes your sense of chivalry goes too far. She's been roaming the swamplands like a gypsy ever since grammar school." Isabella patted the carriage seat. "Sit next to me, Jonathan."

Jonathan reached up and squeezed her lace-gloved hand.

Rachael bit her lower lip. Jonathan, the name fit him.

"Rachael will add a bit of color to our drab day, my dear."

So that's it. She was an amusing diversion to his quintessential life. She wrapped the remnants of her dignity around her and chastised her foolish heart. She'd been foolish to think anyone from his social class could be anything but a snob.

"Rachael, won't you join us?" Jonathan said.

"My shirtwaist and part of my skirt are still damp. I might get Isabella wet. I have not far to travel. The walk will do me good."

"I did not mean to imply —"

"Thank you, sir." With a proud lift of her chin, she continued, "Your kindness is greatly appreciated." She gave a lighthearted nod toward Isabella. "You're as lovely as ever, Isabella. I do not believe you've aged a day since the last time I saw you."

A smug smile escaped Isabella's thin lips. "Thank you, Rachael. I wish I could repay the compliment. To do so, though, would only give you false hopes."

"Then I thank you for your frankness." Rachael squared her shoulders and turned into the wind, her skirts billowing around her legs.

She heard Jonathan's horses neigh and then the rhythmic notes of hooves on the dirt road. Her slender fingers caressed the dandelion on her bonnet, and soon her laughter echoed in the mists around her. Jonathan was no different than any other man of her acquaintance, and she was better off knowing it.

✤ ✤ ✤

"Rachael?"

The noise of heavy footsteps, murmurings, and laughter swelled like the tide. "Rachael," the voice said again. Rachael turned, craning her neck, and then stepped up on her log seat.

She watched a woman's figure, round as an apple, zigzag toward her through the throng of people past the entranceway. "I'm so glad I found you before the revival began."

"Mrs. Rumpson, how good of you to invite me into your home for the evening. Mother has provided our supper." She lifted up her basket. "Moist, but nourishing."

Mrs. Rumpson scanned the gathering people and clicked her tongue. "Have you ever seen such a crowd? I doubt we'll get a bit of sleep. Oh, how I wish my house wasn't next door." Her bird-like gaze landed on Rachael, and she gasped. "Why, child, what happened? Your shoes are caked with mud and your dress." She clicked her tongue again. "And, oh my, that hair."

Rachael stepped down from the log, feeling her ringlets in what she imagined in tangled disarray, dampening her shoulders. She removed her bonnet and handed it to Mrs. Rumpson.

"Did you check for ants before you placed this on your head?" Mrs. Rumpson stared in disbelief at the sodden dandelions hanging limply on the brim.

"It's much too cold for ants." Rachael maneuvered her heavy tresses back into her chignon and reached for her bonnet. "I thought to bring a bit of spring with me. Don't you think the flowers add a bright and cheerful contrast to my dowdy straw hat?"

"Well, when you put it that way…"

Rachael placed the bonnet on her head. "Propriety is all the way one looks on it — as with life." Jonathan proved a disappointment, but God hadn't. He'd provided a rescuer the precise time she needed one. Her gaze landed on a dainty form adorned in blue standing not more than four feet away. Isabella? Here?

"Really, Jonathan, why your sudden desire to change our plans is baffling. Revivals are for commoners. The inside of this tent smells foul. Oh, this is too absurd."

"I found my way again at one such revival. It will do you good."

Then Rachael saw Jonathan. His back was to her, but she couldn't mistake that voice or those broad shoulders — an arm's length away. What is he doing here? She dove, kneeling beside the half-hewn log seat and hunched her shoulders behind the ample Mrs. Rumpson.

"We shall leave if you wish, Isabella." Jonathan turned, gazing at the crowd. "But why not give this revival a chance? Being born-again is a choice only you can make. Come, let us find some seats."

"What are you looking for down there?" Mrs. Rumpson whispered.

"I, I, well, I dropped something." Suddenly, a shadow fell over Rachael. She gasped. How would she explain her actions to Jonathan this time? She looked up.

Saul Spiker's hair shone in ebony waves across a generous forehead and in strict opposition to the rest of his countenance. He pushed it back impatiently and smiled into her startled eyes, offering his hand to her.

"I thought I saw a coin," she said.

"No need to explain. I am well aware of your… interests, Rachael." Saul picked up her bonnet, his gaze sweeping the flowers on her hat as he handed it to her.

Rachael frowned back into Saul's teasing face, then scanned the area for Jonathan. Not seeing him anywhere, she got up and dusted off her skirts. "As I recall, Mr. Spiker, you have a few oddities of your own."

"That is why it is so easy for me to understand yours, Miss Rothburn."

Rachael sat down on the log seat, sniffed, and glanced at Saul.

Saul Spiker's frame was bone-thin, with knees that jutted beneath his trousers and long thin fingers that never relaxed. His one desire was to seek God's guidance as to the purpose of his birth. Rachael often wondered if he might not be too edgy to wait long enough to hear God's reply.

Mrs. Rumpson leaned across Rachael, extending her plump hand. "How do you do? I'm Mrs. Rumpson. And how did you come to meet Rachael?"

"Rachael is a former classmate of mine at Pratt Academy."

Rachael noticed Mrs. Rumpson's change of attitude. With every extra candle on Rachael's birthday cake, Mother brought another matchmaker into her life. Her face grew warmer. All she needed was to have Jonathan and Isabella within hearing distance. She glanced around. Oh, why should she care what he or Isabella thought?

"Rachael, who are you looking for?" Mrs. Rumpson asked.

Rachael turned to study the stage as if diverting her eyes would induce Mrs. Rumpson's eyes to follow. "Shouldn't the revival have started by now?"

"I wish it would never begin — at least not next door to my house. The noise and people trampling my roses is such a nuisance!" She gasped. "Oh my, I can't believe… I don't mean a word. Not a word. We need revivals, only elsewhere." Mrs. Rumpson placed a hand to her open mouth. "Oh, dear, I declare, my mouth flows like stale syrup, not at all to my liking." Mrs. Rumpson fanned her flushed face.

Rachael laughed. Saul joined in. "I don't believe I've ever heard you laugh before, Mr. Spiker."

"It is a welcome relief, Miss Rothburn. A good laugh certainly relaxes the face muscles, does it not?"

Mrs. Rumpson looked hopefully from Rachael back to Saul. "Yes, now where did I leave off? I declare, I'd lose my head if it wasn't fastened on my neck." She clapped her hands together. "Oh, I remember. Are you aware of Rachael's desire to become a missionary?"

"No," Saul said.

"Her mother and I are always telling her to wait."

"Wait for what?" Saul said.

"Until she meets a handsome young man like you." Mrs. Rumpson turned toward Rachael, winking and tilting her head toward Saul. "Then we'll see where her feet lead her."

How humiliating. Averting her eyes from Saul's, she spotted Jonathan sitting five seats down from theirs. She gasped. Had he heard Mrs. Rumpson?

"Miss Rothburn?" Saul leaned forward. "Is there something wrong?"

Rachael shook her head. "You were saying, Mr. Spiker?"

"I was at Amity and heard a Reverend McCray talk about the church's pressing need for missionaries in this new Oregon Territory."

"I was at Amity too." Rachael couldn't believe it. She and Saul shared the same passion for missionary work. "Wasn't it exciting to hear about Marcus and Narcissa Whitman?" Rachael hugged her Bible. "Someday I'll teach the Indians about the saving grace of our Lord Jesus like Mrs. Whitman."

Saul's eyes lingered on her Bible and the mud caked on her bodice, then he placed a finger beneath his high, starched collar. "With zeal like yours, you'll have no problem finding safe passage."

Rachael blushed. Then noticing Saul's heightened color, she felt a stab of sympathy for him. How did men cope with something so tight around their Adam's apple?

"Uh, the American Board of Commissioners for Foreign Missions is planning for another missionary group to leave shortly," Saul said.

"Really? My name is on their roster. I should be receiving a reply soon."

Mrs. Rumpson leaned forward, concern written like a map across her forehead. "Rachael, have you told your parents about this?"

"I implore you, do not disclose this to Father." He would not receive the news well from her, let alone, Mrs. Rumpson. "I shall alert Father as to my plans to become a missionary for this new Oregon Territory as soon as I receive my papers."

"There is really no need to alarm the Senator or his wife, Mrs. Rumpson." Saul smiled back at her reassuringly. "The ABCFM is sending missionaries this month to the West. I have already been contacted and am making my plans to leave as we speak."

"Well, it is a relief to me knowing Rachael has not received her papers. Perhaps this Board of Commissioners considers it as absurd as I that a lone woman should travel to that heathen land. Oh, there's Mrs. Brown." Mrs. Rumpson jumped up. "She has my umbrella. Mr. Spiker, will you escort me please? The crowd is so large and the footing so uneven. I fear I might fall."

"Certainly, Mrs. Rumpson."

Rachael hardly noticed them leaving. This can't be true. Why hadn't the ABCFM contacted her? Jesus, You promised. You said nothing is impossible for You. She closed her eyes, recalling Mark 11:24, "What things soever ye desire, when ye pray, believe that ye receive *them*, and ye shall have *them*." The sharp voice of Isabella broke her concentration.

"You look as if you've seen a ghost," Isabella said. "Perhaps it's the dandelion ghost?"

Rachael looked up.

"I couldn't help overhearing your conversation, very unfortunate you have not heard from the Board." Jonathan's eyes gazed into her face. His look softened, but pity oozed from his lips.

Rachael lifted her chin feeling like a prize fighter on his final round. She would not allow the pity in Jonathan's eyes to waver her resolve to rise above this temporary setback. "No, Isabella, it's not the dandelion ghost, but the Holy Ghost I'm seeking." Then she recalled Jonathan's earlier remarks. "Are you leaving? Don't you want to renew your faith? A born-again experience will give your life meaning."

"I don't belong with these…" Isabella whined. "I mean, we… don't belong." Isabella leaned into Jonathan's shoulder, declaring her claim to him.

Isabella wouldn't understand. Rachael didn't want Jonathan or any man. Her only desire was to go west. She squared her shoulders and smiled. "I will travel west and become a missionary."

A lopsided grin curved the ridged lines of Jonathan's lips. "I wish you an abundant crop, Miss. Rothburn." A wry twinkle filled his deep blue eyes, fixing them on Rachael's face. "Believe that ye receive *them*, and ye shall have *them*."

Her face grew warmer beneath his arrogant gaze. Was he mocking her in wishing her an abundant crop? Rachael turned away. Oh, the impertinence.

chapter two

"You listen to your wife, Mr. Brown," Dr. Jonathan Wheaton said to the lean man stretched out on one of the mattress beds that lined the poor-man's ward of the city hospital. "Another fall off the wharf and your heart might stop altogether. Quit drinking."

"What's a wife to do when she sees her husband going down to perdition?" Maggie sniffed, slapping her husband's shoulder.

Wooly chest hair peaked out from the collar of George's dingy white hospital gown. He crossed his thick forearms and shrugged. "It's hard to work with the boys at the wharf and not join in a little toast on payday." George's bottom lip puckered forward like an unruly child.

"You goin' to follow them to the devil 'cause that's where they're headin'?" Maggie's tears ran uncontrolled down her cheeks. "Georgie, listen to reason, we left Ireland so we could worship the way God intended and give our children a better beginning to life than we had."

"I give ya my paycheck, what's wrong with a wee sip?"

"You call it a wee sip? So drunk you fell off the pier? Where were your chums when you needed them?" Maggie sniffed, then blew her nose. "There's the world we see and the world we don't — that is till Jesus plucks us up… Besides, how am I goin' to live without you snuggled alongside me? Don't you want to see the little ones grown?" She buried her head on his chest and sobbed.

That's the kind of love Jonathan wanted… a woman who would fight for his soul and his worthless hide. That missionary thing he heard Rachael talk about sounded like something he should look into.

George's callused hand swiped his cheek gruffly. His stern jaw wavered as a batch of tears ran down his weathered face. "Aw, ain't fair, you know what your tears do to my insides."

Feeling the intruder but not wanting to leave, Jonathan knew he had found his fulfillment. His reason for being a doctor was to help the helpless. As Maggie put it, till Jesus plucked him up. "You listen to Maggie and I won't be seeing you back here again."

The assistant's shoes tapped a snappy melody on the stark white floor. "Here, Doctor, this came for you and I brought your mail."

Jonathan accepted the envelope absentmindedly and tucked it and the mail under his arm and hurried to his office. As he emptied the envelope, crude maps of the frontier territory unfolded in his fingers. Ever since he read about the Lewis and Clark expedition, Jonathan itched to explore the frontiers of this new western expansion. It wouldn't be long now. Hmm, he could become one of those missionaries and serve the Lord spiritually and medically. "I'll write the necessary papers to the Board today," he muttered.

A letter tumbled down with the day's mail of reports. He slit the envelope open:

> Dear Dr. Wheaton,
>
> I was sorry to learn of your loss. I knew your dear departed mother for over a decade and have recently learned from your stepfather that you have returned to set up your practice in Buffalo. Please accept this invitation for dinner with us on an evening of your choice.
>
> I feel it imperative to explain the reason for the invitation to be taken as it is given from a father's concern over his eldest daughter.
>
> My daughter Rachael is nearing her twenty-second birthday. She is a genteel woman of fine upbringing and stature, with a dowry of sufficient proportion, awaiting the right husband.
>
> I am, your most humble servant,
> Senator Arthur Rothburn

Jonathan fingered the water-marked parchment. Could Senator Rothburn's daughter be the same Rachael Rothburn he just met? He let the letter flutter to his desk like a wingless bird as he grabbed his appointment book. Rachael, a senator's daughter who enjoys tramping about in the lowlands of Buffalo like a common servant girl? Let's see, he had surgeries scheduled for tomorrow; however Wednesday afternoon was available. A home cooked meal would sit well and he knew he'd enjoy the company.

He chuckled, recalling how Rachael had fought back when that upstart adolescent spouted his vile innuendos at her, and then the brief conversation he'd had with her at the revival. That little conversation had his blood boiling and caused him to toss and turn all night. Rachael Rothburn was well endowed indeed, in more ways than one.

Weaving his hands together like a prize fighter, he smiled. Sparring with the feisty Rachael would prove entertaining. He'd better play it cautiously. He didn't want marriage. Not with his exploration of the West. No, he didn't want anyone entangling him with her dreams when he had a trunkful of his own. But dinner would be nice, especially if this Rachael proved to be the same woman who liked picking dandelions.

Rachael's mother bustled into the kitchen and shut the door that led to the hallway and vestibule. "Your gentlemen suitor has arrived. He is quite charming. Please make an effort to invoke his favor. Your father has included a sizable dowry."

Rachael removed the soup from the stove before it bubbled over and felt the tension in her bosom swell like that boiling pot. "Tell Father he can use that money to fund my expedition out west. I was going to tell you both at dinner. I've sent a letter to the missionary board stating my requests. I should be leaving this month."

"Yes, I know." Her mother reached into her pocket and handed her a letter. Then placed a hand to her forehead where a dark curl streaked with grey had fallen. She shoved it back beneath her mobcap.

Rachael skimmed the letter. "The Honorable Senator Rothburn and Mrs. Rothburn." One line stuck out from the rest: "Marriage required." This cannot be.

"Now, dear, let me get that apron off. If I had known Father had invited a guest for dinner, I would not have allowed our cook and Matty an afternoon off. Really, we must not keep the young doctor waiting." Her mother surveyed her. "I am so glad I told you to wear the blue dress, it does wonders for your eyes and figure."

"I look like an over-stuffed peacock. And this plunging bodice makes me look way too desperate." The cozy kitchen with its aroma of spices and baked bread coupled with the noise of the crackling hickory and bubbling pots would heighten the taste buds of the ficklest appetite. Rachael's was unaffected. She hungered for the lost. "I don't know how I'll do it, but I will go west as a missionary some day."

Her mother fluffed up one of her leg of mutton sleeves. "It is a decision you are ill-equipped to make. Rachael, you are of gentle breeding —"

"If God wanted me to marry, he'd have given me a different body. Not one that overshadows most men and gives others the wrong impression about me. I shall put a stop to this immediately." Rachael blew through the swinging doors like a potential thunderstorm into the parlor where Father and the unknown guest awaited her.

"Well... look who cannot wait to join us." Senator Arthur Rothburn's lapse in speech obscured his loss for words. He beamed at her. "Dr. Wheaton, may I introduce Rachael, my eldest."

The tall man dressed in the fashionable brocade waistcoat extended his hand. Engulfed in the doctor's firm grip, she was relieved to see her hand was still attached to her arm when he decided he'd given it a hearty enough shake.

Rachael scowled up at him and gasped. Jonathan! Would he tell her father about Bobby McGuire and his bullies? Father must never know. It would confirm his fears and the need for a husband. She needed to choose her words carefully.

"Well, well," Jonathan's gaze appeared to swallow her whole. "It is you —"

"Dr. Wheaton." By his look, she knew he thought her daft. "How nice to meet you."

Her father leaned toward her like a sapling caught in a thunderstorm. "I get the feeling you two have met before."

Rachael forced herself to hold Jonathan's gaze and held her breath.

"I could never forget such a lovely face." Jonathan sounded much too curious.

"Let me tell you about our Rachael." Father placed his thumbs into his breast pockets and tilted his head to one side like an amiable cockatoo. "She's every bit of five-foot-eight and her sturdy build wards off sickness."

"Father!" Rachael felt her cheeks burn with humiliation. Father never admitted her full height of five-foot-nine. His embarrassment about her size only intensified her self-consciousness. How could she make any man happy? She averted her eyes, watching as each of her siblings promenaded into the room.

Her two brothers, Mark and Harmon, hesitated before Dr. Wheaton, sending her a sympathetic smile. Her sisters, Jane, Martha, Joyce, and little Anna, curtsied, then Jane grabbed five-year-old Anna by the hand and all six ran into the kitchen.

Father continued to rock back and forth on his heels. "Well, Dr. Wheaton, what are your thoughts of our Rachael?" Father waited. No response came from Dr. Wheaton. "She isn't the willowy sort. But you can see that for yourself. That she's strong." Father's expression held a calculating keenness, and his smile did not reach his eyes. "Rachael's height complements yours. You are both very statuesque." Father chuckled deep in his throat, rubbing his hand along his chin. "And she can bear you many heirs."

Rachael swallowed the bitter taste of it all and drew in a long, slow breath. Who was this stranger wearing her loving father's clothes, displaying her as if she were a potential brood mare on the auction block?

"Well, uh..." Father rubbed his chin. "Do you enjoy hunting, Dr. Wheaton?"

"Hunting and fishing are passions of mine. And you, Miss Rothburn?" Jonathan's face bore the crimson shadow of a blush.

Before Rachael could get out a word, her father's booming voice interrupted her. "Why, yes, Rachael is very good with the rifle, aren't you, dear?"

Mother's voice echoed across the room. "Mr. Rothburn, I am in need of your services."

"Well, I'll leave you two to your... uh, conversation."

"Alone, at last." Jonathan bent over her and she swam in his shadow. He was a man of a considerable breadth and height. No wonder he had plucked her so easily out of the water.

"That dress is very becoming to your hair and eyes." He boldly swept her form with a gleam of his own. "It complements your attributes... pleasingly."

The heat of a blush worked its way from the wide neckline of her afternoon dress to her face. She stepped away, tilted her head, and glared back. "I wore it to please only Mother."

He chuckled. "Your eyes, they appear blue, but I daresay there is another color looming within their depths."

"Would you like to check my teeth next?" she whispered. How dare he? Father commanded her respect, but Dr. Wheaton was treading on quicksand and about to feel the full force of her temper if he stepped any further into this barbaric ritual — an arranged marriage indeed. Convenient for Jonathan, who would acquire an added fortune, a warm bed, and a namesake.

"So what color are your eyes?" Jonathan stepped closer.

Rachael's face grew warmer beneath his bold gaze.

"They are hazel, a greenish-greyish color," Mother replied with a discerning smile from her position near the door. Then like a general reviewing his troops she observed her brood as they all paraded into the dining room for dinner.

"I can see that now." Jonathan bent closer. "You clean up well, Miss Rothburn, well, indeed."

"Forget our first encounter ever took place," Rachael whispered, looking at Mother and then to Father. "Mention it to no one."

Jonathan nodded his head, bowing at the waist. "It is as you wish."

Mother breezed her way back through the swinging doors of the kitchen, and returned with a large soup tureen adorned with antique handles of solid ivory and gold lily scrolling etched on the fine bone china. "Jane, you can bring in the pitchers of tea and milk. Arthur?" Mother looked at Father and patted her linen cap trimmed with lace and tied beneath her chin.

"Yes, yes." Father glanced at his pocket watch. "My dear, you never cease to amaze me." Father extended his pocket watch toward his guest. "See here, Dr. Wheaton. Mother has fulfilled both her duties as cook and hostess with remarkable punctuality. You can expect similar skills from our Rachael."

Rachael dug her nails into her palms and prayed for patience. The meal would be over soon and Jonathan would go home. Then she would be rid of him.

"May I?" Jonathan pulled out Rachael's chair.

"All right, children, sit down. It is time to say grace. Father?" Mother bowed her head, Father prayed, and then they passed the steaming plates of fresh bread, broiled fish, and homegrown beans around the table. Baby Ross, who had eaten earlier, played with his wooden spoons, banging them against his high chair. Anna, who'd just acquired her grown-up chair, elevated with plump pillows, couldn't resist demonstrating to their guest the correct way of banging.

Martha leaned across the table to lock glances with Jane. Her auburn tresses fell dangerously near her half-consumed soup. "I think Rachael and Dr. Wheaton make a handsome couple, don't you, Jane?"

Rachael's startled eyes met Jonathan's, then shied away. *I don't believe my misfortune.* She bent down and buried her spoon into her clam chowder. His nearness caused her appetite to evaporate. She felt his eyes surveying her; she dared not look up. She forced a spoonful of soup into her mouth. Her knotted stomach protested.

Jonathan chuckled, and dabbed at his clean lips. "Does Rachael always eat with such gusto?"

Jonathan covered Rachael's shoulders with her fur-trimmed cape lined in satin, allowing his hand to linger long enough for her to feel the warmth of his fingers, then turned to retrieve his own coat. His boots echoed across the wood floor and Mrs. Rothburn's voice followed his heavy thoughts. "Go on, Rachael, a walk after dinner will do you both good. Dr. Wheaton has asked to see Lake Erie. If you hurry, you might catch the sunset mirrored in the lake."

As he returned to her side, Rachael pulled her cape closer to her form and squared her shoulders, as if preparing for a chilling interlude, her head taking refuge within her hood. He opened the door and paused to inhale a deep breath of the crisp spring air. He motioned her out then shut the large oak door behind them.

He gave Rachael a thorough perusal out of the corner of his eye. Her long flowing brocade dress resembled a bell, swaying to the movement of her strides. It was as he had suspected. Rachael Rothburn was capable of making her own decisions in accepting the hand of a suitable husband.

"You know you have a very erect manner of walking, Miss Rothburn. I noticed that the morning of the revival. Some might consider such deportment haughty."

Rachael stopped.

That got her attention. "I find it graceful, almost royal in its dignity."

Rachael's turbulent eyes scowled back. "I find this conversation distasteful, Dr. Wheaton."

How dare she throw his regards back at him like that. "Distasteful is a strange word choice when someone has paid you a compliment, especially since that person rescued you. Wouldn't you agree?"

"You may recall, Dr. Wheaton, I did thank you for coming to my rescue." Her quiet voice held no apology.

"Yes, indeed you did."

"Thank you for not revealing the incident to Father… I trust you have not done so?"

"Your secret is safe with me, Miss Rothburn." There was something about her that made her irresistibly intriguing. "Could you find a more suitable word to replace distasteful?"

She pivoted, facing him, her hands drawn in fists by her side. "Next month I shall be twenty-two. I am a spinster. I am without hope of redeeming the reputation of the Rothburn name. What choice of words would you have me use?"

Her words so vibrant, he knew they hurt her deeply to disclose. Though ten years her senior, he understood her feelings of abasement. His father's abrupt death, his mother's rejection, and his uncle's iron-fisted discipline made him feel abandoned, banished from being a son of worth to a boy starved for affection. What had been his sin for his mother's repulsion? Or was it his father's abandonment through death that had caused his mother's flight into another man's arms? Should he tell Rachael? No. He would never disclose his feelings of abandonment to her or any woman for fear of their rejection. He set his jaw, masking his emotions, willing his arms not to sweep her into his comforting embrace.

She searched the depths of his eyes, her gaze earnest. "By your look, you agree with my parents. We need to hurry. I know of a shortcut we can take." She resumed her long strides toward their destination.

Leaving the brick pathway, Rachael ducked onto a shallow foot path to the left that dipped and turned toward a dense forest. Jonathan watched her sway and turn with the agility of a doe in flight, whereas he, like a cumbersome bear, managed to get slapped with every available branch and twig that happened across his path. He laughed and the loudness echoed in the floral tapestry of pink, crimson, and violet hues that filled the sky before them.

"Isn't it lovely?" Rachael spread her arms to include the broad expanse of sky and water.

You're lovely. Exciting. Even her moods were pleasurable. "I apologize for laughing. I hoped the woman I rescued from those ruffians and Senator Rothburn's daughter would be one and the same." He reached for her hand. "I would think you would want me to tell your father about those ruffians."

"I am capable of taking care of myself." She jerked her hand from his grasp and hid it within the folds of her dress.

"Have you ever been to England, Miss Rothburn?"

"No. America is my home, and the only place I wish to travel is west. I want to be a missionary."

Jonathan snorted.

"Is something wrong?"

His lips curled with skepticism. "So you're planning to traverse the uncharted wilderness to save the savages. There are many female acquaintances of mine that have this romantic idea of championing a cause like Narcissa Whitman and seeing new lands."

"Mrs. Whitman has my enduring respect and admiration. But I do not entertain the thought of becoming like her. I am the vessel God has created me to be. We are different in our manners, but the same in our love for our Savior."

Rachael flashed him a look that could have frozen water in July and Jonathan rolled back on his heels. His gaze probed hers. "I see. It's become a passion for many young women recently reborn, figuratively speaking of course. But you're different." He stepped closer. The scent of lavender and roses, earth and water intoxicated his nostrils. "This Second Awakening of religious principles has filled the pews of many a church up and down America, but one has to wonder if it's sincere, this charismatic movement."

"Praise the Lord." She stepped away, and walking along the lake, tossed her words over her shoulder as a person would a bone to an obstinate pet. "That is all I have to say to you on the subject, Dr. Wheaton."

"What, Miss Rothburn, do you have to offer the Indians? Brought up in a mansion, daughter to a senator, with parents who adore you?"

"I feel God is drawing me to become a missionary."

He watched Rachael walk to the sandy banks of the lake and look out at the waters gleaming in the sunset. He remained silent for a moment, then drew up beside her. "Do you know how to bake bread with only a handful of provisions?"

"I am a teacher by profession. An older gentleman, versed on wilderness techniques has taught me and my class about the pioneers who tamed this region. I will employ him to teach me more survival techniques." She hugged her arms to her chest as if to barricade her heart from ill.

"It will help. Do you know how to harness a team? Have you driven a buckboard that's like a covered wagon in handling?"

"I often harness and drive our family's carriage to church."

"I was referring to a team of mules."

"What use would a team of mules be here? But I'm eager to learn."

"There isn't time to learn, especially on the trail."

She turned her gaze back to the darkening waters of Lake Erie. "If God wants me to go west, He will find a way for me to get there."

Rachael's profile displayed her gently sloping forehead, a sharp nose, and stubborn chin. An uncompromising face, but a noblewoman's all the same, a noblewoman needing nurturing. Yes, he'd seen that character before, mirrored in the eyes of George Brown, that determination to survive. He studied her face, gleaming in the lapse between the end of day and the beginning of night.

Rachael's pure innocence, her willingness to accept the unknown and to follow her Savior to the ends of the world, he couldn't help but respect her... and fear for her safety. She would be safer witnessing to the poor and downtrodden of New York, not the blood-thirsty heathens in the west. "You'll wilt like your confounded dandelions. Wither in the harsh winters and the hot dry summers of the wilderness. Wilt and possibly die with only good intentions for a marker placed over your grave."

"Better to wither beneath adversity than wilt in dreams of what might have been." Her hazel eyes sparkled back at him.

His mind battled from present to past as he pictured her sitting beneath the budding cherry tree. That could have been the end but for the strange coincidence of having Senator Rothburn's invitation sitting on his desk. Only, he didn't believe in coincidences. "I see now why Jesus has called you to the mission field, Miss Rothburn, and I am beginning to see why our merciful Savior has had us meet. It is an honorable undertaking to care for the downtrodden of our forlorn New York slums. I can arrange this for you."

A slight breeze sent the poplars' rustling leaves to sway their music down to them. The lapping waves washing on the sandy shoreline bathed their ears in its soft rhythmic beats. She stood there, her head held high and aloft with her hair blowing in the breezes. "God wants me to become a missionary in the Oregon Territory."

He turned toward the lake.

"What? You do not think God capable of it?" Her quiet voice held no reprimand.

"I think God has better things to do than to answer our whims."

"I will win souls for Christ, I feel…" She tapped her chest. "It's here, deep in my heart."

Jonathan stared into the deep waters of Lake Erie, seeking an answer to his troubled thoughts that whirled from experience to indecision. Hers was not the same genteel style he was accustomed to. She was in a class all her own. Her beauty came from within.

He turned. Her brown hair floated about her shoulders, playing with the breezes coming off the lake. In the setting sunlight, flecks of reddish highlights gleamed of her vitality. She lifted her chin as if to absorb the breeze fully. He'd never met a woman who had the ability to change the course of his destiny. No, it couldn't be. The thought was explosive. "Not that I don't understand your… desire. You see it has been my deepest wish to explore the West. I'm leaving within the month on an expedition." He swallowed past the sudden thickness in his throat. "That is the reason why marriage is an impossible choice for me."

Rachael lay awake staring up at the plaster cherubim scrolls of her ceiling. Tears rolled unheeded down her cheeks as the twilight moon seeped its silver rays through her bedroom window.

She pictured the beautiful Isabella with her golden curls who hardly made a shadow within Jonathan's fine ebony carriage. Who was Rachael in comparison?

Father's comments at dinner referring to her size caused a burning flush to sweep her countenance. She wiped her tears away with the back of her hand, recalling the stroll to Lake Erie. To Jonathan she was nothing but a tall, stout spinster. She buried her face into her pillow and sobbed. Oh, how embarrassing… Father couldn't pay Jonathan enough. Not anyone enough to wed her.

chapter three

*M*iss Rothburn. Miss Rothburn." The maid's white apron
flapped like a kite without a tail against her stark black
uniform.

"I'm over here, Matty." Rachael pushed the tray of seedlings aside
and brushed the dirt and mud off her gloved hands and stood up.
Whatever could be wrong? In long, quick strides she met their maid
on the garden's cobblestone walkway.

"You have a gentlemen caller — a Mr. Saul Spiker." Matty put a hand
to her middle, slightly out of breath.

Was that all? "Tell him I am indisposed and not receiving visitors."
She had no interest in callers.

"But your mum has invited him into the parlor, and when I last
looked, he was supping on tea and scones."

Rachael turned so Matty could not see her disappointment. What
better way to appease Father than by receiving every suitor who called.
Besides, what if Father had sent him? "I will join him momentarily."

Rachael used the servants' stairs to reach her bedroom unnoticed.
Gazing into her mirror, she shuddered. Her hair was wet and disheveled from her morning romp through the woods. April's showers and
the warm weather had made the foot trails muddier than normal this
year. Her shoes and the hem of her skirt were caked with dingy black
stains from the paths she had wandered.

She changed into a fresh cream and yellow dress, and after attempting to tame her unruly locks, wrenched a bonnet on them and smoothed her curls beneath its brim.

"There." She frowned at the scowling reflection in the mirror. If her raiment did not affect the desired response in her suitor, Mother's discerning look would be quick to reveal it to her. Mother she never needed to worry about. Rachael chuckled, then made her way to the parlor.

"Mr. Spiker, how nice to see you again. What's brought you here on such a dismal day?" Rachael curtsied.

Saul rose from his chair and bowed. "It is always a pleasure to find an excuse to visit you, Rachael." His dark eyes searched hers.

Avoiding his look, Rachael turned toward Mother. "Saul spent most of the time at the revival watching over me." She walked toward to the cluster of sofas and chairs decorating the formal blue and green parlor. With its cooling shades, it was a restful haven during the hot summer months. During the brisk winter months, a cheerful fire in the mammoth stone hearth sent its red glow across the sky blue wallpaper of seagulls and clouds.

Mother smiled, and as always a lovely aura of warmth accompanied it. "Thank you, Mr. Spiker, for taking care of my headstrong daughter."

Rachael laughed. The morning romp had renewed her hope. What a difference from yesterday. "Mother, I am a product of you and Father." She sat down between Mother and Mr. Spiker.

"Yes, I'm certain of that. You are much like great-grandmother Sutton in temperament. More tea, Mr. Spiker? Rachael, I'm sure you would like a little tea to drive away the chill of your morning walk."

"Yes, Mother. A little more cream than usual, please."

"Mr. Spiker, Rachael has not stepped far away from her youth. She prefers milk over tea and romps in the woods instead of sojourning down rose-strewn walkways."

Mr. Spiker slapped the arm of his chair and leaned toward Rachael, his eyes staring into her face. He glanced down at his teacup and saucer, then set them on the side table. "Mrs. Rothburn, I've spoken to your husband and request a moment with your daughter."

Father couldn't have, not her friend. The rapid thumping of her heart and her pulsating temples conveyed the truth to her unwilling mind. The atmosphere of the room felt bleak and depressive like the weather outside. Even the blue wallpaper took on a dismal look. Rachael gulped down her tea, placed her cup on her saucer, and handed it to the waiting Matty.

Matty gathered up the dishes, placing them on her silver tray, and followed Mother out of the parlor door. Mother hesitated. The regal arch of her head nodded in Rachael's direction. She drew the large oak doors shut.

The noise of those mammoth doors closing with such finality echoed in Rachael's ears. She kept her gaze fixed on her hands, which found a safe burrow within the folds of her dress.

Saul knelt down on one knee before her, placing a hesitant arm on one of the elbows of her chair. "Miss Rothburn, I hope I am not catching you totally unaware as to the intentions of my heart, for they are long overdue."

Rachael bit down on her bottom lip. Father. How could he? Not Saul, too. Has this man seeking God's heart fallen to materialism? Was no one safe from Satan's sting? Had the knowledge of her sizeable dowry aroused his feelings? Was that why he found he was in love with her?

"We have known each other a considerable time. Your desire to become a missionary is likened to my own. Do you not find this amiable?"

"Yes, you are well aware of my feelings." Her eyes avoided his and she crammed farther into the restricting high back chair.

"God is calling me to a mission of servitude among the Indians. The Board has contacted me for the expedition, Rachael." Saul reached for her hands, clasping them into his thin, clammy fingers. "I have learned they desire married couples only and immediately I thought of you."

"Oh, Mr. Spiker..."

Saul placed his index finger on her lips. He smiled, rising from his perch on the rug, still clutching her hand in his clammy grip, misunderstanding her exclamation.

"Mr. Spiker, there is more we should know about each other before assuming this is the course which our Good Lord intends for our lives. A union between a man and woman needs to be more than a business arrangement."

Saul's mouth gaped open. "My proposal has come as a shock to you, but I thought..." He dropped her hand and stepped away.

Like a canary given its freedom, Rachael sprang to her feet, and in one swishing movement of her long skirts, rushed toward the bay window, releasing a quivering breath.

"I can imagine your misgivings." Saul's footsteps reverberated against the polished wood floor, echoing the pulsating rhythm of her heart. "The gossip about me at the Academy is alarming to a lady of your station. I wish I could erase any doubt as to its truthfulness."

Rachael searched her memory for the strands of gossip overhead at the library while preparing lessons for her students.

"Sadly, I must concede the gossip is true." The warm breath of his whispered words into her ear startled her. "My mother is a godly, well-educated woman who reared me in a godly home. My father couldn't read or write. Mother did the best she could to teach him, but he enjoyed the brothels more than books." Saul's fingers raked through his hair. "Dear mother did what she could to keep food on the table, even begging for work at her father's business. She was too proud to accept charity, especially from her high and mighty well-to-do relatives."

A bitter sigh escaped Saul's lips. "Oh, try and understand. When your father wrote me I couldn't help thinking, well, that it might be a message from God."

Rachael's thoughts swirled out of control. Father had finally found someone he could pay to wed her. Humiliation welled up within her.

Saul turned and with heavy steps walked toward the fireplace where flames wrapped the logs with red-orange fingers. "I thought you of all people would understand. You can imagine my astonishment when my father, with his lady friend on his arm, came to the Academy to belittle me, demanding money."

"I never dreamt the scandals relating to a certain professor was... you?" Her petticoats rustled about her legs as she rushed to Saul's side. "I'm so sorry."

"I don't want your pity, Rachael. I want your love. I do not feel myself unworthy." Saul stared into the fire. "Like my mother is not unworthy of a loving and faithful husband. He spitefully used her and then discarded her. You see, the only money my father got was my mother's dowry. My mother refused to share her inheritance and used it, instead, to send me to college. He got even with her and me by taking a mistress and blatantly parading about the city with her."

Saul grabbed the poker and stabbed the log until embers of red and gold spiraled upwards, his mouth drawn into ridged lines. "Am I not the same man that bent a knee before you a moment ago? Am I not the same man to which a hundred students prattle their Bible verses? But will I be the same man to Senator Rothburn when he finds out about my father? Will he find it questionable for me to wed his daughter? Will having me as a son-in-law upset the fair balance of his English heritage?" Laying the poker aside, Saul looked at her, his eyes softened as they beseeched hers.

"I stand before you, to implore your fairness, and your heart, dear Rachael. I feel God is drawing us together to perform His work in the mission fields." He reached for her hand, entwining hers with his and bent down on one knee. "You are more beautiful than any woman I have ever seen. See how our hands melt one into the other? Allow me to become your husband so I might entwine my love with yours and perform in Christian faith God's missionary work in this new frontier."

chapter four

octor Wheaton, Deacon Cambridge of the American Board of Commissioners for Foreign Missions to see you."

Jonathan laid aside a patient's chart and rose from his desk as his secretary and Deacon Cambridge entered the office.

"Dr. Wheaton." A man barely reaching Jonathan's shoulder covered the distance between them and stuck out his hand, shaking even before Jonathan took his bone-thin fingers into his grasp. "I remember your mother well, knew her for nearly forty years. She was a fine lady. I was sorry to hear about her death."

Jonathan searched his memory and the man's face. "I'm sorry. I can't recollect my mother mentioning your name."

"That's understandable. Now, I'll get right to the point. We of the Board feel blessed by your sacrifice, your willingness to dedicate eight months from your practice to venture with Reverend McCray and take our missionaries to the Oregon Territory."

"Wait." Jonathan held up his hand. "What about Reverend Park? He is the person who is most knowledgeable. And, the way I understood it, we were to go ahead of the missionaries and return the following year."

"The Board has decided Reverend Park is not physically fit to handle the journey. Reverend McCray is both knowledgeable and fit for the expedition and has ventured out as far as the Platte River. He's acquired Reverend Park's maps and two Pawnee Indian youths to aid you in this venture. The Board wishes to have the missionaries begin their journey this year.

The most desirable site lies southwest of the existing missionary site."

"When do you want me to leave?" Jonathan rubbed his palms. He could feel the virgin soil of a new territory beneath his feet. Just think, this time next month he would be seeing the primitive frontier that few white men had ever witnessed.

"The sooner the better. Can you be ready by April 10? Reverend Mc-Cray wants to spend a week with you. To get you acclimated before going west. You are to meet him at eight o'clock, Monday morning, at Lake Ontario's shipping dock. From there you will travel to Canada. McCray has located a French Canadian who was part of the Lewis and Clark expedition. He has a trading post in Oshawa and can tell you more about the terrain and what you will need to pack and prepare for."

"Really? Why the man has to be —"

"Sixty, he's living with some Indian tribe. You'll be picking up your supplies for the expedition as well."

Jonathan plopped into his chair, glancing over the half dozen files of patients. "I understand we must be in Liberty, Missouri, by May if we are to have sufficient grazing for our livestock during the journey and make it over the mountains before the snow. Did you bring the papers I asked for? The application I requested to become one of these missionaries?"

"Yes, we are delighted you want to be a part of this Great Awakening." Mr. Cambridge opened his briefcase and withdrew a piece of paper. "But it is with regret that we cannot process your application."

"Not process…" Jonathan rose, thrusting his chair back so hard it spun across the room like a child's toy top. He loomed his six-foot, six-inch bulk over the man who now sat cowering in a chair. "I'm paying for the equipment and supplies to make this trek. Do you realize how hard it is to get a doctor to take on my patients?"

"Dr. Wheaton, if it were my decision, I would not hesitate to give it to you. But rules must be upheld. You are not married. The stipulation is that all missionaries must be married couples before receiving assigned positions. You will be taking the missionaries, two couples — yet to be determined — and, of course, per your recommendations. Once they are settled, you will have to return."

"I seem to recall this country is free."

"You are free to do as you choose, but you will not be able to be part of our organization."

Jonathan punched his fist into his hand and walked toward the window. "You mean, I'll be setting up the missionary sites, but I won't be able to be one of the missionaries? And you mean by missionaries, a husband and wife? You think women of our society capable of this excursion?"

"Correct. The Pilgrims brought their families, which included their children." Cambridge's chest swelled with importance. "Our association is world renowned. We cannot bend the rules. Unmarried men and women in the wilds would be scandalous."

"So, if I marry before I leave, I can be one of the missionaries, seeing how I am funding the complete expedition?"

"Well, when you put it that way. You will be moved to the top of our list."

Rachael. She would make the perfect wife. He could regain some of his money for the expedition from her dowry. And what a wife, beautiful, intelligent, and… willing. He chuckled. Maybe not so willing, but he could win her over. His hand went to his chin, recalling their walk to Lake Erie. She might refuse his proposal, ending his chances of becoming a missionary. He would have Rachael's father do the proposing.

Cambridge fidgeted with the papers he had pulled from the briefcase. "About your application, Dr. Wheaton, you are not married, and due to your need to leave in all haste, I see no way for you to meet our requirements."

With the quick even strides of a large cat, Jonathan stared down at the top of Cambridge's dwindling hairline. "Deacon Cambridge, let me see those papers."

Jonathan whipped the papers from Cambridge's hands, and with a stroke of his pen, handed them back to him.

Cambridge blinked. "I see that congratulations are in order."

"My betrothed and I will be married this week. She is as eager as I to serve this Second Great Awakening in the new territory, and I shall meet Reverend McCray on Monday."

Cambridge rose to his feet, steadying his shaking hand before clasping

Dr. Wheaton's. "I've heard Reverend McCray is a hard man to deal with, especially on the trail. But I doubt you'll have any problem, Dr. Wheaton."

* * *

Rachael did a half twirl in the Rothburn parlor. The peaceful and serene setting of the room had become a hubbub on her father's entrance. His heavy footsteps and loud exclamations sounded through the room like a thunderstorm. "I forbid you to marry him."

"But, Father, it was you who invited Mr. Spiker to court me. I sought to please you."

Her mother held a handkerchief to her lips, stifling her sobs.

"Mother, don't cry. Our daughter would never humiliate us this way."

"I don't understand, Father, we are Christians. Christians do not harbor ill will toward one another. What has Saul Spiker done that is so wrong? His father he cannot help. If anything, we should commend him."

Her mother looked down at her tear-drenched handkerchief and nodded. "She is right, Arthur. What cause do we have to condemn this young man, a young man zealous to perform God's work? We should be ashamed of ourselves."

Arthur patted his wife's hand. "There, there, Margaret. I don't slight the young man. I commend him for his gallant efforts to rise above himself, but, Rachael, you will not understand our feelings until you have children of your own."

"Yes, Rachael dear." Her mother sobbed. "It is so."

"Mother dearest, I will never do anything to offend you or Father. I will always love you both dearly. No matter where my Savior may lead me, I will always love you."

"Ooooh." Her mother held the lace-edged handkerchief to her lips. "Then you do plan to marry this young man and go with him to that heathen land." Tears floated across her once clear eyes, big tears that sent rivulets down her swollen cheeks.

Rachael's lungs ached as if they would burst. She could not go against her parents' wishes, their pain too much for her to bear. "No, not if you and Father do not want me to."

"Did you tell Saul you would marry him?"

"No, Father, I only promised to tell you of his intentions and of his disgrace. He is the humblest of men." Her father took a deep breath and expelled it, then locked his hands behind him. He gazed out the window as he rocked on his heels.

"The only one suitably matched for you is Dr. Wheaton," he said.

"But, Father, I've just met him."

"He is well suited for you, Rachael. Your mother and I knew Jonathan's mother for over a decade."

"Jonathan's father was a strong-willed man. I could never understand how his mother could allow her brother-in-law to take Jonathan to live with him after his father's death," her mother said.

"Yes, but it did the lad well." Her father added. "Dr. Jonathan Wheaton bears a fine name. You could not do wrong by wedding him and you will grow to love and respect him, Rachael. Trust me in this matter."

"But I want to be a missionary and Saul shares my desire. Saul is humble. Jonathan is prideful and headstrong. I cannot see how you could have missed these faults in his character."

Father rocked on his heels more violently than before. "Your perception is questionable, daughter. How did you arrive at such an assessment?"

Rachael walked to the window, finding solace in the gentle green hillside. "He threw my missionary plans back into my face, making me feel unworthy." She bit out her words through clenched teeth, but wanted to scream out the truth. To invoke the hurt Dr. Wheaton had with his glacial indifference to her. He thought her unworthy of him!

Father's smile broadened. A smothered laugh escaped her mother's lips. Rachael turned, confused. "What is this all about?"

"It seems Jonathan wants to become a missionary, too." Her father closed the distance between them and took her shoulders into his strong hands. "Dr. Wheaton has always entertained the thought of exploring the West. The Rocky Mountains instill the greatest thrill to his adventurous nature. He is funding an expedition and has decided to become one of these missionaries in this place people call the Oregon Territory."

What did this have to do with her? Jonathan made her feel foolish with her vague knowledge about the West and naiveté of the Indians' dialect. She was as finished with him as he was of her. She shrugged off her father's hands.

"Daughter?" Father, head cocked to one side, waited for her reply.

"Oh!" She sank into a chair, staring into the blazing fire. Her emotions sparked like the flames, out of control. So Jonathan was going west and she must remain. "So when is Dr. Wheaton leaving?"

"April 10. He's arranging the preparations with a Reverend McCray."

"Dear, it is Father's greatest desire and mine to fulfill our children's dreams," her mother pleaded.

Rachael rose from her chair and squared her shoulders. It must not be God's will for her to go. She must accept the decision of her parents and of God. "Dr. Wheaton wished me Godspeed and an abundant crop of souls when I told him of my desire to become a missionary, and I shall wish him the same."

"Abundant crop, you say? Yes, yes, Dr. Wheaton mentioned that." Father chuckled. "That is when he asked for your hand in marriage and I accepted most gratefully."

"What?" She plopped herself back into the chair. "Father, how could you? Am I nothing but a piece of livestock to you?"

"You may not see the reasons behind our actions, but some day you will come to understand them." Her mother was quick to come to her father's defense. "Parents want what is best for their children."

Her parents' good intentions tore the breath from her lungs. A marriage of convenience was what her parents proposed, and she was powerless to fight the current of fate sweeping her into this whirlpool of indifference.

Saul. She wasn't in love with him, but she was acquainted with him. He'd said she was the most beautiful woman he'd ever seen. But because of his upbringing, she could not marry him. Strange, he was branded an outcast, not of his doing. She, because of her station in life, was forced to wed a man not of her design, a man who looked on her as a clumsy spinster. She could never be dainty like Isabella.

"Rachael, you will be performing the most admirable sacrifice a young lady of your stature could. You will wed Dr. Wheaton and be the wife he needs to accomplish his life's mission, while complying with the orders of the Most High."

"I cannot believe that God would approve of a unity without love." Her father threw up his hands and looked to his wife.

"I thought you would be pleased with the news." Her mother entwined her slender fingers into a web of indecision. "I could have spent my elderly years contently spoiling my grandchildren, but God made it evident to me that this was not the case for my eldest. Your father and I believe it is God's will that you wed Dr. Wheaton and fulfill your calling with a joyous heart."

Oh, the shame of it. She would only be a wife on paper, until her husband chose to love her. Jonathan had said marriage was an impossible choice for him. What changed his mind? He would abate his repulsion for her in order to achieve his dream to go west. Well, she didn't need Jonathan's love; she would have Jesus' love. "When and where is my marriage to take place?"

Her father cleared his throat. "Dr. Wheaton said the sooner the better for the marriage ceremony. He is requesting this Sunday afternoon."

"This Sunday, the ninth?" Her mother scrunched the handkerchief to her lips, her muffled words expelling what Rachael's thoughts evoked. "This gives me little time to prepare."

Rachael rose to her full height. How dare Dr. Wheaton treat her family with such disregard. "Am I to surmise he sent his proposal to me via my parents? Will he be sending his engagement ring the same way?"

"He's a busy man, Rachael." Her father stroked his chin, in deep thought. "Now, we need to make haste with the invitations. We'll have the ceremony and the reception outside. The weather will be warm enough, I think, once the rain stops."

"But, it will take time to address and mail out the invitations." Her mother looked from her to her father. Preparation was the key to her mother's tranquil world.

"We'll invite everyone by word of mouth."

"Oh, the flowers." Her mother's hands went to her cheeks. "And the wedding dress? There is no time to make one and she is too tall for mine."

"No problem, Mother." Rachael placed a placid smile on her lips. It was clear her parents' concerns were only to wed her off. "We have our dresses from Grandmother's funeral." A sudden twinge of remorse cloaked her mother's face. Rachael hurried on. "I can take the dress with me to perform my duties in the mission field. White would get dirty." She stared at her parents coolly. "There, see how easily everything has been arranged? I am sure Dr. Wheaton will approve of the matching color scheme. Of course I would ask him, only I don't know how to go about reaching him."

She'd dreamed of becoming Jonathan's bride since the day he'd rescued her from Bobby McGuire and his bullies. A marriage of convenience, without feelings getting in the way of duty, was all Jonathan wanted, and true love was now as remote as the stars in the heavens. She had hoped someday he would look at her like he had Isabella. She choked out a bitter sigh. Jonathan Wheaton, her rescuer, was now her jailer.

The brass knocker resounded on the front door. A moment later Matty walked into the room, curtsied, and announced, "Ma'am, a Dr. Wheaton is here."

A man's laughter in the foyer captured the sudden quietness. Not waiting to be shown in, Jonathan's tall build overshadowed the doorway.

Father hurried forward, his arm outstretched before he'd made it across the room. "Dr. Wheaton, please come in, sit down and make yourself comfortable. Our home is now yours." Her father turned. "Matty, tea and scones for Dr. Wheaton."

A confident smile pinched the corners of Jonathan's lips, but his eyes captivated Rachael's. Not even Bobby McGuire had dared to be so bold. She covered her throat with her hand and glanced away.

Was it desire that sent his eyes burning into hers? Did he feel the same pin pricks and goose bumps running up and down his spine when their eyes met? No. That was pure nonsense. She shoved her hands deep into the folds of her dress.

What could Jonathan see in her but a means of getting to the frontier of a distant land? A man with a hunger to explore the unknown and make his mark on history. No, she was just a tool to be used in his determined hands. She bit hard on her lower lip. Her heart pounded against her rib cage. He could never love her; she was much too ugly.

Father glanced from her to Jonathan. "We're finishing up the wedding arrangements."

"Good. I have an appointment with Reverend McCray tomorrow evening. So Sunday afternoon at, shall we say, three?" Jonathan's eyes swept her form like a hot summer breeze. "That'll give Rachael plenty of time to get ready for her new duties, I should think."

From somewhere beyond the edge of her crashing world, Rachael raised her head, and with a proud tilt to her chin she confronted her new tormentor. "I thought you said I was incapable of becoming a missionary? Aren't you afraid I might wilt like my dandelions?"

A brow arched across Jonathan's forehead, a chuckle escaping his determined lips.

chapter five

A repetitious knock on Jonathan's door made him respond in equal haste to the impatient caller. "Come in!" His office door whisked open, banging against the wall layered with his diplomas.

"I'm sorry, Dr. Wheaton," Mr. Cassing said. "But Miss DeSimone —"

"Jonathan, I am in no temperament to be kept waiting." Isabella bustled through the opening in a rustle of brocade and lace, her stiff leg-of-mutton sleeves barely making it through the doorway. She gave the clerk a haunting glance. "That is what I asked you to say to Dr. Wheaton, why are you having such a problem remembering it?"

Isabella's voice grated Jonathan's already heightened senses like coarse gauze on raw skin. "You may leave for the day, Mr. Cassing, and thank you. I'll lock up when I'm finished." Jonathan resumed filling in the forms on his recent patient. "Oh, before you leave, would you be kind enough to contact Dr. White? I need to meet with him tomorrow."

"Will Dr. White be the new physician?"

Jonathan nodded to Mr. Cassing; however, his eyes followed Isabella about the room as she thrust off her cape and tossed it on the deep-cushioned leather chair. She returned his look, then narrowed her eyes at Mr. Cassing, as if to forcibly remove the man from their presence.

"We shall miss you, Doctor."

"As I you. You have performed your duties well over the years."

"It was a pleasure."

Isabella slapped the chair with her parasol. "My, my, how touching."

"Yes, well, good evening, Dr. Wheaton, Miss DeSimone." With a polite bow, Mr. Cassing left the room, closing the door softly behind him.

"I'm beginning to feel I am of little consequence to you, Jonathan. What other reason could there be for your fiancée to be the last to learn of your intended plans to leave a thriving practice to go live in some no-man's land with a tribe of scantly clothed savages."

"It's called the Oregon Territory, Isabella, and the inhabitants, scantly clothed or otherwise, need Jesus." Jonathan rose and stretched. "I do not understand why my decision comes as a surprise. You know my desire to explore the West."

Isabella shrugged, a half-sided smirk sweeping her lips. Her smile resembled a snarl. He walked to the front of his desk, rested his bulk on it, then crossed his arms and studied her. "I cannot place the time I proposed to you," he said, staring at her bare ring finger.

"It was more of a mutual understanding." Isabella raised her slender arm to her hat and cocked her head to one side, displaying the saucy tip of her becoming Paris original resting on her silky curls. "An engagement of intent, so to speak." Isabella's bell earrings set off the stylish picture to perfection, a picture that had more than once bewitched Jonathan. Only this time it did not cause a twinge of remorse.

Rachael and Isabella were opposites in every way. On this, he couldn't be happier. He chuckled.

"What is so funny?" A look of surprise covered Isabella's face like a shade on a window. "When are you leaving?"

Jonathan had posted his intended marriage in the *New York Herald*, so he bridged the subject cautiously. Was her vexation only for him vacating his thriving practice to venture into the wilderness, or was there more? He shook his head slowly. "I will be leaving Buffalo on Monday."

"Don't you think you should reconsider this venture? Surely you're not planning on turning over your practice to this Dr. White?"

"That is exactly what I am doing."

"Jonathan, be reasonable. Once you get this… this hunting escapade and sleeping out in the wide open spaces out of your system, you'll be back. You'll want your practice back, too." Isabella thrust the tip of her parasol onto the wood floor in exasperation. "How can you possibly think of living without money and prestige and leave all this behind?"

Jonathan's eyes swept Isabella's petite form. From the wide and very low neckline of her soft-blue day dress, to her tightly corseted waist, to the layered ruffles gathered at the bottom of her full skirt, to the tiny high-button shoes that peeked from beneath her hem when she lifted her skirts. She made a perfect picture, right out of the *Godey's Lady's Book*. Jonathan's eyes appraised her beauty. There was no getting around that. "Yes, I see what you mean, Isabella. There will not be too many parties requesting my presence once I lose my practice."

Jonathan frowned into her startled eyes. "But, then, I never found much pleasure in parties. I went because you liked them. Lately, the only pleasure I have derived from my profession is when I entered the charity ward at the hospital. That's when the pieces started to make sense to me. I enjoyed doing God's work."

"This whole expedition thing is nonsense. Leave it to some country bumpkin, not a refined doctor like yourself." She tapped her parasol on the wood floor again. "You are a distinguished and active member of the community, a trustee of your church and ordained as an elder. People will remember you, Jonathan, even if you decided to remain in that remote wilderness. But why go?" Isabella walked over and leaned toward him. The scent of her expensive Paris perfume and the inviting fragrances of a woman's body engulfed his senses.

"You don't want to leave me behind, do you?" she coaxed. Her slender finger traced his collar, her eyes liquid as they gazed into his. "I know the American Board of Commissioners of Foreign Missions has been all the rage, but that won't last. This Second Great Awakening will vanish like the last and people will stop saying 'praise the Lord' on every street corner and become civilized men and women again."

"You take your religious beliefs too lightly to satisfy me, Isabella." Jonathan's voice quivered close to uncontrollable. She didn't understand him or his Savior. Or did she take them both for granted, believing they would always be there to run to when she chose? Sadness crept through him, seeing her garments for what they were, materialistic rags that would decay with time. "The Board is an organization sponsored by both Presbyterian and Congregational missions throughout the world. America is a small piece, as you are just a small speck to God's great plan of saving mankind through his only Son, Jesus Christ."

"Yes, yes, yes, Jonathan. I have heard it all before." Isabella rolled her eyes. "I go to church every Sunday — only I haven't become a fanatic like you. Heaven forbid, just because you're bent on destroying your life for these savages, don't pin me with guilt."

He rose to his full height, looked down at her off the bridge of his nose and walked away only to turn back and survey her from across the room.

"I recently entertained Deacon Cambridge of the board. He amazed me with how much of my personal life he knew."

"Cambridge?" Isabella mused over the name. Jonathan knew when she was hiding something; she always tapped her fingers on the closest piece of furniture, as she now did. He smiled.

"I hadn't realized how close you were to my stepfather until I spoke with Deacon Cambridge. I understand now that Mother and my stepfather attempted to build barriers against me going west. What I couldn't understand is how Cambridge thought we were engaged."

Isabella lowered her head a moment, then looked up at him. He watched the gleam of her eyes through thick, sooty lashes. She strolled toward him, swaying her hips, encouraging the brocade and lace hem of her slip beneath her skirts to rustle, altogether feminine.

"I suppose I did reveal my heart before we had decided on our marriage date." Isabella batted her lashes, placing her tiny fingers below her neck. "But what is a woman to do when cornered? I cannot order my heart from leaping into my eyes. I only nodded that I would be happy to wed my beloved Jonathan."

"I have had no intentions of marrying you, Isabella. Our only commonality is in our proper English names. You could never humble yourself to become a missionary."

"Why?" Isabella's face turned an ugly shade of red and she stomped her foot. "Why this passion to grub among the savages? You could be a famous doctor some day. Don't you want that? Don't you want to show your stepfather he was wrong about you? Going to that forsaken land will prove nothing."

"Blame it on the Awakening because it was during one revival that I felt an overwhelming desire to serve Christ. It was He who gave my life meaning. Jesus taught me how to forgive and gave me a reason to draw breath each day." Puzzled, his gaze lingered on her for a suspended moment. "What gives your life meaning, Isabella? Surely it is not the latest fashions from Paris."

"Are we going to split hairs, Jonathan? If we are, then let's not ignore your innermost motive."

"What do you mean?"

"You're not blind. Surely you see as I that you want to live up to your father's name. That is what all this is about." She waved her hands in the air. "A way to glorify the Wheaton name. All this seeking and saving lost souls is only a ploy to get what you really want — admit it."

Jonathan looked away. Can the blind lead the blind? He'd read that parable, *A disciple is not above his teacher, but everyone who is perfectly trained will be like his teacher*... Was it because of his example Isabella had not found Jesus? He lowered his head and said a silent prayer. Oh, Lord, train me to be more like You — even if it takes my whole life.

"I am human — and it would please me to be among the names of those brave explorers discovering new territory, as my ancestors did before me, but my true desire is to glorify my Savior."

"Yes, well, I am sorry about your father. Your dear departed mother was sorry, too, but you will never know how sorry because you chose not to come when summoned."

"I came as soon as I learned of her sickness. I tried to make it back. I rode all night. If you want to blame someone, blame my stepfather for not sending word sooner."

"That is beside the point."

"Isabella, that is precisely the point, but my stepfather can do no wrong in your eyes. You might as well accept the fact. I am going to be a missionary and that is final."

"Oh? How? They only take married couples, and I am not about to go to that... that wilderness for anyone, not even for you."

Laughter bubbled from a place deep within him. "God has provided me with my bride."

"Oh, really, who could that possibly be? I cannot imagine any woman in their right mind consenting to such a preposterous thing as living amongst the heathens in such a desolate land. I believe you are making her up. When Cambridge told your stepfather and —"

"Go on."

Isabella covered her mouth with dainty white fingers, her eyes round as saucers. "Your stepfather cares for you, Jonathan. Your mother did too. You never forgave her for remarrying, nor accepted your stepfather for the caring man he is. I don't understand how you can possibly love those savages, when you don't even love your own family."

"I forgave Mother and Stepfather. I asked their forgiveness the day I accepted Jesus as my Savior. It was they who would not accept my calling."

Isabella fluttered a hand before her face as if swishing a fly. "Come now, Jonathan who is not facing the truth here. You are not married and are lying to pacify the mission's requirements."

"You know my fiancée."

"Me?" Isabella squealed like a piglet caught in a fence. "None of my friends would be so stupid as to venture out on such a mission." Her eyes drew into slits as narrow as her plucked brows. "No, it couldn't be, not — Spinster Rachael. That vagabond who prefers wandering the lowlands and forests of Buffalo to New York's finest shops? Don't you know, people of propriety think she's common? You couldn't stoop so low."

Jonathan snorted. "Low? She comes from a prominent family and is far above the women I have socialized with before. She will become my wife, Isabella, in the true sense of the word."

Isabella stamped her small foot. "As long as she's willing to accompany you to this no-man's-land, you'd have married an Amazon. Are you so certain you want such a woman to adorn the famous Wheaton name?"

chapter six

*R*achael, dressed in her knee-length linen chemise, corset, and starched petticoats, walked in from her mother's bedroom unnoticed by her sisters. Today was her wedding day, only she didn't feel like a bride. A commodity, perhaps, but not a bride.

Sixteen-year-old Martha watched Jane complete the alterations to Rachael's dress, the draped ebony folds across her lap. "Dr. Wheaton is so dreamily handsome. I wonder. Do you think they've even kissed?"

Kissed? That was the last thing Rachael was concerned about. She'd be happy just to get along with him for ten minutes without arguing.

The fragrances of lavender, lilacs, and roses drifted from the cut flowers on Mother's vanity. Mother's words flashed through Rachael's memory. She shuddered. The church required consummation to legitimize the marriage. If she did not consummate her vows, Jonathan could decree a petition of divorce, which would cause her father and the Rothburn name grief and humiliation.

Jane looked up from her sewing. "From what I've overheard Mother saying to Father, Jonathan was brought up by his bachelor uncle. I wonder if he understands women of gentle upbringing like our sister."

"Rachael is sour on men." Martha shoved a strand of hair behind her ear.

"That is not true. Rachael's just shy. Besides, when it comes to being attracted to the opposite sex, it's a matter of choice." Jane, tying the last knot on the beads she'd strung on Rachael's dress, poked her needle into her pin cushion. "I can't imagine how I'd feel if Father arranged my marriage to a perfect stranger and then expected me to share my sheets with him."

Rachael lifted her chin. Jonathan Wheaton would not have his way with her, and he would soon learn of that. He didn't bother to give her a proper proposal of marriage, so why should she honor her part of the vows? Besides, Jonathan wanted to go west as badly as she, he would not ask for a decree of divorce. With a proud lift of her chin, she drew a ragged breath then cleared her throat.

Martha gasped, elbowing Jane. "Sis, how long have you been standing there?"

"Long enough."

Jane's voice sounded anxious and much too curious for Rachael's liking. "The proposal is the most romantic time in a girl's life. When William proposed, I felt like I was being lifted on a puffy white cloud of love and —"

"Rachael, did Jonathan kiss you after he proposed?" Martha waltzed around the room on her own puffy white cloud of daydreams. "He's so dreamy, so tall and handsome."

Rachael cast her eyes on her mother's sculptured ceiling of cupids carrying bows and arrows. Pish posh. She didn't need or want a husband. "I received my proposal through Father." Rachael turned toward the Queen Anne full-length mirror and stared at her reflection. Her heart lunged within her chest as if trying to escape. She was going to a strange land with a stranger who didn't love her. A cold chill started at her neck and worked its way down her spine. Would Jonathan demand she fulfill those duties and force himself on her?

"Don't you think Dr. Wheaton is handsome, Rachael?" Jane's gaze flitted from Martha to Rachael. "There's a man's gentleness, his concern over your welfare. The loving way he helps you across a bridge. Oh, there is much more to love than physical…"

Rachael stared into the mirror not seeing her image but, instead, the naïve girl who chose to leave behind everything she knew and loved for the unknown. Martha was right. She was sour on men — especially Jonathan. He was in love with Isabella. Why didn't he marry her? Isabella was gorgeous and genteel and her parents didn't need to provide a dowry for her to find a husband.

Jane slipped her arm around Rachael's waist and whispered. "Don't marry Jonathan if you don't love him."

"What choice do I have? If I don't marry Jonathan, then my hopes of becoming a missionary in the west are gone." Tasting the bitterness of the fate that awaited her, she met her sister's gaze and forced herself to hold it. "Besides, if I didn't marry Jonathan, Father would only marry me off to someone else. What has love got to do with marriage when you're over twenty? You're eighteen, Jane, and now that you're engaged, Father would be concerned about what the neighbors will say taking you down the aisle before me. No. It is best I marry Jonathan."

Jane looked down at the mourning-turned-wedding dress. "I don't understand why you wouldn't let me redo your graduation dress. At least that was ivory and the satin material did wonders for your figure. People will think that you're not excited about marrying Jonathan and —"

"Ah…" Rachael sneezed, her stiff-boned corset strung so tightly she could barely inhale.

"You're not used to wearing a corset, dear Rachael. You'll get used to it." Jane smiled. "We must dress pleasingly for our men."

"I would enjoy my wedding more if I wasn't corseted so tightly. I dare not sneeze again for fear the fastenings of my fashionable bodice will pop off completely."

"They're much stronger than you give them credit for." Jane motioned for Rachael to lift her arms. "No, toward me… higher than that."

The fabric floated over her arms, draping her waist and hips. Jane fluffed up the pleated panels of material that trimmed the gown around the bodice and the large gigot sleeves.

Mother, clutching a vase of flowers, stepped through the bedroom door and stopped mid-stride. A sob escaped before she could stifle it.

Rachael pretended she hadn't heard. "Mother, you look lovely. I like the way you've done your hair."

"I've brought fresh calla lilies for your wedding bouquet. And remember your train. If you're not careful, you could get it caught under someone's foot and rip the delicate fabric." Mother walked to her dressing table and set the flowers down, then opened a large jewelry box. She drew out her pearls and draped the necklace around Rachael's neck. Rachael felt Jane pulling her hair, twisting her locks into corkscrew curls.

She couldn't remember a time she'd been fussed over like this. She peeked into the full length mirror. A silky halo of cascading color crowned her head and gave her a queenly appearance. To complement the reddish highlights of her hair, Mother entwined Rachael's tresses with tiny pink roses. A garland of silky white tea roses was added to her dress.

Her mother surveyed her work; her gaze probed Rachael's for a response. "Yes, that will do."

Rachael's thoughts churned like thickened buttermilk. Something was on her mother's mind.

"You mentioned your heroine Narcissa wore black for her wedding. Has it occurred to you that, perhaps, she was unsure of her decision?"

"Dr. Whitman was considerate enough to wait until after his exploratory expedition." Rachael willed her face not to reveal the turmoil of her emotions over Jonathan's lack of gentility, then threw caution to the wind, as she lifted her head in defiance. "Narcissa had eight months to communicate with her betrothed before the wedding." Why did Narcissa choose black for her wedding? She had time to make her gown. Had Narcissa married Marcus Whitman only because she wanted to travel west? No, certainly not. Dr. Whitman adored her. No. There was no comparison whatsoever.

"Today's your wedding day, my daughter. You'll not be only ours anymore. After today, you'll belong to another."

Mother's words sent a pang of regret piercing through Rachael's bosom.

Rachael lifted her face toward the sapphire sky. A hint of a breeze moved the trees that dotted the spacious lawn. The rains and warm temperatures had started the fruit trees blossoming early this year. The white and pink of the budding apple and plum trees added more color to the array of violet and red geraniums and blooming petunias. They were Mother's conservatory flowers, and they dotted the cobblestone walkway with purple, yellow, pink, red, and white.

Her family had worked tirelessly, spreading the word, ensuring she would have the best wedding she could on such short notice.

Awed at the assemblage of friends and neighbors who had come, Rachael huddled behind the rose trellis waiting for her father. Though the roses had yet to bloom, their tiny green leaves were complemented by satin ribbons and bows entwined with baby's breath, which made a perfect peek hole.

The fashionable ladies adorned in stylish silk moiré in mauve and blue, set off with draping satin sashes, chose their seats carefully. She smiled. Both her side and Jonathan's were full. Not one empty chair remained. "Oh, everyone is so beautiful." Bodices trimmed in lace matched their parasols, and hats were trimmed in either Spanish lace or satin decorated with flowers and ostrich plumes. The outfits complemented the ladies' stylish coiffures and the garden wedding scene.

Rachael's fingers felt the glossy smoothness of her black satin dress self-consciously. She portrayed the tall, plain spinster her friends and neighbors imagined her to be. Why fool herself into thinking she could be that delicate, starry-eyed bride she had often admired gliding down the runner toward —

"What are you doing, Rachael, spying on your own wedding?" Father asked.

How handsome Father looked. Laughter bubbled from a place deep within her. "Your waistcoat fits you to perfection."

His stiff shirt front with studs swept toward his slender waist and to his smartly creased trousers and patent leather shoes. His auburn hair flecked with grey and his imposing height commanded a handsome stature. Enough to turn heads. But her father's devotion to her mother never swayed his vision. Could she count on that from Jonathan? Taking her white gloved hand into his own, her father placed it in the crook of his arm. "I don't know why I was so bent on marrying you off. How will I get through the day without seeing your smiling face or hearing your laughter ringing through the house?"

Rachael blinked. Looking down at her black dress… what had she done? Her graduation gown of Ottoman silk with its pearl front and tiny veil of silk roses would have blended with the other ladies. Was she tempting fate choosing black as her wedding gown? After all the saying was "Marry in black, you'll wish yourself back."

Looking down at her hand entwined with Father's arm, she prayed silently. Please Jesus, correct my mistakes. Bless this union. Show me it is your preordained will for Dr. Wheaton to wed me rather than Isabella.

She looked up then and squared her shoulders. She would step out from beneath this arbor and into another life, into another world. Leaving all she knew behind her. She took a hesitant breath as the wedding march drifted toward her on the fragrance of violets and lilacs. Was this what she really wanted?

Jonathan held his breath. Rachael's black gown glowed like onyx in the sun's rays. Two long trails of white roses were fastened down the front of her dress, relieving the sharp black. At her shoulders more white roses adorned each tiny sleeve and a three-stranded mother-of-pearl necklace rested below her soft alabaster neck.

He'd been right that first evening to call her queenly. A halo of curls and roses adorned her head like a crown and she matched the image well, coming toward him with her head held high and her black chiffon gently blowing in the breezes. Her long mesh train floated like angel wings behind her.

As they knelt down together, a sudden eagerness to finish their vows and feel Rachael in his arms overwhelmed him. "Till death do us part" echoed in his ears and he closed his eyes. Lord, please help Rachael to be well equipped and up to the stringent demands of the wilderness.

Her gentle "I do" stirred him in a way he'd not anticipated. Her voice was soft as a nightingale. Like no other woman he had ever known, she invoked more desires than he knew he possessed. He closed his eyes anticipating their first touch, their first kiss, and realized he was shaking. He said a hurried prayer that he would be gentle.

"I pronounce you man and wife. You may kiss your bride."

They rose together, and he bent his head toward hers. She hesitated. She drew away before accepting his hand and paused before meeting his lips. He pulled her to him, his mouth seeking hers.

Her raspberry-colored lips quivered and he longed to give their softness the going over they needed, losing their tepidness in his admiration of her, but he dared not. He lowered his head, barely covering their softness with his. Then his arm swept her waist, hugging her to his side, searching her eyes seeking the same desire. Rachael gasped, and stepped away.

Was she recoiling from him? That could not be. He scowled back. His lenient grasp, now granite, denied her escape. His eyes ignored her pleas and gazed out toward the assembled guests. When their friends rose to their feet, he bowed, hearing their applause and bowed again, then whispered. "Be careful, Rachael, people might think you did not want to wed me. I can ill-afford for my family and friends to surmise this wedding is in name only."

Rachael lifted her chin, inviting his wrath. "Isn't that what it is?"

A shrill voice sang her name across the gardens. Rachael turned toward the sound. Mrs. Rumpson's skirt, an ornate affair of shot silk with velvet stripes of rose pink, green, and brown trimmed with black velvet bands along the hem, swayed back and forth like a misplaced bell. She quickened her pace. "Oh, I wanted to tell you what a lovely couple you make."

Jonathan cut a commanding figure with his black waistcoat and trousers that contrasted sharply with the white shirtfront. The matching neck cloth and high collar complemented his square jaw.

"My, my." Mrs. Rumpson fluttered her fan in front of her face. "Why didn't you tell me about your intended when I attempted to match you with that young man at the revival?"

"Oh?" Jonathan said with a questioning lift of his brow.

Mrs. Rumpson opened her pink parasol, angling it over her eyes. "There, that is much better. I couldn't see your lovely face for the sun, Rachael."

"Who was he?" Jonathan looked from Mrs. Rumpson to Rachael.

"An acquaintance from the Academy."

Mrs. Rumpson waved her lace handkerchief before her nose and Rachael whiffed rose sachet as Mrs. Rumpson's hawk-like gaze flitted about the garden. "It was merely an old woman sharpening her matchmaking skills and needing to be useful, Dr. Wheaton. Rachael did you proud. She was most gracious serving tea on our half-hewn logs and making everyone comfortable before the preacher took to his podium."

"That sounds like something Rachael would do." Jonathan's baritone voice rose with pride. He swallowed her hand into his large palm and released it like a man might pet a dog.

"If my memory serves me right, that gentleman from the Academy was quite smitten with you, Rachael dear. When I heard you were to be married, I thought it would be he standing alongside you."

Jonathan's scowl resembled foaming sea water. Rachael chuckled. He's upset. Good.

Mrs. Rumpson shielded her eyes for a better view of Jonathan's face. "Yes, you are handsome like that young man at the revival." Her brows drew close, matching Jonathan's. "It appears to me rather curious, Rachael, that you did not mention your intended when you were describing your plans. I recall you planned to go alone to this new Oregon Territory."

"You could say, Mrs. Rumpson, that God preordained Rachael and me for the trip."

"Why, who would have thought?" Her face beamed back at them as she bustled toward a group of matrons.

Rachael knew their conversation would not rest long among the three of them.

"Hmm, this Mrs. Rumpson certainly likes to spin a story."

Rachael laughed. "And create her own."

"This fellow student, I don't believe I heard you mention his name?"

"When have we had any time together that would allow me to mention his name?"

"Well, besides the week I'll be with the Reverend, there'll be lots of time afterwards to become… acquainted in the wilderness."

Rachael looked away. Would Jonathan demand his matrimonial rights? His eyes hadn't moved from her face.

※ ※ ※

Rachael and Jonathan paused before the bedroom door and looked at Rachael's two sisters.

"Persistent, aren't they?" Rachael whispered. Ever since Martha's and Joyce's escorts left, they had hounded Jonathan and Rachael's every step, which embarrassed Rachael and heightened Jonathan's attentions.

Without warning, he swept her into his arms. "Oh, Jonathan, put me down. I'm fully capable of crossing the threshold myself." She squirmed in his tight embrace to no avail.

"Am I doing it right?" he asked of the two sisters.

Martha and Joyce, tittering out of control, nodded their heads.

"What are you girls doing up there? Come down here this instant," Mother said from the foyer below.

"Put me down before you drop me." Rachael pounded his chest. He ignored her fists and carried her toward the banister, watching her sisters descend the stairs. Oh, how she wished she could call her sisters back. She felt under matched against this man with arms like steel and a will to match. "Mrs. Rothburn, do you think me incapable of carrying Rachael across the threshold?"

"Why, no, Dr. Wheaton."

"But, Jonathan," Rachael whispered, exasperated at her weakness. "I am too large for such displays of strength."

His admiring eyes swept her face like a warm ocean breeze, his lips a mere breath from hers… she tilted her head away. "My dear wife, you are no more than a feather in my arms." His arms shook, but not from lack of strength, the low tremor of his voice confirmed that. He walked toward the railing and looked down at the Rothburn family and remaining guests. "Our thanks to you, family and friends, for witnessing our vows and the joining of our lives."

"Here, here!" someone said as Jonathan strode back to the bedroom, kicked the door open, and slammed it behind them.

He set Rachael down on the patterned rug of the guest room, his eyes not leaving her face. The potent smell of freshly cut lilacs wafted about the room. Shafts of evening light from the full length windows cast long shadows across the rug.

Rachael's heart thumped an erratic beat in her ears. Her legs felt queasy. She grabbed one of the ornate four posters of the featherbed for strength. He was so strong. She turned from his gaze and stepped away, then stretched out her arm for the small bouquet adorning one pillow; she held it to her nose. Jonathan hasn't been rough; he's been gentle. Hearing the soft steps of her husband, she relaxed. "Isn't this flower lovely? Its beautiful fragrance has filled the room with the scent of spring." Rachael held the spray out for Jonathan to smell, shyness overtaking her emotions.

"You're lovely."

Did he mean that? His dark brows lifted as his soft eyes met hers. He brushed his hand against her cheek, a groan followed, and a sudden intake of breath. Her own breathing had ceased to function rhythmically since he'd swept her into his arms. He drew his face toward hers and stroked her cheek again. She closed her eyes, reveling in his touch. Her husband. She'd dreamt about this moment, but never believed it could ever be, not for her.

His hands drifted to her dress. With ease he unfastened her buttons. Then his fingertips drifted over her upturned chin and down her neck, encircling her with his hands, drawing her closer. A sigh escaped her lips and the deeper sound of Jonathan's followed. He pressed his lips to hers, softness and firmness fused as one. She didn't want it to stop.

"Rachael." He breathed her name, releasing her lips only to draw breath before claiming them again, pulling her closer as he wove his hand up her spine, entwining his long fingers in her hair, pulling out her hair pins. Rachael shook her tresses free and Jonathan groaned, imbedding his hands into her silken locks, exploring her with his lips as he swept her into his arms.

Walking toward the bed, he laid her down, his fingers brushing the puffy sleeves down over her shoulders.

Realization brought its icy fear of the unknown. "No," she whispered in the thickening darkness. She drew away from his touch into the folds of the featherbed. He bent closer. Unable to loosen his hold on her, she tried to turn her head sideways, but he forced her face forward, kissing her forehead.

"Don't. You're frightening me."

"Rachael, Rachael." He looked at her. "You're beautiful." Taking a shaky breath, his head plunged forward to kiss her throat. His lips trailing to her —

The taunting eyes of the town's bullies lurched before her mind's eye. Jonathan's eyes gleamed into hers much like a hungry wolf as he flipped the buttons of his shirt open revealing his muscular chest, his carnal desires all too evident.

She'd forgotten the one ingredient she desired most of all — Jonathan's love. Using the sudden lapse in physical connection to her advantage, she swung to her feet. Her bare toes curled into the rug beneath her, as if to hide from Jonathan's lust. She couldn't — no, she wouldn't — consummate her vows with a stranger.

She clutched her mourning dress to her bodice. "You... you hardly know me —" Sobs peppered her whispered words and echoed in the still room. "I'm more than a body. I have more... to give... than... why can't you see that? Lust will never take the place of... true love. Leave my room until you can properly bed me, sir!"

The wind from the open window whipped her dress about her legs. Jonathan looked from the empty white sheets to her. "You know I could demand my matrimonial rights."

"I think not. Are you forgetting our journey west? You need me." Clutching her dress, she ran to the safety of the dressing screen.

She didn't look out until she heard the bedroom door close.

chapter seven

achael and her brother Harmon walked up the rickety wooden steps and knocked on the cabin door of Harry Betts. No reply. She turned to leave.

"You lookin' for someone, miss?"

Rachael spun so fast the heel of her shoe fell into the crack between the old boards of the porch. She bent to dislodge it as she spoke. "Mr. Betts?"

"That's me." Mr. Betts squinted, his mouth drawn in a resolved frown. "You got business here?"

Shielding her eyes from the early morning sunlight, Rachael extended her right arm.

Mr. Betts' curly grey beard could give Saint Nicholas competition. However, that was where the similarity ended. A tattered hat and breeches to match, boots strapped with bailing wire around sole and leather completed his appearance. Her hand grabbed his dirt-encrusted fingers and the rough-as-sandpaper palm.

"Mr. Betts. I'm Rachael Rothburn-Wheaton and this is my brother Harmon. We spoke some years back. You provided lessons on pioneer survival techniques. Remember, you came to my classroom and spoke with my pupils?"

"Your what?"

Rachael took a deep breath. "You always referred to me as Becky."

He put his gnarled hand to his chin and rubbed. "Now I remember. Sorry. Forget a lot these days."

"I'm leaving to go west shortly. My husband is making the arrangements. He wanted me to acquaint myself with driving a team of mules."

"Well you've tickled my innards with your go-to-meeting speech and flattery. Why on earth would you want to go to the wilderness?" Diverting his eyes from Rachael, he gazed at Harmon. "Can't you convince your sister to stay put?"

"She's been bent on becoming a missionary ever since I can remember, sir. No use trying to change her mind."

Mr. Betts perused her from top to bottom and back up. "Lady, from what I see, you haven't a snowball's chance in July on surviving."

"Sir, that is why I am here. You do not know me or my conviction to spread the Word of God to the Indians. God will provide me with the ammunition I need to teach the Word. You must provide me with your down-to-earth experience of the wilderness."

Harry Betts' mouth dragged open and a smile spread across his bearded chin. He stretched forward, fingering the fabric on her coat.

"First of all, this won't do. You've got to have clothes that can hold up to any kind of weather. There aren't any fancy dress shops across the Great Divide. Step on in and I'll see what I might have. Maybe I still have an old leather apron of my wife's lying around you can use to harness the team. I know I could sure use some help around here — might be we can work out a deal. I give you some free education and you can give me some free labor." He chuckled. "Could be I'll come out the winner on the agreement."

Rachael's shoulders felt as tight as a string on a bow. She rolled them in an attempt to alleviate some of the tightness. She was used to harnessing the Rothburn buggy horses; however, harnessing Harry Betts' six-mule team was a different matter. She never knew she possessed so many muscles that could all hurt at the same time. Even her skin ached.

After five days of harnessing and driving Harry Betts' mules, and then learning how to drive cattle, she was thoroughly saddle sore. The only good thing about this was that he had said she was a natural on horseback. She couldn't confess she already knew how to ride. Every compliment Harry Betts gave her she cherished. He was sparse on praise and liberal with tongue lashings whenever she didn't accomplish her tasks in proper pioneer fashion.

Her shooting lessons with pistol and rifle came easily, due to the fact she had gone hunting with her father and brothers. Still, it gave her a sense of accomplishment she had never experienced before. Quail, pheasant, and rabbits became an easy target for her. That is when she could find them. Soon she was learning how to make snares for small game. Harry Betts had already taught her how to lay out the skins for tanning and how to sew the pelts, making them into hats and mittens.

"You might think this isn't necessary, what with your husband and all, but you never know what might happen in the wild." Mr. Betts was careful to never get her in harm's way and this she often wondered about.

One day while stalking a deer, Rachael came across a big buck. The deer turned toward her, but she was downwind of him, and he didn't seem to notice her. She took a bead on him and heard a growl. The buck took off. She turned in time to see a black bear come charging at her. Harry Betts took him down with one well aimed shot.

"Why'd you wait so long to shoot?" Betts smelled of venison and bacon grease, and she wasn't so sure if he didn't plan on taking a bite out of her, he was that angry. "You've got to be quick or instead of it being your supper — you'll be its!"

"I'll… I'll do better next time. I promise, Mr. Betts."

"Right. No next time if you don't. Let's get the mules and drag its carcass back to the cabin. I'll teach you how to skin it."

She'd become as good almost as Mr. Betts with the Bowie knife. She wondered while being elbow deep in the carcass of a deer or bear what Jonathan would say if he knew. Would he be proud of her? Or, would he, like Father constantly did, tell her every day that this wasn't necessary? Did they really think she'd always have a man around to do the hunting for her?

When would the ministering to the Indians take place, between baking her bread, scrubbing her clothes in the river, or gutting a deer?

"Here now, I'm going to show you what you have to do to make jerky." Rachael smiled down at the man who stood only as tall as her shoulders. He'd become her trusted friend. "Did your wife know how to do all of this?"

Harry Betts beamed. "She could pick a fly off our milk cow with her rifle at twenty yards. She mostly liked shooting out the feathers on Chief Arrowhead's war bonnet." He laughed. "Betsy was a fury to be reckoned with when you got her riled up. See, there's always something to drag a man away from his cabin. Betsy had to fend for herself one winter. Me and a group of neighbors had ridden out to save our cattle. Then we got boxed up when a snow storm hit and to top off our predicament right pretty, the injuns came swooping down on us. I got clear, but a lot of the men didn't make it.

"I recall one woman. Her and her mister came from Pennsylvania, a right pretty gal, but spindly. My Betsy took one look at her, shook her head and said, 'Why lands sake child, you've hardly got enough meat on your bones for the buzzards to eat.' Her mister didn't make it and come spring we found out that she'd gone plumb mad. Her children were all dead, starved to death."

"Mother, please come in." Rachael set down her quill, resting her hands on her desk. Mother entered, her hands buried in the pockets of her printed apron, the heels of her low boots tapping a rhythmic beat across the wood floor. She chose the high-backed Windsor chair facing Rachael's desk, plopped down, and ran a hand over her coiffure, then tucked a loose strand of hair beneath her cotton cap. Mother rarely sat and never without a purpose in mind.

"What's wrong, Mother?"

"Do you think all this practice with that mule skinner is something you will use?"

Rachael picked up the quill she'd been writing with and set it back into the ink. "I feel the Lord might have led me to him. And as Mr.

Betts would say, 'Plan for the worst and be glad it never happened.'"

"I know of some herbs that can provide medicine and food." Mother drew out notepapers she'd made into a paper book tied with yarn. "I've listed them in here with their description and a picture of the plant."

Rachael took it, thumbing through the pages. "This is perfect, Mother." She'd worried she'd forget something. "I'm certain I will need this."

"We're planning a farewell party for you. Everything has been arranged. That way our family will be together one last time. Jane wanted it to be a surprise, but I thought you might want to know."

"A surprise?"

"And I came up here to give you this. A letter came from Jonathan."

Rachael's fingers shook, recalling her wedding night. She tore open the envelope and read, *"Rachael, Supplies and our passage are purchased. Will be on the ferry at Lake Erie in Buffalo tomorrow morning. Bring a wagon. Your husband, Jonathan.*

chapter eight

Rachael walked halfway down the steep hill, searching the Lake Erie shoreline and boat dock. Seagulls glided back and forth in the sun-drenched sky as if playing with the sunbeams dancing on the river. She looked out at the hustle and bustle of the thriving harbor recalling Mr. Betts' words.

"Back in the 1700s this was all nothing but a dirt trail used by the Indians and wild animals. Me and my Missus would come down here and she'd do her washing while I stood guard with my musket."

Would the Oregon Territory grow and prosper as this region had? Yes. And she and Jonathan would help carve a spot out of that wilderness for other families to follow as Harry Betts had here.

Harry Betts said their most worthy opponents would be deprivation and exhaustion. Few had the gumption to conquer it. Rachael sank down onto the grass-covered bank. "Dear Lord, send Thy angels to protect our steps, for as it is written 'he shall give his angels charge over thee, to keep thee in all thy ways. They shall bear thee up in *their* hands, lest thou dash thy foot against a stone.'"

She watched men clad in business suits, farmers in overalls, and frontiersmen in buckskin coats and pants stroll down the pier looking, just as she was, for their friends and loved ones.

Rachael contemplated her reunion with Jonathan. It seemed as if eight months had elapsed, but it had been just eight days. She'd reread the closing words of Jonathan's letter several times. No emotion. Was he still angry because she had refused his advances? Would he demand his matrimonial rights to consummate their vows before leaving for the West?

One man, who had disembarked from a boat, stepped away from the crowd. He was tall in stature, clad in a buckskin fringed shirt and breeches. He wore a wide-brimmed hat that shielded his eyes. Firmly grasped in the long fingers of one hand was his flintlock rifle and a knapsack made out of animal skins. Could that be Jonathan? She couldn't imagine him wearing buckskins, let alone carrying an animal skin knapsack. His gaze met hers.

She blushed, opened her parasol, and turned around to climb back up the steep hill to the safety of her buckboard. What must this stranger think of her boldness? What would Jonathan say if he knew?

"Madam, may I be of assistance?"

The tall man she'd admired stood at her elbow. She ducked her head. He extended his arm, then rested it to his side. "I'm afraid I'll get your fine clothes mussed."

She stiffened. "Thank you, sir, I got down here by myself and am quite able to return." She stumbled. Her heels slipped on the dew-covered grass. Teetering out of balance, she wobbled sideways as a gust of wind blew at her parasol and suddenly she was falling — right into the awaiting arms of this backwoodsman. "Forgive me. I can't believe I could be so clumsy I — Jonathan?"

He laughed. "I'm glad I spotted you when I did." His voice dropped an octave lower and held no reprimand, though she felt she deserved it. "You have a knack for getting into predicaments, and I like being there to help you out of them." He carried her up the hill, his eyes sweeping her face, as if convincing himself it was she. "Have you lost weight?"

"Well, if I have, it's due to my worry over you."

He stopped. "You were worrying about me?"

Their faces were so close, so very close. Rachael's heart thumped like a caged bird against her ribs begging for freedom beyond her bars of inhibitions. Her eyes eagerly sought his… a questioning brow rose above Jonathan's eye. "I trust this physical contact has not wounded your delicate disposition."

Is he mocking me? "You can put me down. I am quite capable of walking up a hill." She placed her hand in the crook of his offered arm as they continued walking toward the wagon.

The lean muscles of his forearm hardened beneath her fingers and there was something in his eyes that had not been present before. "Besides your… clothes, something else has changed about you." Her breath exploded in an excited gasp. "Yes, I see now, you have brought back the untamed wilderness with you."

"I did, Rachael, yes, I did." Jonathan's deep baritone rang like a resounding trumpet in the early morning mist. Her words had unleashed his excitement that now poured over her head like liquid gold touched by sunlight, brimming with the riches of human imagination.

"You'll like the Reverend McCray. He's as big as life. Why right now, he is on his way with two Indian boys to locate the fur company, in hopes of traveling with them." He held up his hand. "See that? I learned how to dig out a canoe with a hatchet. I've got the calluses to prove it."

Rachael chuckled. "I can see for myself how much you hated it."

Jonathan's eyes glowed. "It gave me a hunger for the wilderness, Rachael. McCray says it'll need a hard hand, a gentle one, too, and a determined will before we can tame the unknown, but it's going to be worth it. It's like…" He pointed up. "Like traveling to the moon, the wilderness is that unknown. You can't imagine the wonders." Sunlight drenched the brim of Jonathan's hat in colored prisms of light like one of Mother's crystal chandeliers radiates the candlelight. He had stumbled across his God-given destiny.

"Rachael, cholera greeted us on the banks of the Mississauga and Ojibwa Indian camp past the Oshawa trading post. What those poor Indians would have suffered if the Reverend and I hadn't been there, only God knows." Jonathan grabbed her hand and kissed her fingers. "Only we were there, my dearest. The word 'providential' kept entering my thoughts while I treated those natives. Yes, God does rule the affairs of man and the Great Physician is sending us to the far corners of this unknown country to witness to His starving people." He turned his face away from hers as if he was embarrassed for her to see his expression, afraid to share all his emotions with her.

"I witnessed a peek into Christ's amazing grace. The Reverend Mc-Cray's sermon came from his heart and the Indians responded with a thirst I have never seen in the people here."

Lifting his head toward the sun, Rachael watched him thirstily drinking in the life-giving sunlight. His voice was just a whisper, as soft as the breezes that stirred her hair.

"When I accepted Jesus as my personal Savior, I don't know that I felt what these Indians did. I wonder, leaving all our earthly possessions behind, if we might not come to understand God's grace in our lives better."

He turned, grabbed her hands and squeezed them. "Think of it, we'll be the ones seeing God's spirit awaken in man a thirst to be born into His family. Reverend McCray says the Indians are hungry. Their souls are starving but they don't realize they're starving. Given the opportunity, they'll lap up the Good Word like a cat laps up milk. That's how the Reverend puts it. Oh, that I might be found worthy of such an enterprise."

Reaching the wagon first, Jonathan stretched out his arm. His warm fingers grasped hers firmly and he pulled her towards him. His eyes searched hers, caressing her face like the morning sunlight. "I am sorry, Rachael, about our wedding night." His voice had a melody she'd never heard. Anxious and apologetic, yet wildly magnetic, it drew her to him like Sir Arthur to Lady Guinevere. "I never meant to frighten you. Can you forgive me?"

Jonathan's trying to understand me, my trepidations. "You're not angry with me?"

"No." His gaze lingered on her face. "I'm only angry with myself." He bent closer.

He was more man then she'd ever known. Painful bashfulness overwhelmed her senses. She restrained his lips from coming closer and turned her head. "Jonathan, I… I hardly knew you before. You were a stranger then and now —"

"I'm no longer the well-groomed doctor?" Jonathan laughed and the sound of it echoed down to the docks. People walking by looked up.

Leading her toward the buckboard, he placed his things in the back and helped her in. "We need to pick up the supplies I left on the dock. And, you will never guess. I met a couple leaving for the Canadian wilds for a missionary trip, but I convinced them to join us instead. He's a minister, Rachael, and his first choice was to become a minister west of the Rockies, so you can imagine his elation of acquiring the position of his dreams. They are New Yorkers like us."

"It will be like taking a part of home with us." Rachael clasped her gloved hands. "I did so hope for a lady companion on the trip, one I could share my journey with."

"You will like her. She is a quiet, gentle woman. Yet, I sense a strong interior beneath her humble demeanor."

"Oh, I'm so excited. Just think, tomorrow we leave."

❊ ❊ ❊

While Jonathan unloaded the buckboard, Rachael tiptoed up the stairs. She wanted a moment with her mother and sisters that must last her a lifetime.

She stood unnoticed in the open doorway of her mother's sitting room and drank in the red velvet drapes, rich tones of mahogany, and fragrances of lavender and lilacs. Jane was waltzing around the large room to the tempo of her fairytale dreams.

Rachael forced a lighthearted laugh from her trembling lips, her eyes memorizing Jane draped in her shiny satin wedding gown. "You look like an angel, Jane. I wish I could be here on your wedding day." Her words wobbled on the threat of tears. "I have some good news. Jonathan and I are leaving for Cincinnati tomorrow morning. Isn't that wonderful?"

"No." The always frank Joyce ran toward her and clutched Rachael's skirts. Joyce hugged Rachael with such fervor she found it hard not to give in to her emotions.

"I don't want you to leave us."

Rachael laid her head on Joyce's and hugged her close. "I know, dearest. I don't want to leave you either."

Joyce looked up and gasped, pointing to the tall mountaineer-looking man clad in buckskins filling the doorway with his broad shoulders. "Jonathan?"

Mother jumped up, forgetting her sewing basket. The contents tumbled onto the rug. Rachael ran over and bent down to retrieve spools of thread, needles, and scissors.

"Jonathan, you've changed." Mother's screeched voice sounded like a trapped blue jay. "I… I suppose the reality of Rachael's leaving has just hit me. To this far off frontier with a man I hardly… know. I'm sorry, Jonathan."

"Well, if you want to know what I think." Martha set her sewing aside and rose from the gold tapestry settee. She walked forward and circled Jonathan. "You're even handsomer than before. It's like those clothes were made for you."

"I can see your ancestors in you." Jane looked over Martha's shoulder, holding up Joyce's book. "See, Jonathan, this is a picture of your great-great-grandfather in Jamestown, Virginia."

A worried look clouded Jonathan's blue eyes. "I pray I can fill the shoes of my great-great-grandfather. I guess I shall know soon enough."

Jane cupped slender hands about her well-powdered cheeks. "Oh, the ball! Mother?"

"Oh, dear, I guess I should have asked your permission before planning it. But, I did not want my eldest to leave us without a proper fond farewell."

Jonathan frowned. "But the Reverend has told me we are nearly a week late."

"Tonight, it will be tonight." Martha jumped up, unable to suppress her excitement.

Jonathan's brows poked together in confusion. "So — the invitations have been sent out? For this evening, how did you know of my return?"

Jane handed the invitation to Rachael. "When Rachael received your telegram, we hand delivered the invitations, like we did for your wedding."

Rachael read it out loud, "Would you do us the honor of being present for a fond farewell ball to be held at 1223 W. Maple Drive for Rachael and Jonathan Wheaton this 17th day of April at 6 p.m."

chapter nine

_R_achael touched the rose Jonathan had placed in her curls, then trailed her hand down her bodice to the small tapered point at the front of her corseted waist and inhaled. She rehearsed her speech a half dozen ways. Maybe she worried over nothing. Isabella may not come.

With the last guests' arrival, she and Jonathan walked into the large parlor. Jonathan stood ramrod straight, clad in his buckskins, allowing his eyes free reign through the tangled groups of men and women dressed in elegant ball attire.

Crystal chandeliers sparkled with the brilliance of Solomon's palace, and polished wooden floors and tall banisters gleamed with the deep richness of fine cherry wood. Spacious, yet welcoming, the room had a large stone hearth that blazed a cheery fire. A settee with ball-and-claw feet nestled within an alcove nearby, offering an invitation for semi-private interludes to the couples. At the opposite side of the room the members of the band tuned their instruments.

"We will be leaving our families and all our worldly possessions behind, Rachael." Jonathan's gaze was so earnest, so impassioned she felt his hurt. "Am I being selfish allowing you to venture into these unknown hardships?"

"Memories cannot be left behind, just as God's spirit, once invited to dwell within one's heart, cannot depart."

He kissed the top of her gloved hand. "And what are earthly riches in comparison to God's?"

Father strolled passed them to the lead musician. The musician nodded his head, set down his glass of punch, and walked to the center of the stage. A table waited with his violin. He picked it up carefully, cradling it like a father cradles his child, his gifted fingers guiding the bow skillfully. The other musicians hurried to his side. "Gather your ladies fair. The ball is about to begin."

Rachael smiled into Jane's and William's faces. Wherever Jane went, there was William. Their love for one another showed in their slightest glance. If ever there were two people hopelessly in love, it was Jane and William. A pang of regret poked Rachael's heart. Would she and Jonathan ever love like that?

As the swaying notes of the waltz filled the high arched chambers of the cherry paneled room, thirty couples dressed in the most elegant of fashion swayed and dipped to the eloquent tempo of the music. When the waltz ended, the violinist announced a reel.

Her brother Mark elbowed his way to her side. "Jonathan, would it be all right with you if Rachael danced the reel with me?"

Jonathan's brows rose in obvious surprise. "I was sure you were going to ask that strawberry blonde over there who's been giving you the eyes since the ball began."

"Oh, I will, but I need Rachael to get me in step so I don't do something silly like flattening Rosemary's shoes with my big feet."

Jonathan chuckled, sending a glance toward Rosemary, then winked at Mark. "I'll try to keep her busy until you can take over."

"Jonathan, you will be much too busy performing your host's responsibilities to me. Rachael dear, how is married life?" Isabella's icy blue gaze sent a chill up Rachael's spine, as did her emotionless words.

Jonathan wrapped his arm around Rachael's waist and she immediately felt the warmth and comfort of his touch. He smiled down at her.

"What a sweet display of affection. Rachael's enormous height does complement yours, Jonathan." Isabella clasped her small hands together at her waist. A move which drew the viewer's eyes to the plunging neckline of her scarlet gown. "Rachael dear, are you putting on weight, or maybe… Jonathan, have you been keeping secrets?"

Jonathan's hearty laugh mingled with the musicians' instruments. "When we decide to begin our family, I'll make sure you are one of the first to know."

Isabella drew out her fan and slapped it open on the folds of her brocade ball gown, then waved it before her face, her chest rising and falling with her rapid breath. "Are you going to ask me to dance or not? I've never been a complacent wallflower and do not intend to be one this evening."

"Sis, the dance is about to begin."

Rachael followed Mark to the dance floor, relieved to be out of Isabella's company.

As the ball progressed, beads of perspiration broke out on the most carefully powdered foreheads. The doors leading to the gardens were flung open, and the dancers begged for more. Rachael kept step to another reel, or so she tried. Mark's feet sometimes got tangled with hers.

Mark's thick hair had fallen into his eyes. He attempted to shake it away. Rachael smiled, and with the back of her hand, stroked his wayward bangs back into place.

"Sis, I'm going to miss you. Those people out west don't understand what we're giving up letting you go."

Rachael watched Jonathan and Isabella dance gracefully around the room.

"Don't worry, Sis." Mark followed her gaze. "Jonathan's crazy about you."

"Jonathan's tastes lean to petite ladies. I am neither."

"Don't get in a huff over the Isabellas in your world. Jonathan's made up his mind. He wouldn't have married you if you weren't his type. Look at him. He's wearing his frontier clothes. Telling everyone in the room he's shedding his old self, ready for his new life. He doesn't care what others think. He's a man's man. He's not going to allow a group of people like the mission board to rule his life. He'd have found a way around their rules. Only, going through Father insured you couldn't say no to his proposal."

Rachael gasped. "When did you become so confident and wise?"

"I owe it to you. Remember James 1:5? 'If any of you lack wisdom, let him ask of God, that giveth to all liberally.' You'd always say that when I felt I wasn't smart enough."

"Oh, Mark, I pray what you say is true." She watched as Jonathan bent lower, whispering something in Isabella's ear. Rachael swallowed, her throat dry and scratchy.

"You're a lot prettier than Isabella."

"Right, and a head taller, too." Rachael guffawed. The reel ended and they made their way to the punch table. She accepted the glass he extended toward her. "You had better ask Rosemary for the next dance before someone else does." She raised the glass to her lips. She must learn to distance herself from humiliation, then choked on the punch. Mark's eyes had hardened beneath his scowling brows.

"Sis, you trust God but hold little trust in yourself. You believe in God, now believe in yourself, then the true you will come out and flourish."

"That's quite philosophical."

Mark swiped his hair off his forehead. "Yeah, well, Mother and Jane are always saying that."

"They are? I never thought it was I inhibiting God's design for my divine destiny." As Mark walked over to Rosemary, Rachael noticed Isabella lead Jonathan toward the gardens and decided to follow them.

"It is more private at the gardens than standing outside these windows." Isabella's voice grated on Jonathan's nerves. She looped her arm through his and glanced toward the gazebo and gardens a few yards away.

Jonathan gazed at the towering three-story house. The massive Tudor mansion of stones and bricks blended well with the stones and granite patio and steps.

Isabella patted his arm. "It will be a change, don't you think, for one like Rachael, brought up in the splendors of all this, to leave it? After all, Jonathan, you and I never had a family to speak of. It's evident that Rachael's family loves her. I think I could adapt much better to living in that wilderness than Rachael. After all, we only have each other, what with me being an only child."

"I have brothers and sisters, too."

"You have one brother and one sister and the rest are half-brothers and half-sisters. Even your full brother and sister you never got to know."

Jonathan grimaced. "My past is behind me." He hoped she caught his meaning.

"You never really had a mother. After all you were little when she passed you off to your uncle." Isabella snuggled closer. "My, it's gotten chilly, don't you think?"

"No, I don't."

Jonathan's thoughts were on Rachael. Had he told her how beautiful she looked tonight? He had planned to, remembering the Reverend McCray's words about the needs of young brides. Isabella was right about one thing. He missed his mother's wisdom. He couldn't manage to do anything right when it came to Rachael.

She had come down the stairway in an ivory gown with mother-of-pearls running its length and breadth. She'd taken his breath away. Her shoulders bare, but for the gigot sleeves that hugged her shoulders like a glistening shawl. With her crown of curls cascading around her ivory complexion, she resembled an angel.

That was when he knew. She was his morning light, his evening moon all rolled into one. He closed his eyes and breathed in the wind sweeping off the lake. He was blessed beyond his earthly dreams.

"Jonathan." Isabella poked at his buckskin tassels. "I don't believe you've heard a word I've said."

Jonathan's narrow smile raised the drooping corners of his grimace. "Actually, I haven't."

"Really?" Isabella's bottom lip protruded. Her sharp nails dug into his buckskins.

"What are your nails made of? Granite?" He pulled her fingers off his arm. "Isabella, why are you still here? I'm a married man. You are wasting your time, valuable time, my dear, that you should be directing toward an available male."

Isabella smirked. A look that did not flatter her.

"Are you trying to tell me that you are a married man in every sense of the word?"

Jonathan's eyes dove into hers. "You need to return to the dance and I to my wife's side." Bowing gallantly from the waist, he added, "I allowed you to lead me here so I could say good-bye, Isabella."

Drawing her fan like a man would a sword, she slapped the fan open. "That's what you think. I determine when a relationship is over, Jonathan. I alone. I'll not lose you to an ogress. You haven't seen the last of me."

Jonathan turned from the woman whose obsession for him had become his thorn. If anyone was an ogress, it was Isabella. The moon ducked behind a cloud, as if to escape her wrath.

What was that? A woman's form shaded within the consoling shadows of the mansion — Rachael? What was she doing crouching there?

chapter ten

labaster pillars and green ferns complemented the red velvet tapestry that graced the tall windows and plush accommodations of the Cincinnati Hotel. Jonathan had attained a two-bedroom suite with a connecting parlor. Rachael bit her bottom lip. Was he thinking of her comfort, or was this arrangement due to their previous argument about her spying on him and Isabella in the garden?

"I determine when a relationship is over, Jonathan, I alone." Isabella's words haunted Rachael and caused her little sleep. Jonathan argued that if she hadn't been eavesdropping, she'd have nothing to worry over.

She glanced over her shoulder, searching the faces of the well-groomed ladies in the hotel restaurant. She wouldn't put anything past Isabella and had voiced her concerns to Jonathan. Occupied by the pending trip, he had not given her concerns a second thought.

"I cannot imagine what is detaining our missionary couple." Jonathan drew out his pocket watch like a cowhand would a six-shooter and frowned into its face.

"Patience, husband." Rachael picked up the menu, scanned the entrées, and smiled. This afternoon they would depart for St. Louis. They couldn't leave too soon to please her.

Jonathan patted her hand absentmindedly. How handsome he looked today in his grey pinstripe suit. Her eyes flitted from him to the ornate room, recalling how hard it had been for her to convince her exuberant husband to shed his buckskins. Noting the crystal chandeliers, gleaming goblets, and sparkling silver crests on the cutlery decorating the table linens in this noted Queen City of the West, Rachael was glad Jonathan had listened to her recommendations.

The rugged West was but a passing memento in Cincinnati. Refined and elegant as any eastern city she was acquainted with, she felt that Cincinnati could no longer hold the title of City of the West. Rachael glanced at her husband. Understanding warmed her heart. No wonder he was impatient to leave. He longed to breathe into the Oregon Territory the spirit of hope that only God could give a heathen land. The western border had expanded to encompass the unknown regions stretching beyond St. Louis.

Jonathan thumped the linen tablecloth. "I've got to get our tickets for the steamer. Now where do you suppose — Oh, there they are." Jonathan jumped to his feet.

A tall man, thin in stature with a shadow of a woman whose height came to the man's chest walked toward them. Rigid in posture and dressed in black, the two newcomers lugged heavy suitcases. Rachael braced herself, glancing down at her cream blouse and velvet-blue travel suit. Eager to make a good impression, she rose and stood alongside Jonathan.

"Rachael, may I introduce Saul and Beth Spiker."

Rachael sucked in her breath.

Saul's eyes swept her face, and Rachael noted the sharp declaration of his brows just before his glance swerved from Rachael to Jonathan.

The tiny Beth with the doe-like eyes sent Rachael a warm smile that more than made up for Saul's stony countenance. "You must excuse Mr. Spiker, he's had a terrible upset stomach from our bumpy train ride to Cincinnati. But he is much improved."

Jonathan accepted Saul's response without a second glance. "Is this all your baggage?"

"Yes. Our household items are at the dock."

"That's fine. Please join us. We were about to order." Jonathan glanced toward Rachael. "Please order for me. The porter and I will take ours and the Spikers' baggage across the street, and I'll get our tickets for St. Louis." He turned to Saul. "I shall make sure our accommodations will be suitable for our wives."

Their waiter, seeing Jonathan leaving, came forward. Ordering was somewhat a hurried affair. Afterwards, tiny Beth rose. "Will you excuse me please? I have need for the powder room."

A narrow smile swept Saul's face as he rose, then nodded. After his wife's departure, he resumed his seat.

Beth's departure filled Rachael with dread. *What is wrong? This is certainly not the same Saul who proposed to me.* As Beth turned the corner of the gold-leaved wallpaper and walnut door frame, Saul leaned toward her. She was glad the table separated them.

His black eyes, like two burnt coals, gleamed into hers. "Say nothing to Jonathan or Beth about my father or knowing me. Do you understand?"

"But why?"

"Say nothing, Rachael. Promise me," he urged.

Confusion over Saul's attitude fell like a damp shawl on her shoulders. "I give you my word. But I see no reason to hide the truth."

Beth returned to the table in better spirits than when she had left. "I can't believe how beautiful this hotel is. Have you seen the ladies' room, dear Rachael?" Her small lace gloved hand flew to her tiny mouth. "Oh my, I hope you do not mind my impetuous greeting?"

Rachael laughed. "Not at all, if I might have the same liberty and call you dear Beth, for I have grown affection toward you on our first meeting."

Jonathan's return melted away their conversation, his mood as infectious as sunlight after a storm. Rachael gave a silent prayer of thanksgiving for his return. She avoided Saul's eyes throughout their lunch. Still, it was not in her makeup to cower before bullies. There would be another confrontation with the sour Saul. She was sure of that. Next time she would be ready.

The spray from the mighty Mississippi moistened Rachael's face. She leaned over the railing, straining to see past the fog, wanting to be first to see the gleaming buildings of St. Louis.

It had rained throughout the day yesterday and twice they had come fast on a sandbar. A layer of fog floated over the waters like little misplaced clouds. The steamer's bell echoed in the fog, warning other steamers of her presence on the river. She searched the distant shoreline.

Rugged bluffs rose along the bank to their left and the low plains and lush green grasses of valleys and trees dotted the banks to their right. To Rachael they hummed a sonnet of adventure, but the same could not be said for her companion, especially as the winds grew stronger, whispering of a storm barking at their heels like an impatient wolf.

Beth groaned. Her voice quivered with pain. "I feel so sick. Perhaps I should go to my cabin."

Rachael wrapped a protective arm around the woman's small shoulders. "We shall both go, if you prefer, dear Beth." She was such a frail thing.

Beth's doe-bright eyes gazed into hers. "We will be as sisters, Rachael dear, for we are sisters in Christ Jesus and shall be the only English speaking women west of the Rockies. That is, except for Narcissa Whitman and Eliza Spalding. Oh my." Beth cupped her cheeks between her gloved hands, her eyes as large as saucers. "That will certainly limit our gossip."

Rachael laughed as both women hugged each other. Beth was three years older, yet Rachael assumed the guardianship role without compromise, due to her size and strength. Beth, however, had proven to be the wiser of the two. "Beth, have you ever met Narcissa?"

"I am proud to say I have."

"What is she like?"

"She is lovely, both inside and outside. I met her at a women's aid meeting. She was so excited, so filled with the Holy Spirit. It radiated from every pore. She is the reason I decided to come." Beth leaned against the rail as the wind whipped around their forms. "Sometimes I feel we women hold a dual duty on earth. First we must mother our offspring, and then seek to mother the lost. Narcissa made me realize, too, that when a Christian woman follows the call, whether it be taking care of her own family or traveling into the belly of the wilderness, it has to be something that our Savior should decide — not her alone."

"How do you know when you are following God's requests and not your own desires?"

"That's a hard one for me, too. Oh, of course, some pastors might disagree. But I always felt you'd find the answer in here." Beth tapped her heart.

"I am so happy Saul has found someone like you to heal his wounds."

"Wounds? Did you know my husband before this voyage?" Beth's voice grated Rachael's heightened senses. Why had Saul hidden his past from Beth?

"I met him at the Academy. We were students there."

Beth's voice sounded relieved. "Oh, then, I do understand. Saul told me about that ugly rumor circulating the school." Beth grabbed the railing as their steamer swayed from the swell of a passing boat.

Beth tipped backward. Rachael grabbed her by the waist and then braced herself, as a foaming white wave washed across the starboard side of the boat. The steamer skimmed the turbulent waters of the mighty Mississippi without compromise, the spray wetting their faces and clothes.

"I… I think I am still recuperating from my miscarriage."

"Miscarriage?" Rachael blurted. She shook her head. It was none of her concern. "Come, let us find a chair."

"No, no, it is good for me to stand." Beth rested her hand on Rachael's cheek. "I am so relieved that our Lord has chosen you to be my sister."

Rachael squeezed Beth's small hand, the warmth of her touch lingering on her cold cheek. "I can see why Saul fell in love with you. I feel we shall become fast friends, for life and eternity."

"Yes, I feel it too. Please, tell me more about my husband and his days at the Academy." Beth held Rachael's gaze, searching her face. "Saul is a quiet man, not used to disclosing issues close to his heart. I have learned to be patient. My husband shall, when he is ready, tell me more of his past. Of that I am certain."

What would God want her to do? Foamy waves slapping hungrily at the steamer's hull echoed in the lapse of words. Rachael wiped the spray from her face. How would Jonathan react when he learned of Saul's proposal to her? That she held confidential information regarding Saul's life? Was that what Saul was afraid of?

The boat rocked and heaved sideways. Rachael braced Beth with her own body, nearly falling herself. "That was close. We need to find a place of shelter." Grabbing Beth, Rachael crossed the swaying deck to the safety of the rooms. A wave crashed over the railing where they had stood.

The wind whipped Rachael's skirts about her legs. It was all she could do to support Beth and remain on her feet. River water washed over her boots, the scents of fish and limestone offended her nostrils. Lifting the latch, she guided the frail Beth inside the cabin.

The wind howled like a lone wolf at her heels, banging the door against the wall. She threw her weight on the cabin entrance, and looked around.

She gasped. This was not the dining compartment — it was the men's saloon. "Beth, we can't stay here." A card game was going on in the far corner of the room. At the mahogany bar a number of men turned their shallow gaze on them. One smirked and then elbowed the man to his left.

"Nonsense, I'm not going out there again." Beth walked toward the nearest table. "We'll stay here until one of our husbands finds us."

"This is most improper."

"Dear Rachael, we'll be doing more improper things than this crossing the wilderness."

Someone whispered an obscenity. Rachael didn't need to hear the rest of the conversation to know that it was of a derogatory nature — and aimed at them.

"Here, Beth," Rachael coaxed her into a chair far from the men.

"What'll it be?"

Rachael looked up at the pudgy face of the saloonkeeper as she removed her gloves. "Could we have tea, please?"

"This ain't no tea room. It's a saloon."

"The weather has grown ugly. If we could rest here until our husbands find us, we would be most grateful." Beth's little face beseeched the scowling bartender.

"You're the missionaries, ain't ya?"

"Yes," Beth said.

The man shook his head, wiped his hands on the soiled dish rag, and then tossed it over his shoulder. Rachael leaned back in her chair. The potent smell of whiskey and tobacco erupted from the saloon-keeper's mouth. "You ladies don't know what you're getting into. Those savages know nothin' but rapin' and killin'. Get back to where you came from and forget this foolhearted venture."

"I understand your concern, and I concede." Beth sent him her brightest smile.

"You do?"

"Yes, I do. I would undoubtedly feel the same as you, sir. That is, if I were not on a first-name basis with my Savior."

"Your what?"

"My Savior, Jesus Christ. You see He is sending us and that makes all the difference."

"What?"

"Jesus wants everyone to know about His love and forgiveness. You see that man over there?" Beth said.

"Yep, that's Butch. He can wrestle any man to the floor with one hand behind his back."

"Yes, no doubt. But do you see that demon looking over Butch's shoulder?"

The bartender scowled. "No, but neither can you."

"The world you do not see is as real as Butch over there."

The bartender raised his big calloused hand in front of his face. "That's missionary stuff."

"No, it is not. It's real. If you or Butch should die today, then that devil over there would become plain enough, and this floor beneath your feet would fade into oblivion."

A gust of wind stirred the tablecloths. Someone had entered. A shadow loomed over them.

"I trust you are taking good care of my wife and her friend."

Rachael sucked in her breath. Saul's chilling gaze choked back the happiness she felt to see him. Maybe she should wait for Jonathan.

"I was telling your wife about the grave danger she's facing." The bartender jerked his head toward Rachael.

Saul glared back at her, then moved to stand near Beth, resting a comforting hand on her shoulder. "My wife may be small, but she is strong willed."

"You're sure enough right about that one. That little lady packs a wallop and a half." The bartender wiped his mouth with the back of his hairy hand. "Lady, you sure do speak some powerful words, thinking stuff, you know what I mean?"

Beth smiled. "Come to our cabin when the saloon closes. I can give you some literature to read."

"Can't read."

"Then I will read it to you," Beth brightly replied.

The saloonkeeper blinked, then nodded.

"I wish to return to my stateroom, Mr. Spiker." Beth rose. Her quiet, yet commanding voice broke into the snickers of the men sitting at the table behind theirs. "We attempted to remain where you told us, but it became much too hazardous to do so."

"I do apologize. My business took longer than I expected. Am I forgiven?"

"Of course," Beth said in a gentle tone and then added, "Don't I always, Mr. Spiker?"

Rachael felt like an intruder of their affectionate reunion and bent her head in the excuse of smoothing the folds from her pleated skirt. "Is Jonathan's business complete?"

"Not entirely. He asked me to bring you."

"When shall we reach St. Louis?" Rachael asked.

"In the morning. If all goes well, but this storm may delay us."

The force of the wind from the opened door caused Rachael to take two steps back. She lowered her head and plowed her way after Saul and Beth. Down the slippery corridor, Rachael clung onto the railing of the boat as Saul led Beth to their cabin.

Saul pushed open their door and helped Beth in. Rachael hesitated.

"Come in, dear Rachael," Beth said with such a beaming face that

Rachael felt warmed by it. "We haven't had our tea yet."

"But what of Jonathan? Perhaps I should look for him."

"He'll find you here, enjoying the companionship of friends. After all, Jonathan did ask us to get to know each other better," Beth said.

"I'll get the tea." Saul hurried toward the alcove.

Rachael glanced down the corridor for Jonathan.

"Rachael, can you help set the table?" Beth, near exhaustion, removed her coat with difficulty. Rachael hurried to her side.

"Beth, perhaps you should go and lie down until the tea is warmed." Beth placed a hand to her stomach. "Yes, I think I shall. Mr. Spiker, please make our Rachael comfortable while I rest. If that nice bartender stops by, awaken me."

Rachael followed Saul into the small alcove that the maid had earlier stocked with tea and sandwiches. A fresh brew was waiting. She prepared a tray for Beth, garnishing it with a spray of lilacs from the vase sitting in the small cabin. "I have our tray almost complete."

Lifting the tray, she held it out to Saul. His hands stayed firmly at his sides. "You take it. I won't be staying." He took a step closer, his large hands doubled into fists, his arms rigid at his sides. "Did you tell my wife about my past?"

"Only that we both had gone to the same Academy."

"I have buried my lineage and my feelings for you, Rachael. I never wish to dig them up again."

Was he implying he wanted to keep this lie alive? "I realize my father and I have hurt you. Though I feel the beam in Father's eyes is larger than my own, I am equally to blame." Rachael cradled the tray in her arms. Did Saul know about Beth's miscarriage? Of course, he must. "Saul, I feel it's wrong to withhold the truth from Beth and Jonathan. Can't you see… No, I see you cannot. We have to tell them. We are living a lie if we do not."

Saul's eyes burned into hers.

"So your father wasn't perfect, neither is mine." She hurried on. "You proposed to me because you wanted to go west. Jonathan would understand that. His actions were the same as yours. The sin is in not telling them the truth, as if we held feelings other than friendship for one another… Oh, please don't look at me like that."

Saul turned away. His shoulders hunched. Was he reliving her refusal of marriage?

"Jesus is still training me to be His disciple. God knew who would be the best partner in life for us. Saul, we must obey Christ. We are not behaving Christ-like in keeping this from our spouses."

"Their knowing will cause them heartache. We must pretend it never happened." His face drawn, Saul's eyes were void of emotion.

Rachael rose to her commanding height. "Which of the two secrets are you referring to, Saul, your father's sins or your proposal to me? This omission will grow into deception. No. Please, release me from my oath, Saul, I beg you. It was wrong for me to promise you."

"So now the pupil has become the teacher? I will do the telling. In my time."

"But —"

"Rachael, do not argue."

"I will pray for you, Saul. Pray that you will forgive my father and me — and that you will forgive your father."

Saul scowled. "Remember the rest of Luke 6:42: 'Either how canst thou say to thy brother, Brother, let me pull out the mote that is in thine eye, when thou thyself beholdest not the beam that is thine own eye? Thou hyprocrite.' Remove that beam from your eye, Rachael. You are no better than I." Saul hesitated, his hand on the doorknob. "I'm the innocent party here. Of the deceit from my father and my unforgiving high-and-mighty Christian brothers."

Glad that she still held the silver tray, she clutched its sides so hard her knuckles turned white. A knock and the familiar voice of Jonathan caused a sigh of relief to escape her lips.

"Come in, Dr. Wheaton." Saul grasped Jonathan's hand in a firm shake. Like a chameleon changes color, a smile replaced Saul's scowl, astonishing Rachael at the stark change. What had changed Saul? He had spoken to her as if he hated her.

chapter eleven

*J*onathan glanced up from the clerk's chest-high reception desk at the majestic St. Louis Hotel just as Saul and Beth walked through the broad stained glass oak doors. Rachael followed a few steps behind. Why hadn't either Saul or Rachael mentioned they had attended the same academy? Why had he found out this fact from Beth?

The clerk followed his gaze. "Is that tall, stately lady your wife?"

"Yes, and I was unable to give her a proper honeymoon. Is there any way I could book your bridal suite?"

The clerk whistled softly. "I'll see if I can get you the one with the balcony overlooking the river."

Seeing Jonathan, Rachael smiled. Her face lit with a radiance that transfigured her countenance. His heart did a somersault at the thought of having her to himself for the entire evening. Something about Rachael had changed. She sparkled with life, with a glow altogether irresistible.

"I have witnessed many ladies grace this threshold, but your wife is the loveliest I have seen for many a year." The clerk rested his hand over the small bell located on his counter and hesitated.

Jonathan had seen that look before, a look that said, I wish she were mine. He wanted to hide her from the clerk's eyes. Rachael walked forward and stood quietly by Jonathan's side.

The clerk rang the small silver bell on his cherrywood desk. An older man with grey hair and stooped shoulders dressed in a red and black uniform stepped forward. "Take Dr. Wheaton and his wife to the bridal suite in the east wing, please."

The bellhop picked up their bags and led the way down the carpeted hallway. Like a rare stone uncovered at long last, Rachael's eyes sparkled into Jonathan's. Was it fear of denial that held his love at bay? He wanted to give her the little hugs he'd seen Saul give Beth. Those little social affections appeared easy for Saul; why was it so hard for him? Rachael's skirts gently swished about her legs and the sound intoxicated him. He needed to touch her, to know she was real and not just a figment of his imagination. He looped her arm within the curvature of his own. "Did you enjoy your walk?"

"Yes, but I would have all the more if you had accompanied us on our sightseeing tour." Rachael's hazel eyes gazed at him. "Jonathan, how much longer will your business dealings take?"

"It is finished." He heard the catch in his voice before he could stop, his chest swelling with remorse. He had spent the majority of the afternoon seeking a wilderness guide and had come up empty. They had lost the companionship of the American Fur Company because the company had decided to start a week earlier. The days McCray and he had lost due to the cholera epidemic in Canada had not helped.

Reverend McCray had devised an alternative. He and the two Indian boys, Matthew and Luke, had left from Canada for the city of Liberty, on the Missouri River. They hoped to catch up with the fur company and ask them to wait for the missionaries before leaving for the frontier. McCray was confidant all would go well and promised to send Jonathan news. Jonathan was firm with his feisty partner. He would not jeopardize the ladies or place them in harm's way. If the American Fur Company proved incompliant… well, he would be forced to abandon the pilgrimage and return Rachael and Beth to New York. The men would go forth and set up the missionary sights and return for the women the following year. But that wasn't something he wanted to worry Rachael with right now.

She stirred uneasily by his side. "I am glad to see the color back in your cheeks." He patted the top of her hand. "Now, where would you like to dine tonight?"

"Oh, it doesn't matter to me. I think St. Louis is enchanting."

The bellhop opened the door to their room, turned and smiled. "So you're the missionaries heading west?"

"Are we that obvious?" Jonathan handed the man a shiny gold piece.

"Thank you. Well, we heard you were coming. Good luck to you." Halfway back down the hallway the bellhop stopped. "Dr. Wheaton?"

Jonathan paused before shutting the door and waited.

"Did you hear about the *Diana*? A terrible loss, it was." His earnest gaze held Jonathan's.

"What happened?"

"Snagged herself in the shallow water and sunk. It was tough luck for that fur company."

"Wasn't that the boat you said you wanted to go on, Jonathan?" Rachael's voice sounded worried.

Jonathan's gaze shifted from her to the bellhop. "*Diana* had left by the time we made it to port."

"Truly Providence is ordering our steps." Rachael choked out her relief. "Oh, dear, and think how disastrous it must have been for those aboard."

"At least the boat snagged herself in shallow water and no lives were lost," the bellhop nodded. "She's lying up for repairs someplace between here and Liberty. Most of her cargo got wet. Well, thank you for the gold piece." The bellhop held up his square hat in salute.

"Jonathan, does that mean we will be traveling with the fur company on our way to Oregon?"

Jonathan smiled at the delight mirrored in her eyes. "It'll certainly make them easier for McCray to find."

"And to think, Jonathan, we were willing to go the journey alone, but now the Lord has assured we shall go with appropriate security after all."

The wind lacing through their opened balcony door drew Rachael like a magnet. Her slippers echoed on the bricks of the patio deck, the breeze stroking her hair as the moonlight danced on blue-black waters and windswept white-capped waves of the Mississippi.

"I brought you your cape to keep the dampness at bay." Jonathan's warm hands lingered as her cape floated down around her shoulders.

She barely breathed, afraid that any movement on her part would send one of them fleeing from the uncertain emotions that were often too confusing to explain with words. She leaned her head on his strong chest. He rested his head on hers, his breath hot against her cheek.

She closed her eyes, allowing her sense of touch full mastery. His warmth wrapped her like a shroud and sent her flesh burning with desire. Was this what love felt like? Why God had said man and woman would fuse into one? She never needed a man's love — until now. She needed Jonathan's.

Immersed in the moon's glow, the quiet ecstasy of God's plan for a husband and wife washed over her. Jonathan's breath stirred her hair and she nestled deeper into the crook of his shoulder. Isabella is gone. Then doubt lifted its serpent's head and entered her thoughts. Did Jonathan desire her inner beauty? Did he respect and adore her the way she had seen him with Isabella on that first encounter at Jonathan's carriage? Or, was her desire to become a missionary blinding her eyes to her husband's demeanor? No! This is real. This is love.

"Rachael, I understand you and Saul were acquainted with each other before this journey." His voice rose ever so slightly and held an icy edge. "Were you students at the same academy?"

Rachael closed her eyes, praying for God to grant her the right words. "Yes, Jonathan. I didn't think that it mattered."

"I would have liked to receive the news from you, not Beth. How long have you known Saul?"

"Four years. He was a student and one of my religious teachers at the Academy."

A rap on the door broke into their conversation. "Four years? Neither you nor Saul acted as if you had known one another. Why the secrecy if all you shared was a few books?" Another rap on the door seemed to punctuate his question. "We'll have to finish this conversation later." Jonathan gave her a lingering embrace and then stepped over to the door.

"Saul?" Jonathan opened the door wider. "What are you doing here?" Jonathan trailed Saul's gaze to Rachael like a hound dog on a scent, one brow raised questioningly above his shrouded blue eyes.

She hugged the cape closer to her form and shuddered as Saul's look drifted to her and nervously back to Jonathan.

The candle sconces sent an eerie glow over the curvatures of Jonathan's face. "Yes?"

"There's a boat in port that will take us up the Missouri. They are leaving within the hour."

"I must repack our things." Glad for a reason to escape, Rachael hurried to their bedroom. She wished she had the nerve to confront Saul about her promise. She clutched the doorpost of the bedroom and glanced back. She needed to tell Jonathan everything, before he assumed the worst.

Saul's stern monotones broke into her thoughts. "Dress warm. The night air is chilly."

Jonathan's stormy eyes met hers, his chin stuck out like a granite boulder and he slammed the door shut on Saul's departure.

The moon shining a beacon of light across the darkened waters of the Missouri River gave Jonathan the feeling they were stealing away, far away from the carefree and fun-loving city.

An ache filled his chest. He'd missed his opportunity to share St. Louis with his bride. He could have taken her along with him as he finalized the plans of the voyage. She might have liked that. He knew he would have enjoyed the day much more with his lovely wife by his side.

He regretted his decision asking Saul to be his wife's chaperone. It was clear now that Saul was more than pleased to do so. He had himself to blame if Saul chose to command more liberties than Jonathan deemed necessary.

Rachael leaned over the railing; the dots of spray on her hair sparkled like jewels in the moonlight. Her eyes glowed back into his.

"Every bend in the river brings us closer to the Oregon Territory." The tips of her fingers were red from holding onto the railing with such fervor. He grasped her hands into his. "You need not hold on so tightly, my dear." She was like a child captured by the adventure and unable to suppress her excitement at whatever awaited them around the next bend in the river.

"Oh, Jonathan, it's all so beautiful."

Homes twinkled back at them, on waves of goodbyes as their steamboat glided up the river. "I do not want to miss not one building, not one boat. I feel like this is the last of civilization I shall ever see."

"It is." He felt a twinge deep in his heart for her. "What lies west of St. Louis is the wilderness."

"I won't hear the chime of church bells echoing their refrain on Sunday mornings. Or a lady's and gentleman's laughter mingling with the soft mellowed refrains of violins." Rachael sighed. "There will be no more balls amidst the splendors of sparkling crystal chandeliers."

He would never forget that evening when Rachael gaily breezed down her parents' stairway looking like an angel in her ivory gown of flowing silk... All left behind to journey to the unknown. He glanced up toward the heavens and sighed. Did Rachael understand how different the life she had decided on would be? There was no retracing their steps. Both of them had decided on a course that would change their destiny. A destiny of harsh climates and loneliness, deprivation and servitude, a destiny they prayed preordained by God.

Jonathan covered her shoulders with his arms. "Are you warm enough?"

"Oh, yes, now I am." Her eyes filled with such longing, that his breath escaped in one gasp. "Dear Rachael, what is this longing I see in your eyes?"

"It is for many things." Rachael looked out at the river. The gentle breezes stirred her hair and she lifted her chin. "We are leaving all we have ever known, and will soon embark on the mission of winning souls for our loving Savior. Oh, Jonathan, we have gained far more than we have lost. But how shall I convey what is in my heart and not sound preachy? How will I tell the Indians about the Light of God's redemption when all they have known is darkness?"

"You care about these, these primitive natives that much?"

"I feel half awake, in a sort of dream where this isn't happening. Do you ever feel that way? When what you have wished for all your life is about to come true?"

He held her gaze as his hand stroked her upturned chin. A breeze lifted her hair and floated her curly locks about her head. "Yes, I think I know what you mean." His sigh matched hers and she nestled back, allowing her head to rest on his shoulder.

A pang of guilt interrupted his thoughts. Rachael's innocent declaration revealed a missionary's heart. Whereas his desires were twofold. Truly, he desired to witness to the heathens about Jesus. But his first great love was to explore the unknown as his great-grandfather had done and uphold the Wheaton name.

The hours drifted by without notice. Jonathan listened to Rachael tell about her youth and the years between them vanished as the night turned to dawn. They watched the first rays of the sun peek across the waters, lifting the darkness that had encompassed their lives with a stroke of a hand. "God had a plan all along for us to meet." His lips grazed her forehead and she sighed, arching her neck.

"How admirable are thy works, O Lord of Hosts." Jonathan whispered.

Locked in each other arms, Jonathan closed his eyes.

"Ah, excuse me."

Jonathan felt Rachael's body go rigid. "Yes, Brother Saul."

"The sun is coming up."

"We know. Rachael and I have been watching its progress."

"Well, I thought it would be a perfect time to begin our prayers."

"But of course. Rachael and I will be there shortly." He watched Saul retreat to the other side of the boat, then turned and kissed Rachael's forehead. "Come, dear, we must not keep Saul waiting."

"Why not?"

"He's our minister and deserves our respect at all times."

"Must all his requests be honored?"

Holding her at arm's length, he searched her once smiling face now turned into a scowl. "Rachael, why would you ask such a question?"

※ ※ ※

Their journey up the Missouri River went smoothly with only one stop to take on more wood. They docked at Liberty on April 26. Rachael would never forget the date because that day she placed her first toehold on the rugged western frontier. She laughed, recalling the clamor of the merchants holding out their wares for her to see and the smell of fish, horse flesh, and fresh air that intoxicated her nostrils. The excitement of that thriving western town was contagious. The hustle and bustle of men bidding for livestock at the corrals had spurred Jonathan and Saul into purchasing six horses, fifteen mules, twenty head of cattle, and five milk cows. Purchasing the wagons had proven quite an enterprise.

After loading the wagons they had gone a day's journey northwest of Liberty and set up camp. They had yet to join Reverend McCray and the fur company before beginning their journey in earnest.

Rachael stroked the mane of her bay mare. The mooing of the milk cows and the brays of the mules filled the morning with their noise just as the sunlight peeking over the crest of the plains chased away the darkness with a pageantry of scarlet, orange, and golden beams.

"It is as I had envisioned." Jonathan's eyes shined into hers, clutching in one hand the lead lines of two mules he purchased. In the other hand were the reins of his horse. He nodded his head toward her mare. "That horse's coat matches the reddish highlights in your hair like a shiny penny."

She smiled up at him.

"Allow me to introduce you to Matthew and Luke who the Reverend McCray and I met in Canada." Two Indian boys stood a distance behind him. They had arrived in their camp before sunrise. "They've brought word that the Reverend has located the American Fur Company at a place called Council Bluffs. They are not willing for us to join them. He says he needs my help to… persuade the fur company. I'm leaving to go there now."

"But, Jonathan, how will you find them?"

"McCray sent a map." He held it up for her to see. "There is plenty of grazing land here and water for the livestock. Matthew and Luke will stay and help Saul in making you and Beth comfortable until my return."

The youths examined the animals. Nodding over this and that horse and finally came to the mules Jonathan had purchased. "Very bad mule." Matthew shook his head like a dog ridding itself of dust and slapped the lead line on the mule's neck. Dressed in buckskins and moccasins, his straight black hair trailed to his shoulders and down his back. The other boy, Luke, who could have been Matthew's twin except for the small blemish above his left eye, scowled back.

Rachael looked from the mule to Matthew and Luke. "I can't see anything wrong with him. He's got four legs and a nice long black tail."

"Can't catch buffalo." Matthew pointed to the mule, then the horse.

Jonathan chuckled. "Then Rachael should ride the horse instead?"

Matthew crossed his arms, his bottom lip protruded forward. "Yes, horse good in catching buffalo. Mules too slow."

She stroked the black neck of one mule. Why hadn't Jonathan told her of his plans earlier? He had not relinquished the information regarding the fur company until it was absolutely necessary. The way he coddled her she felt more like a child than a wife.

"May I come along?" Rachael asked.

"No, I must travel quickly. I will ride north to the Moses Merrill Mission and tell Reverend Merrill where you are camped. The youths say the Council Bluffs region is not too far from the mission."

Rachael bit her bottom lip, forcing a smile. There was nothing she could do to keep Jonathan by her side. She must accept her fate, just like the poor animals that were as unworthy as she to question their station in life. She gave one mule an affectionate hug. "Yes, just a beast of burden that will pull our wagons and do our bidding without reprieve."

Matthew and Luke nodded.

Saul, astride his horse, trotted up with Beth on her horse by his side. "You leaving, Jonathan?"

Jonathan swiped his hat on his buckskins. Grit peppered the air. "I wouldn't be in such a hurry to see me go, if I was you."

"The sooner you leave the sooner we can be on our way west." Saul scowled. "I still say we can travel better without this fur company."

Throughout breakfast the two men had acted like Mother's roosters. Rachael watched Jonathan struggle to keep a smile on his face.

"Need I remind you that I am funding this trip? Take care of the women, I shall return in three days." He reached for Rachael's hand and squeezed it.

With the cloud of dust created from Saul's retreating gelding, Jonathan turned. He tilted her chin up and searched her face, then muttered words meant only for Rachael. "Whatever secrets you are hiding within the prisms of your heart, may God direct you. I pray this brief separation will do us both good." He kissed the top of her nose, jumped on his horse, and galloped away.

Rachael stepped forward, her hand raised to shelter her eyes. He was gone.

The saddle creaked beneath Beth's weight. The scent of freshly cleaned leather floated in the air. Beth cleared her throat, but Rachael could tell by the concerned look in her eye that Beth had overheard the conversation between her and Jonathan.

"I believe my horse is a bit thin. Saul had a time finding a saddle that would fit him. Does that mean that he shall be a hard keeper? I feel I could reach clear around his belly if I had a mind."

This conversation was only a means of diverting Rachael's thoughts from Jonathan to something lighter. "Will Jonathan will be safe traveling alone in this wilderness?"

"Jonathan can take care of himself, have no fear of that." Beth rested back in her saddle and chuckled. "I declare, I like the spot Jonathan picked. We are a day's ride from Liberty to acquire more flour and supplies when the supply boats dock again."

Beth's good humor complemented Saul. She possessed the perfect temperament to Saul's solemn disposition displayed the evening before in their tent.

Their tent. Rachael laughed. Her vision of the trip was laughable and totally different from reality. They'd been through days of turbulent waters. Drunk foul-tasting water and eaten fouler-tasting food. Now, the tent she'd dreamed of sharing with Jonathan was a community tent, large enough for everyone to sleep in.

The tent was made of bed ticking and arranged in a conical form with a center pole and fastened down with pegs. Jonathan said it would keep out the cold and give the ladies protection and privacy.

She and Beth had giggled like two sisters preparing their beds and spreading out on the ground their India-rubber cloth that often served as a raincoat. Then they laid down the colorful blankets Jonathan had purchased in Canada. He explained they would place the blankets over their saddles every morning and ride on them during the day.

"You're excited to be underway. I can see it in your eyes," Beth said.

Rachael laughed. "Yes, but I wish Jonathan would allow me to go with him to find the fur company."

"I wish I had your appetite for adventure... and your health."

"Dear Beth." Rachael laid a hand on Beth's saddle, sympathetic to her feelings. The oil Saul used to soften the dry saddle moistened her finger tips. Beth was as fragile as her saddle.

"Do not worry so about me." Beth patted Rachael's hand. "I only wish I had more padding."

"Like me?" Rachael laughed. "Beth, for the first time in my life, I am happy with my frame." She slapped her hips. "I have just enough padding to make me comfortable."

"I am glad to hear that. Besides everything else that is wrong with me today, my stomach is still a little upset from drinking that awful river water."

"You should have accepted the spring water Jonathan and I brought. It was refreshing and a tonic to my stomach. I feel wonderful."

"It shows in your radiant complexion." Beth leaned toward Rachael. "Of course it always helps to be in love."

In love? Am I? Is Jonathan in love with me?

"What's wrong, Rachael?"

She needed to divert Beth from the reason for her chagrin. "I wish

I was more like you. Very resolute. You never complain, but bear with fortitude each and every trial that comes your way."

Beth waved her hand in front of her face, shooing away the stubborn mosquitoes that buzzed from dusk until full sunlight. "Save your pretty words. The journey has not yet begun. We shall see if I live up to your glowing acclamation. I fear both of us will be praying for Christ's victory over adversity. After all, our weaknesses are made perfect in His strength alone."

Rachael knew the small hardships they had endured so far were mere anthills to the mountains that lay ahead. "Yes, we shall soon discover what mettle we are made of."

chapter twelve

on't let them get under your skin, Jonathan." Reverend McCray nodded toward the frontiersmen. "Lafayette could likely help the situation, but he won't. Wants to see what you're made of, whether you stick it out or hightail it back East."

"Well, one more trapper that curses me, then throws a rotten egg at me is going to feel my fist down his throat."

Jonathan scrubbed at an egg stain then lifted his buckskin jacket to his nose. "Whew!" He threw the coat into a thicket.

McCray chuckled. "You'll get fouler smelling the longer you're out here so get used to it. That bride of yours won't be able to stand you downwind."

The howl of a wolf mingled with the clang of the frontiersmen's tin cups and whisky jugs. An Indian village stood a stone's throw away. A squaw glanced up from her fire. Her long, braided hair dipped over stooped shoulders; her eyes stared at him from a gaunt face. The smoke of her campfire spiraled before her form and into the sky like a mournful eulogy. Her teepee made from the bark of trees and buffalo skins flapped in the afternoon breezes like a sail on a ship. Two Indian braves squatted in a drunken stupor near the entry and rolled their heads in his direction.

So much for the white man's influence on the Indian. Jonathan got up from his log seat, picked up his coat, and slipped his arms into the buckskin. A trapper walking by nudged his companion and chuckled.

Lafayette, the boss and head man of the American Fur Company expedition, had ignored his men's actions, from throwing rotten eggs at Jonathan to giving the Indians bad whisky. Jonathan had worked up a personal vendetta toward this half Indian, half Frenchman since they locked eyes on each other two days ago.

Jonathan grunted. He was beginning to think he'd grown horns and a tail the way these fur men treated him. He'd hoped looking like these frontiersmen would demonstrate his willingness to conform to their customs. Customs indeed. What did he have to do, lose a mouthful of teeth and learn to drink that foul smelling liquor they consumed by the barrel?

"I'll go down to the stream and get a bucket of water for our coffee pot and washing. Why don't you unpack the rest of our supplies," McCray said.

"Make sure you get that water up stream," Jonathan warned.

Before he could finish unpacking, McCray returned with the water. Grabbing the coffee pot and the pouch of coffee beans, McCray squatted before the fire. "Here, make yourself useful and grind up these beans."

"With what, my teeth?"

"Use the handle of your revolver. Make it as fine as you can or else you'll be picking out coffee shells from between your teeth."

McCray dropped the coffee granules in the water and set the coffee pot down in the hot ashes. Then he reached for his black iron skillet, dropped sow belly in the pan, added two buffalo steaks and with a twist of his wrist, tossed the meat in the air, and caught it with the skillet. "Now, hand me that bag of flour by your leg."

Dropping two handfuls of flour into a small bowl, he reached into his shirt pocket and pulled out a small pouch and sprinkled in a couple pinches of salt, then added buffalo fat from the steaks. Blending, he formed silver-dollar size cakes and dropped them into the hot iron skillet. The cakes sizzled, spewing puffs of smoke in the windswept air. McCray grabbed his pot holders and lifted the steaming coffee pot. "We'll let the grounds settle a little before I pour you a cup."

"That meat smells good." Jonathan's stomach rumbled in agreement.

"Best smell there is after a day's ride." McCray placed a steak on Jonathan's tin plate.

Jonathan's mouth watered in anticipation.

"Now we got to have us some beans to make the flavor come out right." McCray snatched Jonathan's plate from his fingers. Jonathan slapped his jaws shut before a groan escaped. Now he knew what a dog felt like when deprived of a nice juicy bone.

McCray shook the pot of beans simmering in the fire, then flipped the cakes until both sides were golden brown. "We got a meal here fit for the finest houses in St. Louis." The smell of that steak and cornbread made Jonathan's mouth water like a starving coyote's.

McCray grabbed Jonathan's arm, now half way to his mouth. "I declare. We forgot to pray. He grabbed his Bible, flipping the pages. "Food and even medicine is a heap more effective with the Almighty's blessings sprinkled on it. Okay, here is what the Lord's been whispering in my head since you got here. 'Because thou hast made the LORD, which is my refuge, *even* the most High, thy habitation; There shall no evil befall thee, neither shall any plague come nigh thy dwelling.'"

"Amen." Jonathan couldn't argue with that. God was testing his patience both inside and out. He chuckled, his hand feeling the heat of the tin plate as his eyes devoured its mouthwatering treasures.

Leaves rustled from the thicket bordering their campsite, a voice as wild as a grizzly bear's followed. "Glad to see you still got a sense of humor, greenhorn." Lafayette's lips parted in a smirk between his black curly mustache and two-inch beard. "How do you want your eggs tomorrow?" He let out a loud belly laugh.

Jonathan ignored him and bit into his steak, rolling the savory morsel around his mouth before swallowing, then sipped his coffee. He leaned back and smacked his lips. "Good coffee, McCray, and one delicious steak."

Lafayette spit out a wad of chewing tobacco, missing Jonathan's boots by an inch. "You know Dr. Whitman?"

Jonathan spooned some beans and glanced up. "Know about him, but never met him." He swallowed down the savory mixture.

"Well, I've got one up on ya. Me and my company took him and Reverend Parker to the Rendezvous the year before he brought his Missus." Lafayette chuckled. "He took his eggs pretty good, too. Thought you'd like to know. We don't want a cub shadowing Dr. Whitman not to get his fair share."

"I'm sure Jonathan appreciates the compliment," McCray said. "He plans to live up to what the Whitmans have done."

Jonathan avoided Lafayette and McCray's looks. He didn't know when he left New York how much people expected him to be like Whitman. He didn't like it. He didn't need to follow in the footsteps of someone he'd never met. Living up to the expectations of his uncle and the Wheaton name was enough.

It was every man's character for himself here, and it was the first time in his life he wished his sir name did not begin with a W. It was too close to Marcus Whitman's. That was part of the problem. People thought he and Marcus were related. Jonathan hoped they were, through the blood of Jesus. If he wasn't right with his Savior, the devil was sure to take advantage of him in this harsh, wild land.

"How about it, Lafayette? You going to help my group get across the Rocky Mountains?"

"I'm still considering… Say, we're short of hands." Lafayette squatted in the dirt next to Jonathan. "Are you up to chopping down a few trees we need for rafts?"

Jonathan swallowed down a piece of steak. "Could be."

Lafayette got up, and turning on his heels, walked away as silently as he had come. His moccasins hardly made an imprint on the mossy turf.

"Might be a good thing." Jonathan rubbed his chin. "This might help Lafayette's men accept me."

"Humph! Nothing short of a miracle will do that." McCray tossed his leftover coffee in the fire, then waited for the hiss to subside. "They've got it in for you. You watch your back."

※ ※ ※

Jonathan's arms and shoulders burned like fire. He swung his ax in rhythm to the other men's, ignoring the blisters festering on his hands and the burn of his taut muscles. Up before daylight, he'd had time for only a cup of coffee. Now nearly mid afternoon, his stomach growled in protest.

"Timber!"

Jonathan blinked up against the bright sunlight. A whine split into the thuds of the axes and the hundred-year-old tree crashed to the ground. A cloud of dust spiraled upwards blocking his view of the tranquil blue sky.

Resting on the handle of his ax, he reached into the waist of his breeches for a handkerchief to wipe away his sweat. As he shook it open he noticed the stain. He'd used this handkerchief to wipe Rachael's face the day he rescued her from those bullies. He smiled, recalling how she tried to move away from him when he attempted to wipe the mud off her cheeks, so irresistibly vulnerable and so innocent. Saul's face poked into his thoughts. Come to think of it, vulnerable and innocent weren't good characteristics to have, especially out here.

What was wrong with him? So Rachael and Saul went to the Academy together, so what? Mrs. Rumpson's words during their wedding reception cut into his thoughts as sharply as his ax sliced into the trees. "That gentleman from the Academy was certainly attracted to you, Rachael. Quite smitten. When I heard you were to be married, I thought it would be he standing alongside you." Could Saul be that man?

"Hey, you plan on resting on that handle all afternoon?"

It was Pierre, the French immigrant he'd met in Canada on his trip with McCray. He'd been hounding Jonathan's heels all day.

"Let up, Pierre." McCray approached Pierre from behind. "Work detail is to report to camp."

"Timber!" The warning came too late. The branches of the tree crashed down on Jonathan. Everything seemed to spiral out of control as he fell to the ground.

McCray's soft prayers soothed his ears like a moist towel wrapping his throbbing head. Jonathan groaned. Excruciating pains shot through his body from toe to thigh. "My leg."

McCray bent over him, pulling the branches away.

Jonathan glanced over his shoulder. One leg was bent backward. The other leg trapped beneath a multi-armed branch.

"Move those branches as gently as possible." Jonathan panted. He slowly moved his leg. "It's not broken. I can bend it." McCray worked to free Jonathan's arm. "Ow! I'm okay, see, I can move it." Jonathan sat up and let his head clear, then got to his feet with aid from McCray who brushed away the dirt and debris from Jonathan's chest.

Laughter echoed down to them from the top of the hill. Half a dozen of Lafayette's men pointed and guffawed.

"I don't think your friends are too upset over their miscalculation," McCray said.

Jonathan rubbed his arm and looked up.

"Serves you right." Pierre held up his fist. "You missionaries are all holier-than-thou Bible peddlers."

Jonathan grabbed his ax, set his teeth, and focused on the eight-inch tree trunk, then gave a well directed blow to his new obsession, the woods echoing his hit.

"What are you doing? Haven't you had enough?" McCray asked.

"Got to keep working. Got to… take my anger out on this tree instead of Pierre's face." Only, it wasn't Pierre's face Jonathan saw. It was Saul's.

※ ※ ※

"Here." McCray drew out the white canvas rectangle tent from his pack. "See if you can remember how I put it up."

Jonathan tossed down the wood he'd gathered, reached a thumb up to his forehead, and scratched. "I think every mosquito in the west is in the woods tonight. You want the tent up before I start a fire?"

"I'd help, but I've got to prepare my sermon." He shoved a piece of wood toward the bundle Jonathan had dumped on the ground. "Go ahead, pretend I'm not here, and let's see if you've learned anything."

"I have hands covered with blisters to prove I have." Jonathan bit down on his lower lip and glared at the prostrate minister lounging with pencil and paper against a tree trunk. "Sometimes I feel more like your servant than your partner, McCray."

McCray glanced up at the sky. "Feels like rain. We could get a downpour any time. Best put up the tent first."

He could be as bull headed as Jonathan's uncle, and there wasn't any use in turning up the dirt between them. After all, what example would that set for the frontiersmen and Indians?

Jonathan examined the young saplings bordering the timbers for a potential center pole for their tent. Grabbing his hatchet, he walked over and with a few swings felled one. He wasn't looking forward to bunking inside; the six-foot base left his feet dangling out the entrance. Besides, McCray sounded like a bear in hibernation once his head hit the ground.

Jonathan spread out the tent, running the poplar through the hole made for it along the top, then staked the tent and wedged it down firm.

"If you're goin' to let that greenhorn put up your tent, don't expect it to last through the night, especially if we get wind," Lafayette said as he approached McCray.

"Lafayette, tell your men there will be a sunrise service tomorrow." McCray glanced up from his paper, then continued with his writing.

Lafayette chuckled. "You goin' to have liquor?"

"We don't believe in spirits."

"There's hardly anything between the ears of these men. Why mess up what little they understand with complicated things like the hereafter?"

"Because no one has a choice about death." McCray pointed his pencil at him.

Lafayette studied him, his eyes shining back at McCray like two burning coals. "I came here to tell you missionaries I'll help you to get to Umatilla Valley."

"We'll be powerfully grateful."

"Here's my hand in it." Lafayette stuck out his arm toward McCray. "I'll have to stop off at Fort Vancouver to drop off my pelts and livestock, then me and my men will take you to your valley."

McCray nodded to Jonathan. "This is your expedition."

Jonathan stood up, dusted off his palm, grabbed the hardened, calloused hand of the frontiersman, and nodded. "We'll leave tomorrow and get back to our women —"

"You'll not make it." Lafayette dropped Jonathan's hand like it had burned his. "Big powwow. News is Osage and the Iroquois Indians are on the warpath. I expect to see Pawnee and possibly a Blackfoot war

CATHERINE ULRICH BRAKEFIELD

party. The Blackfoot'll ride hundreds of miles on a raid for horses and guns. Wait until the Indians finish their smoking and trading. Then leave. Or else, you'll be meeting your lady folk without your hair."

"We left our women near Liberty. Are they safe?" Jonathan grabbed a look at McCray.

"That ain't my concern... Look. There's a man named Moses Merrill. A missionary for the Otoe tribe. That man has quite a reputation for fair play. I'll get one of my men to ride over to his place, it's just below the Corne de Cerf, he'll let your women folk know what happened."

"Reverend Merrill." McCray rubbed his ear. "He's studied the Otoe language and translated parts of the Bible for them."

"And I can't believe I'm helping more of you do-gooders." Lafayette's voice brimmed with distaste. "You leave whenever the mood fits. I'll not stop you. I'm giving you fair warning. There's strength in numbers. Me and my men are heading two miles northwest to the stockade. We'll weather the war drums there."

"We'll do as you say," Jonathan said.

"Now, here's the way I figure." Grabbing a twig from a nearby tree, Lafayette bent down and drew a map in the dirt. "The Corne de Cerf, where the Elkhorn River joins the Platte, is about a day's ride from here. The junction of the Platte River and Loup Fork is another thirty miles farther. 'Cause it's the season of high waters, I'll give you four and a half days to reach Loup Fork, which is about here. That'll be a tough one, with this high water and all. My company will give you and your women protection through the Pawnee villages, here." He drew several X's in the dirt. "If you're not at Loup fork by the fifteenth of May, we're moving on. Or else we might not reach Fort Vancouver before the snow flies."

McCray wiped his brow. "We have to return to our party first."

"Hmm," Lafayette fingered his black curly beard. Jonathan held his breath. He couldn't allow his group to travel farther if he didn't get the protection of the fur company.

Lafayette's black eyes seared into Jonathan's. "Well, you helped me get my rafts, guess I can wait another four days. But no more, you understand? I plan to leave Loup Fork by the twentieth of May."

chapter thirteen

*J*onathan bolted to a sitting position. "Ow." He blinked up at the sapling frame of the tent and rubbed his throbbing temples. The hollering continued. "Do you hear that?"

"Yeah." McCray had both boots on before Jonathan could even find his. A volley of gun shots split the silence, and loud whooping punctuated the noise. Head down like a snorting bull ready to battle a matador, McCray bolted through the small tent opening. Jonathan followed.

"What's going on here?" McCray demanded.

A stocky man with a full beard held a wash basin crooked in his burly arms. Pierre stood alongside him, pointing a finger at McCray. "You think you too good to associate with the likes of us?"

McCray shook his head.

"Then why you not drink with us?"

"It's against our religion."

"Religion no reason."

"It's reason enough for us." McCray lowered his chin, crossing his arms.

"Drink." The crowd yelled.

"We appreciate your hospitality, but no thanks."

"You refuse our liquor?" Pierre stepped to within inches of McCray. "We do."

Pierre lifted a dirty hand and motioned the men closer.

A gunshot rang a warning bolt through the crowd. Then another shot rang out. The men parted like sage grass in a heavy wind as Lafayette stepped forward.

Dead silence.

A bullfrog croaked. Another answered.

Lafayette looked at McCray, then Jonathan, and turned toward his men. The fringes of his buckskin jacket waved in the sharp breezes of the night as he scowled back into the bearded faces of his men. "What's going on here?"

Pierre melted into the crowd, leaving the man with the large basin of alcohol in his arms to stand alone.

"Captain, this alcohol is for Reverend McCray and Dr. Wheaton, but they're refusin' our hospitality."

Lafayette growled deep in his stomach, then turned to McCray and Jonathan and whispered, "Can't you bend a little? The boys don't mean no harm."

"We answer to a higher authority. We do not want to offend anyone, but I and Dr. Wheaton must obey God. Our God is a jealous God and He can do more harm than all of you. The Scriptures warn us 'And fear not them which kill the body, but are not able to kill the soul; but rather fear him which is able to destroy both soul and body in hell.'"

"Pierre not fear your God. I will put that basin to your lips and see what God does." Pierre grabbed the basin, the liquor sloshing across his arm as the other man released his grip. Like a rattler's warning before it strikes, the hisses of the men followed.

Lafayette held up his hand and waited until the men were silent. "Your poisonous venom ain't any good for the likes of these men. Christians aren't like any other varmint on earth." His frown deepened. He whispered to McCray again. "What if I wet your lips with the brew?"

McCray's face looked like it was chiseled from granite. "I'd like to accommodate you, Lafayette, but no thanks."

Lafayette snatched his coonskin cap from his head and threw it to the ground. "Your temperance principles are going to dig your grave early!"

"It's because of our love for our Savior, Jesus, who died for our sins."

"If He died for your sins, then, why not take a sip? Ask His forgiveness later. Why take a chance of dying here before you can do any good out yonder?"

"Compromising one's principles begins one step at a time and will lead a man down the wrong path, away from our loving Savior's arms. Jesus didn't compromise his Father's words. He died on the cross for us and He's all the spirit we need."

Lafayette picked up his cap and with one sweep of his arm, motioned his men to return to their tents.

"But what about this here liquor?"

"It's more for us to enjoy." Lafayette turned, hat in hand. "You, the Reverend Park, and Doctor Whitman are cut from the same cloth."

"What do you mean?"

"The men did the same thing to them. They refused to drink it, too."

A pair of rotten eggs flew toward Jonathan and McCray and landed in their campfire, spitting egg juice on the dying embers.

A chorus of chuckles sounded from the darkness.

"Watch your backs." The voice sounded like Pierre's.

※ ※ ※

Jonathan, McCray, and Lafayette's pack train of six wagons, fifty men, and 200 horses poured into the stockade.

McCray jerked his head toward the different tribes. "Those are Shoshone. Look yonder, that group's Flathead. We're going to have some trading going on for sure."

"My, they're a proud looking lot," Jonathan said. He didn't think there could be that many Indians in the West.

A grey bearded man astride a paint horse rode into view, his rifle cradled in the crook of his arm. His neck boasted a polished bear tooth necklace, and perched on his head was the glassy-eyed face of a grizzly.

"That's a mountain man." McCray placed a hand on Jonathan's arm, stopping his horse.

The man's mule was laden with beaver, fox, and bear pelts. Jonathan recalled McCray's words the night before about the solitary existence these men led. The mountain man looked at him and his mouth moved.

"I believe he's forgotten how to form the words." McCray frowned.

A man rode up and slapped a fur-toting man on the shoulder. "Here's a man for ya. Why, he's half bear and half horse, tougher'n hardwood and the ugliest cur this side of the Rockies!" The mountain man squinted back, placing a wary hand on his rifle. "And he can out run, out shoot, and whip any man here."

"Jim? That be you?" the mountain man replied.

"Who did ya think it was?"

The man squinted, measuring him with his glance. "Sure enough, Bridger, I thought I heard tell about a Blackfoot killin' ya' a while back."

"Nah, I'm too ornery to die. But he left me his calling piece. See that?" He turned his shoulder toward the man. "That Blackfoot arrow is still there — likely it would have killed any other man, but I've got me a powerful hunger for livin' and don't feel like turning up the dirt just yet."

They were everything Jonathan imagined these mountain men would be.

"Come on." McCray motioned with his arm. "We need to set up camp."

They rode a bit farther and found a spot close enough to the brook to carry water and far enough from the others to get some sleep. McCray leaped off his horse and unpacked his saddle bags. "Go unpack the mule. I'll start the fire. I think I could eat a whole side of venison all by my lonesome."

Jonathan chuckled. "And I could eat the other half, skin and all."

"That comin' from you... well Doc, you don't just smell like us, you're beginning to sound like us. Lay aside that tent and let's fry us up some side meat." Looking upwards, McCray's mouth broke into a grin. "We could sleep beneath the stars this evening, if you have a mind to."

Jonathan heard them before he could make out what was happening. Whoops and hollers of a half dozen Indians and bursting through the throng of teepees ran a spotted pony with a maiden crouched low, heading straight for them.

"Look out, Jonathan!"

Jonathan lunged, grabbing the pony's makeshift bridle of burlap and rope. The paint reared, grazing Jonathan's forearm, and the Indian maiden slid off the pony's back, creating a puff of dust as she hit the ground. "She's been beaten." McCray pointed to the welts on her arms and legs. He rose from his crouched position and looked over toward the village. Jonathan retrieved his medicine bag and knelt over her. Long sooty lashes fanned her bronze face, the skin beneath her buckskin skirt glistened white in the setting sunlight.

McCray whistled low. "Might be we chewed off more than we can handle." He watched a group of braves gallop their ponies toward them.

She grabbed Jonathan's forearm, her eyes pleading. "Please... help... me."

McCray knelt beside her. "You're not Indian. How —"

"Taken captive. Blackfoot kill father... mother... my sister." Sobs wrenched her shoulders that trembled beneath Jonathan's comforting hand. "Blackfoot kill sister last moon."

The thundering hoof beats and neighs of the approaching Indians' horses sliced into the conversation. "Let me do the talking." McCray blocked the men's view of the girl. Jonathan opened his bag, produced a jar of poultice and dabbed it on the girl's welts. She winced, but didn't cry.

A muscular brave sprang from his pony, raising his tomahawk. "Mine!"

"What seems to be the problem here?" Lafayette's boot kicked up dust as he squinted back at the brave.

The brave put his fist to his chest. "Mine!" Then pointed to the girl.

"What did the girl do to deserve those welts?" Jonathan scowled back.

The brave ignored Jonathan and pounded his bare chest. "Mine!"

The girl scampered to her feet like a wounded pup and cowered behind Jonathan, then spit on the ground near the brave's feet and spoke something in Blackfoot. Based on the Indian's response, Jonathan surmised the comment wasn't flattering. The brave doubled his hand into a fist and shook it at her.

Jonathan turned to Lafayette. "These welts need attention or they will fester. We need to set up that tent and keep her here overnight so I can doctor them."

"You don't ask for much, do you, Doc?" Lafayette spit out a jaw full of tobacco.

"The girl's white." McCray whispered from the corner of his mouth. "What?" Lafayette looked at her closer. "Well, I'll be." Lafayette turned and spoke a few words in Blackfoot. "Could be you could buy her, if you've got enough whiskey, that is."

"You know that ain't happening." McCray pulled at his whiskered chin. "There's got to be a solution we're not seeing."

The brave raised his hand chest high and swiped the air with his fist. "There's your answer." Lafayette nodded toward the brave. "He means to beat the girl until she agrees to marry him, even if it means her death. If he can't have her, then no one will." Lafayette crossed his arms and rocked back on his heels.

The girl grabbed Jonathan's arm, her eyes pleading her case. "If he won't sell her, what's left?"

"You can fight for her." Lafayette shrugged. "It's their way. It'll be a fight to the death."

"I'm a married man."

"She'll be yours to do with as you want. And by the looks of things, she's not going to complain."

"Jonathan doesn't have any experience fighting Indians." Like the lines on a map, concern wrinkled McCray's brow. "He's used to saving lives not taking them."

"Might be I can get one of my men to do the fighting." Lafayette looked around. "But, then, I'm not sure she wouldn't be better with that brave than one of my men."

The brave stepped forward, spit on the ground and raised his fist, then spoke in his native tongue.

"Either way you choose, that buck ain't plannin' on you leaving here alive." Lafayette nodded toward the Indian.

Clad only in buckskin trousers, Jonathan made his way to the center of the circle Lafayette had drawn in the dirt, a tomahawk Lafayette had given him in his right hand. Jonathan had had a quick lesson from the frontiersman Jim Bridger. In return Jonathan promised he'd remove the arrowhead from Bridger's shoulder. That is, if Jonathan survived the fight.

He crossed his legs in circular strides locking eyes with the Indian. He lunged. Jonathan side stepped. The Indian circled, then jumped, arms spread eagle. His knife whizzed past Jonathan's face. The Indian screamed and his braves replied.

Sweat poured from Jonathan's scalp. He took a deep breath. Watch, wait for your chance, and strike hard. Strike to kill. Jonathan blinked. Killing was against all he'd been taught, but he had to. He had to kill in order to save this girl.

Rachael's beautiful face appeared. Pretend it's Rachael I'm fighting for. A war cry erupted like hot lava from the brave's throat, a gurgling cry full of evil. The Indian plunged Jonathan to the ground, straddling him like a horse. The brave's muscles rippled beneath his bronze skin like iron in a hot fire. His breath smelled like raw meat. His knife gleamed in the sunlight as his eyes appeared like fire straight from the pits of Hades.

Jonathan blocked the Indian's knife hand. Dry blood spots on his sharp knife declared his capability to kill. Down, down to Jonathan's throat the tip of the blade sparkled in the sunlight. Jonathan gulped, his arm shook. Strength seeped from his arms like water from a cracked bucket. Was this how his life would end? God, help me!

One bold move could either free him or sink the knife in faster. It seemed his only chance. He thrust his leg up and forward and unlocked the brave's hold. They rolled around in the dust.

Jonathan wrestled and wrenched forward, pinning the Indian down with his body, one knee on the brave's knife hand and the other on his chest. Jonathan raised his tomahawk. The Indian's life would be over the instant he sent the blade through the jugular vein — I can't. I gave my oath. Jonathan punched him in the jaw and jumped up. His heart felt like it had taken residence in his throat. He swallowed, then spit. "Get up."

The brave sprang to his feet. Jonathan wiped the clean blade on his buckskins and turned to leave.

"Look out!"

Jonathan turned. The brave's black hair whipped Jonathan's cheek;

he was pushed off balance. A pain ripped through his right arm. He fell hard onto his back. The Indian jumped on top of him. Jonathan pushed against the Indian's chest. The Indian smiled and raised his arm, ready to strike. Jonathan arched his back and kicked. With a burst of adrenalin, he swung his wounded right arm still clutching the tomahawk, and sank it deep into the brave's jugular.

"You okay?" Bridger's bearded face was two inches from Jonathan's. "You sure you can do this? I understand if you want to wait a day or two."

Jonathan laid out his surgical equipment. "Haven't got a day. We're leaving this morning. Got to get back to my —"

"That little bride of yours. McCray told us you haven't been wed long, must have been hard leavin' her." Bridger squinted through one eye at Jonathan's bandaged arm. "You strong enough to do this cutting?"

"I'm fine." A jealous jab hit Jonathan in the gut. In this wilderness, there was no telling what could happen to a woman. Alone, night after night.

"Then what's wrong with you, Doc?"

"I've never killed a man before."

"There wasn't anything you could've done. He'd probably have killed you even if you did return his property."

"Do you need another drink before we begin?"

Bridger lifted the whiskey bottle and guzzled down half. Jonathan poured the rest on Bridger's shoulder. "This is going to hurt."

Jonathan eased his surgical knife into the soft flesh and probed around the bone until his knife struck the arrowhead. "How long did you say this was in there?"

Bridger grunted. "'Bout a year, I reckon. Doc Whitman took out the one that was three years old."

"A lot of cartilaginous substance has grown around it."

"What?"

"Scar material. If you're planning on keeping the arrowhead, I'll need to boil it clean."

Bridger panted. "Get it out. Don't... care... about a... trophy."

Jonathan held the arrowhead up to the sunlight. "It's all of three inches long."

Bridger let out a sigh of relief and rested back on his blanket. Beads of sweat dribbled down his forehead, brows, and eyes. "Excuse me, Doc, for sweating like a pig on slaughter day. I could feel you draw that thing out. It feels mighty pleasant to be rid of it. My arm feels three pounds lighter."

Jonathan nodded and patted him on his good arm, then reached for a bottle of whiskey. "This is going to sting a little." Jonathan glanced up at McCray who'd walked into the tent. "Hand me my knife. Make sure it's hot —"

"Oww! I tell ya that hurts."

"I'm going to dust it with some antiseptic and stitch it up."

Once finished, Jonathan needed a breath of fresh air. A group of men had congregated outside the tent. "Bridger will be fine. The operation was successful."

"Could you do the same for me? Got me an arrowhead here." Lafayette pointed to a spot in his thigh. "It's been there two years."

Jonathan felt the area. "I can feel it. But I can't promise anything, could be probing into that leg might give you more pain."

"I'll take my chances."

These mountain men had extraordinary power to overcome pain and deprivation. If he could give them a little comfort, then, by the grace of God, he would. "Give me thirty minutes?"

Lafayette nodded. "Name your price."

The girl Jonathan had saved approached him.

Lafayette smiled. "Might be a wedding gift is called for."

"Wha. . ."

She looked up at Jonathan and nodded.

"I'm married." Jonathan looked at Lafayette and then at her.

"Why you fight for me... take life... if you not want me?" Her doe eyes looked up at him questioningly.

A deep-throated chuckle escaped Lafayette's smirking lips.

Drawing her away from Lafayette and the gossiping tongues of the other trappers he motioned for her to follow him. Safely away from the men, he turned and gazed into her liquid-brown eyes. The girl had proven to be hard working. She'd toted the wood for the fire and tended to their horses, singing like a lark throughout the day. McCray had nicknamed her Singing Dove.

"I would have moved a mountain, or died trying, if it would have meant saving any girl's life. There was no other way. I had to kill that brave. I thought you understood that."

"I do not please you?" Her downcast eyes fluttered toward his.

Slender of form, her black hair flowed down her shoulders in thick braids. Though white, she knew only the Indian customs. Her red lips pursed toward him as her liquid eyes seemed to swallow his whole.

His frown deepened. A woman's language is universal. "McCray and I plan to see you settled with a nice white family."

"I no girl. I woman, nineteen, woman's desires. I feel." Her hands went to her beaded front. "My heart yearns for yours."

Jonathan rocked back on his heels. She was more grown than he realized. He stepped away and crossed his arms. Her shoulders sagged. Her doe eyes beseeched his. There had been enough hurt in her life.

"I seven, my sister thirteen when taken captive."

Jonathan's stomach sank. What if this happened to Rachael on their journey west? He swallowed. His throat still dry. He scratched out his words. "I'm married. My wife and I will be missionaries beyond the Rockies and make a home for ourselves there and teach the Indians about Jesus."

Her face brightened. "Me help."

"Yes, I suppose you could." Jonathan swallowed the bitter taste of regret. God, please keep Rachael safe.

"Then Singing Dove come? Be happy if with you." She touched his forearm, where the Indian brave's knife had cut him, stroking it with her fingertips.

"No," he stated firmly.

"You afraid of Singing Dove? If love is strong for this Rachael, nothing I do change it."

chapter fourteen

*R*achael brushed a strand of hair away from her forehead and rolled her shoulders. Her back felt tied in knots. *Where are they? They've been gone seven days. What if…* Spotting a figure, she galloped forward, hoping it might be the kind and understanding Moses Merrill of the Otoe Indian Mission or one of his Indians with another message from Jonathan. Reining up, she attempted to hide her disappointment. It was only the sod farmer, Ben. "Have you heard any news about my husband?"

The man squinted up at her. One eye halfway closed, he sent her a near toothless grin as he removed his hat displaying his grey hair. "Missus Wheaton, as I told you yesterday, could be a heap more days before your husband returns."

Rachael sat back on her saddle and squinted into the horizon. She'd been up since dawn riding in hope of seeing Jonathan's tall figure riding toward camp. Was it already the eighth of May? It was hard to track the days and hours with nothing but wind whipping her clothes and the sun beating down on her head to greet her each morning. She'd dreamt about Jonathan last night and had felt certain this would be the day her beloved would return.

"I reckon you might as well settle in another night." His good eye worked its way to her face. "Frettin' gets ya nowhere. Be patient." He fingered the brim of his well-worn hat stained with sweat. "It's a big land out yonder. He'll show up when you least expect it."

"Thank you. You have been more than patient with me and my bothersome questions." Resuming her ramrod posture, she turned to leave. "But if you should hear any news about my husband and Reverend McCray, we're camped over there." Her hand, adorned in her smooth leather riding glove, pointed in the direction of their camp. She wasn't fooling him. He knew she was scared silly. Why hadn't Jonathan sent word that he was okay?

"Ah..." the man stammered.

"Yes?"

"Word is Mrs. Spiker is sick. Heard tell she nearly fell off her horse. It's rough country. Worse if you're sick."

"Mrs. Spiker is well enough for the journey." Rachael prayed her tone displayed more confidence than she felt.

The man wasn't being cruel, just truthful. Getting Saul to admit Beth might need more assistance as the traveling grew harder was a problem she didn't wish on her worst enemy. "Thank you." Nodding in finality, she turned her horse in the direction of their camp.

"You sure can act a heap uppity when you get it in your mind," the man yelled after her.

Uppity? Me? Rachael lifted her chin and urged her horse into a canter. Just because she didn't whimper every time things went wrong and tried instead to do something about her situation? She could understand it if he called her stubborn — maybe, sometimes — but uppity? Never. She slowed her horse to a trot and strained her eyes to outdistance her mare's hooves. She was coming to a prairie dog field.

These tiny animals made their homes by digging holes into the soil and barked whenever something came too close to their little dug outs. If they didn't happen to be home, their homes became dangerous to a four-legged animal, often big enough for a horse's hoof to stumble into.

A noise of horses running through the fine blades of grass sounded like Mother's shears ripping a silk dress. Jonathan? No. Close to twenty braves on horses galloping north, parallel to her, silhouetted the blue sky. She ducked her head towards her mare's glistening neck, coaxing her horse to a small, windblown sand dune layered with prairie grass.

The braves were not more than thirty feet from her. Their bright feathers and headdresses bobbed from their proud heads. Their long brown legs straddling the bare backs of their ponies moved in poetic rhythm to their horse's strides. One brave glanced in her direction.

"Ah!" She clamped her hand over her mouth and sucked in her breath. The brave slowed his paint horse to a walk, turned and galloped toward her. His sharp nose, covered with dark war paint, glistened in the sunlight. He scowled at her, displaying white teeth that looked even whiter against his copper-colored skin. Their eyes met. His lips curled into a snarl.

Rachael spun her horse eastward and whipped her horse into a run. There was nothing poetic about that face. Goose bumps rose on her skin as she contemplated his arm grabbing her from the safe haven of her horse. "Oh, dear God, help me. Don't let that brave get me." If she got to camp, would Saul have time to get his gun?

Her horse tripped. Rachael choked on the dust from her mare's fall that nearly jarred her out of the saddle and rolled herself clear. A prairie dog barked at her. "Hush." She whispered crouching next to her horse's heaving flanks and peeked over the saddle. A puff of dust trailed behind the paint's hooves. The brave had turned and galloped after his comrades. Rachael stood up. The wind whipped her riding skirt and howled like a lone wolf in her ears. Where is that war party going? Oh Jonathan, I wish you were back. Rachael shuddered.

She knelt down, entwining her fingers that wouldn't stop shaking. "Thank you, Jesus, thank you. Oh, please, Lord, send Jonathan home to me safe and my horse sound enough to ride."

She wrapped her hands around her mare's neck and urged her up. She neighed, then got to her knees and stood. Rachael ran her hands down her mare's leg and hoof. "Good girl. Now take a step." She patted her neck, then urged her horse forward. Her mare limped for a few steps.

A prairie dog from a distant hole rose up on its hindquarters and barked, as if reprimanding her for her stupidity. She had to admit, she agreed with the little thing.

Shaking, Rachael mounted and trotted the last mile toward camp.

The ride gave her time to think about what to do next. She wouldn't tell Saul or Beth. It would only worry them. Besides, Jonathan would be home soon. After all, nothing had happened. God had protected her. She recalled Psalm 91: "He shall call upon me, and I will answer him: I *will be* with him in trouble..." She brushed at her sleeve and fished in her thoughts for something happy to think about. She was safe, alive, and her mare was fine. More to praise God about.

A whiff of buffalo chips and meat met her nose a few yards from camp. What would sister Jane think if she knew they used dried buffalo dung to cook their supper? She envisioned Jane wiggling her upturned nose in protest to that. Rachael laughed.

"What is so humorous?" Saul's sunburned face puckered a frown.

Dismounting, Rachael removed her gloves. Her mare's soft, velvety coat beneath her fingertips provided a comforting tonic to her distraught nerves. She patted the mare's neck affectionately. Saul had been out of sorts for days now. It took both Beth and her to keep him in a pliable temperament. "I was thinking about my sister and what she would think about our choice of fuel."

A small chuckle escaped Beth's lips. She lay huddled in front of the fire on a pallet of blankets. Her face drawn in pain, nevertheless, she smiled up at Rachael. "It is amusing, I must agree."

"How are you feeling, Beth?"

"Better now that you have arrived. Did you learn any news?"

"No one has seen or heard from them." She plopped down on a crate next to Beth. "Ben said not to get our hopes up. It could be a couple more days. You don't think anything happened to Jonathan and the Reverend, do you?"

"Unlikely." Saul pulled at his cotton pants. His knees were popping through his trousers and the sleeves on his coat were ragged looking. A few strings dangled off his elbow, dangerously close to the fire. He tore them off, poked at the fire, then laid the buffalo meat in the frying pan and placed them on the red-hot chips. "Jonathan's too good a hunter to get lost. I hope he comes back with something else to eat than buffalo. I'm beginning to hate the smell of it."

Beth covered her nose. "It's the smell of the chips, dear."

Rachael chuckled. "You must admit, buffalo goes a long way to ful-filling our needs, what with eating their meat and then cooking on their waste… I bet Beth could make you a patch, maybe even a set of trousers from their hide with not much work, or else, I could."

"I'm fine the way I am, thank you." Saul scowled.

"Cotton doesn't wear well in this wilderness and your clothes were already worn when we began the trip," Beth said.

"That's why Jonathan chose buckskin. He says it get softer with use. I'm planning on making a riding skirt with the next buffalo killed." Ra-chael slapped at her green-velvet skirt that seemed to enjoy gathering spoonfuls of dust and coughed. Harry Betts' wife's clothes had been too short and small for her and there had not been time to make new clothes.

Saul stood to his full height, lean and rigid, his black hair and be-ginning beard darkening his stark features. He was a fearful-looking man when he was upset.

"A man of the cloth should stand apart from other men in honor of Him whom he serves."

Beth sighed. "Saul, the knees of your pants are wearing through. I told you before we began this trip that you need to buy new clothes. Soon this 'man of the cloth' will hardly be wearing enough to be decent. Let me darn them this evening before there is no cloth for me to darn."

"I can darn them." Saul poked the fire, sending burnt-orange sparks drifting into the air. His voice now a whisper as his eyes covered his wife. "You rest and gather strength, Beth." He laid the poker down and reached for another blanket, laying it across Beth's shoulders. "The In-dian boys took the mules and went to fetch our milk cows that wan-dered off. When Jonathan and McCray return, I am sure we will have to ride hard to make up for lost time."

Rachael ate her breakfast quickly. She liked to give Saul and Beth time to be alone. Beth's gentle nature was like a tonic to Saul, whereas, Rachael's irritated him. She stood up and brushed the crumbs off her riding habit. "I'd better tend to my horse."

Rachael unsaddled her horse, then tied a red apron around her skirt and walked over to the picket line. She counted the rest of their herd as the animals grazed. Six horses, fifteen mules, twenty head of cattle, and three milk cows, plus the two Matthew and Luke were out looking for. A rumble filled the air. The ground shook beneath her feet. Was it an earthquake? The horses neighed and started to canter around their small stockade. Buffalo? No, not again. The noise of thousands of hooves drew closer. She ran back to the camp. Winded, she gasped for air. "What — is it a buffalo stampede? This one sounds close. What should we do?"

Saul rose from the fire he was tending and stared out. "I don't see them." As if in reply the noise grew closer. He bent over and poked at the fire. "They're far enough away right now. I don't think we're in danger. If I fire any shots that just might stir them in the wrong direction."

Rachael drew breath, listening, her ears drumming with the beat of the brutes' hooves. A shot rang out. Beth got up, took Rachael's hand in hers, and said, "That shot came in the direction of the Ben's place. Do you think they'll trample his sod house? Oh the poor man, he hardly has enough to keep body and soul together as it is."

"Foolish man, one shot won't scare them into submission. They're wild brutes and we're in their domain." Saul poked fiercely at the fire. "Well, at least we'll have plenty of dung."

Beth and she exchanged glances. "Let's get a better look, shall we?" They climbed up a small incline. Rachael strained her eyes against the sapphire blue of the sky and looked westward for the first sign of a wooly head to appear. They'd only seen the herds from a distance. They had never come this close before. The thundering, rumbling noise was gone. The herd had stopped to graze.

The excitement of seeing and hearing something beyond grass and the wind whistling past her ears, even if it was a herd of buffalo, was better than sitting around all day waiting for the sun to descend. Rachael could see the same thought was going through Beth's head.

They scrambled up another hill, then bent down to their knees. Panting, Rachael dug her fingers into the soft dirt and looked up past the grasses that whispered about her form like a thousand humming birds alighting on Mother's petunias. She glanced at Beth and chuckled. The herd, no more than 100 yards away, grazed peacefully. The bull leader lifted his massive head, looked toward Rachael, and snorted. The other hundred or more cows continued to graze. One younger bull, just thirty yards away, shook his head.

Wide in the chest and narrow in the buttocks, black tufts of curly hair rose around his massive neck like a robe. Horns poked from his forehead like a crown. His beady black eyes surveyed the perimeter. The buffalo lifted his nose in the air and snorted.

He gazed at her. Then pawing the ground, he lowered his head, his big nose blowing steam like a locomotive, and galloped toward them.

Rachael gasped. "Run, Beth! We're upwind."

chapter fifteen

*R*achael huddled beneath her blankets, shaking, listening to the soft snores of Beth, and pretending Jonathan would be in bed soon to hold her safe and secure in his strong embrace.

"Rachael?"

"Jonathan?"

"No, Saul."

Rachael sat up, her eyes trying to penetrate the darkness.

"Are you alright? I mean, I couldn't sleep for worrying about you." Saul crouched over her.

"We shouldn't have gone up there." Rachael whispered softly, fearing their talk would waken her friend. "Beth's not well enough. I would never have forgiven myself if any harm had come to her."

"Do you really care for her as much as you pretend to?"

"There is no pretend. She is like the sisters I miss, and she's a kindred spirit in Christ. I can well see how you fell in love with her."

"Rachael, my dear Rachael." Saul said, kneeling before her. She could just make out his face. "I've been thinking over what you said. Have you disclosed anything to Jonathan?"

"No, I made you a promise. I will keep it. But, Saul, we need to. Before Satan finds a way to use it against us. A truth untold because you fear the consequences, especially to a spouse, is a lie. A lie, Saul, and we can't be partners in a lie. It is sure to destroy the love Beth and Jonathan have for us. You don't want that for Beth. I don't want that for Jonathan."

His hand captured hers.

"Dear Rachael, are you happy?"

"Yes, Saul, you need not fear on that account."

"Then I am happy for you." He kissed the tops of her hands.

The tent flap flew open.

The moon's rays cast silky moonbeams of light into the dimness. Rachael looked out, the rays shining on her face. Blinking, unable to see clearly, she tilted her head. There in the opening standing like a colossus with the moon rays glowing all around him —

"Jonathan!"

"What's going on here?"

"Nothing." Saul, frozen, hadn't removed his hand. It was locked on hers. Rachael pushed him away.

A low menacing noise erupted from Jonathan's throat.

Poking her head out of the tent entrance, Rachael scanned the campsite for Jonathan. Where was he? Disappointed, she grabbed her sacks of flour and salt, and stepped out of the tent, toward the campfire.

"Good morning, ma'am." A tall man, with hair the color of a blazing sunset, wiped his hand on his fringed breeches and extended his arm to her. "I'm the Reverend Samuel McCray at your service. And this here is Singing Dove."

"How do you do, Reverend McCray and Singing Dove." Rachael grabbed the reverend's outstretched hand. "I had my doubts you were real."

McCray slapped his chest as if to assure her he was a flesh and blood man and laughed. "Well, I'm sure glad to be making your acquaintance. I heard a lot about you from your husband. I thought he was bragging, but I can see now, he weren't."

"Thank you, sir. I'm in fresh need of that compliment this morning. You wouldn't by chance know where Jonathan is?"

"Believe he's cleaning up down by the creek. Anything I can do?" McCray's piercing eyes reflected the sky. The smells of saddle soap, lye, and tumbleweed swept past Rachael's nose on the breeze that swept the smoke from their campfire westward.

He wasn't bad looking for an elderly man. Curly hair worn shoulder length, a pale half-moon around his jaw where once whiskers demanded residence, and a big lopsided grin and shiny white teeth bespoke of McCray's pleasing disposition.

Rachael could see at first glance McCray was a man used to keeping secrets. Her heart yearned to unburden hers. After all, he was a minister. He'd know what to do, but she'd promised Saul. "Did you ride in with my husband last night?"

"I did." He nodded slowly, his eyes hadn't left her face.

"Funny, I didn't see you when I left the tent last night looking for —"

"We camped down by that river yonder. I didn't see the need to wake you all up, coming in after the midnight hour."

"That was very considerate of you." Rachael hesitated, her mind wrestling with the need for spiritual advice. Feeling the Indian woman's eyes, she smiled back. "Singing Dove, what a lovely name."

"She acquired it from Jonathan and me, after Jonathan rescued her from a Blackfoot brave who'd decided if she wouldn't marry him, no one else would either. He was bent on beating her to death." McCray chuckled. "Guess you could call him a sore suitor."

Rachael studied Singing Dove. Her long, dark braids accentuated her heart-shaped face and shone like a blackbird's wing in sunlight. Her doe-skins fringed with tiny shells complemented her petite frame. Her large expressive eyes stared unblinkingly at Rachael. Then her full lips broke into a shy grin that displayed even white teeth amidst glowing skin and high cheek bones.

Jonathan rescued her? "I'm very glad Jonathan saved you." She's beautiful. Rachael felt a stab of jealously tingling her scalp. She turned and looked around the campsite for something to do to slice through the silence that followed. "I see you have the coffee on."

McCray filled a cup and handed it to her. "Got some biscuits, too, already made, and some side meat. I'm about ready to fry the eggs while waiting for the Reverend Moses and his party to come." He chuckled.

"Jonathan made us ride hard all night. He had a burning desire to get back to you." Squatting down, he looked up at her and winked. "There wasn't any way he was goin' to wait till sunup to ride in here if he could make it sooner. Nearly wore our ponies' hooves off."

Rachael's heart leaped like it would come out of her chest. Jonathan had been eager to get back to her — and then he caught Saul holding her hand.

She lowered her eyes, sipping her coffee. Shame wrapped its dirty fingers around her cowed shoulders. What could she say to Jonathan to right this, but the truth?

Beth bustled out of their tent, her nose sniffing the air, one hand still pinning up her hair. "Is that fresh coffee I smell?"

Matthew and Luke had just come from feeding the livestock and reached for a hot biscuit. McCray slapped the Indians on the tops of their hands with his wooden spoon. "Wait for the prayer before you dip your paws in my pot. I thought I taught you better than that, especially before the lady folk and Reverend Merrill."

"Yes, Reverend." The braves sat down. McCray looked up at the Reverend Moses, his two Otoe braves, the sod farmer, Ben, and nodded his hello. "A bit hungry, I'm expecting, that's the reason for Matthew's and Luke's lack of manners."

"Yes, indeed, they are very good boys." Beth smiled into Matthew's woebegone expression. "I can vouch for their Christian manners. They spoke very highly of you, Reverend McCray. Saying in their broken English that you didn't care if you preached to a hundred or just two. The braves told of you baptizing them and how they have come to believe in this man named Jesus from the way you and Jonathan saved that poor tribe in the Canadian wilderness."

"Yes, ma'am. The Great Physician was truly with us in healing those people. Here's you a cup. Filled it to the brim."

Beth sat next to Rachael and reached for the piping hot coffee offered by McCray and sipped. "Mmm, delicious, now all that it needs is a touch of milk."

"Right here, dear Beth." Saul held a bucket of fresh milk clutched in one fist and a bucket of water in the other.

McCray slapped his breeches with his free hand. "Well, I'll be, all the niceties of a farm, right here in the midst of the wilderness."

"Help yourself, Reverend."

"Don't mind if I do. I haven't had milk with my coffee for a time… Now, I expect we can say grace. Food always tastes a might better with our Good Lord's blessings sprinkled over it."

The sound of sizzling eggs in a hot skillet always reminded Rachael of home. She felt a momentary easiness and relaxed her tense shoulders, but it was not to last for long.

"My biscuits and eggs are most likely not as good as you ladies' cookin', but it does set well on an empty stomach. Saw your buffalo over yonder. Whoever did the shooting was mighty good."

"Rachael did," Beth's small voice replied.

Rachael wished she was an ant and could scurry under the log she sat on. She'd much rather forget the incident with that buffalo.

Beth walked over to her husband, her plate in hand, then folded her skirts about her legs and settled into the seat Saul had prepared for her, layered with buffalo hides and Indian blanket. "Our Rachael single handedly shot the biggest bull you ever want to see. Of course, that being the first buffalo we'd ever seen close, I guess some could argue that he wasn't so big, but he was to us."

Beth patted her husband's arm. "He certainly did look that way, didn't he, Mr. Spiker, charging down on us like he did?"

"What?" said a deep voice behind Rachael.

Rachael looked into the irate face of her husband for the second time that morning. She jumped to her feet. Was he mad because she'd killed the bull? "It isn't what you think, you see, I didn't mean to kill him."

Jonathan's brows arched above his astonished eyes.

"You sure did." Beth chuckled. "You should have seen her, Jonathan, she was out for blood."

Saul clicked his tongue on the roof of his mouth. "Sure does make a man's skin crawl when you think how a woman can change into a —"

"Killer in a blink of an eye?" Beth's gaze probed Rachael's. "That bull had it coming. All Rachael and I wanted to do was take a peek at his cows. He had no right to get mad. Well, she fixed him good. She's going to make a riding skirt out of his old hide." Beth looked around at the crowd of men that had formed. "Serves that bull right, tearing after two defenseless women like he did."

"Don't look like one was too defenseless." The reverend chuckled. "Does it to you, Jonathan?"

"Saul, where were you while all this was happening?" Rachael touched Jonathan's arm. Its steeliness matched his voice.

"Me? Cooking their food. I happened to look up and there on the horizon what do I see, Rachael trying to carry my wife, and this big black brute of a buffalo tearing after them. I grabbed my rifle and ammunition and ran toward the hill. I saw Rachael flutter her apron at the bull telling him to get. Well, he stops and looks at her, rocking his head back and forth, like he was kind of puzzled at what to do next. That gave me time to get there. Then the big brute starts to paw the ground. You could see the dirt flying beneath his hooves. Then Rachael yells at the top of her lungs for Beth to run. Beth yells back, 'No.'"

"What happened then?"

"Next minute I know I'd bumped into Rachael, knocked her and my rifle into the grass. So I grabbed Beth and started to run, that's when I heard a shot —"

"Why, Jonathan, you didn't tell me your wife knew how to shoot." Mc-Cray grinned and slapped his breeches with the palm of his hand. "Did you teach her? But, of course — good idea, came in handy, didn't it?"

Silence.

Beth looked at Rachael and blinked. "Rachael dear," she said in her soft, gentle tone. "You finish the story, seeing how you're the one who did the killing."

Her skin felt hotter than a July sun. All she wanted, all she prayed for, was Jonathan's arms circling her, assuring her that he wasn't mad at her. Oh why hadn't she told him about Harry Betts? Now there were two things separating them.

"You knocked her to the ground, Saul?" Jonathan's cheeks flamed with anger. "And she still managed to take a bead on the beast before it got to her?"

"No, no you see, it was an accident. I didn't mean to, everything happened so fast. I would never hurt Rachael."

Jonathan's jaw turned hard as granite. His eyes blazed into Saul's. "I'm certain of that."

"She didn't stay in the dirt long, Jonathan." Beth's tiny head looked up and turned from one man to the other, like a child would do looking to console two combative adults. "Why, she jumped up like there were springs on the soles of her boots, with a death grip on that gun."

Beth jumped to her feet, pantomiming Rachael's actions. "She swung that big gun to her shoulder, and waited. I held my breath, afraid that brute would maul her before — Jonathan, she was as cold as iron in the dead of winter. She knew it was her life and ours in the bullet of that gun. Then the shot rang out. It sounded just like a cannon.

"Saul told Rachael to stand back. We both thought the beast would land on her. But she just stood her ground. Just stood there. The bull's head hit first and sort of skidded across the dirt and then she told Saul to hand her more bullets. She reloaded that gun, calm as you please, placed her boot on his heaving side and finished him off. Just like that."

Rachael pressed her body closer to Jonathan's. She blinked, the sunlight stabbing her eyes, and smiled. One tell-tale tear made its way down her cheek.

Jonathan's big thumb wiped it away.

McCray cleared his throat and stood up. "Say, are you the Reverend Saul Spiker?"

"Yes."

"Well, I'm pleased to be making your acquaintance. I'm Reverend McCray. I came with Jonathan."

"We've been waiting for you."

"You a reverend?" one man asked from the crowd of onlookers. "What kind of church you run... the Skedaddle church?"

The man next to him elbowed his partner. "That's a good one. The Skedaddle Church 'cause he likes to run."

Saul guffawed. "Look, I was trying to get my wife to safety. You don't think I was going to leave Rachael there. I admire her. I always have, why, I would never do such a thing. Jonathan left her in my care."

Jonathan's shadow loomed over Saul. "Stay away from my wife."

chapter sixteen

*J*onathan looked out at the travelers assembled before him. The crate he stood on creaked, as if complaining under the burden of his weight. Staring down at the crowd, he realized he'd been as cranky as that creaking crate. Bullying them rather than being the kind of man that a person would want to follow. Well, he better change before the only one following him was Rachael. And she had to because she was obliged to. He chuckled in spite of his ill-humored mood.

Rachael stood at the front of the little group. Her soft alabaster skin shone with vitality in the sunlight resting on her head like a halo. Singing Dove stood just behind Rachael. He could only imagine the horrors Singing Dove must have endured. The best way to keep the women safe was to become a large caravan, no matter what the cost. Only, he wasn't sure these frontiersmen were much better than the hostile Indian tribes they would encounter on the journey.

He raised his arms. A hush settled on the group. "The fur company wants us to meet them at Loup Fork by May 20. For us to do that, we're going have to travel some fifteen miles a day to make up for the days we lost getting back here. Reverend Merrill and his colleagues from the mission are willing to help us ford the Corne de Cerf. Then we'll be on our own."

Murmurs swelled around him like a passel of humming birds aroused from sleep.

The Reverend McCray lifted his hand. "We're going to need the fur company's help going through hostile Pawnee territory. We've got the

Platte and Loup Fork to ford, and we've got to do it without any loss of livestock."

"But the ladies," Saul protested.

Jonathan scowled at Saul. Just whose wife was he worried about? Lowering his voice, he murmured, "Be careful, Saul, you're treading on quicksand."

"May I speak?" Reverend Merrill looked around the group.

"Certainly." Jonathan climbed down from the crate and offered it to Moses Merrill who didn't hesitate.

"Do not despair. I and my Otoe friends will help you. There is a barge that can take you and your animals safely across the Corne de Cerf. The Elkhorn and Platte confluence will be the most difficult of the three rivers you must cross this side of the Rocky Mountains. The other two rivers will not be deep and the cattle can swim across.

"What Doctor Wheaton says is true." Moses banged his fist into his palm. "At all costs, get the protection of the fur company. There is a murmur of an uprising among the tribes. Of course, no one knows if anything will come of this. But we must learn from our past mistakes. Some of the tribes you'll encounter are peaceful; however, there are also hostile tribes that will kill your men and take your women, treating them worse than slaves. The journey ahead will take every ounce of strength and stamina you have, but God will get you through." Reverend Merrill climbed down.

Rachael came up beside Jonathan and McCray. "What can I do to help?"

"You and Mrs. Spiker need to fasten down everything in the wagons."

Rachael took off at a run to Beth's wagon, then ran back to her wagon.

McCray chuckled. "She's got energy, that little wife of yours. A willing heart and a heap of spirit."

"Yes, she does." Jonathan's voice sounded edgy even to his own ears as he choked out a bitter sigh. A pang struck his heart like a hammer, recalling Saul's fingers locked on his wife's hand. Why hadn't she refused his advances?

Several minutes later Jonathan made his way to their wagon.

"Jonathan," Rachael panted, out of breath. "I've fastened everything down. Come see." Climbing into the wagon, she opened up the flap.

"You thought it necessary to fasten down my pinstripe go-to-meeting suit? I'd rather have that wash down the river."

"I'll not have us be completely uncivilized." Rachael placed her fists on either side of her slender waist. "Besides, it becomes you. I want our children to see their father in something other than buckskins."

"Children?" His hands cupped her cheeks, his eyes searching hers. What secrets lay within the prisms of your heart, my love? Rachael diverted her gaze to the wagon.

"I'll be back in a minute," he replied in a gentler tone. "I'd better check on Saul."

"Can I come?"

Rachael's soft palms in his callused ones made him sharply aware of her delicate nature, a gentlewoman needing protecting. He grabbed her at the waist and swung her down with one easy motion. They walked side by side to Spiker's wagon. "Beth, I need to take a look inside. Do you mind?"

"Not at all. Saul is fastening down the last piece of furniture." Beth's face beamed into Jonathan's. "You ready to ford our first river?" Beth's eyes landed on Rachael like a mother hen with her chick. "Rachael gave me a boost of enthusiasm earlier."

"So I see." Jonathan chuckled. "Saul?" No answer. He jumped inside.

"I'll get it done without you gawking at me." Saul's hands visibly shook. He wiped a stream of sweat from his brow.

Jonathan jumped down from the wagon and grabbed Rachael's arm. He'd seen Saul's type before; he knew about cold sweats. Saul had run out on Rachael when that bull attacked. Would he do that with Jonathan? Resolve quickened his pulse. As they headed back to their wagon, he picked up his pace, then stopped. He cupped Rachael's cheeks with his hands and deepened his gaze. If there was any deceit in her, he would see it. "What was going on last night? Why was Saul kissing your hands?"

"It wasn't like that."

"All I know is I nearly ran the hooves off my horse trying to get back to you and wasn't expecting to see the two of you… together. So, I'd like to know if you have an explanation to offer me."

Dappled sunlight filtered around the canvas-covered wagons and onto her face. He felt a shiver pass through her body, but she held his gaze with her own. "He was asking me to forgive him for the way he acted when I killed the buffalo."

Rachael's skin seemed to burn his hands. Or was it his jealousy that made his hands feel red hot? Jonathan dropped his arms. After all, Rachael could have been gored by that bull if Saul hadn't run up with a gun. Jonathan hadn't been there to defend her. He should be thanking Saul, not accusing him. What had come over him? He turned and walked the rest of the way back to their wagon. Rachael matched him stride for stride. Her words came in gasps. "Don't… you believe… me?"

His gaze lingered on her upturned face as he fought to control his temper. Concentrate on the river crossing. God, please forgive my jealousy. I have no call to feel this way. Still, no matter how he tried, he could not forgive her. Women. Could there be just one he could trust?

Rachael ran ahead of him. She struggled to climb into their wagon.

"Rachael." Jonathan grabbed her by the waist, lifting her into his arms. Her warm body folded neatly into his arms. He held her close, a soft, wet cheek brushed against his, he searched her face.

"Oh, Jonathan." Her eyes wide, her pink lips slightly parted, as if ready, waiting for his next response. A deeper pink tinged her cheeks to scarlet. "I, I didn't, I mean we didn't do anything wrong. I would never dishonor you."

Tell her. Tell her how much you missed her. He swallowed. That would make him weak kneed, as his uncle would say. He lifted her into the seat and climbed in beside her, recalling his own cold sweats of fear and his uncle's irate voice.

True to Reverend Moses Merrill's words, he and his people helped them cross the Elkhorn confluence. Jonathan was grateful for the barge, even though it took several trips to get wagons and animals across. He didn't know how they would have managed otherwise.

It was with regret when they bade the Reverend good-bye. The work he had accomplished with the Otoe tribe was remarkable and evident to Jonathan that the natives loved the sincere Moses. Reverend Merrill's missionary school and efforts in translating parts of the Bible into the Otoe language had furthered Christianity.

Jonathan glanced at Rachael, quietly sitting by his side. What if she found out that the reason he wanted to become a missionary was for personal satisfaction of edifying the Wheaton name in this new frontier? He consoled himself with the knowledge that his medical experience would further Christianity more by saving lives, than being a humble and contrite disciple seeking God's will. But that knowledge did not help his soul and the fact that his quick temper was a detriment to displaying a godly Christian attitude.

Last night, tossing and turning, unable to sleep, he had lit the lantern and opened his Bible. The book had fallen open to Genesis 27:12 where Jacob confronted his mother about pretending to be Esau in order to obtain his father's blessing. "My father peradventure will feel me, and I shall seem to him as a deceiver; and I shall bring a curse upon me, and not a blessing." Jonathan pondered this. Is that what God was trying to tell him, that he needed to tell Rachael the truth?

He had deceived Rachael's father into thinking his dream was to be a missionary, just as Jacob had deceived his father into believing he was his older brother, Esau. Jonathan had accused Rachael of being unfaithful to him because he had seen her and Saul together the night he had returned from Council Bluffs. The words of Matthew 7:5 were painted in red letters across his mind's eye: "Thou hypocrite, first cast out the beam out of thine own eye; and then shalt thou see clearly to cast out the mote out of thy brother's eye." How could he lead the lost to Jesus if he was lost?

The next morning, sitting next to Rachael on the wagon seat, he realized he must look as terrible as he felt.

"Jonathan, what is ailing you?" Rachael looked with alarm into his face. "You look as if you have seen a ghost."

Jonathan coughed and reached for her hand. His conscience pricked him as if he'd stepped into a burr patch. Had God provided this moment for him to disclose the truth to his wife? He gave her slender fingers a squeeze. "It is nothing."

"Very well, I shall wait until you feel more secure with your conscience." Her soft words held no reprimand.

He was not fooling her, just himself.

"The farther we travel west, the more grassland dunes I see. What do you suppose created such a physiographic region?" Rachael asked.

Jonathan chuckled "Such a difference from the river and Liberty that we left behind some two weeks ago. I suppose it was the wind blowing across the wilderness that created these magnificent dunes." He waved his hand in front of his face. "These bothersome gnats aren't happy with driving the cattle mad. They have to bother us as well."

"We're traveling along the river, but when do you think we'll find a clean water hole?" Rachael drew the brim of her hat down across her brow and licked her lips. "I never thought being so close to water could make me thirstier."

Jonathan slapped the reins across the lead mule's rump and rested his elbow on his raised leg. "I must agree with the livestock, the muddy, stinky water of the Platte does little to quench my thirst."

A rolling landscape of windblown deposits of silt met his gaze and he strained to see past the sand bluffs. Only the Indians on their spotted ponies broke up the monotony of the endless terrain. That and seeking the next water hole, the next place that would shelter them for a restless night's sleep. He, Saul, McCray, Matthew, and Luke took watches throughout the night for an Indian raid.

The curious bands of Pawnees hadn't managed to steal any of their livestock. That had been a miracle in itself. At least the Good Lord heard Reverend McCray's prayers.

"Is that rapids I hear?" Rachael looked at Jonathan and then turned her eyes toward the horizon.

The foaming waters of the Platte filled the broken silence between them. With every step of their mules' hooves their wagon came closer and closer to the banks of the river.

"Giddy up." Jonathan slapped the reins, He drew his hat over his forehead, watching the Indian ponies peeking in and out of the dunes. Why hadn't they made their move? What were they waiting for, a larger hunting party before they swooped down on them? He prayed Rachael hadn't noticed them.

"We've got to get our mules in the river. Once they go in Saul's mules will follow. Ours must not hesitate."

The lead mule took a step into the swirling waters. The swelling water slurped around the mule's legs and the sandy river bank. Jonathan's second string of mules balked, braying loudly.

"Something's not right." Jonathan handed Rachael the reins. "I'll tell you when to come." He held his hand up at Saul. "Hold them up. I'm going in to check the depth."

Jonathan stripped down to his pants. Avoiding the mule droppings and the heavy ruts made by Lafayette's wagons, he waded into the river, he plunged out of sight, and bobbed back to the surface. He swam at a diagonal toward the opposite shoreline and waved his arms. Plunging back into the frigid waters, he came up panting.

Rachael covered his shoulders with a blanket. Jonathan leaned over the wheel of the wagon and gasped for air. The cold water and physical exertion had knocked the air from his lungs.

Saul ran up. "What are our chances?"

"I… wish there was a tree… something to tie a rope across."

Saul smiled at Rachael. "Keep that blanket ready."

Saul stripped off his shirt and headed back to his wagon. Jealously stabbed at Jonathan's heart. He did not care to see the muscles Spiker had hidden beneath his loose clothing. Jonathan looked at Rachael. Her eyes were full of concern — for him or for Saul? Jonathan reached in the back of the wagon for the lead line and hooked it on the mule's bridle.

Rachael chewed her nails like a school girl.

"You need help?" Singing Dove had quietly walked up. "Me swim."

Jonathan dragged in a ragged breath and gulped in a deep breath.

"Tie your horse to the wagon. Rachael might need help handling the team if they get skittish."

"Yes, me do."

Jonathan plunged into the turbulent waters again, his sights on the opposite shoreline. Feeling his way across the slippery rocks and avoiding the drop offs, he led his mules across. Just a few more steps. He motioned with his arms for Saul to start his team. Saul was gasping by the time he reached the opposite shoreline.

"How are Luke and Matthew going to know where to drive the cattle across?" Rachael asked.

She was right. Jonathan's legs felt like lead. He leaned over, resting his arm on Saul's shoulder. "We need to help get the cattle across."

Saul groaned and lay down on the bank, panting like a dog. "Let me… catch my breath."

"Can't afford to lose a one to this current, especially the milk cows."

"Let him catch his breath, Jonathan." Rachael climbed down from the wagon and handed Saul a blanket.

"Thanks."

A groan fought its way to Jonathan's throat. Why did she always protect Saul?

The wagons and livestock across, Rachael grabbed her quilt and scrambled down from the back of the wagon, hugging the layers to her bosom. "Jonathan, here… " He ignored her and continued to gaze into the fire, his shoulders wrapped in Singing Dove's bright red and orange striped Indian blanket. Rachael bit her lower lip.

Singing Dove squatted in the dirt between her husband and Mc-Cray, her dark eyes looking first at Jonathan and then McCray like a devoted lap dog. To Rachael's strained nerves the noise of McCray sipping his steaming coffee sounded like the hissing of a coiled snake. She crushed the blanket to her chest, and shifted from one leg to the other. "Reverend, would you like a blanket?"

"No thank you, ma'am." He smiled up at her, then turned to Jonathan. "I figure we are about two, at most three days behind the fur company. You want me to have Matthew and Luke ride ahead of us. Tell the company to hold up? That we might need their help?"

Rachael sucked in her breath. Why don't they say they are worried about the band of braves that had been following them now for two days? She had pretended, for Jonathan's sake, not to notice, but all the while they were crossing the river, she had her rifle near, loaded and ready.

Damp clothes and perspiration mingling with the odor of wood smoke assaulted her nostrils. Saul, with a crate in one hand and Beth on his other, guided her to sit on the crate, then sat down on the grass near his wife.

"We don't need the fur company, Jonathan. We've done nicely without them so far." Saul cupped his hands around his tin cup and stared into the coffee as if it was speaking to him. "Those trappers don't care for us to tag along in the first place."

What was Saul saying? They had waited for over a week while Jonathan and Reverend McCray rode off to Council Bluffs to find the trappers and convince them to help. Of course they needed them. Hadn't he seen the Indians?

Rachael rushed back to the wagon, fearing she'd blurt out hasty words she would regret later. She grabbed four tin cups and returned to the fire. The bubbling hot coffee sizzled against the cool rims of tin. She handed some to Matthew and Luke, their eyes not leaving the delightful brew they never tired of drinking, then poured coffee for Jonathan and herself.

"Need men to help find watering holes and grazing for cattle." Matthew sipped his brew, his eyes peeking over the brim.

"Need scouts." Luke held the metal cup close to his chest as if gathering both warmth and wisdom. "Need scouts to mark trail and —"

"For what? Just head west, and follow Lafayette's wagon tracks and manure. How hard can that be? As for water, looks like there will be plenty of that." Saul's monotones grated on Rachael.

"Platte murky, not good for drinking. Need men. Protect." Matthew pointed to her and Beth.

"The boys are right, we're riding smack into hostile Indian territory. They don't take kindly to white men, but the women they might enjoy. Beg pardon, ma'am," McCray said. "If you want a synopsis of just what kind of life your missus could have with their likes, ask Singing Dove. Those braves don't give up on what they want. I just hope those braves trailing us get tired and find something more exciting to do."

chapter seventeen

*J*onathan you look so exhausted." Deep crevices of fatigue around his eyes and jaw line made his face look haggard. He had asked no more questions about that night and Saul, yet she knew it haunted his thoughts.

He smiled and kissed the tops of her fingers. "I thought the fording of Loup went well, didn't you?"

"It was quite an accomplishment. I so appreciate Matthew and Luke swimming across and tying a rope to the trees on the opposite bank to guide our little caravan across." Rachael punctuated her words with light conversation, hoping to ease Jonathan's worries. "You really should not push so; you will make yourself sick with worry."

In reply, Jonathan slapped the reins of the lead mule, urging the animal to walk faster. "It's the twenty-third of May. We have not reached Loup Fork. Lafayette and his group will have moved on. We've got to catch up to them. And we can't afford to cross the Rockies later than September. We've got over a thousand miles or more to go before we reach our final destination of Umatilla Valley." Jonathan's bloodshot eyes searched hers. "We're so close to that tributary, I can smell the water from here." He motioned for Matthew to ride over to them. "Matthew, how are the cattle doing?"

"They stumble, need rest. Need water, need feed." Patting his stomach, he said, "Be full for crossing Loup Fork. Need energy."

"Rachael, can you follow Lafayette's tracks?" Jonathan's voice sounded anxious, one brow rose questioningly above his bloodshot eyes.

"Why?" She knew that look. What was he up to now?

"Because you and Saul could go on. McCray is out scouting. I'll stay back with the boys and help them drive the livestock in. Think you can manage?"

Rachael sucked in her breath. "Just Saul, Beth, and I?"

"I don't see any other way." His gaze seemed to sear her face like a red-hot griddle.

Something was troubling him. Why wouldn't he tell her? "You know I —"

"Tell me what I don't know. Did Saul teach you how to shoot? What other things have you failed to tell me?"

His voice grated the air between them.

She drew in a long, slow breath. "If you recall, Father told you I was a good shot." She looked down at her hands and grimaced. She needed to tell him the full truth. "After our wedding I hired the mule skinner Harry Betts to teach me the skills of a frontier wife. If you recall, you accused me of not being equipped to handle the rigors of the wilderness." She gazed into his stormy eyes and cringed.

Jonathan shook his head, as if coming out of a trance. "I guess you thought you did the right thing. Well, can you drive the team?" His blank eyes gazed into hers.

"I want to stay with you." She choked out a bitter sigh. Jonathan's jaw set itself like a steel trap. Oh, Jonathan, we have so little in common. Wouldn't you know that the one thing we both possess would be our undoing — our stubbornness.

Jonathan climbed down from the wagon, untied his horse from the back of the wagon, and rode off.

Jonathan! Her heart cried, but her rigid lips would not allow her sobs to escape. She lifted her chin and picked up the reins. "Giddy up."

As the hours drifted along, the sun made its lazy descent down the crest of the bluffs. There would be no time for supper this evening. It couldn't be helped, but what she wouldn't give for a cup of cool spring water. She thought of having a pity-party for herself, then laughed at the thought. She'd be the only one attending. "Lord, I had hoped to surprise Jonathan with what I'd learned." Harry Betts was right. He said her husband might think she did it because she didn't trust him to be around when she needed him.

Was Jonathan mad at her because she'd proven she didn't need him to protect her? All the same, she'd done the right thing. If Harry Betts hadn't taught her, she would have panicked seeing that buffalo charge, and she and Beth might have been morning exercise for that bull's horns.

She wiped at her tears. Of course she needed Jonathan. She'd have to wait. Wait on the Lord's timing... for His direction. "In all thy ways acknowledge him and he will direct thy paths." Like a mother's hand, the moon's light quietly lit the darkness before her.

Oh, how large the sky. How bright the stars, gleaming like diamonds on the velvety black draping of the night. Oh Lord how great is Thy handiwork... Lord, I'm laying my marriage before Your feet to be built on Your rock. Your rock of love! So when the floods of our human weaknesses and the waves of human adversity beat against our house, it will not fall.

The hoof beats of Jonathan's horse echoed in her ears even before he made it to her side. He held out his tin cup to her. "Here, this should go down well for our supper."

Sipping the liquid, expecting river water, she looked at him astonished. "It's milk."

He chuckled deep in his throat. "Thought I'd surprise you."

She drank it down in large gulps, then handed him the cup.

"I'll get some to Beth. I'll try and bring you back more, if I can."

She looked around the corner of the wagon in time for the full moon to shine its brightness on Jonathan leaning over his horse and reaching down to milk the cow tied to her wagon.

Rachael chuckled over Jonathan's new method of milking a cow, then wondered if he'd thought of giving himself a cup of the nourishing milk. Most likely he hadn't, not until she and Beth had had their fill.

It was after midnight when they stopped. They made their make-shift beds beneath the stars that night.

"There isn't enough energy between the eight of us to pitch a tent." Saul grunted.

"But, there is always strength for prayer." Beth looked at her husband and then bowed her head.

A hush washed over their little party and McCray removed his hat. "Thank you, Lord, for bringing us safely through the river today. Be with us tomorrow as well and all the days of our lives. We pray this in Jesus' name. Amen." They said their goodnights and went to bed.

Rachael lay down next to Jonathan. The warmth of their bodies beneath their Indian blankets eased her aching muscles. Soon she fell asleep.

She awoke to a chilling breeze sweeping its disturbing fingers through her hair and an empty spot beside her that sent chills running up and down her spine. Where had Jonathan gone?

Careful not to awaken Beth or Saul, she crept out of her blankets. She hadn't gone far when she heard voices beyond a clump of trees. That was Jonathan's voice. The night chill wrapped her cowed shoulders. She shivered. A premonition of what she might see and hear stopped her. I can't. I can't spy on Jonathan again. She turned to leave.

"My Jonathan."

That was Singing Dove!

Rachael craned her neck to see beyond the leaves. In her mind's eye she pictured the two of them locked in each other's embrace. Please God, help me. Don't let the devil worm his way into my thoughts and create jealously and distrust. A shuffling noise followed.

"There. Are you sure you want to stay here?" Jonathan's words were weighted with tiredness and impatience. "It's too far away from the camp."

"I prefer."

"Well, if you're sure, I'll be over the rise."

"Jonathan, your wife, she lucky."

"Hmm. Well, good night, Singing Dove."

"Wait, my ankle, you look at?"

"Can't this wait until morning? I told you there doesn't appear to be anything broken. Here."

Rachael heard the sounds of the leather clasp opening and knew it was Jonathan's doctor's bag.

"Take this. Now get some sleep. If that ankle is still giving you trouble in the morning, I'll bind it for you."

Rachael hurried back to her pallet, fearing that at any moment she would hear Jonathan behind her and he'd demand to know what she was doing up.

Jonathan knelt before Rachael. Her soft breathing, her peaceful face like a tonic to his frazzled nerves. God, help me. The vision of Singing Dove running for her life from that Indian brave had awakened him more than once. Lord help me keep Rachael and Beth safe and reach that fur company in time. His hand felt the warm softness of Rachael's arm. He knelt down to kiss her sweet smelling flesh, then shook her awake.

"What?" Rachael shrugged off Jonathan's hand. "It's still night."

"The sun will be up soon." Jonathan knew his gruff exterior felt more like the thorns of a prickly pear. Not the actions of a loving husband. But he couldn't afford to look weak. At least his uncle had taught him how to get the most out a person.

"Here, drink this milk. I want to get to the fur company before they break camp." He had everything packed, the mules harnessed, and the horses saddled. He had done it to afford Rachael and Beth more sleep.

"What's the hurry?" Saul rubbed his eyes with the back of his hand.

"You okay, Beth?" Jonathan asked.

Beth's paleness stood out sharply in the darkness, but her smile reassured him. "I'm fine, don't worry about me."

Jonathan patted her hand. "We'll rest when we get with the company. I want to be with them when we go through those Pawnee villages."

"It's still dark." Saul scowled. "How are we going to know if we're headed in the right direction? We could be moving in circles for all you know."

"McCray knows this area like the back of his hand." Hadn't it entered Saul's head yet what was at stake if they didn't join the fur company? At least ten more Indians joined the party that had followed them from the first Loup. What were those braves up to? McCray thought they were just looking for buffalo. What if they weren't, but were planning to ambush them instead. "Move out and be quick about it. That's an order."

"You forget your place. You're a doctor not a trail boss," Saul said.

"Move out, Spiker, and quit complaining. We've got to make up for lost time. If the cattle and the women can stand it… you can."

Rachael rolled her shoulders and lifted her hand to massage her neck, trying to relieve the ache between her shoulder blades. While working with Harry Betts she thought she knew every aching muscle she owned. But she met a few more sleeping on the hard ground and sitting on an even harder wagon seat.

The hours drifted by. The prairie grass waved in the ever present wind and the creaking wagon lulled her into a stupor. She nodded her head… the buzzing flies woke her with a start. "Oh, my." She shook her head, now throbbing with pain at the center of her forehead. "Good boy." Her lead mule had stayed faithfully to the trail before him. She glanced upwards. Nearly the noon hour.

"Step up the pace, Rachael. We can't afford to stop for lunch." Jonathan galloped ahead. The stench of sweating mules and the buzzing, persistent gnats and flies kept her arms circling her head and fanning her face. The sun looked bigger out here than in Buffalo. It beat down unmercifully, driving away the prairie wind. Oh, for a cool breeze to caress her sunburned skin, sticky with perspiration. Only the prick of the incessant insects kept her awake. She dreamt of that big white bath tub back home and how good the Saturday night baths felt. The warm water filled with scented rose petals, and Mother's sweet smelling lavender soap washing away the weeks of grit and grime from her flesh…

What was that? She stared to her left. Indians? Their ponies churned up dust on the distant sand dune not more than a mile away.

She sighed and bit down on her lower lip to keep from screaming at Jonathan. Her newest anxiety was watching Jonathan and Singing Dove riding together. Singing Dove was a determined little thing. Rachael had to give her credit for that. Always within eyesight, Singing Dove glanced occasionally toward her, as if getting pleasure from the knowledge that Rachael saw them — together. Probably Jonathan and Singing Dove were too preoccupied with themselves to notice the Indians.

She noticed another cloud of dust about a mile ahead. Was it the fur company's caravan? It had to be. Rachael stood up and waved her hands. "There they are and just in time!"

Jonathan galloped up, his eyes blazing into hers like a prairie fire. "What is all the hollering about, Rachael?"

"Over there!" she said, pointing toward the dust. "We made it." She craned her neck and closed her eyes only to open them in astonishment. "What's that?" Two rivers converged with one another, spilling over their banks like feuding families. Murky brown foaming waves tossed around debris lapping up more land in their battle for supremacy.

"We have to go way over there… to the other side of that tempest-tossed and frightful-looking body of water?" She plopped her bottom down on the hard seat. "Hospitable, that fur company."

Jonathan laughed so hard he had to wipe his eyes with the sleeve of his buckskins. Rachael suspected it was mainly due to relief. "Yes, accommodating, to be sure."

She smiled at the boyish look he gave her, drinking in the brief interlude they shared. "I guess I should be used to crossing rivers by now. But *that's* a river? It looks like a piece of the Atlantic."

"Here the North and South Platte River join. Looks big, but nothing we can't handle." His now serious tone caused her to search his face. Was he trying to give her, or himself, confidence?

"And when you have to forge it… it does seem to grow, does it not?"

"Well, I have your horse saddled. You want to ride over with me?"

"Yes. I'd much prefer straddling my horse over being tossed back and forth on this wagon seat."

"I can see your point." He chuckled.

"Wait here." Jonathan plunged into the river with one leap of his horse's strong legs and swam to the opposite bank. She watched as he spoke with two of the riders from the company. All three urged their horses back into the river.

"We're going have to keep going. The fur company will help us get across, but they are planning a full day's ride." He took in a deep breath, his brows drawn close. It was evident he was worried about her.

His bloodshot eyes sent a pang to her heart. "I'm stronger than you think. You'll see." She sat straighter, then cast a wary eye back to the next wagon and a groan fought its way to her lips. "What about Beth?"

Beth barely made a shadow on the wagon seat. Saul stared back at Rachael, then looked over at his wife and nodded. He was concerned about her too. Rachael turned. Jonathan was looking, but not at Beth. He was staring at Saul.

"Quit dawdling. Whip those mules into shape, woman!" The wagon boss's dust-covered face scowled at Rachael. He galloped back down the line, cracking his whip and looking hard at anyone that dared to meet his fierce gaze.

Rachael's shoulders felt like a mass of muscle spasms. It never occurred to the trail boss that her arms ached and her hands could barely hold the reins. Her back drew up ramrod straight. It was all the energy she had left, but she refused to allow this bully to defeat her. Her team of mules was an extension of her.

He scowled down at her before she could draw another breath. "They have been traveling since before sunrise." They were hard-working mules and willingly gave her all the strength they had. They deserved the bearded wagon master's respect.

"Well, aren't you the feisty one."

"My mules can't speak for themselves so I do their speaking for them." Rachael's eyes flashed back at him.

"Don't say? Well those high-handed manners will get you nowhere here. Remember that, and keep moving. Or I'll be obliged to put you in the back, breathing our dust."

Rachael watched the man gallop away. Oh, dear Lord, what has Jonathan got us into? She spotted him riding not twenty yards away, alongside Singing Dove.

"You can call me nosy, Mrs. Wheaton, if you have a mind to."

She had been so busy watching her husband and Singing Dove she hadn't noticed Reverend McCray ride up.

McCray tipped his hat to her. "I feel compelled to tell you." He nodded his head toward Jonathan and Singing Dove.

"Tell me what?" Rachael blinked back her tears.

"It's like this, Mrs. Wheaton. Singing Dove thinks she's in love with your husband. All she's known is a Blackfoot buck that thought he could beat her into liking him. You can imagine what it does to a man's pride to know a gal as pretty as Singing Dove looks at him like some kind of a god."

Rachael flipped the reins back and forth. "I... I don't know what to do."

The Reverend nodded his head toward Saul's wagon. "Be honest."

"I... I would. Only I promised Saul I wouldn't tell Jonathan." Rachael choked out a bitter sigh. "I've made so many mistakes in the short time we've been married." She met his gaze and forced herself to hold it. "I wonder. Do I have a right to stand in the way of Jonathan's happiness?"

McCray's expression held a calculating edge. "Do you love Jonathan?"

Rachael looked away. She wanted to scream Yes! With all my heart, but her pride would not allow her. She opened her mouth only to shut it, assuming a pose of indifference. "What are Jonathan's feelings about me?"

"Mrs. Wheaton, you need to come to grips with yourself before you can help your husband." His words abraded her emotions like the sandy wind on her skin. 'What therefore God hath joined together, let not man put asunder.' What I'm seeing are two stubborn people, one highly proud and the other highly jealous." Reining his horse, he pivoted and galloped away in a puff of dust toward Jonathan and Singing Dove.

chapter eighteen

*A*fter a week of watching the seventy odd men of the caravan Jonathan would rather chance the Indians than ride alongside these desperate traders who hadn't seen white women for a decade or longer.

"So our paths cross again, Wheaton." Pierre stepped away from the group, his dark face next to Jonathan's. "At Council Bluffs you gave me much amusement with your wood chopping. This time you bring your little *chérie*." Pierre put a dirty hand to his lips and kissed the air, the smacking noise loud enough for the whole camp to hear.

"Your chérie, she is as you say, like a succulent peach… *oui*? Ready to be plucked and eaten."

Jonathan lunged for him. McCray grabbed his arm and blocked his way.

Jonathan looked past McCray to Pierre. "You keep your dirty hands and eyes off my wife, you understand?"

"Ah, I tremble in my boots." Pierre's eyes grew blacker, his mouth growling the words. "You keep a close watch on your little chérie, closer than your own gun there." He shot a glance at the leather belt fastened to Jonathan's hip. "I've warned you." Then he pointed at McCray. "If I can't get Wheaton one way, Pierre will get to him another."

"Why you —" Jonathan lunged for him again, but McCray was quicker.

Pierre mounted and rode away.

"Get a hold of yourself, Jonathan."

He tried to shrug McCray off, but he held on like a wolf with a bone.

"We've got to get through that Indian camp." McCray whispered. "Pierre wouldn't be stupid enough to do anything before then, so we've got time to work out a plan."

Mounting up, they drew their horses up when a familiar voice yelled their names.

"Say, is everything all right?" Lafayette slapped Jonathan's back in greeting as he rode up.

"I guess you two are in pretty good standing." McCray chuckled.

"I never forget a favor." Lafayette moved his leg out of his stirrup. "No more pain in my leg, now that arrowhead is gone. I'm good for another ten years before I feed the worms."

"Are you ready to do something about where you're planning to spend eternity?"

"You don't give up, do you, McCray?"

"Think of it this way. Jonathan is in the body-mending business and I'm in the soul-mending business. One works well enough until you die and the other works clear on forever . . . eternity, that is."

"You know I don't believe that stuff." Lafayette rested back in his saddle. "And it's best to focus on the now. We're in Indian country. We've got to stick close." He balled his hand into a fist. "We've got some men, but those injuns got more braves and skill. Why I've seen them skin a coyote in two shakes of their knives . . . or a man's scalp in one. White women are rare in these parts. I don't know how they'll react."

"Are you worried they'll try and capture them?"

"I never could understand the workings of a buck's brain, and I don't intend to say I do now. Some of my own men are lapping the dust with their tongues." He removed his coonskin hat and wiped his brow with the sleeve of his fringed coat. His dark eyes bore into Jonathan's like a lance. "I'm tellin' you simple. Don't take your eyes off your wife, Doc."

"Arise, arise."

Rachael yawned and stretched. They had heard that cry everyday for three and a half weeks. Watching the sun crest the horizon, she listened to the braying of the mules' herald another day. The twenty-first day of June promised to be another scorcher like the previous twenty-eight days had been.

The camp of wagons, tents, and livestock sprang to life as the seventy men that made up the American Fur Company became a hive of energy consuming a hurried breakfast, dowsing fires, harnessing their mules, and rounding up 200 animals. Rachael chuckled. With the mules braying, no one in camp could oversleep.

"Rachael, I'm still angry about the way the fur company killed our little calf." Beth drew her tiny hand into a fist. "Not much substance for seventy men. I'll fight them myself if they try and confiscate any of our milk cows."

"Hush, keep your voice down." Rachael wrapped her arm around Beth's shoulders and gave them a gentle caress. The bones on Beth's slight shoulders felt like pieces of kindling beneath Rachael's gentle hands. "I never heard you talk like that before."

"Our milk is our main substance, the nourishment in our tea and our connection with civilization." Beth's lip quivered. "It's the only thing I can keep down. Our barrel of flour is almost depleted. What are we going to do?" Beth rested her head on Rachael's chest.

"We'll keep what little flour's left for thickening our broth. However, that will be the end of our once-a-week cakes." Rachael puckered her lips, deep in thought. "I know, I'll ask Singing Dove what their people do for bread."

"Listen to me. I'm a fine example of a Christian woman. I don't know what I was thinking. Come to think if it, yes I do. I thought when we got with the company they would have all sorts of staples. Guess I thought of them as a sort of traveling store." Beth wiped her face with the corner of her worn apron. "I haven't had a bath for months. I feel downright indecent."

"But the buffalo meat has been nourishing."

"Yes, but having buffalo morning, noon and night, I'm beginning to hate the smell, taste, and texture of the beast. We've cooked it every which way. Only, it tastes the same. Besides, look at the way we have to eat.

"Our table's the ground, our tablecloth is our India-rubber cloth and when it rains, it's our coat. The only dishes we have are our tin basins for teacups, iron spoon, and a plate and our only knife is our dagger." Beth nuzzled deeper into Rachael's shoulder, as a child would her mother. "I'm tired of being a nomad. Even when we camp for the evening, when the food is cooked, we take our blankets and lie down by the campfire."

Rachael swallowed down the bitterness that came like bile to her throat. She always ate with Jonathan on her right and Singing Dove sharing her husband's left. A pang, sharp and deep, pierced her skin. Instead of driving their wagon, he spent most every day riding alongside Singing Dove checking out the cattle, preferring Singing Dove's companionship over sharing the wagon seat with his wife.

Did Jonathan love her or Singing Dove? Rachael couldn't seem to make him happy — could she bear seeing him miserable with her? He would grow to hate her. Wedlock would become a harness of misery and torment, rather than a cherished ring of love and commitment. McCray's words were her only solace. "What therefore God hath joined together, let not man put asunder."

"I know I shouldn't complain. Saul always takes out a trunk or box from our wagon and I sit on it. But the land is so barren. No stones. No trees. Nothing but prairie..." Beth turned slowly around, wringing her hands dismally.

Rachael wet her dry lips with the tip of her tongue remembering their fried cakes the other evening. She was determined to remain optimistic. McCray had chosen that night to draw her aside and confide to her his plan. When the time was right, he'd drive her wagon and keep Singing Dove occupied so she and Jonathan could be alone. A few moments with Jonathan would seem like a piece of heaven had opened up for them. She'd already rehearsed what she would say.

Beth tugged at Rachael's arm and whimpered like a forlorn puppy.

Saul ran up, his hair whipping about his face like a scared colt's. "Did you hear those men whooping it up last night? Jonathan and McCray shouldn't allow them to drink like that."

"Oh, Saul, what can they do in a crowd of seventy men?" Beth fluttered toward her husband and ran her fingers through his locks. "Did you count our livestock like I asked you to?"

"Yes, six horses, fifteen mules, nineteen head of cattle, and our five milk cows. They are all there." Saul shrugged off her arm. "I guess those men were too busy drinking to kill any more of our cattle. Well, we'd best get a move on or we'll be forced to the back, which is like driving our wagon in a sand storm."

Rachael looked at Beth, then Saul. Please Lord, help us and let today be the day McCray drives my wagon. "Saul, we need prayer." They clasped hands.

The wagon master's horse galloped up and stopped two feet in front of them. The horse did a half rear. A cloud of dust descended over them. Rachael closed her eyes and bowed her head.

"What are you doing?" he hollered.

"Dear Jesus, be with us this day and all the days of our lives. Fill us with Your love, yes Your unending and unrelenting love and patience, Lord, amen."

Rachael looked up to see Jonathan sitting astride his horse next to the wagon master, his face unreadable, staring a hole into Saul's black head. Rachael jerked her hand from Saul's like it was burning her fingers.

"Get those things packed up." The wagon master yelled and waved his whip at them. "You holy rollers think I'm kidding. You'll soon find I'm not." Snapping his whip, he reined his horse into a rear, then turned and galloped off.

"Catch up! Catch up!" The black whip curled over the wagon master's head like a rattle snake and slapped the air. Ten wagons, including their two, formed a rigid line of tight formation.

Rachael drew her bonnet down, shielding her eyes from the glaring sunlight. She was fortunate. Her wagon was close to the lead. There was less dust here and she was afforded a ringside seat to what lay ahead.

The pack animals loaded with supplies followed after the wagons, strung like pearls on a string. It all made quite a picture.

"Catch up! Catch up!"

She'd gotten used to the gruffness of the wagon master's bark, gotten used to hearing his whip cracking and splitting the air like a pistol shot. One bearded man, part of the fur company's eight wagons, who had allowed her to move her wagon forward, tipped his hat and smiled. "Mon chérie, Pierre is my name. If I can be of service in any way, do not hesitate to ask." He tipped his hat again.

Rachael couldn't keep her smile at bay. Pierre's brows hovered over his sparkling dark eyes, and he gave her a friendly wink. The other men only frowned at her, so she took the opportunity of Pierre's friendliness to educate herself on the elite of a wagon train.

"Why are there six mules on your wagons?"

"Chérie, because of the heavy load they pull."

"And the cart drawn by two mules?"

"It carries the lame Mr. Jones, the proprietor of the company who always comes. He does not trust anyone, mon chérie, with his investments. That wagon with the fancy plaid emblem on the side is Sir William Drummond Stewart, a wealthy Scotsman. He has brought along his artist friend, Alfred Jacob Miller, to draw the West." Pierre tapped his chest and winked again. "See how important I am?"

Her laugh drew a head out of the flaps of Pierre's wagon. "Watch out for him, Mrs. Wheaton. Pierre is a notorious ladies' man."

"I apologize for waking you, Clem. You must be tired after being on duty all night guarding our animals from Indians."

Clem tipped his hat. "That's all right, ma'am. Never heard a prettier sound than a woman's sparkling laughter. I'd forgotten what it sounded like. I had to get up and tell ya." Then drawing his eyes from hers to Pierre's, he nodded. "He's giving you the once over with his lusting eyes, that's a bad sign. You watch out for Frenchy, you hear?"

Rachael slapped her reins. "Giddy up." She heard the galloping hooves of horses approach.

"What were you doing talking to Pierre?" Her husband's scowling eyes collided into hers. She looked over at Singing Dove, then back at him, sitting tall and straight in the saddle. "Jonathan, do you have time to ride up here with me?"

"Maybe later." With that, he and Singing Dove galloped off.

The morning sweltered into noon as the hot June sun beat down on Rachael. She exchanged her bonnet for one of Jonathan's old wide brimmed hats. Jonathan, astride his horse, poked into view. She was ready. "Do you have a moment to talk with me now? You've been so busy with the wagon train."

Leaning over his saddle, he whispered. "Stay away from Pierre, you understand?"

Confused by his hostility, she blurted, "Why? He's charming and very polite. He didn't mind sharing conversation with me, unlike you." Rachael leaned over to glance behind the wagon. The Frenchman rode just behind them. He removed his hat and did a polite bow with his head.

"Stop returning his looks."

"Jonathan, I really do need to talk to you."

"Why don't you two go for a ride? I'll drive the team." McCray was as out of breath as his horse.

Rachael coughed from the floating cloud of dust McCray's horse had stirred. "I'd like that, very much."

An agreeable smile broke the lines of Jonathan's taunt lips. "I'll saddle your horse."

Jonathan's laughter bubbled forth from a place that had been parched since they first landed at Liberty. He urged his horse alongside hers. The day had turned into a pleasurable outing with Rachael by his side exploring what Lafayette and his men called Chimney Rock, a large cone shaped formation that rose from the ground like a giant solitary soldier. A man with sweeping sideburns and a beard to match sat on a three-legged stool painting.

"Oh, you must be Mr. Miller, the artist Sir Stewart has employed to paint the West." Rachael looked from the man on the stool to Jonathan.

Her eyes sparkled, an air of excitement and anticipation of life about her.

The distinguished man stood and bowed, his eyes gleaming back, not moving from her face. "At your service. And you must be the beautiful Rachael everyone in the caravan has been talking about."

Rachael chuckled. "Hardly. I just have little competition out here."

"Ah, you see as an artist sees, noting beauty others miss. This land is truly magnificent. Beyond the scope of human imagination."

"Indeed. Only a majestic God could so lovingly have painted this tapestry of art for our mortal eyes to behold. What treasures heaven must hold for our eternal soul." Spreading her arm wide, she laughed.

She had the laugh of a lark, capable of smoothing the jagged edges of Jonathan's moods in an instant. Evidently, it had the same effect on Mr. Miller.

Pierre's ugly face and uglier words edged into Jonathan's thoughts. He pushed them aside. He would not let anything disturb the enjoyment he felt being with Rachael and having her vitality for life rub off on him. Getting a glimpse of Rachael's silhouette, his pulse leaped like a bullfrog. She had more curves than a dove taking wing.

"Well, we shall bid you good day, for I am taking my wife for a ride." Jonathan moved forward and Rachael obligingly followed. She wore one of his old hats. That hat never looked like that on him. He smiled, glancing back at her, noticing the painter was still watching them.

"What's the matter, Jonathan?" Her eyes peeked beneath the leather brim and mirrored the bright grey-blue sky above. Her pearl white teeth and sun-rich complexion shone with vitality. No wonder every man in the outfit was love struck.

"We're nearing a Pawnee camp. Act like you did before, Rachael. Don't look at the braves. Treat them with respect, keep your eyes down, and don't try to communicate with them."

"But Jonathan." She heard a drumming of hooves and an answering neigh from Jonathan's horse, then a cloud of dust swelled like a thunder cloud around them.

"Jonathan, I look for you, there is problem with cow." Singing Dove's long thick braids shone bright and silky in the sunlight and her face beamed into his.

A bitter sigh escaped Rachael's clinched teeth and with reluctance Jonathan met Rachael's penetrating gaze. Embarrassed, he lowered his eyes. "We'll talk later, Rachael." His thoughts churned like sour grapes. He'd not noticed, until now, had not realized how many times a day Singing Dove found ways to interfere when he was with Rachael.

He bent down, lifted the wide rim of Rachael's hat, and grabbed a peek at her face. She turned her head away, but not before he'd seen a tear making a path down her cheek. "We'll have our talk, I promise." He gentled his tone. "Go back and stay with the train until I return."

"But, I can come. I know how to drive cattle. I learned from Harry Betts."

"Harry is it?" She doesn't trust me to take care of her. Doesn't she realize she attracts men like a dog attracts fleas? "Must you always question my motives?" He leaned over his saddle and stuck his face in hers. "If I wanted to be partnered with a cowboy, I would have married one. Do as I say."

chapter nineteen

he Reverend McCray provided a sympathetic ear to Rachael's account of the disastrous conversation with Jonathan. She held her resolve, refusing to tie her horse to the wagon, choosing instead to ride astride and independent into the Indian camp.

A group of Pawnee Indian matrons surrounded her. Rachael sucked in her breath and dismounted.

One woman, as round as she was tall with thick silver braids on either side of her melon-shaped face, gave Rachael a toothless grin. Spreading out her arms, she engulfed Rachael like a sweet pea into soup. Rachael laughed and returned the hug.

Matthew put a hand to his chest. "She know my aunt. She happy I going home."

"Oh, tell her we are most grateful for you and Luke. I do not know how we could have come without your aid."

Two Indian braves bowed.

"Oh, my, they are respectful and proud," Rachael said.

"As respectful as in civilized society." Jonathan came up behind her. "The Pawnee call themselves Chahiksichahiks, 'men of men.' Come Rachael, we're going to stay here for the night and need to prepare our camp." Jonathan grabbed her elbow and guided her toward their camp.

Tall and athletic, the Pawnee bore themselves with a quiet dignity and an incurable curiosity. Large oval lodges made of willow branches, grass, and earth made up the village. "Those huts look big enough to house more than one family," Rachael said.

"Very observant, Mrs. Wheaton." Reverend McCray said. "Unlike our culture, the Pawnee descendants are recognized through the mother. When a couple marries, they move into the bride's parents' lodge."

One brave stepped forward. He had to be at least six feet tall, well proportioned and was of fine bearing. His hair was bound in one single braid. "Why is his hair done so?"

"That's called a scalp lock. The hair stiffened with paint and meat droppings, made to stand erect and to curve something like a ram's horn around his face."

She glanced over her shoulder at the brave. The brave's eyes followed her movements.

"They are a handsome sort, for all their pointing and sign language. I do not believe we have to worry about them lifting our scalps." Beth's little eyes didn't miss a thing.

"Look what I got." Saul held out a small leather sack of corn meal.

"Oh, Mr. Spiker. I've been so hungry for a little bread."

"Now is as good as any time. Rachael, go get the skillet and I'll start the fire."

Rachael retreated into the tent and grabbed the utensil. Turning to go back out, she saw the brave with the scalp-lock. He had followed her inside and now stood between her and the tent flap. She clutched the skillet to her chest. Her breath came in gasps as she saw his eyes rest below her neck. Pointing toward the tent opening, she motioned for him to leave.

The brave motioned with his arms, slapping his palm and then pointed to her.

"Yes, we cook with this."

The brave shook his head, slapped his chest. Extending his arm, he handed her three freshly killed prairie chickens.

"Oh, thank you. It will be our first chicken since we left New York. I shall cherish your gift. Here." Ripping off a piece of her petticoat, she handed it to him. "I know it's not much, but your woman might like a piece of fabric from New York."

The brave rushed out of the tent whooping to his fellow braves who stood outside watching. A crowd of braves formed around him.

"Rachael dear, whatever did you give him?" Beth asked.

"Oh, nothing, really, pieces of my dress in exchange for these. . .well, I think they're chickens."

Beth looked down at the birds. "Prairie chickens, to be sure. Saul, is that what you think?"

Saul glanced up from the fire and blinked, smoke circled his head like a wreath. "Could be, you need to ask McCray." Not long after that the three of them had the birds plucked and ready for the pot.

"Mmm, smells delicious. We'll have ourselves some cornbread soon to go with our meat." Beth dropped water into the flour, added a pinch of salt, and kneaded the dough.

"I like it best with a little meat flavoring, Mrs. Spiker. You ever try it that way?" McCray said.

Beth looked at Rachael and winked, then turned toward the minister. "Why, no, Reverend."

Rachael suppressed a smile with difficulty. McCray always had a better way of cooking. It was humorous to watch him trot across from one campfire to another to make sure they were preparing the food the way he expected it. A sensitive culinary chef, he attempted to hide his obsession over how food should be cooked, but to no avail. "Here, let me have that dough."

Saul grunted, placed the chickens on tin plates and handed the skillet to McCray. "Wait, I need to cook the other chicken."

"No, I've got mine warming on the fire."

McCray flavored the raw dough to his liking, patting it into cakes, and then laid the cakes the size of a jar lid in the skillet. "I've got me some beans we can add to our meal."

"I think I could eat that raw." Saul licked his lips as he watched the cakes frying to a golden brown.

Jonathan walked up leading his horse, and sniffed. "Here add this to our dinner. I picked some berries. I don't remember their name, but Singing Dove says they make a right good dessert, once cooked."

McCray took the berries from Jonathan and looked at them, tasting one. "I think they're in the boysenberry family. Hmm, they need to be washed before we can eat them. Sometimes eaten raw, they can give a man a powerful stomachache."

"Well, I'll find out the hard way. I ate quite a few for lunch." Jonathan chuckled. "So far I feel great."

"Will Singing Dove be joining us, too?" Rachael asked.

"Nope." Jonathan smiled and unsaddled his horse. His arm gave with the sudden weight and he let his saddle fall to the ground with a thud, dust powdering the worn seat.

Rachael rushed to help him. Reaching for the saddle he took her hand. She felt his fingers weave themselves with hers, like threads in a quilt, and searched the depths of his eyes, his gaze earnest as was his hand in her own.

"That arm still bothering you?" McCray asked.

"Just a little rheumatism." Jonathan relinquished her fingers and bent to wipe his saddle with the back of his sleeve. Rachael clung to his horse's reins. Overwhelmed by the surge of feelings Jonathan's touch had evoked, her legs felt wobbly. Is this the same Jonathan who was cross with her earlier? What happened?

Jonathan carried his saddle to the campfire and set it upwind of the smoke, then walked back toward his horse. Rachael, bathed in his tall shadow, looked up. He stepped closer. Her breath came in gasps as his drenched her with his warmth. His voice low and deep, he mouthed out the words as if they were part of an unfinished sonnet. "Go sit down by my saddle, Rachael. I'll join you once my horse is bedded down for the night."

Unsure of her own voice, Rachael nodded and did what she was told. Using the saddle as a back rest and cupping her legs beneath her skirts, she looked up to see Jonathan staring at her. He smiled.

Beth was too busy fixing the coffee to notice. "Jonathan, where is Singing Dove?"

"She's having supper with Indian boys' people. Matthew and Luke are very excited."

Rachael sat back on Jonathan's saddle, still warm from his body. She watched him stroll into the darkness whistling, with his faithful horse trailing his heels. That was the most eye contact Jonathan had given her in over a month. Did McCray have something to do with Jonathan's change of mood? She looked over.

McCray looked up from the skillet and winked.

Rachael woke with a start. What time was it? The blackness of the tent met her eyes. Something had wakened her. Jonathan groaned.

"What is it, Jonathan?"

"I... don't know." His groans continued and he struggled to catch his breath. "My stomach."

Rachael listened to his labored breathing. "What can I do?"

"I, I, my stomach." Jonathan fought to speak, moaning. "It's... cramping. Need to get warm... might... ease it."

Rachael grabbed her blankets and wrapped them around him.

"Look in my bag for white powder... dissolve it in some... water."

"Yes, my dearest love." Perspiration dotted Jonathan's forehead. Rachael patted it dry, then bent over and kissed his forehead. Only hours ago, he was consoling her, holding her in his strong embrace kissing her softly until slumber captivated them both. Dear God, please heal my beloved Jonathan. She scrambled to her feet, got the needed medicine, slipped it in her pocket and grabbed the bucket — empty.

She peered out from the tent's flap. Some of Lafayette's men were still up, drinking around the campfire. She wrapped her shawl closely around her shoulders, then stepped out from beneath the safety of their tent.

The fires of the trappers and the Indians sent ghostly spirals of smoke into the bleak night. No sign of the moon. Perhaps that was better. She didn't need Lafayette's men to know she was up — alone. She clutched the pail's handle, and keeping to the shadows, hurried toward the river.

She felt the wind sweeping the trees lining the river banks. The clouds overhead swept past allowing the half moon to glow hazily across the river as it splashed over pebbles and rocks. She waded in, her bare feet tender on the sharp rocks beneath the water. She waded in farther, until she felt the bottom of her petticoat dampen from the cold river water. There would be no way she could boil the water before Jonathan drank it. She didn't what him to contract a disease from dirty water. "Dear Jesus, please bless this water." She scooped up a half-bucket full.

The bushes rustled. Her heart did a somersault. A bear? She took a deep breath. Don't act afraid. Jonathan said animals could sense fear. She forgot to ask him what to do if you couldn't help acting scared. She started up the hill. The bushes to her left rustled, then a low growl. Only, it wasn't the growl of an animal. It was a man's.

"Show yourself, you coward."

The Indian whose eyes had lingered on her that afternoon staggered toward her. He held her petticoat piece between his fingers. She could smell alcohol on his breath. He tossed his jug into the thicket and stepped closer, grinning.

Her heart beat like a drum. Her breath matched beat for beat.

Why hadn't she thought to bring Jonathan's pistol? The Indian had been friendly earlier in the day. Perhaps she had nothing to fear. He staggered toward her. Should she scream? Would it do her any good? She watched as he advanced and she clutched the bucket handle till her fingers ached. The pail was her only weapon.

"Rachael? Where are you?"

"Saul? Over here," she called out.

Saul burst through the thicket, armed with his rifle. He was barefoot, his hair ruffled. He saw the Indian no more than three strides away from her and jumped between them.

"What do you want with Mrs. Wheaton?" Shouldering his rifle, he waved it in front of the Indian's face. "Go. Now."

Rachael cowered behind Saul.

"Me Running Horse. Buy her." He pointed to Rachael. "Mine! We trade. Make my squaw." He held up the piece of cloth from Rachael's dress.

"No." Saul turned and pointed to Rachael. "She has brave. Married." Saul swung the barrel of his gun on the Indian. The Indian stepped back.

"Rachael, show him your hand, your wedding band. Good." Saul waved the barrel of his gun. "Mrs. Wheaton happy. Happy. Smile. Good." Then he motioned the barrel of his gun at the Indian. "Happy married to doctor. You go now." Then he whispered beneath his breath, "Before my finger gets itchy."

"Husband not well. Die." The brave staggered toward her.

"No! My husband will not die."

"What did you do to Doctor Wheaton?"

"Not do." The Indian slapped his bare chest. "He do. Eat poison berries."

* * *

"You're going to be all right." McCray tucked a blanket around Jonathan's shoulders. "I can't figure out how come none of us got sick from the berries."

"Because you soaked them first and then cooked them." The quinine had worked as Jonathan had hoped, but he could hardly move. His stomach was still very sore and he felt weak all over. "The fruit isn't poisonous."

"How about your arm? Did you check for any cuts? I had a scout that thought he had rheumatism, found out he'd gotten cut and it was lockjaw."

"That was the first thing I did. No, it's rheumatism. I feel bad holding us up. Why don't you go ahead?"

"No." Saul sat down next to McCray. "We're a team. I might not see eye to eye with you, Jonathan, but that doesn't mean I don't look at you like a brother."

"I'm glad to hear you say that." McCray's lopsided grin confirmed his words.

Saul looked around. "Where's Rachael?"

"She and your wife are down by the river washing clothes."

Jonathan lifted himself off the pallet Rachael had prepared for him. He managed to move into a sitting position, suppressing a groan. Saul poured himself a cup of coffee, took a sip, and stared into the embers.

"Something bothering you, Saul?" Jonathan reached for the cup

McCray prepared.

"Yeah. I've been wrestling with telling you. But I don't see any way around it." Saul stared into the fire then at McCray. "Rachael isn't going to work out like my Beth. She isn't out of the right cloth to be a missionary's wife. She brings out the worst in these westerners."

"What?" Jonathan narrowed his eyes. "Are you forgetting how the Indians acted toward her? That head Indian woman hugging her? I didn't see Beth being taken in and accepted so quickly."

"Did Rachael tell you about last night?"

Jonathan grunted and managed to get to his feet. He didn't plan on defending Rachael's honor lying down. He attempted to remain calm amidst the turbulence Saul's words ignited; however, he couldn't suppress his scowl. "Suppose you tell me why Rachael isn't cut out to be a missionary."

"I found her down by the river with an Indian."

"She was getting me water. I haven't a clue where that Indian came from, but I'm sure it was no rendezvous."

"I'm not saying that. But, well, there is no easy way of saying this. Rachael is very well endowed. Even in these conditions, Jonathan, she's a holy eyeful."

Jonathan's temper flared like a pot boiling over. He grabbed Saul by the collar of his shirt. Rachael's soft words and her even softer kisses covering his forehead last night spoke more than any sonnets of love could. And to think, he treated her terribly — distant — almost hatefully these past months.

He'd seen the hurt in her eyes when he rode off with Singing Dove. The pain his curt words inflicted on her were worse than a task master's whip. He wasn't proud of what he did. In fact, he hated what his jealously had turned him into. Now here was his chance to flatten Saul's arrogant nose and his nagging conscience in one blow.

McCray's hand tapped his arm. "Is that a Christian response?" McCray's soft words were like a poultice on his wounded pride.

"Saul, none of this is Rachael's fault." Jonathan kept his voice low, attempting to harness his temper. He'd rather hurtle his fist at Saul, instead of words. But he was a true Christian now and came here to do the Lord's work, not appease his pride. He released his hold on Saul. "You want to blame someone? Blame God. He formed her."

Saul swished the hot liquid in his cup.

"What were you doing down by the river, Saul?" McCray leaned forward waiting.

Jonathan glanced at Saul.

"I… noticed her heading toward the river."

"But you didn't notice Jonathan moaning in pain?"

Jonathan glanced at McCray, then Saul. "This is as good a time as any… Saul, I know about you and my wife."

Saul jumped to his feet. "Rachael swore she wouldn't tell you —"

"About your misguided father and your heritage?" McCray was on his feet, too.

"What?" Jonathan looked at McCray.

"So you've come from the Board to replace me." Saul threw down his cup and glared at McCray. "I knew I couldn't trust Senator Rothburn. Don't tell my wife. At least give me that. I lost Rachael when I told her the truth. I don't want to lose my Beth."

"What's this all about?" Jonathan's eyes burned with indignation. He'd hired Saul with the understanding he was an honorable minister.

Saul's shoulders sagged, as if to ward off a blow. "Then if Rachael didn't tell you —"

"I only know what Beth told me, that you and Rachael went to the same Academy," Jonathan said.

Saul collapsed on the crate and buried his face in his hands. "Rachael wanted to tell you, Jonathan. She didn't want to keep anything from you. I made her promise not to. I couldn't stand you knowing I proposed to her so I could be a missionary in the Oregon Territory. She might have said yes if not for her father, if not for *my* father and his elicit affairs.

"My father dirtied the Spiker name and left my mother to try and pick up the pieces of a broken family. Oh, then there are those righteous Christians. They forgive everything but what matters to society. Just don't ask for their daughter's hand in marriage. When I met my lovely Beth, well, she brought hope and love back into my life. I couldn't live if I lost her."

"Let me get this straight." McCray fingered his chin. "You followed Rachael to the stream to ask her if your little secrets were still safe?"

Saul rubbed his hands through his hair. "No, I was going to tell her that it was time to tell Jonathan and Beth the truth. I couldn't bear the guilt of keeping this secret any longer. But I'm too late. I've lost my mission because of something I had no control over. I've lost Jonathan's confidence and my wife's respect by not revealing the truth."

McCray laid a hand on Saul's shoulder. "No one is replacing you. I'm much too old to do the work the Lord has set before you, but you need to ask yourself this: Can the blind lead the blind? Will they not both fall into the ditch?" McCray looked at Saul and then over at Jonathan. "Jesus is training you both for the mission that lies before you. I hardly think anyone cares what your father has done. Jesus was illegitimate, at least to earthly eyes. The Board is more concerned about the man who is representing our Savior. Not their ancestry.

"You're seeing the mote in everyone's eye, Saul, but not the beam in your own. Accept you are a sinner and move on with your life serving the Lord God Almighty."

McCray turned to Jonathan. "Jonathan, as long as you hold jealousy toward Saul, you're not building your house on the Rock. You are both good men. Consider these trials as the Lord pruning you for what lies ahead. After all, 'why call ye me Lord, Lord, and do not the things which I say?'"

"I never even knew when you asked me to join your missionary team that you had wed Rachael." Saul looked down at his hands. "I love Beth. She may be sickly, but she's got a good heart for the Lord and can keep me in my place. I surely need that."

Jonathan squeezed his eyes shut. This can't be. God, tell me this isn't so. Rachael had no choice but to marry him. She had no choice, that is, if her hopes to become a missionary were to come true. And he had never proposed to her — of course, he wanted his own selfish desires over hers. The truth gnawed his insides, like the poison that had not yet left his body. Which one, he or Saul, would have been Rachael's choice? Jonathan looked down at his cup feeling McCray's eyes searing his heart. He turned his gaze toward the trees lining the river's edge. Was that Pierre's face gleaming back at them? He watched the Frenchman bolt toward the trapper's encampment. How much of their conversation had he heard?

chapter twenty

Rachael's eyes fluttered from Lafayette to Jonathan. Beads of perspiration like dew drops covered Jonathan's broad face. Was it their campfire causing the perspiration or a fever?

"Will you be well enough to travel tomorrow?" Lafayette fingered the corners of his beard as he eyed Jonathan.

Jonathan placed his elbow to his side, grunted like a wounded deer and rose from the log he'd been sitting on. "I'll be fine." The tree tops stirred with the whisper of a warmer breeze to come. "I'm feeling the heat of the day, that's all." He wiped his brow with his handkerchief.

"Yeah, right. Bet your guts feel like they're trying to come out." Moving with a quiet grace of effort unusual in a man so tall and muscular, Lafayette walk forward and slapped his hand on Jonathan's shoulder. "Listen. You and your group stay here. Rest. Fort William is less than two days' journey, at the confluence of the North Platte and Laramie Rivers. When my company gets to the fort, I'll have someone from the fort check on your party." Lafayette fingered his beard, as if pondering a better plan.

"My men will skin me alive if I asked them to wait. All they talk about is getting to the Rendezvous. Just follow our trail to Fort William and when you leave Fort William, look for a large black rock about a mile in diameter jutting out of the dirt like... well, pardon my language, ma'am." Lafayette chuckled. "Like a mammoth amount of buffalo dung, yep, that's what it looks like to me.

"Some fur caravans have started calling it Independence Rock 'cause if you make it to that rock before or by the fourth of July, you know you'll make it over them mountains before the snow flies. After you see that rock, watch out for the watering holes. Smell the water before you let your cattle drink it. If it sniffs bad, send them away and whatever you do, don't you drink it. You'll catch up with us at the Rendezvous. Then we'll head out for Fort Hall."

※ ※ ※

Rachael stared out at the horizon and wondered if mountains hid behind that dusty brown haze. For miles in all directions, the stark greenish-brown landscape held a beauty all its own. A hill here, a rock formation there, jutted from the flat terrain. She said a prayer of thanks for the few trees that dotted their campsite. She'd come to learn that in this territory trees only grew near rivers.

Despite the barrenness of the land, Rachael's anticipation of starting their mission grew with every beat of her heart. Tomorrow they would break camp and head for Fort William. She knew Jonathan's lust for adventure couldn't keep him down for long. During the past three days of rest, his strength grew stronger and so did her love for him.

Today had proved as hot as the early morning gnats buzzing around their tent flaps had predicted. McCray and Saul were out hunting. Matthew, Luke, and Singing Dove were watching the herd. Beth and Jonathan were napping.

She grabbed the water pail and a rag and headed for the stream. She set down the pail and plunged the rag into the cool water until it touched the smooth pebbles of the stream. She wrung out the excess water and ran the wet rag across her face, feeling the soothing wetness cool her hot cheeks. She hoped to look fresher than she felt when Jonathan saw her next. She filled the pail and returned to camp to prepare dinner.

A noise from the tent distracted her. She looked up from the fire at Jonathan and smiled. "Our dinner is just about ready, and just about done for tasting."

"Rachael, come here." Jonathan walked stiffly toward the log they used to sit on and plopped down, then motioned her to join him.

"Is something wrong? Do you hurt somewhere?"

"Right here." Jonathan pointed to his heart.

She should have known not to allow him to go down to check on the livestock. But she'd hope the walk would strengthen him. Evidently it had the opposite effect. "Is the pain heavy?"

Jonathan cupped his hand into hers. "Yes, severe." He drew her toward him, wrapped his arms around her, kissing her cheek, then her forehead. "Rachael, there is something you do not know about me. Something I have kept hidden, that I did not want to admit, not even to myself."

A lump as big as a peach seed clogged her throat and she coughed. Would he confess his love for Singing Dove? Or Isabella? She knew this day would come eventually. She slumped down on the log. Dear God, please allow me to accept the truth without weeping uncontrollably. Help me keep calm.

Jonathan's cheek muscles stood out as he clenched his jaw. He sighed. "I overheard your conversation with Mrs. Rumpson about you wanting to become a missionary out west. I had accepted Christ at one such revival, but I never knew what to do with my spiritual commitment, until I met you." He turned, knelt down before her and took her hands in his, palm side up and kissed them gently.

The tingles of a thousand goose bumps washed through her, renewing hope in her aching heart like raindrops on a parched riverbed.

"You were the one who gave me the idea of being a missionary... Rachael, when it comes to being a man of God I'm an imposter. I am short tempered and easily distracted. You and Saul have an unbridled exuberance for doing God's work. I want that exuberance."

"Prayer, Jonathan. Humility and prayer." She felt a jab to her conscience. What had Reverend McCray said? Was her pride getting in the way of her disclosing her own sins to Jonathan?

"All I ever wanted was to not be an embarrassment to the Wheaton name. I wanted my name to be engraved on some stone someday like my great-great-grandfather's." He rose and staggered toward the opposite side of the fire, his shoulders hunched forward. Rachael bolted off the log as if it was burning her. She rushed forward.

"Such foolishness when souls are at stake doomed for the fire pits of hell! Do you think God is mad at me? Is that why I am ill?" Jonathan said, his voice but a hoarse whisper.

"No, Jonathan, your desire is to serve Him." She laid her hand on his back. "Your conscience is pricking you because it is active and alive with the desire to do God's will. I feel —"

"What, dear Rachael?" He turned, sweeping her into his embrace, and lowered his head upon hers. Locked in each other arms, his muffled voice drifted like a sonnet to her thirsty ears.

"I knew you would understand. But can I ever be the man of God I need to be to fulfill this mission God had laid out before us? At times I feel like a fake."

"Why? Reverend McCray told me how you saved that poor tribe in Canada from cholera. Remember Proverbs 3, verses 5 and 6? Hasn't God directed our paths here now?"

He gently pushed her away. Gazed into her upturned face, as if waiting to record the effects of his next words. "My temper is uncontrollable with Saul. Is there something between you both you have not said? Tell me, Rachael, for I have poured out my soul to you. Tell me the truth —"

"Me and Saul?"

He gave her a pained look. Rachael sucked in her breath and rushed toward the security of the log. Does he know about Saul's proposal? What should she do? Should she tell him? But what of her promise to Saul?

"I sense there is something you're keeping from me." His footsteps sounded to the tune of her heart, coming closer with every beat. Panicked, she fished over her hidden secrets. Which one should she reveal first? Her love for him? Saul's proposal? Jonathan had not taken the news of Harry Betts well. She could just imagine how he would take the news of Saul's proposal. She swallowed. Is this deception normal between wife and husband? Lord, help.

"I, thought you would be pleased about the frontier knowledge I acquired from Harry Betts, but —"

"I am." Jonathan's laugh was as husky and golden and warm as the sunlight on her head. Rachael looked up at him curiously.

"I just have a funny way of showing it." He stretched out his hand to her.

"I am relieved to see both your spirits have improved." Beth bustled forth. "Rachael dear, your stew is about to boil over."

❊ ❊ ❊

Rachael flipped the reins over Sassy's rump. "Giddy up! Or you'll get the whip." The mule heehawed back at her. Sassy had taken advantage of Rachael's preoccupation. She chuckled, recalling the first time they met Sassy at Liberty and Matthew had immediately shown his distaste over her. Indeed, the word 'ornery' was a compliment to the mule's disposition. Jonathan had promptly named the mean spirited iron-mouthed mule Sassy.

The dust from Saul's wagon wheels puffed like frothy brown clouds behind him. Rachael coughed. They had set out early the morning of the June 25 and Fort William was but five miles away. She had hoped Jonathan would join her in the wagon and not exert himself. He complained he was no invalid and had ridden up ahead with Reverend McCray to alert Fort William as to their arrival. She was as impatient as her husband to see the fort.

Waving the dust away she stared out at the fifty or so teepees dotting the landscape around the fort. The stockade was made of cottonwood logs and looked to be some 200 feet or so wide. At least that's what Reverend McCray said it was over last evening's campfire. A large Stars and Stripes waved a greeting at her. Nothing looked more inviting to her home-deprived eyes than that American flag. It was a little piece of civilization splattering the blue skies above. "Pick up your feet, Sassy."

Buckskin clad Indians, some wrapped in their colored blankets stopped to stare at her. She touched the rim of her bonnet. "Hello. Nice to meet you."

They stared back. She could feel their eyes on her as she made her way toward the fort. One brave, sitting proudly on his paint pony, galloped alongside her. He took a lingering look at her, then galloped off, whooping about something. His look unnerved her. Where was Jonathan? She glanced down. One woman glanced up from her boiling pot and scowled. The odor was irritating, but familiar. Rachael fished in her thoughts, but could not place the smell. Then it came to her. It was the odor of mule skinner's brew in Liberty.

"Girl, now is not the time to dawdle." She slapped the reins over Sassy's back again. Sassy heehawed and jumped into a half-gated gallop, catching up to Saul's wagon. Rachael chuckled. Right. That Indian's stew pot smelled a lot like mule. "That's what happens to lazy mules, Sassy."

As if the stockade doors had eyes, they opened to bid their wagons entry. Rachael's mouth flapped open like a shade on a window. A cast iron cannon pointed ominously toward the Indian encampments they had just passed.

Jonathan galloped up. "Impressive, isn't it?"

Rachael pointed to the buildings high on each side of the stockade. "What are those?"

"Block houses, the frontiersmen can see for miles from them." Jonathan dismounted, tied his horse to the wagon and climbed up to the seat next to her. "The fur company has already left for the Rendezvous."

"Oh dear, then we are too late and I did want to see just what a Rendezvous was like."

"Don't worry. The Rendezvous can last as long as a month."

Rachael lowered her voice to a whisper. "What are all these Indians doing camped outside the fort? Are they planning an attack?"

"No. These mountain men often take Indian wives and become part of their families." There was a thrill of alarm in his voice, his monotones vibrating with emotion. "The Indians have a mortal horror of the cannon over the blockhouse, the one you saw when you entered the stockade. They believe it has powers to talk and think it sleeps now, but that it could wake up at any time."

"Really?" Rachael rested back in her seat. "And of course, the mountain men and fur companies do not care to educate them."

Jonathan shrugged his large shoulders. "I doubt it would do any good. Presently, the Indians prefer the white man over their own race. The uprisings are always among warring tribes. They come here three or four times a year bringing their peltries to exchange for dry goods. Also for tobacco, beads, and alcohol."

Reining up the team, he climbed down from the wagon and offered Rachael his hand. She saw Saul and Beth being escorted toward a building. She and Jonathan followed them in.

"Ladies we are honored with your presence. Please make yourselves comfortable." A tall man with shiny black hair and a mustache to match offered Rachael a chair with buffalo seat bottom. She hesitated.

Beth looked up from her seat and smiled. "Go ahead, Rachael dear, it is quite comfortable."

The black haired man with the mustache chuckled. "Indeed. Last year we had the honor of Mrs. Whitman and Mrs. Spalding's company. Both quite agreed our chairs were the best they had yet to encounter on their way westward." The man smiled. "Now, what would be your ladies' desire? A hot bath? Warm water enough to do your laundry? You name it, and we shall do our best to accommodate our lovely guests."

McCray, who had followed on their heels as silent as a bird dog, stepped forward. "I believe the ladies are in need of both, and I am glad to accommodate their wishes. But if you do not mind, I shall leave tomorrow to catch up with the fur company."

The Sunday after their arrival they held a real worship service, complete with a fine message from Saul. Jonathan congratulated him on it, and Rachael beamed with pride into Jonathan's eyes. "See, I'm trying," Jonathan whispered back. Rachael praised her loving Savior Jesus who had healed Jonathan, and the Almighty God who blessed their little caravan and gave His angels charge over them to guard them, with the sun by day and the moon by night bringing no hardship near their tents. Just as Saul had preached.

She and Beth had a proper bath and washed all their clothes. Jonathan kept busy, pulling many of their belongings out of their wagon and placing them into the growing pile along with Beth's furniture. Not a memory of Fort William Rachael would cherish. This task eclipsed the fleeting pleasure of her hot bath and clean clothes. And poor dear Beth. Her bottom lip quivered like a child as she witnessed her keepsakes tossed out like yesterday's dishwater. Nonetheless, she held her tears at bay. They had to lighten the load for the trip crossing the Rockies. Beth grumbled that someone needed to build lighter wagons.

They stacked their belongings neatly beneath the eaves of one building hoping the frontiersmen could put some of their things to good use. If not the garrison, the Indians would find some use for them, Rachael was sure.

Rachael managed to save the wedding trunk Jane had given her. She had stuffed a few treasured mementos of her past life inside for her future children to see. However, material possessions didn't matter. Matthew 6:31 proved true. Their heavenly Father provided for all their needs.

She and Jonathan had grown closer after his illness, and Jonathan's attempts to please her in the little things that made life bearable renewed her spirits and her love for him. He accepted the skills Harry Betts taught to her, though she didn't know if Saul had told Jonathan about her and Saul's past. She didn't care. She would not worry about tomorrow, for sufficient for the day was its own trouble. Refreshed in spirit and in body, only God knew what treasures lay before them.

Then before the sun peeked above the horizon that twenty-seventh day of June, they set out for the Rendezvous. A dense fog blanketed the trail, and Rachael wondered how Jonathan knew where to lead the mules. For nearly thirty miles, the trail dipped and curved like a slothful snake with no place to go. The westward trail swelled like the sea, and Rachael grabbed onto the side of the wagon, feeling herself tipping upwards. The slight grade displayed low hanging clouds swimming before her eyes. Peaking like black foam, the dark and mysterious clouds sent a chill coursing through her veins.

"We might be in for some bad weather. Just look how black those clouds are."

Jonathan chuckled. "Those clouds are the Rocky Mountains, the great divide that separates east from west."

She squinted into the western horizon. "Oh, Jonathan, how are we ever going to climb them?"

The hours dwindled away with the scenery changing before her eyes like the seasons of the year. Sunlight ricocheted off the spectacular orange and red sandstone formations that rippled like the waves of the sea on either side of the fur trappers' trail. She tried to memorize every beautiful landscape. Words were inadequate to describe the magnificent brush strokes of God's handiwork. In many places rock formations rose as high as a mountain only to dip into a canyon-like formation of red, orange, and brown hues. She wished she could share it with Jonathan, but he had long ago saddled his horse and ridden out to check on the livestock.

The hoof beats of a lone horse galloped toward her wagon. The springs of her wagon seat creaked as she turned to glimpse her husband's strong profile. The scent of dust, sweating horse, and the bold masculine smell of leather swabbed her nostrils.

His deeper than usual baritone voice sent whispers of terror coursing through her veins.

His ever watchful eyes didn't miss her concern. He patted her arm. "It's going to be all right." His mouth twisted from its grimace into a one of his lopsided grins she had grown to cherish. "We've lost two of our beef cows, that's all."

"How?"

"Remember what the men told us at Fort William about beware of the sweet water?"

"You mean about that folklore of some shipment of sugar being dumped in the river?"

"Yeah. Well, the water's not sweet, but poisonous. We've got to ride on through this spot before any more of our cattle die, or we get sick from drinking it."

Rachael clutched her throat. She had almost stopped her wagon to get a dipper full because of her thirst. Her throat contracted and she tried to swallow, only it was so dry all she could do was utter a dry cough. "But how can that be? It's so beautiful here?"

Jonathan's horse pulled at the reins, as if impatient to leave. Jonathan's whiskered face broke into a grin watching her. He swept off his hat and bent over to kiss her on the cheek. "That just goes to show beauty is superficial, my love, to our inner spirit. Here, take my canteen; I have another. We should be out of here soon." Slapping his saddle, he rode off to keep an eye out for the cattle.

The next day they were up before daylight. Thirsty, Rachael ran her tongue across her teeth, her mouth as gritty as her hands. With apprehension she took her seat on the wagon and picked up the reins, hoping today they would come across some delicious spring water.

To her delight, Jonathan joined her on the wagon seat. What new sights would they encounter today? The early morning fog was so thick she could hardly see beyond her lead mule's head. Then suddenly sunlight stole its way through the mists like a beacon of hope to their weary and thirsty caravan.

"We should be reaching South Pass soon." Jonathan looked around. "People come from all around this territory to the Rendezvous. French Canadian trappers, Indians, and the nomadic mountain men."

Rachael skimmed the horizon. A cloud of mist and a few jagged mountains loomed to the south of their small caravan. The captain at Fort William said this was the lowest part of the Rockies, only around 9,500 feet high. The rest could be as high as 14,000 feet, though no one really knew for sure. That was just his estimate.

Jonathan hadn't heard from McCray or Singing Dove who had ridden ahead, trying to locate the fur company. A rider trotted into sight to the west of them. At first she thought he was an Indian, then realized as he came closer, his beard giving him away, that he was a white man. His horse was as lean as he, an ill-fitted beast with short legs and a large head that looked ready to fall any moment. "Jonathan, who is he?"

"A mountain man," he whispered back. "Try not to stare, probably been up in the Rockies for a year or so, come down to do a little trading."

"How do!" The mountain man picked up the pace and rode up alongside of them. "Excuse me for lookin.' Haven't see a white woman since I left home." He stretched his long legs in his stirrups, standing clear off his seat, as if affording himself a better look at her.

Rachael took hold of Jonathan's arm and smiled back.

"How long ago was that?" Jonathan asked.

"Hmm, 1799, that's when I lit out for the hills."

"The Black Hills?"

"Them and the Rockies. You headin' to the Rendezvous?" Around the mountain man's neck lay a string of animal teeth, and though the day was warm, he wore a fur hat.

Jonathan nodded. "How much farther do we have to go?"

"Full of questions you are? First you have to get through South Pass and the Rockies' Wind River Mountains.

"Well, how much farther?"

"Cast your eyes yonder…" The mountain man lifted his rifle off the crook if his arm and pointed. "Squint your eyes and stare hard to the west. You'll see them rising up in what looks to be a mist, but there they be."

Rachael gasped. As night parted for day, what she thought were clouds was the massive expanse of mountains rising out of the earth like a giant prehistoric beast laid before them.

A deep throated chuckle from the mountain man startled Rachael. "You be missionaries? Like that Whitman bunch that come over last year?"

"Why, yes sir, we are." Rachael smiled. Any semblance to her heroine Narcissa was indeed a compliment.

"I see you take great store in that title. It pleases me a heap to know that." The mountain man lifted his rifle and etched the mountains, like he was drawing their outline. "I reckon the first time I laid my eyes on them, I figured there was no way 'round that heap of mountains.

"Then I met Jedediah Smith. Only God could have preordained that meetin' out here in this no man's land. Jedediah told me a man named Stuart had found a way through where there seemed no way. Called the place South Pass."

The mountain man rested his arm on the crook of his saddle. "Why, them mountains could have divided this land eternally if not for Almighty Himself bending down to give this new country of ours a helping hand." The man sat back up and cradled his rifle in his arms like a babe. "I reckon you missionaries preaching the gospel to usins ignorant about the Hereafter could make a mark on this new country more than the mountain men and explorers. I know Narcissa did that for me." He chuckled. "So howdy do. And ma'am, tell Narcissa I'm a reading that Bible she gave me and enjoyin' it a heap."

"Well, glad you saw fit to join us again, Wheaton." Lafayette stretched out his hand toward Jonathan. Jonathan reached for the callused hand of the frontiersman.

Lafayette raised his hat to Rachael. "Ma'am, frontier life agrees with you. You're as pretty to look at as a sunset after a hard day's work." His eyes met Jonathan's the same instant his callused hand wrapped Jonathan's fingers. The neighs of Indian ponies laden with baskets and trinkets, curses of mountain men, and yelps of pack dogs added to the cacophony of the bustling camp.

"It'll be a scorcher today for sure. We're camped over on the south end of the shanties. Got good access to the river there," Lafayette said.

"Follow me," McCray yelled at Jonathan, not stopping the loping canter of his horse. "I've staked out a good place. Hurry! I don't want someone else gettin' it. Singing Dove's guarding it for us."

As they neared the campsite, Jonathan pulled his wagon alongside Saul's. He noticed a well-built, short-legged man dressed in a plaid shirt standing next to Singing Dove. A thick crop of curly hair fell across his wide forehead and long sloping sideburns that nearly came to the corners of his large mouth framed his face. "I've heard one of you be a doctor?"

"Yes, that's me." Jonathan jumped down from the wagon.

The man kept his eyes lowered and fumbled with the brim of his hat. "My wife is havin' a powerful time birthin' her wee babe." He glanced up, concern creasing his brow. "Can you come?"

Jonathan avoided the man's eyes. He reached for Rachael and gently lowered her to the ground. The noise of Indians and trappers whooping and laughing a distance away filled him with dread, recalling his fight with the Blackfoot brave.

Laugher bubbled up from a place deep within Rachael. A bitter sigh escaped him. Her gaze grew serious beneath his drawn brows. "What's wrong, Jonathan?"

His thoughts churned uncomfortably. He didn't want to leave her side. Yet, what if it was Rachael struggling with the pains of childbirth? "Maybe you could come with me, be my nurse?"

She smiled and his heart did a little flip. Her gaze flitted from the Scotsman then back to him.

"I'm going to make our supper."

Jonathan tipped her chin, his eyes searching hers. How could he impress on her the potential danger? She seemed unaware of her beauty and how that beauty could affect a man. "Promise me you'll not talk to anyone and stay close to camp. These frontiersmen and Indians get rowdy when they start drinking their firewater. You promise?"

Rachael nodded.

"I'll be back before nightfall."

Rachael stirred the big kettle of soup she'd made, remembering Jonathan's concern for her safety. He should be returning soon and she had everything she needed right here. An hour worked into another. She placed the last of the buffalo chips she'd gathered on the fire and wrinkled her nose. A cluster of trees down by the river, their green leaves a bouquet of cooling color amidst the deep blue sky, beckoned to her. Wouldn't it be nice to sit around the campfire and smell wood instead of dung? Maybe she could find some kindling. She could use some fresh water, too.

Humming a tune, she headed down the hill to the river with her bucket in one hand and a strap to tie the kindling locked in her other. The sound of her shoes scrunching the sagebrush echoed in the soft afternoon breezes. Then the gibberish sound of many dialects echoed up to her. She strained to see past the clusters of trees, hesitating, tossing around the thought of climbing back up the hill, toward the safety of the wagons. Who could they be? Perhaps only some people washing their clothes. She would keep to herself and get the water well upstream and away from the debris of the shoreline as Jonathan had taught her.

A group of men clad in buckskins stood no more than a few yards away from the river bank. One left the group and walked toward her. "Ah, mon chérie, it is good to see you."

"Pierre, it is good to see you, too. Did you have a good trip after we left the company?"

"Oui, oui very nice," he said, looking around.

"I must admit, Pierre, I do enjoy hearing an accent of European origin and not the common words of the westerners. Is that why you cling to your nationality?"

"Nah." A tall man with yellow hair stepped forward. "He thinks the ladies enjoy hearing it. Right, Frenchy?"

Rachael walked to the shoreline and stepped into the water, then bent over and dipped her pail into the water.

"Here, allow me." The yellow-haired man grabbed the bucket from her before she could stop him. "I may not have a French accent, but I do have manners."

"Cobb, I will help the mademoiselle." Pierre moved to grab the bucket from him. Cobb shoved Pierre and he fell into the river, a few feet from Rachael. She sidestepped, right into the river, nearly falling. Cobb grinned, extending his hairy arm. "Here, I'll help you."

"No, mon chérie, do not. He will never let it go." Pierre jumped on top of Cobb, hurtling him to the ground. The men gathered around them. Thankfully, they seemed to have forgotten about her. She started once again to fill her bucket. Or had they? She watched a band of men walk down to the river, their eyes fixed on her. Her bucket full, she left the water. Before she could climb the riverbank, the men blocked her way.

One burly man separated himself from the crowd. She backed away. Her shoes grazed the slippery rocks of the river — she didn't look down. Instead, she watched the man with the dirty beard and beady eyes. His eyes gleamed back and then he reached for her.

She sidestepped, inhaled, and dove into the river. Her skirts tangled around her legs. She fought to swim in the direction of their camp, then came up for air, kicking toward the shoreline. Jonathan, please be there.

chapter twenty-one

achael took a deep breath and dove under water again. She couldn't swim much farther, not with her skirt restricting her kicks. Her shoes weighed her down, too. She had no choice but to lose them. She unbuttoned the pleated waist, kicking her skirt free, and watched the fabric float along in the gentle current.

She spotted a sandy knoll that split the river and swam toward it. Coughing, crawling onto the sand, she inhaled deeply. Her heart beat against her rib cage. She peeked upstream toward the shoreline she had vacated. Good. She was hidden from the men's view. Beached like a slimy fish, she removed her shoes. Clutching them, one in each hand, she considered leaving them behind. Would she find another pair as comfortable to replace them? Would her shoes do her any good if she should lose her life? She tossed them down and crawled toward the water. She struck out on a diagonal, keeping her head low, and swam toward a stand of bushes. Reaching the shoreline, she coughed, spit out the film and grit between her teeth, and inhaled deep breaths of fresh air. Once she had regained her breath, she looked around. Wave-washed boulders met her gaze.

This didn't look like their camp. Where could she be? She crawled up the riverbank in hopes of a better view of her surroundings. A distant sound like rapids met her ears. No human sounds. What should she do?

Wiping her face with the back of her sand covered hand, only one option made sense. Pray. God, be merciful to Your servant. Help me. Lead Jonathan to me. Hebrews 11:6 came to mind — without faith it is impossible to please God. She must have faith.

A horse neighed above her. She looked up. An Indian brave looked out at the river. She fell prostrate on the sand, holding her breath. If captured, this Indian brave would make sure his new squaw would lose total identity to the lady brought up in a senator's mansion in New York State. The words of Apostle Paul whispered in her thoughts. By faith the harlot Rahab did not perish.

Jonathan couldn't wait to show Rachael what the Scotsman had given him for payment. He couldn't wait to see the surprise on her beautiful face. Even though beaver was highly prized in the fur market, as soon as the Scotsman drew out the blue fox pelt, he knew she would love it.

Riding into camp with McCray, he looked into their wagon. "Where's Rachael?"

McCray shrugged. "Maybe in Beth's wagon?"

Jonathan knocked on the wagon. No reply. He knocked again. "Rachael?" This time he knocked harder, impatient, "What's going on here? Beth, is Rachael in there?"

Silence. Finally a head popped out. Saul lifted his suspenders over his shoulders. "Rachael's making supper." He climbed down.

Beth's little head poked out of the opening. "Mr. Spiker give me your hand. Saul was asleep, but I remember Rachael saying she was going down to the river to fetch kindling and water… then I must have fallen asleep. I don't remember hearing her return."

Saul went to the kettle and sniffed. "The soup's done, but the fire is out."

"This isn't like Rachael." Jonathan gazed out toward the river, craning his neck to see past the bushes. "Where could she be?"

The noise of the squabbling men along the riverbed struck like an arrow right through his heart. He'd never forgive himself if something had happened to Rachael. He took a firmer hold on his rifle and ran the rest of the way toward the river and the clump of trees that hid from view what he feared most.

"There's our bucket." Saul, winded, grabbed it up.

Jonathan didn't care about the bucket. He shrugged off McCray's hand and stared back into Pierre's hate-filled eyes. "What have you done with my wife?"

The men at the river's bank looked up, smirked, and resumed their search.

Pierre chuckled then continued to nurse his cuts and bruises. A small group of mountain men hovered around the hilltop, looking into the water.

"There it is again. See, I told ya.'"

"Well, get it."

"Go on. You afraid of getting wet, Jake?"

"Thar's no use getting wet when that thing is floating straight to me, is thar."

A piece of cloth floated down the river. What could it be?

Pierre chuckled. "Too light to be a body —"

"Looks like her skirt. You're right Frenchy, she outsmarted us, but didn't I tell ya, I didn't see how she could swim with that thing tangling her legs."

Jonathan's pulse jumped at the man's words. *I should have never left Rachael alone in this heathen land.* He ran to the river. McCray and Saul grabbed his arms.

"Can you get it now, Jake?"

"Yeah."

If they hurt her, if they even scratched her with their dirty fingers… Jonathan fought against McCray's and Saul's arms. "Let me go!"

Jake plopped down on the bank and removed his moccasins. Rolling up his leather breeches, he waded into the river. "Brrr, colder than I imagined." With the stick he'd been whittling, he fished out the fabric. "Yeehaw! It's her skirt. I can only imagine…"

Jonathan made a lunge for Jake, dragging McCray with him.

"Hold up, Jonathan," McCray hissed between closed teeth. "There's too many of them to fight, and besides, we might need their help. Don't jump to conclusions."

Dragging the object from the river, Jake held the fabric to his nostrils. "It still smells of her —"

"You animals." Jonathan's knees went weak as a newborn baby's. "What did you do with my wife?"

Pierre got up from the bank, dusting off the seat of his breeches. "Pierre gets what he wants." His eyes grabbed their way into Jonathan's. "She needs a man like Pierre to awaken her needs." He chuckled deep down in his throat, and rubbed his stubby fingers in anticipation. "What a mademoiselle."

Jonathan lunged at Pierre. Tumbling to the shoreline, the cold river water splashed over their prostrate forms. Pierre plunged Jonathan's face into the water. Pierre's eyes stared down at him through the silt and foam, eyes full of hate and malice pushing Jonathan down, down into the depths of the frigid river. Jesus, give me strength.

Jonathan kicked, hitting Pierre in the groin, throwing him backward. Jonathan spurted to the surface, spit out a mouthful of water and gulped down air, then straddled Pierre like he would his horse, punching him over and over in his face. McCray grab Jonathan by his neck, hoisting him up. Saul grabbed Pierre, holding his arm behind his back.

"You holier-than-thou missionaries don't know how to turn the other cheek." Pierre coughed out his words spewing water and spit. "What's wrong? You don't read your Bible? You suppose to share what you have with others less fortunate. Pierre wanted to be first in the sharing, see?"

Jonathan lunged for him.

"Hang on there, Jonathan." McCray said. "This isn't going to do you or Rachael any good." McCray held firm. "The only way we're going to find Rachael is with God's help. I'm not planning on you muddyin' the waters to His grace now."

McCray's and Saul's prayers weren't going to bring Rachael back, especially with the heathen Pierre a stride away.

※ ※ ※

Rachael lay there, face down, playing possum. Maybe the Indian would ride off. Surely he had better things to do than get off his horse for some drowned woman. Hearing his moccasin-clad feet walking through the tall grass, she held her breath, bracing herself for the sudden thrust of a spear into her back or a knife to her scalp. Dear God, please help me. She pressed down into the soft bank. She didn't hear anything, maybe he had gone. Oh thank You, Jesus.

Then it came again, the shush, shushing of something, or someone walking toward the shoreline. Maybe he's thirsty, maybe looking for a drink of water and hadn't seen her. Her lungs burned for air, but she continued to hold her breath. If only she had died in that current. Better that than being kidnapped like Singing Dove. Oh dear, what had she endured? Jesus, give me wisdom and strength.

Rachael felt the toe of the brave's shoe in her ribs, turning her over. She looked up into his dark, curious eyes, his head tilted slightly to one side. Rising to a sitting position, she clutched her damp legs clad only in her petticoats. His bronze arm reached for her.

❊ ❊ ❊

"Jonathan, Rachael isn't a weak-kneed woman. Hasn't she proven that? Why look how she took down that buffalo?" Saul said.

Jonathan cupped his hands over his eyes, praying the vision of her nude, dead body wouldn't materialize. "You think she drowned?"

"Unlikely, to my way of thinking. The river isn't full and the current is manageable." McCray cleared his throat. "As I see it she got out of those skirts so she could swim to safety."

Jonathan looked up. "Then where is she?"

Silence followed.

Jonathan rubbed the back of his neck. "So what could have happened to her? You think some brave grabbed her?" His hopes and dreams were drowning in a sea of despair. He couldn't imagine his life without Rachael. She had become his reason to wake up, his excuse to rest his weary head next to hers and listen to her soft breath. "She's still a woman. She doesn't know how to handle herself out here with heathen men and her just in her undergarments."

Saul rested a comforting hand on Jonathan's shoulder. "Rachael's got grit. But we've got to find her fast."

"You mean before Pierre does." Rising from the bank, Jonathan grabbed his gun and looked toward the sun. "We've got about an hour before dusk. Let's get moving."

McCray winked at Saul. "I taught him everything he knows."

"Wait." Jonathan put a hand on Saul's chest. "McCray and I will look for Rachael. Look after Beth and Singing Dove. Could be some of those men will think the camp unguarded."

"Right, I'll head on back." A few steps up the hill, Saul turned, his face riddled with questions. "What do I tell Beth and Singing Dove?"

"Just tell them Rachael got lost and we're looking for her."

Jonathan and McCray spread out and searched the banks of the river for some clues. Jonathan wished Luke and Matthew were here, but he had given them leave to seek out their own tribes.

His lovely Rachael could be dead or in the hands of some heathen. The picture of Singing Dove slipping down off her pony's back and crumbling before his feet, swam before his eyes. *My Rachael, abducted by a brave, forced into slavery to do his devious bidding. God where are You? Why did You allow this to happen? What more do You want of us?*

Faith.

The words of Hebrews 12:3 came to his mind… "Consider him that endured such contradiction of sinners against himself, lest ye be wearied and faint in your minds."

McCray's hand slapped his shoulder. "Can't make out any more. It's getting too dark. Might as well return to camp."

"No, we're close. I can feel it… Look here, what's that?" Jonathan grabbed a piece of cloth tangled in some blackberry bushes.

"Is it Rachael's?"

Jonathan's breath came in spurts. "I believe so. Look, it's fresh. See, the bent twigs are still green. Who else could have come this way?" Jonathan knelt to the ground to look for footprints. The thorns from the blackberries clung to his flesh. *Rachael, how these thorns must* have pricked your soft, tender flesh. Dear Jesus keep her from harm.

McCray walked ahead of Jonathan. Jonathan stayed on his knees, tracing Rachael's exit from the river. Yes, she was crawling, crawling up this bank. Jonathan stopped. He touched the imprint where Rachael's body must have lain.

Jonathan looked at McCray, who nodded. They both spotted the imprint of moccasins and then the imprint of a set of large boots — Pierre's?

chapter twenty-two

*R*achael retched from the smell of the dirty cloth the Indian brave wrapped over her mouth. He had stripped it from her petticoat and it reeked with river water and mud. The rope around her neck dug into her soft skin. She wrestled with the rope that tied her arms behind her back. If she freed her wrists, she could escape.

As she staggered behind the Indian's pony, the sharp edges of the rocks pricked and cut her bare feet. She concentrated on the sun as it dipped below the mountains, determined to draw her thoughts away from the ache in her shoulders and arms and the pain of her bleeding feet. How would Jonathan find her in the night? Dear Jesus, where are You?

Rachael bowed her head in shame as she walked between rows and rows of traders and their booths. This must be the Rendezvous Jonathan hoped to avoid her seeing. Trappers stopped and gawked at her. She swallowed the bitter taste of captivity and scrunched her eyes shut, refusing her tears access. God, help Jonathan find me. She heard the traders yelling out their prices and the fur trappers arguing back. The proud brave stopped and jumped down off his spotted pony. Pulling on her neck rope, he shoved her toward a trader.

"What? You want a trade? For what?" A tall, overweight man gazed at her through small beady-black eyes.

She had seen these same French Canadian trappers from her perch on the wagon seat next to Jonathan. Perhaps this man had seen her sitting alongside her beloved. She tried to speak, but her words came out garbled.

His dirty hands grabbed her face. He turned her head from side to side. "Hard to tell in this light. What you do to her? She's muddy and cut up. Is she your slave?"

She shook her head, attempting to use her eyes to speak to him.

"White woman?"

She nodded.

"Where did you get her?"

The Indian pointed toward the river and then motioned with his hands.

"Oh, you think the river god drew her out for you to trade with. Well, I don't need trouble, especially now. Got all I can use." He nodded toward the tents. "Go on down that a way, heard tell there's a fancy-house, might be you can trade her for whiskey there."

Rachael mumbled beneath the gag, working her jaw, trying to get a word out — just one plea for help.

"I don't need the devil mad at me for helping you." He turned his head away, his voice a menacing growl. "I've got to look after my own hide and you know as good as I that the devil will leave his own alone, as long as you don't go crossing sides."

She glanced at the French Canadian then back at her Indian captor. Crossing sides?

She set her jaw and stood her full height. She'd cling to Jesus until her last breath. *God, I will never forsake You or my Savior Jesus like this man has.* Psalm 118 came vividly to her mind. *The LORD is on my side; I will not fear: what can man do unto me? ... therefore shall I see my desire upon them that hate me.*

The devil better hide if he knows what's good for him because God's elect have entered Satan's playground. Send out Your angels to do Your bidding, Lord, so we might perform Your miracles on the heathens that have desecrated the earth You created with Your holy hands.

She was snapped back into the reality of her predicament when the Indian pulled on her neck rope. She stumbled forward, yet managed to give the Frenchman one of her most uppity looks. She was sorry for him. Foolish man, she may be forced into captivity, but she was not destined for the fiery furnaces of eternal hell.

As the Indian zigzagged his pony through the crowd, she dragged one bleeding foot before the other. The rope chafed her bruised neck. Despite her pain, a hope of escape began to formulate. The Canadian said he didn't want to make the devil mad. She needed a man who didn't fear the devil. God, send me a deliverer. As You have said "For he shall deliver the needy when he crieth." Her toe hit a rock and she stumbled, struggling to stay erect. Night attempted to wrap dark fingers of hopelessness around her. She must cling to Jesus. Jesus, hear my cries. I beseech thee. Now was not the time for her to feel hopeless. But hopeful. Lord, I believe You have a plan for my safe escape. "Faith is the substance of things hoped for … without faith *it is* impossible to please *him*." She could barely see. Indian women walked beside her, curiosity painted across their faces. She shivered, then stumbled again. This time, her face hit the dirt with a thud. Dust filled her nostrils and she gasped for air.

"Hold up there. I say hold up!" Someone pulled on her rope and knocked the buck off his horse. She got to her knees in time to see the fist of her captor aimed to hit her. A shadowed form came between them.

A tall man, square of shoulder with wavy blond hair slashed through her rope. Cobb? The two men confronted each other. She saw the steel blades of knives shine in the moon's glow. She climbed to her feet and ran past the crowd that had formed around the two men.

Running toward a tent she ducked around it and bent down, hoping no one noticed her escape. She labored to breath. The pungent taste of the cloth binding her mouth licked at her tongue. Looking around for something sharp to cut her ropes, she crept toward a tree stump. A shiny hatchet gleamed in the moon's glow — an answer to prayer. Shifting it sideways, careful not to allow it to fall, she rubbed the coarse rope binding her wrists against the sharp metal.

The rope slipped from her wrists, and she jerked the gag off her mouth. She rubbed her jaw. Her mouth so dry, she couldn't cry out if she wanted to. The loud cries of the frontiersmen continued. The two men were still fighting. Unsure which way to go, some inner sense told her to stay away from camp, the trader's words echoing in her ears. She was in the devil's playground, with little hope of finding a deliverer in the midst of it.

❀ ❀ ❀

"Jonathan." McCray pointed to the unshod hooves of an Indian pony and the small bare feet of a woman following a few feet behind. Jonathan and McCray dismounted.

"Yep, he's got her and it looks like he's on his way to the Rendezvous." A horse galloped up. Jonathan turned in time to see the fringed buckskin of Singing Dove jump down from her pony and engulf Jonathan in her tight embrace.

McCray clicked his tongue to the roof of his mouth. "What are you doing here? Get back to camp."

"No, me help track." Placing a hand to her chest, Singing Dove implored, "Let me help, you helped me."

"She has a point. After all she knows more about these camps than we do," Jonathan told McCray. He turned to Singing Dove. "Where would an Indian take a white woman?"

"To trade for pony or whiskey, come. See I rode Whisper. We trade back."

"That makes sense. You want her to ride ahead?" McCray said.

"Will that be safe? Won't some buck try and claim Singing Dove?" Jonathan asked.

"Me not afraid." Singing Dove jumped up, kicked her mare into a lope, and was gone.

"Just what we need." McCray coughed as the dust clogged his nose. "Two woman out alone amidst of all these whooping Indians and drunken trappers."

Jonathan's eyes darted to the left and right of the wilderness trail. Whooping Indians, staggering mountain men, and spontaneous brawls filled the dirt path, making travel for Jonathan and McCray slow and treacherous. Mountain men skilled in the ways of the wilds, who had survived beasts and climate, couldn't beat two-legged varmints. Now he watched the hard work of these trappers whittled away from their grasp into whiskey. It could turn any man's adept skills of survival into slothful foolishnesses in a matter of two swallows.

Jonathan could read McCray's thoughts as clearly as if they were his own. How are we going to find Rachael?

Jonathan watched a pack of wolf-dogs pulling a heavy litter of furs. The whip of their master cracked like gunpowder on the dogs. "Get on, you mangy animals."

"You know, McCray, evil is not a matter of skin color, but about the color of our hearts, isn't it?"

"Amen. The only thing that can change the destiny of the human race is the knowledge of Jesus."

A group of Indians galloped through the crowd. Their rifles raised, their war whoops filling the ears of the onlookers. He'd seen at Council Bluffs the braves lying in squalor, drunk from the white man's whisky.

A little man accosted McCray, extending two bottles. "Whiskey? You men want whiskey?"

McCray waved the man aside. Everywhere both white men and Indians bickered in trade, adding to the bedlam. "Looks to me like the men and Indians are getting rowdier. Might be a wise move for you to ride back to camp and check on Beth and Saul."

"Me? It's my wife some Indian has his filthy hands on!"

"That's why it needs to be you. You're angry and not seeing things clearly. The short ride back to our camp will help you cool down."

Jonathan reined up his horse as two men in a fist fight plunged in the dirt before him. One man produced a knife from his boot and slashed out at the other. "That'll teach that injun some manners."

Jonathan turned his horse away. No one spoke. So this is what living in a godless environment was like — brutal savagery. Being a missionary would mean turning the other cheek and watching your backside all at the same time. This place was a nightmare beyond anything Rachael had ever encountered. He would never forgive himself if something should happen to her. He took a deep breath and slowly released it in an effort to calm his temper.

"Alright, McCray, I see your point. I'll head back to camp, tell Saul and Beth where we are, and meet you back here."

"Wait. Look there." McCray pointed toward a large tent.

Jonathan sucked in his breath. There, standing before a tent flap was a white woman with vibrant red hair dressed in doeskins.

McCray approached the woman and lifted the brim of his hat. "Ma'am, we're looking for a white woman, about five nine with curly reddish brown hair."

"We suspect she's been abducted by an Indian." Jonathan raised his hat. "Have you seen or heard of anyone?"

"Can't say I have. You been looking long?"

"Came today, ma'am, could you please keep an eye out?" McCray said.

"What's in it for me?"

"A good word to the Lord." Seeing her smirk, McCray pointed to Jonathan. "You might need the services of Dr. Wheaton before rendezvous is over."

The woman smiled. "Could be. But gold speaks a might better, if you get my drift. I'm not getting any younger."

McCray reached in his pocket and drew out a coin and handed it to her.

She bit down on it. Satisfied it was authentic, she pocketed it.

Jonathan rubbed his fingers along Singing Dove's pony as Beth stroked Whisper's grey mane, talking soothingly to the frightened animal. "I don't care. I'm going with you, Jonathan. Are you going, Mr. Spiker?"

Jonathan should have stayed with McCray. But how was he to know that Beth possessed an iron-clad will beneath that soft exterior?

"Why do you think a few whooping Indians are going to scare me? We will be up to our elbows soon with only these savages as you call them. We might as well get to know them. Now put my saddle on Whisper. She knows where her mistress is and she'll lead us to them, won't you, girl?"

Saul glanced at Jonathan and shook his head. "You are the stubbornest woman I ever did have the misfortune to —"

"What was that remark, Mr. Spiker?"

"Fortunate, I meant, I mean, I said your stubbornness is what I need to motivate me into action, Mrs. Spiker."

Jonathan chuckled, then coughed into his palm when Beth's sharp eyes landed on him. How did Saul manage to control her? He'd never seen this side of Beth before; it made a man downright uneasy.

"Yes, Mr. Spiker, I thought that is what you said." She smiled brightly back at Matthew and Luke. "Now, you sweet boys keep an eye on everything until we return."

"Me go." Matthew turned toward his brother. "Luke stay, watch."

"Oh, but, it has been arranged. I —"

"Me go." Luke smiled brightly, "Please and thank you, ma'am."

"Why, Luke, how nicely said. I thank our good Lord for these wonderful boys He sent to help us to our destination." She gathered up Whisper's reins. "I feel so much better about this trip."

Jonathan led them all back to the Rendezvous. A hush had settled over the area now that the sun had risen. Beth shook her head, clicking her tongue, pointing to the women.

Taos, native wives married to French Canadians, with their children by their side scurried like tumbleweeds, running with their empty buckets toward the river for water. They didn't look up at them as they passed, just hurried along.

"Their quietness speaks more than words. Poor little things. There is much work here for us to accomplish in a short amount of time."

Jonathan bit his lip, recalling how he thought about the women not being able to handle such blatant barbarism. Dear God, please keep Rachael in Your perfect peace. Reining up his horse he said, "Beth, you lead. Give Whisper her head."

"Go, Whisper, tell us where they are, dear beast, and go with God's direction." Whisper walked down the middle of the lane, passing tent after tent. Then the mare stopped before a larger one with a red foxtail attached to the flap's door.

"This is where I left McCray. Now where do you suppose he is?"

"Good, Whisper." Beth gave the horse a gentle pat on her neck.

"Hello in there." Jonathan yelled.

No reply. Jonathan motioned for Saul to circle the tent. Saul jumped down from his horse, and motioned for Matthew and Luke to follow.

A red-haired woman emerged from the tent. "Closed. Can't you see that red tail? Git." Blinking in the bright light, she held up her hands against the sun.

Beth smiled politely back. "We came for our friends, Singing Dove and the Reverend McCray."

"Not here."

Jonathan frowned. "I was here just forty minutes ago with the Reverend."

"And you have our little Singing Dove as well." Beth leaned forward. "I might as well tell you, you'd better produce them."

The woman rested her arms on her generously rounded hips. "What are you going to do about it?"

Jonathan started to speak, but Beth held up her hand. "Stay here and sing hymns. Ever heard of water baptism?"

"What?"

"Get ready to meet your Maker." Beth's eyes blazed. "That red hair of yours might turn the river as red as the Nile the day Moses brought the slaves out of Egypt. We'll find out soon enough. You see, God told me not to leave here until you produced the missionaries who would lead our Lord's creation out of the devil's hands."

"That holy stuff don't scare me."

"Good then you won't mind hearing a few hymns… Rock of ages…" Beth sang out louder than Jonathan had ever heard her speak. He didn't know she could carry a tune, let alone send his ears ringing from the sound.

"Wait," the woman protested.

Saul stormed around the tent and untied the flap.

A sickly aroma filtered through the opened flap. Jonathan recognized the odor of drunken stupor. He jumped down from his horse.

The red-haired woman moved her bulk in an attempt to block their way.

Saul tied the tent flap open. "There. That will let in the fresh air and morning light. Some of those people in there might be dead. Come on, Jonathan."

Muffled noises inside reached Jonathan's ears. The woman tried to block his way. "Leave."

"Not until our curiosity has been appeased." Jonathan struggled to control his temper with the woman. "Step aside."

He stepped over the bodies slumbering in their drunken world, the stench nearly unbearable, and looked into each face before going to the next. Two forms lay motionless. Dead? No, the whiskey was doing its work. A form in the corner of the tent rolled over, shouldering to a half-sitting position. "What you want?" a gruff voice asked.

"I'm looking for the person who owns a black and white paint."

"Wouldn't know, not mine." The man motioned with his head toward the corner of the tent. "Could be hers, I suppose."

Jonathan walked closer, bending over a figure folded in the far corner of the tent. "Singing Dove?" A girl he'd never seen before looked blankly at him and screamed.

"There, there, little one, you need not be frightened of me."

Saul picked up the little child and hurried outside, coughing.

Where could McCray and Singing Dove be? As if in answer to his question, Luke, McCray, and Singing Dove entered the tent.

"They tied up, in the woods," Luke said.

Jonathan coughed. "Get out of here before this stench makes us sick." They left the tent and joined Beth.

"Shame on you." Beth shook her head at the woman. "On top of all your other sins, you are a liar, too?" Her voice brimmed with distaste. "Do you have any idea where you are heading to?"

"I hope the opposite direction of you," retorted the woman.

"Well, you are right on that account." Beth smiled at the girl cuddled in Saul's arms. "And who might this lovely lady be?"

"That's my child. Unhand her."

The little girl cringed, placing her small arms around Saul's neck. Saul patted her shoulders comfortingly. "There, there, is this your mother?"

The girl shook her head.

"Another lie." Beth's look swept over the woman. "My, my, you make a habit of disobeying the Ten Commandments. What do you have to say about this?"

"I say, get out, and take the brat."

McCray felt in his pockets. "Not until you give me back what belongs to me."

"Here." She tossed his change purse on the ground and the coins she had stolen from him. Then tilted her head and screeched out a laugh. "Forget looking for that white woman. She's long gone."

"What do you mean?" Jonathan grabbed her by the shoulders and shook her. "Where's Rachael? What have you done with my wife?"

The eerie noise erupted from the red-headed woman's mouth again.

"So you have sold your soul to the devil." Beth climbed down from Whisper and walked toward her.

"Get away. I'll cast a spell on you like I did to the Indians who thought they could take me captive."

"A spell?" Beth threw out her hands toward the woman. "No dear one, you cannot cast a spell on us. You see, we have Jesus. We are temples of the Holy Spirit. Why don't you try on our Spirit of Peace? God sent his only Son to save you, only you."

"Get away. Don't touch me!"

"Tell me, where is our dear Rachael? What have you done with her?"

"Don't have. I, I…" The red-headed woman whimpered like a child beneath Beth's gentle hands, as Beth stroked the woman's tears away, one by one. "Lord, lead this gentle woman back into the folds of Your loving grace. 'For God sent not his Son into the world to condemn the world; but that the world through him might be saved.'"

"God don't want me. I'm a sinner."

"He wants all His children, dear one. For Jesus says in the Holy Scriptures, 'I came not to call the righteous, but sinners to repentance.'"

Big weepy tears washed down the woman's cheeks. "I wish I knew where this Rachael be." She turned and peered inside the flap. "See the man lying in the corner? He came late last night laughing about seeing a white woman bound around the neck, hauled behind a horse by some Indian brave."

Jonathan stormed into the tent, picked up the man and carried him out.

"Be of good cheer, sister, your faith in Jesus Christ has made you well!" Beth hugged the woman. "Come, sister, let us go to the river and wash away our sins."

"Yes, yes I'll go. Thank you for caring… about me." She turned to the little girl, who nodded at her. "Can my granddaughter join us?"

Beth brought her hands together in celebration. "Why, of course." She bent down and looked into the little girl's eyes. "Dear one, do you believe that Jesus Christ is the Son of God?"

The little girl nodded. "I prayed Jesus would send someone to help my grandmother."

※ ※ ※

Rachael huddled within a small cave along the river's edge to wait for daylight. The trappers and Indians were more interested in their gambling, trading, and whiskey to come look for her.

Surely Jonathan had found her tracks in the dirt, walking behind that Indian's pony. She peeked out of the cave. Daylight. Beautiful sunlight. She let her eyes adjust and listened. A crowd of people drew near the river's edge.

"Shall we all sing, 'Rock of Ages'? Who knows it? Now don't be shy. Brother Saul, why don't you lead?"

That's Beth!

Rachael made her way out of the tiny cave and stepped into the water. Overhead some men spoke in low voices. She stopped. Waited. Silence. She knelt down and crawled toward the beach, her hands and knees wet with the frothy water. She shivered, but not from cold. She sucked in her breath, trying not to make any noise. Slowly, she made her way toward Beth, toward safety. Oh, Jonathan, where are you? Careful, only a little farther —

"Ahhh," she screamed. Someone wrenched her to her feet by the hair. A hairy arm brushed the soft flesh of her bare shoulder and knotted a bandanna around her eyes. Another pair of hands grabbed her waist. Hard, calloused fingers dug into her exposed abdomen. An odor of bear grease, alcohol, and the man's unwashed, filthy body assaulted her nostrils. A third grabbed her wet legs and lifted her clear off the ground. "Let me go. Jonathan! Jonathan!" She kicked with all her strength and hit the man's arm.

"Ouch. You white wench." The man's sour breath and foul-smelling clothes were no better than the other man's. "I'll teach you to kick me."

She sucked in a breath of fresh air and screamed. "Jonathan, help!"

One of them placed his dirty fingers across her mouth. She shook her head, fighting the man's bear-like grip. Someone grabbed her arms and tied them behind her back. She caught a whiff of buffalo and whiskey. She bit down hard. "Ouch! Mon chérie."

"Pierre?"

Another rag covered her mouth. Oh, no, not that again. She shook her head and kicked harder. The sound of horses running through the weeds bordering the river's edge renewed her spirit. She kicked again. The captor released her legs and she heard him splash into the river. Her second captor threw her to the ground. She fell with a thump. The boot of the foul-smelling man forced her body into the weeds, as if attempting to hide her from her would-be rescuers. Oh, Jesus, please bring Jonathan. The sound of the horses drew nearer.

"How dare you touch my wife!"

Jonathan! Rachael heard the grunts and groans of the ensuing fight, but could Jonathan fight off all three? As the fist fight continued she felt someone remove the bandanna from her mouth and eyes and looked up to see McCray. He untied the rope around her wrists and helped her up.

Three masked men ran into the river, staggering and cussing up a storm as they fled. Jonathan started after them. McCray caught his arm and jerked his head toward Rachael.

She shivered uncontrollably beneath their stares that felt like ice-cold daggers on her skin and covered her bare legs as best she could with her tattered petticoat. Her wet hair dripped chilling water down her chest, shoulders, and back. Cringing from the look of pity in McCray's and Jonathan's eyes, she dipped her glance downward, and gathered the tattered remnants of her dignity.

"Rachael." In one swift stride, Jonathan caught her to him. He removed his buckskin jacket and wrapped it around her shoulders. His arms closed around her like an eagle would its babies.

"Jonathan, Oh Jonathan I'm —"

"Oh, my love." He kissed her muddied brow, her tear-stained cheeks, and the throbbing rope burn on her bleeding neck. She clung to him, her tears wetting his shirt.

"I wish I could erase the hours of torment you've endured." Lifting her chin, he smiled reassuringly into her eyes. His lips hovered over hers, caressing hers softly. "My beautiful Rachael," Jonathan whispered, holding her close. "Thank God Beth chose to baptize that woman, or we would not have heard your screams."

"Truly God heard my prayers. Who but God would have known to put you there at this moment in time?"

The noise of approaching horses brought a hot flush to her cheeks. Who could this be, someone else to pity her? Thrusting her arms into Jonathan's jacket sleeves, she drew it close across her bosom. So this is how it felt to return from captivity.

Singing Dove touched Jonathan's arm. "Jonathan, did those men hurt you?" Singing Dove stared at Jonathan in awe.

Rachael swallowed and looked away. Singing Dove always found a way to redirect her husband's attention to herself.

"Rachael, are you all right?" Saul's eyes held only concern.

Jonathan stood there in his gathered poet shirt with his arms crossed, displaying his muscular chest. He looked rugged and regal. Her brother Mark had been right. Jonathan was a man's man — and a woman magnet. Oblivious to Singing Dove, he was too absorbed with frowning back at Saul.

"I'm fine now."

"Nothing or no one can take away your spirit, Rachael. Not Indians, trappers, or lumberjacks." Saul said. "You proved that today."

"All I proved is that I need to be more careful. None of us knows what lies around the bend of a wilderness trail. Only with God's guidance will we survive."

"But our character is our own, Rachael." Saul's eyes shone into hers. "And you have shown your fortitude and spirit admirably this day."

Jonathan turned Rachael toward him and forced her to look at him, then whispered, "For once Saul and I agree. Yes, strength and honor are your clothing, my spirited wife."

McCray grabbed Saul by the sleeve of his coat. "Come on. Let's help your wife with the baptisms and give these newlyweds a chance to get reacquainted."

chapter twenty-three

rossing Bear Creek proved treacherous. Jonathan hadn't expected to encounter such a fast moving current, nor had he expected large boulders jutting out at all angles that could trap wagons and cattle. But that was behind them now.

Jonathan stopped to check his exhausted mules' and horses' hooves. Surely the terrain would soon become easier, the animals needed a reprieve. Traveling had grown more mountainous with every foothold. The trail they followed seemed nothing more than a footpath winding up the side of a steep mountain. So steep, it was difficult for horses to maneuver and their wagon had been upset twice. Worse, the soles of his horses and mules had become tender from stone bruises.

"Jonathan, how are the cattle doing?" Rachael said.

"Remarkably well, I can't believe our milk cows are still giving milk. What with traveling from sunup to nearly sunset or after, they have little time to forage for food."

"At least we have food. What about our meat. Do we have enough of that dried buffalo meat you purchased from the Indians?"

He smiled. Rachael had become a good helpmate to him, reminding him of their needs. "We should be arriving at Fort Hall soon."

Since Rachael's abduction, their relationship had grown stronger. A new thought shuffled forward like a warrior with his arrow drawn. She needed him. Perhaps it was silly on his part, but he felt he'd proven himself to her. He frowned, remembering Saul's continual praises of

Rachael's character. He felt his temper rising.

"Jonathan." Rachael leaned forward and whispered, "Matthew and Luke appear most upset since we crossed the river."

He came back to reality with a jolt. "That's because we're in Blackfoot country." Jonathan narrowed his eyes and scanned the trees and rocks above. "I fear we might lose our Indian help. Not Matthew or Luke, but most everyone else."

"Why?"

"The Blackfeet are vengeful. Because of their hatred for the white man they will torture and kill our Indians unmercifully." Jonathan glanced at her to see what effect his words would have. "They will make us into slaves whose only reprieve is death."

"No windows, except a square hole in the roof. How can they stand not seeing the sunlight day after day and month after month?" Rachael's mouth gaped open as she stood staring at the hewn logs and roofs covered with mud. The peaked chimneys of Fort Hall looked ominous.

"They look out the bastion." Jonathan said.

"The what?"

"The bastion." Jonathan shrugged. "It's like a port hole on a ship, only this hole is just large enough for guns. McGregor did a fine job in equipping his fort."

"So that's why these buildings are all enclosed by a log wall, and the chimneys peaked —in case they are attacked by hostile Indians." Rachael glanced around at the thirty-some Indians that walked within the fort. "But what about these Indians, are they peaceful? There are certainly enough of them here."

"Usually. But the fort is in Blackfoot country, and the Blackfoot never stay friendly for long. That's why I have to leave you here."

"What?" She clutched Jonathan's arm tightly. "Surely you are joking. I hardly know when you're being serious or not."

"I have to leave, darling. I have to make sure the trail we plan to take through the Rockies is passable. Rock slides, snow, these things can change the direction of our travel. There isn't any way around it. You'll be safe here. Do not leave the fort."

"But, Jonathan, we just arrived. Can't you allow yourself a night of rest and leave in the morning?" With Jonathan by her side, the fort was a castle, but with him gone, it became her prison.

"Now, Rachael. We must cross the Rockies before winter arrives. Time is of the essence." Placing his forefinger beneath her face, Jonathan tipped her chin and gazed into her eyes. For a long while neither spoke. "God will not allow anything to happen to His missionaries, and we'll be back in three days, at the most four. If we do not come back in four, I promise you can send Beth after us."

Rachael's laugher bubbled forth. "Who would have ever suspected that gentle Beth would become such a little tornado here in the wilderness?"

"Not Saul, to be sure." Jonathan chuckled. "I get the feeling he is trying to prove himself in her eyes, though such a thing is not required. Beth respects everything he is about. She is just more outspoken when it comes to the Holy Spirit."

"Will Saul be going with you?" Rachael hated it when Jonathan wasn't near. They had become a team, one looking after the other.

Jonathan's eyes turned hard as flint. "No, he will remain to look after you and Beth."

Rachael gave a sigh of relief. "Well, that's good. At least Beth and I will have some protection." Seeing his suddenly stony countenance, she feared this secret he refused to share would weaken and destroy what they'd worked hard to attain. "Jonathan, take me with you. I am nothing without you and I prefer to share the danger with you. Haven't I proven that I am capable?"

"Is that what you want? To be capable, as you put it?"

"Jonathan, I don't understand you at times." She sighed. "Is Singing Dove coming?"

"She is coming as an interpreter. The scout of this fort, McGregor, is coming because he knows the mountains like the back of his hand."

"Of course." Rachael cast her eyes downward. She had known the answer before she even asked it. Please, Jesus, rid me of this jealousy for Singing Dove.

Singing Dove walked forward, her tiny feet barely making an imprint in the dirt. Petite and slender, she moved with the grace of a wilderness creature. Rachael felt like an ogre by comparison.

Unlike Isabella, Singing Dove was kind and considerate toward her. Singing Dove knew through her years of captivity how a woman can feel degraded in a few hours of servitude. Still, that did not dissipate the knowledge that she adored Jonathan. Her liquid eyes stared into Jonathan's. "I am ready," she said, the soft melody of her voice an enchanting blend of Indian and English woven together.

Rachael wished she could make her voice soft, not harsh and opinionated. Slow and mellow, not quick and impatient. She had tried to change. Oh how she had tried, but her anxiousness made her rush ahead of her intentions, causing her to appear boisterous and demanding.

"Mrs. Wheaton, how are you?"

"Very nicely said, Singing Dove." Rachael smiled and turned to see what Jonathan thought of Singing Dove's diction. She had asked to learn proper English, and Rachael enjoyed her gentle spirit. Jonathan hadn't noticed. Singing Dove noticed Jonathan's inattention, too. Rachael patted her on the arm.

A lump as big as a peach seed formed in Rachael's throat as she watched Jonathan, McCray, McGregor, and Singing Dove prepare to ride out of the fort. She bit her lip to keep from crying.

Beth hugged her shoulders. Oh, sweet Jesus, will I ever be able to console instead of always being the one consoled?

"Only forty-five more days left before getting to Umatilla Valley. With this being the second week of August that's a good thing." Beth raised her arms toward the rustic buildings. "And we've got a roof over our heads instead of that flapping canvas. Rachael, our heavenly Father has been good to us throughout our journey."

"Yes, and throughout our expedition, you have been the constant source of my strength." Rachael sighed. "I set out to be like my heroine Narcissa, but I have come to realize I can no more be like her than I can be like you, dear Beth. The Holy Spirit has made me content to be who I am." A *married* spinster who does not know a man's love.

Beth watched as Rachael kept her eyes fixed on Jonathan riding out the stockade gates. "We must put our past desires away and look forward to the days ahead. They will fly by like the wild geese above."

Rachael laughed, listening to the hubbub overhead as a flock of geese flew south.

"Those are all the pretty words I can think of right now. Come, I want to show you something." Beth gathered Rachael's arm and cupped it beneath hers.

Rachael took one last look at Jonathan before he disappeared behind the closing stockade gates, then allowed Beth to lead her toward the cabins.

Beth pointed to the log stools and seats. "Aren't they adorable? And comfortable, too."

"And much better than sitting on dirt." Rachael laughed as Beth sat down, sighing over the cushion that adorned the wooden seat.

"The buildings at Fort William were somewhat the same. But they had windows and we had chairs made of buffalo skins. Here we have stools to sit on, but they are quite comfortable. My, how resourceful these frontiersmen are." Beth shrugged her small shoulders then tugged at a tendril of hair. "I think we should plan a special dinner for the men's return, Rachael. There is plenty of food here to make it a feast."

"I heard one of the fur men say we were short of meat."

"Yes, but one only needs a bit of meat when you have an assortment of fresh vegetables to pick from. Did you happen by their garden brimming with corn, turnips, onions, and even a few peas?"

"Peas? My, how long has it been since I've tasted one."

"The varmints consider them very delectable, too. They have consumed them even before they are fully ripe." Beth laughed. "I really do not think the men folk realize how starved we are for the things we left behind." Beth shuddered. "Of course, I cannot speak for you, but I could do without buffalo meat for a lifetime. That meat has never been a delicacy to me, not like sweet potatoes, black eye peas, and cornbread."

"I agree, Beth. The thought of peas and cornbread makes my mouth water. Did the mice get them all?"

"I confiscated a few from the hungry little varmints, see." She held out her apron pockets. "This is what is left after the mice have had their breakfast."

There was enough for a small helping. Rachael scooped them up, placed them in a bowl and sealed the top.

Beth picked up her sewing, her head bent, her fingers flying, working at mending a hole in one of Saul's go-to-meeting coats. "What do you think of the Reverend McCray and Singing Dove?" Her expression held a calculating keenness.

Rachael stirred uncomfortably in her chair. "I like the Reverend. Jonathan thinks highly of him, giving him the credit for getting us across the plains safely. As to Singing Dove, she is willing to learn the white woman's ways. I think there is hope for her to meet a God-fearing man and settling down. Is that the way you see it?"

"She is willing to conform." Beth set down her sewing for a moment. "Only, I fear the Indian influence might keep her to come fully to the Lord."

"It will feel strange not to be traveling with the large caravan of trappers." Rachael hid her expression from the keen eyes of her friend. "I had hoped we might have converted a few to our Lord."

"We must not worry about that. God has His plan, and we have done our best to set a good example."

"Yes, we must present good examples." Rachael bent over her sewing. This was the first time since leaving Liberty that she and Beth had the privacy to discuss women things. Should she reveal her suspicions regarding Jonathan and Singing Dove? Rachael felt her heart would explode if she did not ask Beth her opinion.

"Beth, do you think Jonathan is in love with Singing Dove?" Rachael could trust Beth to understand and not think the less of her for asking.

"I suppose he does. The Reverend told me Jonathan killed a man for her, though it was self defense. The Indian brave swore he'd kill Jonathan anyway. So he really didn't have a choice."

Rachael's heart skipped a beat. Beth felt it too, that Jonathan was in love with Singing Dove.

Beth stopped her sewing. "I don't know why they didn't give that girl a Christian name. They gave those two Indian boys Christian names. It doesn't seem right to me to be calling her Singing Dove when she's white, does it?"

"Jonathan says she'll not answer to anything else. She is so lovely, so petite, and she has such a sweet way of talking."

"Indeed." Beth smiled. "She is beautiful in every way but one. She needs Jesus to make her complete."

Beth's honesty was shredding Rachael's insides, one piece at a time. She knew Singing Dove needed Jesus. Once Singing Dove accepted Jesus Christ, what would stop Jonathan from desiring her over — I cannot say it. I cannot think it.

Rachael tumbled in a heap to the floor and knelt before Beth. "I'm terribly jealous over her and Jonathan," she blurted and buried her head in Beth's lap, sobbing.

Beth's fingers lifted Rachael's head. "Rachael, your spirit is as gentle as a snow-white dove's and Jonathan loves you dearly. You are his wife. No woman could ever be lovelier to her husband than you to your Jonathan."

Tears streamed down Rachael's cheeks. Doubt had captured her heart. "How can you be so sure?"

"Because I have walked through my own doubts." Beth's eyes grew teary from sympathy, or was it something else? "I can tell you life is our best teacher and experience our best weapon when explaining the healing power of Christ's grace and love."

Rachael recalled their voyage on the steamer to St. Louis. Beth's miscarriage. Rachael felt her cheeks grow warm. Would Beth suspect her thoughts?

"You knew the child I had carried could not have been conceived by Saul. Yet you never condemned, never treated me differently. That's when I knew." Beth smiled.

"Knew what?"

"You were born to a genteel family of high society. You were taught to look down on women of ill repute, of people not born to your station in life. I knew this about you, from Saul. I, on the other hand, knew well Saul's predicament, much like my own."

"You?"

"A member of my own family… had his way with me… by force. Saul was my only defendant. He took me as his wife before I lost the baby and gave the child his name. Without repudiation, without hesitation."

Beth bent over her sewing, her tears wetting the pants she mended. "I like to think that if God had not seen fit to take my innocent baby, he would have grown up knowing he was loved by my Saul, just as if he was Saul's child."

"You are always so cheerful, even in your infirmities. You are the glue, dear Beth, that holds our little missionary caravan together. And you are the one who has endured the most."

Beth's tears formed pools in her large doe-like eyes. "Through the darkest pitfalls, our Savior's light shines through. Jesus never intended that to happen to me, but He did care for me through the ordeal. I understand what a sinner feels like. So alone. The man that did that to me took his life. His guilt killed him, as Satan hoped."

Beth looked out through the open door at the sky, blue and inviting. "I will never allow that to happen again, so help me God, if there is a chance for me to lead that person to Jesus. This life is but a link to the chain leading to eternity."

Beth wiped her nose. "I've got to get these knees darned before Saul returns from the trappers' bunkhouse. He wanted to see if some would attend morning services tomorrow. You know how he is about his clothes." Beth bit off the thread and rethreaded her needle. "Why don't you make sure that room of yours is ready for Jonathan's return? I think it's high time for a soft bed and well… all the comforts availing a married couple." Beth met Rachael's gaze and gave her a wink.

Rachael blushed at her frank words. "Yes, I can do that." She felt the weight of her jealousy leave her shoulders. Beth had known, yet had not judged her. Rachael jumped up and kissed Beth's forehead. "I'll make Jonathan a feast he'll not forget. Remember those blackberry bushes we passed? They are but a mile from the fort."

chapter twenty-four

Rachael worked nonstop on their little quarters for three days. Now on the fourth day, Jonathan had still not arrived. The only thing left to do to complete their celebration was prepare the blackberry pie. This must be the reason for Jonathan's delay. Though Rachael had promised Jonathan to stay within the fort, surely God was giving her His blessings to proceed on this venture. Beth was hesitant. Rachael assured her she would only go halfway down the mountain. Jonathan said he would return the way he left and so retrace his steps to mark the trail. She was likely to meet him on her return. Wouldn't Jonathan be surprised?

Pierre was happy to accompany her. Saul had introduced Pierre to John Bunyan's *Pilgrim's Progress* and showed him the prayer "God be merciful to me a sinner... magnify thy grace in the salvation of my soul." Since then, Pierre had asked her countless questions about Jesus. She knew she should be happy about Pierre's appetite for God's Word, but she could not release her misgivings. She thought he'd been one of the three men who tried to abduct her at the river. He denied it adamantly.

"Please allow me to chaperone Mrs. Wheaton to her little berry patch," Pierre said.

The soldier looked from Rachael, then back to Pierre. "Only if Mrs. Wheaton agrees."

"Is there anyone else?" Rachael asked.

"Ma'am, we are short of men. There has been an Indian uprising to the north," the soldier replied.

Rachael clutched at her collared dress, recalling the stories Jonathan told of how the Blackfoot treat their captives. "My husband and his party — are they safe?"

"Yes, ma'am, as safe as can be expected."

Dear Lord, please send Your angels to protect and guide them.

"Mon chérie, you must not worry. God will protect them, oui?"

Pierre's voice grated on her nerves like trail dust on her teeth. But the only way she was going to get blackberries was to accept his offer. "Wait here. I'll tell Beth where we are going and get my basket and shawl."

"Oui, oui, mon chérie."

She dashed into the cabin and grabbed her shawl, basket, and a knife to cut the stems if needed. Testing its sharpness, she wrapped it in some rags, shoved it to the bottom of her basket and hurried out to the waiting wagon. As she approached Pierre, he stuck out his arm and helped her climb into the buckboard.

The beauty of the landscape created a sonnet of praise in her heart as they past Big Wood River. She smiled at Pierre's jokes on more occasions than not. Pierre smiled and asked questions about God the Father and Jesus His Son. She should be glad, not skeptical. After all, hadn't Saul won their first convert to the Lord? Oh, how great is our Savior!

While Rachael hunted berries, Beth would be preparing a delicious vegetable casserole. They had acquired a little venison and fish to go with their dried buffalo, and the mountain bread they relished would grace their table as well. Rachael bubbled with happiness. This would be like a Thanksgiving dinner after months of coffee, beans, and buffalo meat. She had enough time to pick the berries and make the pie before Jonathan arrived that evening.

"So it has been your lifelong desire to teach the Indians about Jesus?"

"Yes, and the Lord opened up the doors to my dreams."

Pierre's eyes glistened like coal. "It is not like you think, chérie. These Indians have their own religion. They have their medicine men. This heaven you speak of is a place they call their happy hunting grounds. No different."

"Jesus is different from their gods. I do look forward to heaven. I sometimes wonder if I might get there before my father and mother. Life in the wilderness is unpredictable."

Jonathan's handsome face came before her. How she longed to have him here sitting beside her so she could feel his arms around her. The days had been empty without him. She had never felt such love for a man before. God wouldn't allow anything to happen to Jonathan, would he? After all, he was much too valuable to the expedition, and to her.

Pierre pulled up the horses. He climbed down and walked around to help her down with her basket. She accepted his extended hand. "Thank you, Pierre, I will hurry."

His dark eyes avoided hers.

Before long she had her basket brimming with the succulent fruit. Walking out of the patch, she stopped to remove the thorns from her skirt. "I am finished, Pierre. We can return now." Silence met her ears. "Pierre?"

His arm wrapped around her waist as his free hand covered her mouth. The bear grease smell — it *was* him! She kicked him hard in the shin and elbowed him in his gut.

"Oww!" he yelled as he released his grip on her.

She screamed and the echo reverberated through the mountainside. "What are you doing? This is no way to act."

"Ah, mon chérie, I could only admire you from a distance. Now, see what your God has given me? An opportunity to feel your silky flesh. Pierre is patient man when he stalks the deer. So with the woman, too."

"Well, I have very little patience, myself." She backed away from him, looking about for a means of escape. A small brook lay to her right.

"No river here. Yes, mon chérie is afraid, soon she will be crying out my name — in ecstasy. Pierre much better kisser than your husband. You see."

"Never." The wagon was a distance away. Pierre had planned his attack well.

"Ah, my little bunny, looking so frightened. Have no fear. Pierre knows a woman's needs. Consider this a little payment for this afternoon of berry picking." He motioned with his fingers. "Come to me.

You will enjoy Pierre. He has a way with the women. Your screams will turn to squeals of joy."

He advanced on her, like a cat on a mouse. Her hand dipped into the basket and her fingers grasped the knife she'd brought. She was not helpless this time. "Really, Pierre, this is foolish. You know you do not want to harm me."

"Harm? No, no, I would not harm you. After all, I am Frenchman." Thumping his chest, he shrugged. "Enough of talk."

He was on her before she could scream, but she was ready. She slashed at his arm. He drew back and snarled.

"You will pay dearly, mon chérie." He lunged at her again, slapping her with his large hand. She staggered. He lunged again, and she slashed him a second time.

"Ow! You heathen."

"You're the heathen." She dropped her basket, lifted her skirts, and ran toward the wagon.

Pierre ran after her. She dodged him, avoiding his arms and bolted away.

The thundering hoof beats of a horse echoed in her ears. With the sun in her eyes she couldn't see… A man jumped off his horse and wrestled Pierre to the ground. They tussled round and round in the grass. Rachael made good her escape. "Help me. Someone help me. Oh, dear Jesus, help me!"

"Rachael!"

She stopped.

"Jonathan?" She stumbled forward, her hand across her forehead, shielding her eyes from the sun's rays. Is it, could it be — "Jonathan!" She ran to his outstretched arms and melted within their sheltering comfort, weeping. "Jonathan!" Tears ran down her cheeks. His eyes filled with tears for her. He caressed her face. She flinched, but did not draw away.

"You have a welt there. Did he strike you?"

"Yes. I… I was going to make you a blackberry pie. I, I'm sorry."

The thundering hoof beats of more horses rang like a bell in the quiet afternoon. "There, Rachael, you're safe now." He glanced up.

"McCray, go on ahead. Take Pierre back with you. Rachael and I will come in the buckboard."

Pierre moaned as McCray got him to his feet. "I don't know what happened. I would never harm Mrs. Wheaton. We were merely playing a little game. Hide and seek, I think. Is this not what you named it, Mrs. Wheaton?" He shrugged his shoulders. "A misunderstanding. Mrs. Wheaton misunderstood Pierre. Pierre forgives her."

"Misunderstood? Jonathan, surely you cannot believe him over me."

Jonathan held up his hand. Rachael swallowed the bitter taste of Pierre's deceit, restraining her sobs.

"Go, Pierre, never approach Mrs. Wheaton again."

Jonathan guided Rachael into the buckboard, then returned to pick up her basket and grab the berries that had fallen out. He handed the basket to Rachael, got in the wagon and took up the reins. He ached to stroke her tousled curls and kiss away the smudges of dirt on her soft cheeks, but Pierre's innuendos were too fresh in his mind. Rachael's welt and swollen eye were convincing evidence Pierre was lying, but it did not erase the fact Rachael had come here, alone, with a man like Pierre. What did she think would happen?

His heart broke into a thousand pieces, seeing her berry stained hands folded in her lap. A deep groan fought its way through him, begging for release. Like a child who had been bullied, she was trying not to cry and act brave enough to warrant praise and not criticism for her actions.

"I believed Pierre when he said he was saved." Rachael swiped her nose. "And… I told Beth it must be God's plan for me to pick blackberries. I'm still such a babe in Christ. Will I ever stop seeking *my* desires and reasoning it is God's will that I satisfy my own whims?"

"We are both guilty of that." He patted her hand. "Still, you are closer than I to becoming what the apostle Paul strived for Christians to become."

Unlike him, Rachael believed in the inherent good of people, expecting God's love to shed His light over mankind. Jonathan set his jaw into a rigid line, not wanting to understand. Not wanting his love for her growing deeper. Innocence like Rachael's could get her killed.

"This land is too primitive for you, Rachael. You need to be where you can go and pick wildflowers and berries to your heart's content without being threatened."

Rachael snuggled next to Jonathan, resting her head on his shoulder. "I was threatened in New York. Remember, you had to save me then, too."

A chuckle escaped without his consent. "So I did."

"Jonathan, I always hated being tall instead of petite like Isabella or Singing Dove, but Jonathan." She wrapped her arm around his and held him close. "If I was like those girls, I could never have fought off Pierre's advances."

"What are you saying?" His emotions swelled out of control. "You didn't expect that?"

"Heaven's no." Her lips puckered downward, her expression horrified at the thought. "I didn't want to go with him. But he was the only one that could come and the soldier wouldn't let me go out alone. I wanted those blackberries." She pushed her bottom lip in thought, like a child would do to explain her way out of a predicament. "Oh, I know I have gotten myself into quite a few… predicaments. But you've got to stop thinking the worst of every situation I get into. It's me, Jonathan. Take me as I am." Holding up her basket, she smiled. "They're bruised, but I think I can still manage to make you a pie."

He laughed. Dear Lord, how can I possibly stay angry at such a woman? "I noticed a slash on Pierre's forearm. The only other female I know who could do what you did would be Singing Dove."

"Pierre planned this. I should have realized he wasn't being honest. He asked me about Jesus and about our missionary work. I thought he had accepted our Savior. That he'd become Saul's first convert."

Jonathan frowned into her large, moist eyes. "You could never convert him, Rachael. The only thing he desires is you." He pulled her away and held her shoulders, then glanced at her downcast face. "You've got to stop being so naïve."

Rachael looked up with eyes that bespoke their love for him. The soft, yielding flesh beneath his grip overwhelmed his senses. His breath caught in his throat, but he managed to stutter out, "Rachael, I'm going on to Umatilla Valley, but you will be returning east with the next fur caravan."

chapter twenty-five

*J*onathan fastened his eyes on his plate. He blamed himself for not courting Rachael like he should have. He could only imagine what her delight and willingness would have been had he proposed to her properly. Would he have seen desire in her eyes? He would never know.

"Rachael worked for days sweeping and washing down the cabin." Beth's glance darted from Jonathan to Rachael. "Removed every cobweb off the walls and ceiling, washed your bed linens, and aired out the feather pillows. And look at this beautiful bouquet she made."

"Rachael has a soft spot for wildflowers." Saul smiled across the table at her. "I remember that dandelion hat you wore to the revival. Remember, Rachael?"

Rachael looked up. "Yes, I remember it well. That was when I learned about you wanting to be a missionary. Isn't it surprising how our Lord works out our dreams and His plans so beautifully?"

Jonathan stabbed his fork into his meat. So it was Saul that Mrs. Rumpson referred to. What was it she called him — 'smitten' wasn't that the word she had used?

"You've got yourself a hard worker in Rachael." Beth coughed, choking on her food when Jonathan's stormy eyes swept hers. Beth wiped her nose with her handkerchief. "I declare my nose wants to run like a sugar maple."

"Are you feeling any better now that you rested?"

"Yes, thank you for asking, Reverend McCray. But I'll feel much better once we arrive at our valley home, and Rachael and I can set up our housekeeping."

Jonathan looked up. Had Rachael confided in Beth about him wanting her to go back East? Was that why she mentioned their Oregon home? Was that why the air seemed filled with tension or was that his own discomfort pricking him?

"Your pie's delicious, Rachael." Saul looked at Jonathan. "She got the crust done to a perfect light brown color, in spite of that old stove. I don't know how she managed."

"I nearly burnt our bread." Beth wiped her mouth with one of the napkins she had removed from her trunk.

"Beth, the bread is done just the way I like it. I was afraid I might have put too much sugar in the pie."

Saul sent an encouraging grin. "It's perfect. Everything is perfect, Rachael."

Of course it was. Jonathan glanced at Beth. He and Beth had more in common than he realized.

Rachael bent her head close to her plate, as if to hide her black eye. Still, it was hard for Jonathan not to admire her. She wore her black wedding dress and her hair shone in the soft glow of the lantern. Like a halo done up in soft curls around her head. He had to give her credit for not backing down to Pierre. But that bruise around her eye — no, he'd made the right decision. Rachael did not belong here.

"I think I have already begun to think of this place as home. Don't you?" Rachael's mouth pulled into a familiar grin. "New York is so far away. Even the evenings are pleasant here, with the door wide open. And the mountains are beautiful. I wish I could paint like Alfred Jacob Miller. I'd send their beauty back home to Mother and Father to enjoy." Her mood grew solemn. She leaned close to Jonathan and whispered, "Whatever happens, I shall cherish the experiences I have shared with you — all." She sat straight in her chair and looked at each person around the table.

Her beautiful eyes held such pain. Was she memorizing their faces? Jonathan's heart skipped a beat.

"This feast was better than I have ever eaten in the Hotel Cincinnati,

my compliments to our two lovely hostesses." McCray bowed his head.
"I've been trying to decipher if you two couples could make a mark in
the wilderness, become successful at winning souls in the devil's playground, so to speak. Do you want to know my opinion?"

"Yes." Rachael leaned forward. "We welcome your honesty, Reverend McCray, and I will cherish your words, flattering or not, and wherever the Lord may lead me, I shall be content."

McCray smiled. "Beth, there couldn't be a better wife for our serious
Saul. You manage to make the sharp edges of his tongue easier to digest."

Saul nodded, reaching for her hand. "So you think I have a chance
at reaching souls equal with my wife?"

McCray chuckled. "Yes, if you're willing to listen to her quiet heart."

Jonathan squirmed in his seat. He felt like he was sitting on a cactus
plant, dreading the prick of McCray's sharp, truthful words.

"Rachael, you and Jonathan are molded out of the same cloth, both
stubborn and proud. Yes, our Good Lord has proven He's got a sense
of humor, placing you together. God must figure that locking the two
of you in matrimony will do what might take Him years to produce."

Jonathan stabbed a piece of pie and forked it into his mouth. He'd
rather pretend he choked on a piece of pie, instead of McCray's words.

"The Lord needs you two… smoothed and polished, your stubborn
wills in obedience to His commandments. You won't be obeying your own
determined wills, but the Lord's declaration of his Son's saving grace."

Jonathan's mouth dropped open. McCray was right. He couldn't let
Rachael go, he couldn't. Sending her home was like sending a part of
him back in defeat. Besides, he loved her. He needed her to complement himself, to tell him when he'd overstepped his boundaries. Jonathan reached for her hand and kissed it. He knew what needed to be
done. Yes, it was all so clear now. He needed time alone with Rachael.

McCray looked pleased. "So, trail boss, when are we heading out?"

"In about two days. Only we won't be heading out together." He'd
been pondering two different trails over the steepest part of the Rockies. He had talked to McGregor about that very thing this morning.

"What?" Saul looked up from his plate and gulped down his bite of pie.

"Saul, you will be going with McGregor. He knows these Rockies like the back of his hand. McCray and Singing Dove will accompany you. Rachael and I will wait and leave with Lafayette and a few of his men. We'll take the livestock with us."

Rachael sprinkled the few wild rose petals she had found along the south side of the cabin into her bath. Watching them fall gently into the water, she stepped into the tub and taking the soap and sponge, she drizzled the water over her shoulders as her thoughts drifted to Jonathan.

Jonathan was a man after God's own heart, and like the biblical David, he had shown the struggles of a man wrestling with nature, with good and evil of the battle life hands a man. He knew it wasn't in God's plan for her to return east. Lying in the water, she watched as it rippled about her body. The warm water washing over her soothed her tense nerves. God planned for her to finish her mission in the West and live out her years married to a man she loved and adored. Only God could plan it so well.

Refreshed and clean, she stepped out of the tub and reached for her cloth to dry herself. Hearing heavy footsteps outside the door, her heart stopped. Her body still moist from her bath, she turned her back to the door. Jonathan was out checking on the livestock. Was it Saul? She thrust her arms into her robe, wrapping the ties about her waist. Hearing a sudden gasp, she turned.

Jonathan shut the door and laid his bulk against it.

"I didn't expect you back so soon."

"I can see that." Jonathan couldn't take his eyes off of her. The robe did little to detract from her roundness, her gentle curves and her long, silky hair that shone like an auburn sunset about her sloping shoulders. "Would you like me to leave?"

Rachael hesitated, a slow flush sweeping her cheeks as she shook her head. Her eyes sparkled and a soft smile crossed her full lips. "I'd like you to stay," she whispered.

"Why?"

"Because, I…"

"Yes."

"I never want to be apart from you again." Her eyes locked onto his as she disrobed and tiptoed to him.

Jonathan glanced down at her, kissed her upturned lips and reached down, swooping her into his arms. He carried her to the bed. The white sheets blended with her alabaster skin, and contrasted with the tanned hands and arms where the sun had darkened her. He bent down and kissed her soft white neck and the sun-kissed lock of hair that fell across her lovely shoulder.

His lips traveled downward.

Rachael groaned, arching her back.

Her rose-scented skin invited his pleasures. The moment he had dreamt of had arrived. He inhaled deeply, caressing her hair with his hand as he peeled off his shirt, his trousers.

Her eyes widened, watching him, her lips parting, her hand held high, inviting his pleasure. "Rachael!"

She embodied everything he'd ever desired in a wife. Refinement, gentleness beyond his highest expectations, and a genuine love for Jesus. McCray was right. They were stubborn and proud. They were also opposites, she soft and gentle and he rough and unyielding. Christ's love woven into their marriage commitment had made them one body.

He smiled, thinking it had taken long enough for him and Rachael to come together. United as one as they had promised before friends and family, it had been worth the wait.

She could send his blood boiling with the thought of her at times. Make him go mad with jealously over her. But when he looked into her eyes, he went weak at the knees. Yes, she had been worth waiting for. He rested back on his pillow and closed his eyes. His last thought before drifting off to sleep was of Rachael's sweet smelling hair.

Rachael stirred. "Is it time to rise?" Cuddling his neck with her cheek, she kissed it.

He hugged her closer to him. "No. We have a moment longer." She snuggled back into the crook of his body, nestling her head on his chest. He took a deep breath. *Thank You, Lord, for the woman You have given me. Pray let us always serve You humbly and in love.* He kissed Rachael's forehead. He understood better the reason why married couples went on a honeymoon. That time alone together was precious.

Time alone. Perhaps... Memories of a foggy boat pier washed over him. His mother kissing him goodbye, refusing to look at his tear stained cheeks, and fluttering her handkerchief in surrender to his stepfather's wishes.

Jonathan was eight years old then, but he could still taste his salty tears as they dripped down his chin, the feeling of rejection burning his flesh red in the frosty air.

He shuddered at the memory and clutched Rachael. She nuzzled him, her breath stirring his chest hairs with her soft sighs. Jonathan looked down at her face and ever so gently kissed her forehead and sighed.

He recalled the Reverend's warning. "Ask God's and Saul's forgiveness for being jealous for no reason." He wasn't jealous of Saul. But was jealousy at the root of his the decision to split the wagon train?

Why do you call me Lord, Lord, and do not do the things I say?

God, why can't I forget Saul's anguished face admitting he proposed to Rachael? If she held no feelings for Saul, why didn't she confess that to him the day of his illness? He'd given her the opportunity.

Well, McCray may disapprove, but he would have his alone time with Rachael to prove to her he was the man for her. Then their love would blossom like a rose bud.

Yeah, right, McCray had told him. *Or are you trying to prove that to yourself?*

Dear God, forgive me. I'm asking for a little time. I need to have some time with Rachael — alone.

chapter twenty-six

*R*achael couldn't see. She fanned the air as swarms of mosquitoes buzzed about her head, their stings inflicting her body with welts. She tried not to scratch, but the pain was unbearable. She felt she would go mad with the incessant itching and pain.

She positioned her horse alongside Jonathan's and mimicked what he did as they drove the cattle. She watched one cow, her udders full of milk, kick at the mosquitoes. The cow kicked and mooed, looking at Jonathan, as if asking him to give her some relief from the blood-thirsty insects.

"I hope the cows do not run mad because of the mosquitoes," she said.

Jonathan grunted, riding over toward the cow and flicking the mosquitoes off with the branch he'd snapped off a tree. "I thought Lafayette knew the lay of the land better than to head us into this inferno."

"Will we be at Port Neuf soon?"

"Yes." He smiled. "Strange name for a fort."

Rachael looked across the hovering bodies of the mosquitoes that looked more like black clouds than insects, and sighed. Then the cloud seemed to dissipate and the widest river they ever forded on horseback came into view. Rachael's stomach churned as she watched the water splash across rocks and boulders.

"Keep the team moving, Rachael. Don't let them stop or we'll never get them across."

She rubbed her arm across her face. Blood oozed down her arm from her mosquito bites.

"Come on." McCray pointed to the opposite bank. "Let's get across. We'll stay at the fort tonight and you'll get your first full view of the Snake River there."

She was glad McCray had persisted in accompanying her and Jonathan. He'd proved a valuable ally and friend to her already.

"We're making good progress." Jonathan stood in his stirrups and looked out over the body of water. "That's the American Falls on the Snake River."

Their roaring pulsed like her own heartbeat. "I can't imagine their size. How will we ever get across?"

"This one shouldn't be so bad. But this is the beginning of the falls along the river. We'll have to be careful that the horses and cattle don't crowd. There's a ledge on which we can cross."

This one? What did that mean? Rachael held her breath as if doing so would help her and her horse become thinner as they walked across the narrow ledge. The roar of the falls deafened her as the spray from the water whipped over their bodies and beat against the rocks and boulders below.

She let out her breath. Her face and hair were drenched, her eyelids heavy as the spray misted her eyesight. She and her horse had crossed to the other side. She could only imagine how her horse felt feeling the welcoming solid ground beneath her hooves. She glanced back.

The pack mules bunched, one trying to pass another. Clutching the high collar of her dress, she silenced her cry. Jonathan spurred his horse back across the ledge to retrieve the pack mules.

"Jonathan…" Her cries caught like a fish in a net in the noise of the falls.

Jonathan trotted up the rock formation and grabbed two pack mules. One tied behind the other, he led them across the ledge. Suddenly Pierre pushed forward on Jonathan's flank. It appeared that Pierre began to struggle with Jonathan. Jonathan's horse's neighs split through the noise of the falls like a death shriek. His horse reared. Rachael screamed as she watched the pack mules plunge over the falls, spiraling head first through the water.

Their braying echoed down the steep mountainside, then drowned in the foaming waters beneath. Where was Jonathan? God, help him!

There he was, riding through the foaming sprays of the waterfall. His fluid largeness ripped the fog in two. "Jonathan!" She kicked her horse forward, reaching for him, sobbing, clutching him to her. "That could have been you."

He brushed her forehead with kisses, then jumped off his horse.

"That's the last time you're going to cause me trouble," he said as he approached Pierre. He pulled Pierre from his horse and threw him to the ground. With one carefully laid punch, Pierre lay silent.

※ ※ ※

Jonathan smiled. Rachael patted the mule's head, and swabbed its cuts. "This gash is particularly deep. Come take a look at it, Jonathan." Rachael had recovered from the incidents at the falls remarkably.

He stopped emptying his saddle bags and went over to see. Rachael was always doctoring either him or the livestock. "He'll mend. I can't believe that he didn't do worse going over the falls the way he did."

"I wish the other mule had survived." She sighed. "How much farther do we have?"

"I don't know." Jonathan placed his hand in the small of his back, stretching upwards, and looked about. "It is beautiful here, isn't it? Lafayette choose a good place to stop for the night. This place will help us and the livestock rest from the ordeal of the falls."

Long grass waved in the soft breezes of the morning. Their hungry animals, nearly twenty mules and horses in all, grazed contentedly. It appeared the livestock had put aside the harrowing adventures of yesterday and sought only to feast on the grass of today.

Jonathan thought he could learn a lesson from watching his livestock. What was it Jesus said about not being concerned with any worries that might lie ahead? He grabbed a deep whiff of fresh air filled with the scents of fish and clover. The Bible verse he sought to remember escaped him. Anyways, he was enjoying this little bit of paradise.

Rachael glanced beyond him for a short moment, then met his gaze full on. "We could learn from God's creatures, Jonathan. I am recalling Matthew 6:34 'Take therefore no thought for the morrow: for the morrow shall take thought for the things of itself. Sufficient unto the day *is* the evil thereof.'"

He chuckled. Rachael had begun reading his mind more and more lately. He wrapped his arm around her shoulders.

"Hmmm, Mother would often do that very thing. Did I ever tell you that?" she said.

"No. What very thing?"

"Every time my sisters or I got a little anxious, Mother would come over and hug us. Just keep her arm around us without saying a word."

He gazed into her eyes.

"She didn't need to say anything. We could feel her love enveloping us."

He kissed the top of her head, then searched her eyes. Can you feel my love? He wanted to shout it to the tree tops. Yet, something, someone held him back and kept him from saying more. "I was thinking of resting today, it being the Sabbath, and only our Good Lord could have found a finer place to enjoy the day."

"These six straight days of travel have made our poor animals footsore. But there are blessings around every corner if we take time to notice them."

"Yes, this will be a good place to give ourselves and our animals a much needed rest."

"But —" She nodded toward Lafayette who was busy packing up.

"Lafayette wants to leave this morning. Well, we'll see." Jonathan walked toward McCray sitting on a boulder near the falls. He hesitated before taking another step.

"McCray, what's wrong?"

McCray's tears floated across his eyes. He blinked, then waved away Jonathan's concern. "These are tears of joy. I opened a letter from home I'd gotten at the fort. I forgot I had it. Can you imagine? Or maybe it was preordained that I read it now. Anyhow, it's starts off,

Our prayers go before you from your beloved church, Reverend. Without your sacrifice of comforts left and lives daily offered, our Savior's

work could not progress. Your missionary work is the heart of love, edifying our Savior, Jesus Christ.

"I must admit, it takes a man's breath and makes him humble to know that so many people believe in what we're about."

Like a magnet, Jonathan was drawn, his conscience pricked concerning his feelings toward Saul. "You still think I acted against God's divine orders by separating the party?"

McCray rose from sitting on the boulder. "Well, seeing how you brought it up." He led Jonathan to the river's edge. "If you feel that-a-way, you need to get down on your knees and ask God's forgiveness."

"I didn't mean to alienate you or God by my decision."

McCray looked out over the Snake River. "I don't believe you did, but the question you need to ask the Lord Almighty is, did you do it according to His will or your own? You can't expect God's blessings to come if you're acting for yourself."

※ ※ ※

Rachael woke from her nap with a start. For a moment she did not know from what. There it was again. It was coming from the wagon. Getting up she peered into the darkened interior. "What are you doing, Jonathan?"

"Got to lighten the wagon. Saul and Beth's is much smaller and lighter than ours. I cannot believe we managed this far."

"But those are your clothes. You'll need your suits. You can't afford to throw out a single one. How will you ever buy others?"

"I have my buckskins. Don't know why I brought suits in the first place."

"But Saul wears his. We're civilized beings, Jonathan. We're coming here to tame the heathen. Not for the heathens to rub off on us —"

"You're thinking about what I did to Pierre the other day." Jonathan turned his turbulent scowl on her. She looked away. "He had it coming. You of all people should know that. Why, if I hadn't come along when I did at that blackberry patch, I cringe to think what might have happened."

Rachel wrapped her shawl closer around her shoulders. She had felt the same. That is, until she had prayed. She could not explain it to herself, let alone to Jonathan.

Something had swept over her after she offered God her sincere cry for forgiveness over her assailant. In that moment, the Holy Spirit swept her memory clear. Pierre's lies that peppered through the camp that she had wanted his advances did not give her concern.

She and God knew the truth. Watching Jonathan, seeing his anxiety over Pierre, and knowing she was to blame for Jonathan separating their ministry caravan told her more plainly than words that Jonathan did not wholly believe her. Saul did. Silently, Rachael prayed for God's guidance. How can I show Jonathan my love and devotion, Lord?

Saul may have been right to cling to his Eastern ways. Perhaps not conforming to the wilderness helped him cling more to his Christian beliefs. She looked up at Jonathan still rooting around inside the wagon.

"Jonathan, we need to put before these new converts a set of morals they cannot argue. Part of this is being who we are, remembering where we have come from and that we represent our Savior."

Jonathan frowned. "Don't worry, Rachael. I'm sure at least one of us will keep the heathen ways at bay," he said and retreated into the wagon.

"But..." The thought continued to plague her, why had Jonathan split up their caravan? It was like splitting the sword of God. Reverend McCray was right to worry. "Jonathan why did you split up our caravan? After all, Jesus said 'For where two or three are gathered together in my name, there am I in the midst of them.'"

A large banging sound came from deep in the wagon. Rachael jumped. Like a grizzly disturbed from hibernation, Jonathan's scowling face appeared from the tent flap. "If you must know, I wanted time alone with you. To have some semblance of a honeymoon. Humph! Big chance of that here. This is not exactly what I had in mind."

Rachael drew her shawl around her as if it was her armor. "Especially after giving in to Singing Dove's protests and allowing her to join us instead of going with Saul and Beth. I thought of you as a man after God's own heart, a regular David of the nineteenth century. How ridiculous."

Jonathan stomped back into the wagon. "I never tried to be anything but me." He threw out more items.

Rachael looked down at their discarded things. "It's a little like bringing a piece of home with us, is it not?"

"It would have been better for us not to have brought so much in the first place. Only what was necessary. It's too much materialism at the expense of our animals." He stared down at her. As if daring her to dispute his words.

Jonathan was right. She recalled how she covered her eyes as their wagon crossed the falls. Even though this little paradise was an oasis to their weary and foot-sore animals, the worst seemed to await them around every bend.

Jonathan disappeared into the wagon again. Rachael could hear him milling about. Then he jumped down, dragging her trunk. "I'm afraid this will have to go. I know it means a lot to you, but — we have to lighten our wagon."

"It's our wedding trunk, Jonathan. Jane gave it to us as a present on the eve of the farewell party. There hadn't been enough time to prepare ours so my dear sister gave hers to us. Some of the contents I haven't even had time to explore for fear my emotions would run away with me."

"It is the custom of the country to possess nothing, and then you will lose nothing. Look at my books." Jonathan held one up for her inspection. "I can't tell you how many times I have packed and repacked these. Now look at them. The pages are so wet I doubt the ink will be legible once they dry."

Jonathan was being realistic. She, on the other hand, wanted to listen to her heart and wrap her past around her like a cozy shawl. Once these cherished things were gone, all she would have left of home would be her memories — memories now fading like the ink on Jonathan's worn medical books.

She placed her hands on the trunk's scrolled top and gently ran her fingers across the top. How she would miss this memento of home. One lasting remembrance of her past.

Jonathan removed his hat and stared at her, then beat his hat on his buckskins. He turned to gaze out across the formidable miles and miles of wilderness. "It's a good burial site below the falls, there, for your little trunk. Most likely it will become a cherished keepsake for one of the Diggers' lodges.

"Diggers? Who or what are they?"

"They're the Indians of the Snake River area. They're called Diggers because they live on roots during the winter and salmon during the summer."

"Then at least someone will have use of it."

"What is that?" Singing Dove had approached unnoticed.

Rachael blinked back her tears. Singing Dove had sought for every opportunity to learn about her own race that growing up with the Indians had not afforded her. She was an intelligent student who desired to learn "the white woman's ways" as she called them. She accepted everything except a proper Christian name and baptism. Talk of the Trinity caused her to seek an escape. She would get up from her seat near the fire and hurry into the outer darkness of the camp's glow. Her behavior baffled McCray.

Watching Singing Dove's eager eyes lavish her trunk gave Rachael a sense of comfort. "Shall we see what is inside?" The thought sent a flood of tears pooling in her eyes.

Throughout the months across the miles, she comforted herself that she would find a quiet moment once they settled into their new home to explore the trunk's innermost regions. Exclaiming over its contents within their new cabin would be like sharing their new home with her family. Now the wilderness had robbed her of that opportunity.

Rachael knelt before the trunk and taking a key from around her neck, opened the lid. Dishtowels, red and white wash rags, a yellow sun bonnet, and a pair of green and burnt orange garden gloves greeted her. She smiled, looking at her rough work-worn hands.

Then she spotted another key lying between the garden gloves. She took it and inspected it. "This key must belong to the trunk, too. Maybe it's a spare." She tried it on the latch. "This is much too small for this large slot."

Singing Dove knelt beside her on the moist ground. There was another compartment below the first. "Here, Singing Dove, hold these for me." Now that the towels and clothes had been removed, she saw the second compartment and the key hole. She opened the second drawer that lay hidden before unsuspecting intruders. The top came off easily in her hands. Laying it down, she unfolded a white wedding gown with mother-of-pearls and intricate lace.

"What is that?" Singing Dove touched the fabric and then drew her hand back, as if afraid it would bite.

"My mother's wedding dress. I thought it was for Jane — Jane was trying on her gown... Mother was finishing it the day you returned from Canada, Jonathan. They made Mother's wedding gown over... for me." She smiled into Singing Dove's attentive eyes, and then back to Jonathan. "Remember what Mother said?"

Jonathan frowned. "No, should I?"

"Oh, you do, Jonathan, I can tell you do? Mother said, 'Do you think every man and woman marries for love? Life's biggest decisions are made in our innocence. How can the impetuousness of youth understand the depth of love? Or is it commitment, one to another, that binds the heart after romance is replaced by reality?"

Rachael clutched the wedding dress to her bosom. "Singing Dove, I got married so quickly there wasn't time to make a proper wedding gown for me. Here. Take my mother's gown and wear this when you meet God's choice for you."

"I do not know if this could ever be." Singing Dove looked at Jonathan. "I think my heart will always be bound for another who cannot share my happiness or my love."

Rachael blinked. Jonathan's chagrin and the sudden change of his countenance were obvious.

"You women get this settled. We need to get packed and on our way."

"Yes, my Jonathan." Singing Dove scooped up the dress. "I will pack it carefully on my mule."

Rachael had to know. She could no longer ignore the silent looks and unspoken words. Fearing the answer, yet needing to ask. "Who is it, Singing Dove? Who is it your heart cannot forget?"

chapter twenty-seven

Jonathan hitched the mules to the wagon instead of the horses and climbed onto the wagon seat. He hoped he did the right thing. After all, his mules had traveled over twenty miles a day for two weeks now, could his faithful mules cross this tempest-tossed body of water?

Lafayette wanted him to mount his wagon on the canoes he'd provided him and paddle it across. He didn't much care for that idea. After all, he'd lightened the wagon. McCray said if he wasn't going to use the canoes, to use the horses. But his horses were unshod and foot worn.

Rachael turned before entering the river and smiled reassuringly into his troubled eyes. Mounted on Singing Dove's horse due to its favorable height, she guided the horse forward.

Singing Dove followed next to Rachael.

The fast moving river stretched before them. A half a mile wide of the fastest moving current he'd seen since the mighty Mississippi. Twenty foot logs bobbed about the river like cork in a bottle of champagne, but it was more shallow here than anywhere else.

Jonathan let out a sigh of relief as Rachael and Singing Dove successfully reached the opposite bank.

Now Matthew, along with an Indian boy Lafayette provided, had the job of herding their cattle through the rough waters. Matthew confided to Jonathan last evening that he missed Luke who had gone with Saul and Beth. Jonathan could tell just by watching that Matthew was having problems with his new help. Lafayette had his hands full trying to get his own animals across without losing any. Jonathan couldn't expect help from any of Lafayette's men.

Matthew's dark eyes glanced his way and then motioned for Lafayette's Indian boy to follow him into the icy-cold water. Always before when a stream needed crossing, Matthew and Luke would strip off their shirts, wrap them around their heads, and jump into the water, guiding the cattle.

Jonathan took a deep breath. Lord, what have I done in my jealousy over Saul? Please forgive me, and do not punish the others for my foolishness. Please guide us all safely across.

He looked down at his hands, callused and leathery from months on the trail and recalled how Rachael had caressed the beautiful white satin and lace folds of her wedding dress with her own rough hands. He couldn't escape the longing in her eyes, all the more painful recalling that black dress she'd worn on their wedding day. He'd cut deep into her feelings. Would he never learn to think of Rachael first? Then there was Singing Dove. Her obsession for him troubled him. Even Rachael had noticed.

The trappers' cries alerted him. Mounted on the fleetest ponies, Jonathan watched three Indians Lafayette used as scouts enter the river. All he could see were their heads bobbing in the white-capped waves. The horses snorted. The Indians were hallooing, with Matthew in the lead. He fought to keep their livestock together against the mighty current of the Snake River. And then Jonathan saw the most beautiful sight. He blinked. The Indians triumphantly ascended the opposite bank with cattle, mules, and horses all intact.

Now it's my turn. "Giddy up." Jonathan cracked the whip above the mules' heads and descended into the current. The water swirled against the sides of the wagon, and he worked to keep the wagon upright. Suddenly, they were floating down the river, the wagon caught in the current. Before Jonathan could correct the mishap, the wagon fell sideways, tossing him into the river. Quickly he emerged from beneath the wagon bed, coughing and gasping for air, reaching for the reins. Then his shirt sleeve got caught on the wagon, pulling him down into the dark swirling water.

* * *

"Jonathan!" Rachael screamed from the opposite bank. "Help him, Matthew."

Matthew and four Indians dove into the water. They plunged through the frothy waves swimming in strong strokes toward the wagon. The mules strained to move forward despite the wagon floating sideways. The Indians dove under the water.

Rachael searched the water for any sight of Jonathan. Then he and Matthew burst above the water, gasping for air as they emerged.

Lafayette's men, mounted on horses, threw out their lassoes. Matthew and the Indians tied them to the wagon and with the help of their horses the men on the bank were able to upright the wagon and pull it toward the bank.

Jonathan swam toward shore.

"You okay?" Lafayette patted him on the back.

Jonathan coughed up spittle. "Yeah." He checked his mules and took a look at his wagon.

"What you got?" Lafayette walked over.

"A severed wheel."

Lafayette slowly walked around the wagon. "Got one back here, too." He glanced up. "Pierre, is this your handiwork?"

Pierre shrugged. "So?"

"I've had enough of your shenanigans, Frenchman. Fix this. And fix it right, or I'll whip your hide in shreds, you understand? Don't give me that look, both me and the men are tired of you. You've made us another day late." Lafayette's face turned beet red. "One of you men go and see what these woods have to offer us in the way of deer or antelope. One of you Indians rustle up some fish."

Rachael wrapped a blanket around Jonathan's shivering shoulders.

"Tha-that river water is co-cold."

Singing Dove ran to gather kindling and started a fire for Jonathan and the Indians to warm by while the wagon was being fixed.

Rachael coaxed Jonathan from his watchful diligence of the wagon and up the bank to the fire. "Do you think Saul and Beth made it okay? One of the men said the south end is the only way to come, and that this side was terrible and nearly impassable."

Lafayette smiled, coming up behind them, tipping his hat. "Ma'am, your friends are ahead of us, a day's ride away. They don't have the livestock to contend with. But you're right, the worst is comin'." He swept his hat brim toward the mammoth space of mountains looming in the far distance. "Gotta climb over that distant mountain peak to the Blue Mountains. Wish we didn't have to wait. Don't like waiting, with winter slappin' our heels."

Rachael sat down next to McCray and Singing Dove. She had opened the Bible Rachael had given her, one of the many treasures that lay hidden at the bottom of the trunk. Singing Dove stared at the pages, turning them slowly.

"You take." Singing Dove motioned for Rachael to take the Bible.

"Why? You will need it. It shall become a source of strength to you. Trust me in this."

"Read, please, find where your…" She made the sign of the cross. "Jesus?"

Singing Dove nodded. "Where tells about love. Reverend McCray say God brought Doctor Jonathan." Singing Dove tapped the Bible. "You show me where."

Rachael looked at the Reverend McCray. "Perhaps the Reverend would."

McCray got up, his coffee cup in his hands. "No, I think it is high time for Singing Dove to hear it from another woman."

Rachael took the Bible from Singing Dove's fingers. Surrounded by ministers, she'd never dreamt that she would be asked to lead someone to the Lord. She marveled as to God's perception, the way He had led her to this day, this moment with Singing Dove.

She bowed her head. Sweet Jesus, what if I say the wrong thing and Singing Dove flees into the nearest stand of trees like always? Her thoughts turned a direction she didn't want to go. Was Jonathan playing a part in Singing Dove's infatuation for him? Lord, show me the truth. Laying the Bible in her lap, she gathered Singing Dove's hands into her own. "First, we must pray, Singing Dove, for the Great Holy Spirit to descend on us like a white dove with His wisdom."

Rachael prayed, took a deep breath and plunged forward. Singing Dove's eyes grew as large as goose eggs as Rachael explained about the Father and His Son who came to earth to teach them and then to shed His blood for their sins, and about the Holy Spirit who lived with them after they accepted Jesus into their hearts.

"God our Father knows you, Singing Dove, even if you do not know Him. He loves you enough to seek you. See right here Jesus tells a parable about a lost sheep, and how He rejoices when He finds that lost sheep. 'I say to you that likewise joy shall be in heaven over one sinner that repenteth, more than over ninety and nine just persons, which need no repentance.'"

Singing Dove rested her hands in her lap, watching Rachael. She closed the Bible and swallowed past the sudden thickness in her throat. "When I first married Jonathan, I did not know him well enough to love him like a woman should love her husband. Through Jesus I learned. Now I love Jonathan with my whole body."

"I love him, too. Can we share? It is the Indian way, if head wife agrees?"

Rachael wanted to know the truth, but it stung all the same. She swallowed hard and pressed on. "It is hard to share a heart, is it not? When a man and woman are married by our God's commandments, they make a promise to God that they will love, honor, and cherish until death do they part."

Singing Dove's brows rose above her startled eyes.

"They become one heart. Someday you will meet the man God has planned for you. Then all the words I have spoken to you this day will unfold before your eyes and you will know they are true. That man will redo the parts of your life that have hurt you. He will make you complete and you will understand the Holy Book's wisdom."

"Doctor Jonathan did all this for you?"

"Yes." Rachael's gaze held hers. "I understand your confusion better than you know."

Singing Dove's expression changed from surprise to concern to pleasure. "Teach me about this Jesus. Teach me to love." Her voice swelled an octave, to a whisper seeing Pierre.

"Mon chérie." In the campfire's glow Pierre eyes gleamed down at them. It was obvious he'd been listening. "Teach me, too, how to love like Jesus does."

"Are you willing to pray with us?"

Pierre nodded.

"Shall we bow our heads? Now repeat after me." She sent out a silent prayer, then took a deep breath. "Dear God, I admit that I am a sinner and in need of Your forgiveness. You sent Your only begotten Son, Christ Jesus, to suffer the punishment that I deserve. Please help me all the days of my life to turn from my sins and live a life that pleases thee. Thank you, Father, for your gift of eternal life and for the hope I now share with Singing Dove and Pierre. Amen."

※ ※ ※

"I don't care what you say, McCray. Rachael should have learned by now not to trust that Frenchman."

"Jonathan, you have got to let go of your infernal jealously over Rachael." McCray slapped his hat down into the dust. "She's witnessed to Singing Dove. The girl has accepted Jesus as her Lord and Savior. Give your wife credit for what she is, a God-fearing Christian woman who knows the power of the Holy Spirit. Did it ever cross your mind that she'll be able to do what I couldn't, bring these heathen trappers to the Lord?"

"No!" Jonathan's voice echoed down the mountaintops that he and McCray had just climbed. Spruce trees grouped in clusters like green grapes dotted the mountain, a purple hue in the sparkling sunlight of clouds so low Jonathan felt he could pull one down. Oh, how I want to believe Rachael is as innocent as she pretends. Believe that she would have selected me over Saul. But why would she? He was seeing more clearly his shortcomings mirrored in the Reverend's eyes.

"What is eating you? I'm not leaving this mountain until you tell me."

"It's nothing you can help me with." Jonathan's hands felt weighted down like ten pound irons as he patted McCray's shoulder. "Don't worry. Keep an eye on Rachael and Pierre. I don't trust that skunk, especially now that he hides his disguise behind Christianity."

"You've got a right to worry. Let's get moving before we have to wait another day to finish crossing these mountains."

※ ※ ※

Mountains. As far as Rachael could see. Lofty and majestic in their stance, reaching upwards as if to touch the beard of clouds that dotted the twinkling blue heavens. Had Jonathan lost his way in this maze of mountains and trees seeking the next passageway?

"Mon chérie, do not worry. As you say, Jesus will watch over your husband, yes? We are entering what my people call the Blue Mountains. Are they not divine?"

Cliffs and ridges, trees and more trees, like a chain of deep green that turned blue in the afternoon, and each mountain they crossed had been more dreadful than the first. Rachael bowed her head. After two weeks of traveling the mountains westward, all she had left to give was prayer and thanksgiving. Had not God protected Jonathan and their little caravan thus far? "Yes, Pierre, God will watch over my husband and us, and see us safely through."

God answered her pray expediently. Out of the haze of a mountain's crevice, Jonathan's hair glistened with the sunlight that poured across his shoulders. Sitting tall in his saddle, his hand lifted to her in salute.

Pierre moved his horse closer to hers. "Mon chérie, see? He has made it safely back."

Rachael urged her horse forward. She searched Jonathan's face, praying he could read in her gaze the love in her heart. "What's wrong?"

Jonathan leaned over in his saddle, looking past Rachael toward Pierre. "What were you doing standing by Pierre?"

"I wasn't. He rode up to me. Please, Jonathan, we must trust in the saving grace of our Lord, mustn't we?"

※ ※ ※

Rachael felt the mountains pulling them like a current, engulfing them beneath, like the waves of the sea. Would they ever find their way out? Despair nipped at her heels. With every step of her horse's hooves, the mountains grew taller. They had to abandon the wagons. Everything they owned was on their mules. Narcissa had called these mountains Mount Terrible. Rachael agreed.

Now the twenty-fifth of September, they'd been within the clutches of mountains and trees for over five weeks, camping beneath their snow topped pinnacles. Every mile brought the realization of the mountains' magnitude and depth. There were gaping cavities around every corner, majestic rocks that angled upwards toward the impregnable heavens — as if trying to touch the beard of God.

The horses climbed and climbed. Lafayette was often unsure as to where the pass lay through the mountainous region. "I thought for sure the pass was over that ridge there." Lafayette looked skyward.

Pierre tilted his head backward. "Wait here, I'll have a look."

"No. This is my expedition." Jonathan kicked his horse forward.

"Please, Jonathan, allow Pierre to try. You've been climbing all day. You and your horse must be exhausted." Rachael's pleas were to no avail. Jonathan would not relent. He seemed set on proving himself, but to whom? She watched him leave and turned to McCray for solace. "Reverend, what is troubling my husband?"

"The Doc?"

"He is the only husband I have. What is he hiding from me? I feel you know, but are hesitant to tell me."

McCray patted her gloved hand. "Keep praying. We need the Lord's help to get us through these ranges. Whether Jonathan likes it or not, we're going have to bed down again in the mountains."

chapter twenty-eight

Jonathan dismounted and marked his trail. They had scant food supplies left. A small bag of flour and a few pieces of salmon. They heated the snow for their water, both for themselves and their livestock. They had killed a steer for meat and eaten what they could of it and packed the rest carefully. What lie ahead of them? With winter fast approaching, he needed to sustain his herd for the long months ahead.

The horses, mules, and what remained of the livestock were living on wild sage. He'd combed the mountains until his horse's hooves were bleeding. He'd worn his boots down in spots that he was treading on sock. He tethered his horse to a tree and climbed up on a boulder to look out.

Every twist and turn of the mountains became more confusing. "God, I know you are angry with me, but please don't take it out on the rest of them." He dropped to his knees and clasped his fingers. What did the apostle Paul say? "For the good that I would I do not; but the evil which I would not, that I do." What was the matter with him? His past was behind him. His future would be determined by his lustful desires or his desire to do God's will. Which would it be? "Please, Lord, forgive me. Thy will be done, now and forever."

As he looked up from his prayer, he saw the sunset filtering through a pass he thought led to nothing. "Of course, that's why I didn't see it. The sunlight played tricks with my eyes." He'd not seen what now was so evident.

Jonathan looked up to where the mountain peak appeared to touch a low hanging cloud. *Dear Lord, has that been my trouble? Have I stopped looking up and so have lost my way?* There it was, the valley he was looking for where the Umtilla Indians lived. Lofty mountains covered with clusters of pitch and spruce pine trees, surrounded the circular plain. At the foot of mountains swirled the Columbia River. Beyond he could make out two distinct mountains, Mount Hood named after a British naval officer and Mount St. Helen named after a British diplomat. Both mountains were conical in form and separated from each other by what must be a sizeable distance.

All he had to do was cross some half dozen peaks to get to Umatilla. Hearing a noise in the thicket, he turned. Pierre emerged.

"Is Rachael all right?"

"Yes, she the only woman I know that could resemble a beautiful angel in this." He swept his arms over his head. "As you say, conditions?" He chuckled deep in his throat.

"What are you getting at?" Then the Reverend's words slapped Jonathan in the face. *Give Rachael a chance. It might be the Holy Spirit will use her to reach these men for Christ.*

Pierre's gaze held his. "Men like us don't understand women like Rachael."

He hoped Pierre didn't sense his uneasiness. "I understand you're a saved man. What do you mean by that remark?"

Pierre fingered his holstered revolver. "Saved? Oui oui. Since I was a little boy, my mama she tries."

"What are you saying?" Jonathan's words caught in his throat like a bone. *Just as he thought, Pierre had tricked Rachael and Jonathan into believing he was saved.* Jonathan glanced over at his horse, his gun sat in its holster. *What a fool I am. With me dead Rachael would be free.*

Pierre stepped closer, his right hand resting on his revolver. "I never believed in this God or His Son, until your wife explain. She opened my eyes." He paused. "I came to thank you. I see there is a heaven and a hell. Jesus show me light. Made me see this jealously for your friend, Saul and, too, you have this jealousy for me? No? I was very bad man, no more. Pierre… big sinner. No more. Pierre Christian." He walked over and slapped Jonathan on the shoulder and smiled. "Why do you not tell Rachael you have this knowledge about Saul's proposal?"

Jonathan sat back on his heels. "How do you know about that?"

※ ※ ※

The beans bubbled over the open fire. Rachael removed the pot and placed a cover to keep them warm.

"Rachael."

She looked up, her husband's scowling face met her gaze.

"I know Saul proposed to you." Jonathan's hands were drawn into fists by his sides.

She closed her eyes against the threat of tears. I just knew this would be the way he'd respond. She rose from her knees, and walked to the opposite side of the fire to check the coffee. Why did he care if Saul proposed? After all, he thought proposing an inconsequential act. "What do you want me to say?" She tried to appear calm, inwardly her heart was pounding like a war drum. She wanted to scream in his irate face, I didn't want his proposal — but I did yours! She grabbed a pot holder and reached for the pot of boiling coffee. The men glanced their way. Had Jonathan's words carried to their itching ears on the persistent wind in these mountains?

Jonathan stared out over the deep prism of rocks, cliffs and miles of trees. Singing Dove stood a small distance away. Oh, why does Jonathan continue to pretend? It's as clear as the rocks over Singing Dove's head. He even came down the mountain with Singing Dove, walking side by side with her like strolling lovers.

Rachael walked over to him with the coffee pot in one hand and his cup in the other. "Jonathan, what does it matter? You never even bothered to propose to me. You had Father do it for you. Yes, Saul proposed to me. He… we had known each other for some time and we shared the same dream. Why should it matter to you that he proposed first?" The steaming brew hissed like a snake into his cup's cold, metal interior. As cold as Jonathan's eyes.

"You're right. It shouldn't."

For a breathless moment Rachael thought her dream might become reality. That Jonathan would take her into his arms, kiss her, and tell her how sorry he was for not giving her a proper proposal. That he loved only her and had never loved Isabella or Singing Dove.

"We'll talk later." His voice as void of emotion as his eyes. He turned and sat down at the men's campfire and stared into the fire.

That night, the snow floated down on her prostrate form, dotting the velvet blackness. The coldest night in her life. She shivered and tossed her blankets over her face. In a sort of groggy trance between sleep and wakefulness, she waited for Jonathan to share her bed, but he never appeared. Was he with Singing Dove? The thought caused instant rage within her bosom. She knew in her heart he would be loyal to her and refuse to share Singing Dove's bed, but what she didn't know was if he wasn't sharing his thoughts with her. That was almost as equally sinful, at least to her.

"Rachael, stay in your saddle. I won't allow your horse to fall."

So Jonathan won't allow her horse to fall, yet she'd slipped and slid twice on the half-inch of snow that blanketed the mountainside while trying to fetch him his breakfast, and he hadn't said a word then. She looked away when he glanced up at her, but she'd noticed his square jaw was set as if in granite. Nor had he attempted to explain where he was all night. It was cold. The saddle felt like a block of ice and her husband's attitude didn't help to warm her.

Sloppy wet snowflakes fell on her hair and lashes. She couldn't believe that back home she would always make an excuse to be out in the first snow of winter. How innocent she had been then. Jonathan shivered. Yet, she could see sweat beading his brow. She bit down on her bottom lip hard enough to feel a pin prick of blood. What's wrong? Part of her wanted to win this silent struggle of domination over the other.

Is that what a Christian wife should do?

Jonathan led her horse up the jagged cliff trail, his hand that held the reins shaking. "Jonathan, you are not well. You ride and I'll walk for a spell."

"I'll be fine, Rachael, just don't move. The trail is very slippery and your horse is doing everything she can to keep from slipping."

They were now descending the steepest mountain they had ever climbed. Like a winding staircase, she could feel her horse's haunches slide as her front feet braced against the turn and in places, her horse was perpendicular. Her poor horse dreaded the hill as much as she did. What of Jonathan? How was he staying up? "Jonathan, you might slip, please I can handle my mare, you do not need to lead her."

Jonathan chuckled. "I am not leading her, she is leading me and holding me erect all in one. My horse is much too foot sore to bear my weight. The Reverend is bringing him."

The path became extremely stony. "What is that covering the slope? It's not like any rock I've seen before."

Jonathan reached down and grabbed a couple, feeling it between thumb and forefinger. "Looks like chips of broken basalt."

"Jonathan, we need to check out this next turn, can Rachael wait here?" McCray yelled.

"What choice do I have?" she said, smiling.

Jonathan smiled back. His deep blue eyes twinkled at her. As tranquil blue as the sky, but when she broached her inhibitions to him, no doubt would turn as turbulent as storm clouds sweeping the mountains above his shoulder. "Wait."

"Yes?"

She bent over her horse and whispered. "Where were you last night?"

"Checking out the trail, and… McCray and I had a lot to go over."

"Then… you weren't with Singing Dove?"

Jonathan snorted. "Of course not. She was sleeping in her blanket." With that he disappeared with McCray.

He and McCray returned quickly and the procession continued on. Their horses' feet, unshod, were tender and stumbled often. Jonathan climbed on foot every place that could give him a foothold to see past the next mountain peak. No wonder he was stiff. He hadn't lain down all night. Rachael knew the weight of his decisions had a lot to do with his exhaustion and sleeplessness. How had Saul and Beth fared? Jonathan would never forgive himself if anything happened to either. Her heart cried out to him, knowing it was because of her.

Jonathan had silently carried the burden of Saul's proposal. Rachael closed her eyes. Why hadn't she told Jonathan herself? Why? Why didn't she tell him last night that she thought of Saul as one of her brothers? But she hadn't. Instead, she stood there gawking at him. She could blame no one but herself. God forgive my foolish pride.

She ached to tell Jonathan how much she loved him, but… she looked down at her hands holding the reins of her horse, then to the bowed head of her husband now taking her reins.

"Jonathan, why did you walk down from the mountain alongside Singing Dove last night?"

"Did I forget to tell you? She tracked Pierre. She was afraid he was up to no good, so she followed him." He chuckled. "With a pistol hidden in her skirt."

"Oh?"

Sweat dribbled into his eyes, he wiped it away. "Singing Dove didn't believe in Pierre's conversion. I hadn't either. I'd as soon forget that I didn't believe. Pierre's a changed man, Rachael. He told me so last night and he says he has you to thank for that."

"But I never manage to say what I should, when I should. I'm much too proud and —"

"I shouldn't jump to conclusions. These fur trappers need Jesus as much as the Indians do. I'm too quick to judge, proud and very stubborn."

She bit down on her quivering bottom lip. Not so proud now. His head was down and his shoulders bent, as if he carried the full load of guilt and jealousy on his shoulders. If only, she'd been honest from the beginning. Dear God, please forgive Jonathan and me. She knew God would forgive her, but could she forgive herself?

"Jonathan, you look so tired."

"I'm fine." His breath came in gasps, "It's the elevation."

"I… about that proposal of Saul's. Well… I didn't —"

Her horse tripped and Jonathan fell to his knees from the sudden thrust. "Easy, girl," he murmured as he rose, patting her neck. "Guess I need to concentrate more."

"Jonathan, I could use your help over here." McCray motioned him over. "The pack mule is limping. He must have picked up some of this black stuff. I'll need you to steady her while I hoof pick her foot."

"Okay." Jonathan hesitated. "You'll be all right until I return?"

Rachael nodded. How she longed to say the words so close to her lips. Her chin quivered. She clamped down on it, holding it firm. That secret was the last of her pride. How could she give it up? She would be vulnerable before her husband, vulnerable before the world without her pride.

Lord, it's easy to ask forgiveness, but so hard to give over one's sins. Help me, Jesus. She glanced back. Jonathan moved cautiously toward the front. There was only a small path, small enough for one animal to go through at a time. One of the mules brayed and in that split second, Jonathan went flying from the impact of its hooves to his chest.

"Jonathan!" His name echoed down the mountainside.

He landed with a thud on a precipice. He'd not fallen into the abyss. Thank you, Jesus! McCray scrambled down the mountain, a rope tied around his waist. He hoisted Jonathan on his shoulders then motioned for Matthew, Lafayette, and Pierre to pull them up.

McCray knelt, laying his ear on Jonathan's chest. He looked up, and shook his head.

"No! This cannot be." Rachael bent down over Jonathan's lifeless body, listening for a heartbeat.

"Oh Lord, You've brought us so far. And to end like this? Please let Jonathan live. I need his love, Lord." He was so still. She stifled the sob burning her chest. "Help me, Jesus. Help me accept whatever you decide. Dear God, please let Jonathan live. Please, God, let him live." A spark of light sent its rays over an iridescent cloud, the snow drifting down like cotton. Gently, she pressed her mouth to his one last time.

Jonathan gasped. Rachael cupped her arm around his neck hugging him to her chest, kissing his forehead, wetting it with her tears. Jonathan's eyes fluttered open.

"Oh, Jonathan, I love you so much it hurts. I don't care if you can never love me back like you did Isabella… like you do Singing Dove. I love you. Ever since you fished me out of that terrible mud hole back in Buffalo. I… I was determined not to love you. Then I was too proud to admit it. I was too proud to tell Father, but he and Mother knew. They knew like Jesus knew. I loved you the first time our eyes met that day beneath the brim of my dripping bonnet, and I'll always love you."

A slow smile swept Jonathan's face, "Well, it took you long enough to admit it."

Rachael sat back on her heels, appalled he would return her heartfelt confession in such a sarcastic way. "Are you saying, you knew all along I loved you?"

"I'm saying to the love of my life that I spent all of last night praying God would have you love me the way I loved you. Only God could have made you confess it now. Come here." His arm drew her close, but she didn't need any invitation.

Eagerly she sought his lips. Snow floated down around them and the hoots and hollers of the men filled their ears. Snowflakes instead of rice and the sincere echoes of man's elation, not even a pipe organ could sound so good.

chapter twenty-nine

Rachael looked out over Umatilla, more beautiful than she had imagined. For more than six days Saul and Beth had waited impatiently for Rachael and Jonathan to share their exploits with them. But Saul had not been idle. He'd put up their tent and had even made a table out of logs as well as a few chairs. A half dozen logs, ready to make into their winter cabin, were neatly stacked next to a clump of pine trees.

"Rachael, you should have seen Saul riding that Indian pony. He looked like Ichabod Crane with his black coat flying behind that paint horse."

"Well, the only way I could ride the thing was at a gallop."

"And did you notice the camas growing so beautifully along the mountains?" Beth exclaimed. "Here, I brought a few with me. The Indians showed us how to dig them up. They are very sweet. See, it almost resembles an onion in shape. But, Rachael, I hardly expected the taste. It doesn't taste like an onion at all. It tastes much sweeter, sort of like a fig."

Rachael, hesitant, bit into the fruit. "It's delicious." She chewed off a larger bite and handed it to Jonathan.

"Isn't this country wonderful? Fruits of all sorts grow in abundance here. We are going to spend our lifetimes learning about this beautiful wilderness."

Jonathan took a bite. "How do they cook this?"

"The Indians dig a hole in the ground, and throw in a heap of stones," Saul pantomimed the process. "Then they heat the stones until they are red hot and cover them over with green grass. They place the camas in and cover everything with dirt. When they take them out, they are black as coal. They eat them through the winter months."

Rachael lifted the onion-looking vegetable to her nose and smelled it. "Amazing."

"Well, come on." Jonathan reached in his saddle bags for string. "We've got to mark out our cabins. Lafayette and his men have promised to chop down trees for our cabin."

"Timber!"

Jonathan chuckled. "Lafayette's men are already at work. Now, where would you like our first house to be, Rachael?"

She started to speak —

"Wait." Jonathan rushed forward and planted a kiss on her cheek. "Hold that thought. Let me get my stakes." He was as eager as a school boy entertaining the thought of summer break.

Rachael laughed from pure joy. Jonathan had confessed to her that he'd never loved Isabella or Singing Dove. He had loved her the first time he'd seen her in that pathetic looking bonnet. He'd followed her to the revival, hoping for another glimpse of her — where he learned of her missionary plans. The more he learned about her, the more he loved her.

Beth and Saul clutched each other's arms, laughing and hugging one another, enjoying their delight.

A noise coming over the rise captured her attention.

"Now what might that be?" Beth walked up the hill arching a palm over her brow. "It's someone in a buckboard," she hollered back to the others.

"Must be the neighbors." Rachael ran up the hill, breathing in the crisp fresh air. "Only I wasn't aware we had any."

"Whoever it is, they're in a hurry. Look how that buckboard is turning up the dust." Beth shielded her eyes from the bright sunshine.

Lafayette joined them. "My eyes must be deceiving me, but I don't think I could ever forget that form. The only man I ever saw sit a horse like that is Dr. Marcus Whitman himself."

"What?" Jonathan bolted out of the tent and up the hill. "Don't tell me I'm finally going to meet the man I've been walking in the footsteps of since I left St. Louis."

Lafayette chuckled, and slapped Jonathan on his back. "Got to admit, you didn't do too bad yourself. Me and the boys were bent on breakin' you. You've got the same stuff as Marcus."

The wagon came closer and Rachael's heart jumped to her throat. "Then, could that be Mrs. Whitman in the buckboard?"

"Who are those other people?" Beth asked.

"Must be the Reverend Henry Spalding and his wife, Eliza. They're the missionaries who came out with the Whitman's."

"Oh yes, they settled in the Nez Perce country."

Rachael touched her hair. "Jonathan," she whispered, "how do I look?"

"That's the first time I ever heard you ask that question. Not even on our wedding day. What makes this meeting so special?"

Rachael bit her bottom lip. "Narcissa's my heroine. She was the one who inspired me to try, to believe that if she could cross the Rockies, then I could, too."

Beth nodded in agreement. "I have a hunch that Narcissa and Eliza will inspire more women to achieve their dreams, believing that with Christ all things are possible."

Lafayette's men sat down to enjoy a meal of pork, venison, cabbage, turnips, onions, milk, tea, and bread and butter. Jonathan and Rachael looked around their makeshift table and thanked God for the rich blessings that had brought them safely through the perilous months.

Smiling at little Alice, Rachael realized that not only were Narcissa and Eliza the first two white women to cross the Rockies, Narcissa had done it while pregnant.

She felt humbled to know that God had cared enough to make her and Jonathan welcome in their new valley home complete with so many attending.

Singing Dove wore her white woman's dress, a lovely aqua-blue print with large gigot sleeves that came to a slender point at her wrist.

Rachael had painstakingly altered the dress to fit Singing Dove. She had allowed Rachael to comb out her braids and lay her dark hair softly down her back. She sat demurely next to Rachael, imitating everything she did during supper.

With the dishes washed and put back away in the Whitman's buckboard, Singing Dove handed Rachael a package carefully wrapped in animal skins.

"Mrs. Wheaton, I have a present for you."

Rachael smiled at her. "Thank you." She placed the big package on their makeshift table. "This is unnecessary. Your lovely presence is enough of a present." She blinked, looking around at the crowd that surrounded her. Her heart felt as if it would burst with joy. Stroking the soft beaver pelts, memories of the journey's hardships fell away like the morning mist.

Lafayette, standing alongside Jonathan and McCray, nodded and fingered the brim of his hat. "It was the Whitman's who planted the seed in my head that I needed to change and then when you and Jonathan came along… Well, I couldn't ignore that tiny sliver of hope any longer. You sure made a believer of me, Mrs. Wheaton, with your determination not to become bitter. Not even when that Indian got a hold of you, you kept your loving spirit. Never thought I'd admit I was a sinful man in need of a Savior."

Lafayette looked up then, his eyes wet. "Because of Jesus Christ, I can beat my own rotten nature and keep Satan from gnawing on my heels." He bowed his head and sniffed. "I'd like to invite you to my baptism."

Lafayette looked over at McCray and nodded. "McCray here is goin' to do the honors. He always did have a hankerin' to hold my head under water." A round of laughter greeted his words. "It's good to know that if our paths never cross after this day, I'll be seeing you all in heaven."

"Oh, yes, Mr. Lafayette, where Jesus Himself shall dry our tears." Beth's small hands clapped in glee. "Open up your present, Rachael."

Rachael pulled the cleverly sewn beaver wrapping away and to her amazement Mother's wedding gown with the mother-of-pearl beading and delicate white lace and satin glimmered before her in the sunlight.

"Oh, how lovely!" Narcissa fingered the soft glistening fabric. "I have forgotten how lovely lace and satin were. Isn't Rachael's dress beautiful, Marcus?"

"I wish your wedding dress had been white and not black."

Narcissa placed a small hand on her husband's chest. "I assumed you wanted me to be practical, Mr. Whitman." She reached for his arm, cupping her hand around his. "Why didn't you tell me you had a romantic nature beneath that hard exterior when I married you?"

A delighted smile curved the corners of his mouth. "Because, I didn't have one until after I married you, my love."

"I do have something in common with the famous Dr. Whitman," Jonathan said, smiling at Rachael.

A shiver of delight passed through her at his touch. "I think our Lord has given us a second chance, Jonathan. And you still have your black suit."

He bent down on one knee and kissed her hand. "Rachael, will you do me the honor of becoming my lovely bride?"

Dumbstruck, she covered her heart with shaking fingers. Was this really happening? "Oh, Jonathan… you proposed." He did love her. "Yes, Jonathan. With all my heart."

He chuckled. His eyes darting around the crowd. "She didn't think I could ever get my stubborn knee bent to do it, but with God all things, even pride, become manageable… Saul, will you do the honor of marrying us? McCray, would you give Rachael away? Singing Dove, could you be Rachael's maid of honor. Now, all I need is a flower girl." Jonathan laughed, bending down to little Alice. "Could you be our flower girl?"

Alice, chewing on her fingers, looked up at her mother.

Narcissa chuckled. "Well, you could hand her the flowers, but I don't know if she'll carry them or eat them."

"Sounds like Jonathan has planned this for quite some time." Saul chuckled, winking at Singing Dove. "You have any part of this?"

Singing Dove beamed at Rachael. "I no longer Singing Dove." She gazed at the crowd, lifting her head with a queenly poise much like Rachael's. "My name is Sara."

"Just Sara? Isn't there a last name?" Beth's eyes sparkled into hers.

"In time, when Jesus reveals him to me."

Pierre removed his hat. Revealing his clean face and groomed hair, he smiled shyly at Sara.

Saul, clutching his Bible, raised it high above his head in a victory grasp. "What a cause for praise and gratitude. Rachael, who would have thought I would be your minister in this Oregon Territory and be marrying you?"

"How true. We could never have planned this nor found our perfect mates without the help of our Lord and Savior." Jonathan laid his hand on Saul's shoulder. "Can you forgive me for my blindness? I can see now that the Lord's will was for you to share this ministry. He led me right to you, but I couldn't see past the log of jealously in my eye. Forgive me."

"Certainly, brother. I was calling everyone a hypocrite but myself. It's remarkable how clearly one sees the wisdom of Christ's words when you listen with your heart and not your mind. Forgive me as well and here's my hand on that."

"Our Lord has prepared His disciples for just such a day." Marcus beamed like a benevolent father would. "Isn't that so, Reverend Spalding?"

"It most certainly is, Brother Whitman."

"I'll provide the entertainment while we wait." McCray stepped onto a stump that had been used as a seat earlier.

"Hurry, Jonathan, we need to get dressed." Rachael gave him a little nudge.

Up the hill toward the tent she went with Jonathan following. A small yellow flower growing in a clump of weeds caught her eyes. She rushed over, bent low, and smiled. "Look what I have found, a dandelion."

Jonathan chuckled. "Look there's a bunch of them growing next to this tree. Stubborn little flowers, aren't they?"

"Not wilting beneath adversity. Remember, Jonathan, our first meeting?"

"I shall never forget it. It changed my life, Rachael dear."

Reverend McCray's words floated up to them.

Rachael grabbed her dress and hurried into the tent to change.

Jonathan stood outside. Rachael knew he was listening to the Reverend's words just as she was.

"Through the flood waters and mountainous trials, I watched as Jonathan and Saul grew to become disciples of God. My sermon comes from Luke 6:45 and John 1:11. 'A good man out of the good treasure of his heart bringeth forth that which is good; and an evil man out of the evil treasure of his heart bringeth forth that which is evil; for of the abundance of the heart his mouth speaketh. And why call ye me, Lord, Lord, and do not the things which I say? Whosoever cometh to me, and heareth my sayings, and doeth them, I will shew you to whom he is like: He is like a man which built an house, and digged deep, and laid the foundation on a rock.' The Rock of God's word." McCray paused, flipping the pages of his worn Bible. "Jesus 'came unto his own, and his own received him not. But as many as received him, to them gave he power to become the sons of God... Which were born, not of blood, nor of the will of the flesh, nor of the will of man, but of God. And the Word was made flesh, and dwelt among us (and we beheld his glory, the glory as of the only begotton of the Father,) full of grace and truth.'"

Rachael hurried out of the tent, dressed and ready. How different she felt about this wedding ceremony than her first. Her hands touched her cheeks; they felt flushed. Oh, how exciting. What a difference being in love can make. She smiled, listening to the conversations, echoing laughter, and excitement about her, and strolled back down the hill toward her friends.

Lafayette spoke with an exuberance that made Rachael appreciate God's love even more.

"It's like you said, McCray." He slapped his leg in affirmation. "It truly is that-a way. Wagons before yours, except for the Whitman's, had every animal taken from them. Greenhorns, like yourselves, knowing too little but believing they knew enough, were left on foot in this dangerous country and perished when a wolf pack or hostile Indians got a hold of them."

Beth held out her small finger and chided. "We only lost four horses, a mule, a couple of cows, and three calves. One of which your men confiscated unlawfully."

"Well, I'll be... you still recalling my lack of judgment, ma'am?"

"God even preserves us through our lack, Mr. Lafayette, through this dangerous and lengthy journey into the unknown," Beth said.

Lafayette pondered this. "I can't get over how you came through it. I never saw the like. We didn't even come across a war party."

"We nearly encountered a war party the day before we met you, Mr. Lafayette," Rachael said.

"I was sure praying they wouldn't attack." Jonathan squeezed her hand.

"I wonder, do you think God's angels camped around us when we claimed Psalm 91? Is that the reason they never attacked us?"

Lafayette slapped his hat across his buckskins. "McCray, if you don't baptize me here and now in Jesus' army, I'll do it myself!"

McCray laughed, placing his hand on Lafayette's shoulder. "How about after the wedding? It's October 7. Remember it, Lafayette. That's the day God's angel wrote your name into the Book of Life."

Rachael touched the hat Narcissa brought, put on the gloves Beth gave her, and accepted the bouquet of dandelions Jonathan picked. In the distance she heard the song of a lark. Soon they would have a cabin of their own. Jonathan planned to dig down deep enough to hit solid rock. Yes, they both were founded on the Rock. Only, first she and Jonathan had to be willing to listen and obey. That had been the hardest part. Yes, God's promises were waiting.

Reverend McCray placed her arm in the crook of his. One of Lafayette's men started to play "Amazing Grace" on his harmonica as she walked toward the altar that overlooked a beautiful babbling brook. The trappers, mountain men, Matthew, Luke, and sweet Beth stood to one side. On the other side, stood the Whitman's, the Reverend Spalding, Eliza, and the Cayus, along with a few Umatilla Indians nearby.

Little Alice, in a small wooden wagon pulled by her mother, tossed out flowers from her chubby little fingers. Sara followed. Rachael felt the gentle, yet strong arm of the Reverend McCray lead her forward. Tall and straight as a tree, Jonathan waited. His broad shoulders etched against the backdrop of a blue sky and majestic mountains. The dream she'd prayed for was hers to live. Jonathan loved her, only her and God. They were a threefold cord, with God at the center.

Rachael glanced at her bouquet and smiled. Though she always chose the large perky dandelions to adorn her bonnet, God used a wilted dandelion to bring Jonathan and her together. Wasn't that just like her loving Jesus to use the broken and beaten to send out His message of love.

CROSSRIVER

If you enjoyed this book, will you
consider sharing it with others?

• Please mention the book on Facebook, Twitter, Pinterest
or your blog.

• Recommend this book to your small group, book club,
and workplace.

• Head over to Facebook.com/CrossRiverMedia, 'Like'
the page and post a comment as to what you enjoyed
the most.

• Pick up a copy for someone you know who would be
challenged or encouraged by this message.

• Write a review on Amazon.com, BN.com, or
Goodreads.com.

• To learn about our latest releases subscribe to our
newsletter at www.CrossRiverMedia.com.

CATHERINE ULRICH BRAKEFIELD

Catherine is an ardent receiver of Christ's rejuvenating love, as well as a hopeless romantic and patriot. She skillfully intertwines these elements into her writing as the author of *The Wind of Destiny*, an inspirational historical romance, and *Images of America, The Lapeer Area*. Her most recent history book is *Images of America, Eastern Lapeer County*. Catherine, former staff writer for *Michigan Traveler Magazine*, has freelanced for numerous publications. Her short stories have been published in Guidepost Books *Extraordinary Answers to Prayers, Unexpected Answers* and *Desires of Your Heart*; Baker Books, Revell, *The Dog Next Door*; CrossRiver Publishing, *The Benefit Package*. She recently spent three weeks driving across the western part of the United States, meeting her extended family of Americans. This trip inspired her inspirational historical romance, *Wilted Dandelions*.

Catherine enjoys horseback riding, swimming, camping, and traveling the byroads across America. She lives in Michigan with her husband, Edward, of forty years and her Arabian horses. Her children grown and married, she and Edward are the blessed recipients of two handsome grandsons with another grandchild on the way.

www.CatherineUlrichBrakefield.com
www.Facebook.com/CatherineUlrichBrakefield
www.Twitter.com/CUBrakefield

GENERATIONS

What happens when God steps in to change one man's life?

MORE GREAT BOOKS FROM CROSSRIVERMEDIA.COM

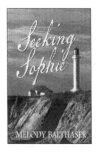

SEEKING SOPHIE
Melody Balthaser

Indentured servant Sophie Stalz stabs her master to protect herself from rape. Escaping through the Underground Railroad, she now finds herself stranded on an island in the hands of a stranger. Surrounded by the sea, Jackson Scott just wants to be left alone with his memories. His fortress crumbles when Sophie shows up on his doorstep. As her master is *Seeking Sophie*, can Sophie and Jackson build a life together free from their past?

FINDING BETH
Linnette R. Mullin

Three years ago, Beth Gallagher lost her brother, Josh, in a tragic accident. Grief-stricken and estranged from her father, she turned to the one man her brother warned her about – Kyle Heinrich. Now she's discovered his dark side. She flees to the Smoky Mountians to clear her mind and find the answers she needs. Will she have the resolve to follow through? And, if so, what will it cost her?

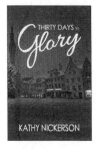

THIRTY DAYS TO GLORY
Kathy Nickerson

Catherine Benson longs to do one great thing before she dies, while Elmer Grigsby hopes to stay drunk until he slips out of the world unnoticed. Against a Christmas backdrop, Catherine searches for purpose while fighting the best intentions of her children. She gains the support of her faithful housekeeper and quirky friends. Elmer isn't supported by anyone, except maybe his cat. When their destinies intersect one Tuesday in December, they both discover it is only *Thirty Days to Glory*.

WHERE HOPE STARTS
Angela D. Meyer

Karen Marino is a professional success, but her marriage is in shambles. When her husband, Barry, shows up drunk at her restaurant, she loses both. She returns to her Midwestern home to sort through her options. But instead of answers, she finds an old boyfriend waiting for her, an angry brother bent on revenge, and a family full of secrets. Can she find her way back to the place *Where Hope Starts*?

48973469R00157

Made in the USA
Charleston, SC
14 November 2015